*Prequel to the Janaforma Trilogy*

# DANCE *of the*
# WARRIOR
# *and* WITCH

*Prequel to the Janaforma Trilogy*

# DANCE *of the*
# WARRIOR
# *and* WITCH

## Martha Fawcett

JANAFORMA PRESS

Davidsonville. Maryland

Text copyright © 2013 Martha Fawcett

Janaforma Press

Davidsonville, Maryland

www.marthafawcett.com

Cover image created by Duncan Long

Library of Congress Control Number:
2013953808

ISBN: 978-0-9890636-4-7

Printed in U.S.A.

First Edition

## DEDICATION
*To Adam, son and chemist extraordinaire!*

.

# CONTENTS

# ONE

## PART I: THE SHARDASKO WARRIOR

I am a Shardasko Warrior
Mindful of the First Adaptation
Truth is my responsibility and karmic legacy
My disposition cooperates with me
I accept each new situation
I am at peace with myself
I am moderation
Loving kindness
Constancy
Kinship

Darkness was squeezing all light from the sky. The last dull rays from the sun Gearthot disappeared behind the craggy ridges of the Tyburnian Mountains and a moment later, the Sutcay Tay Valley slipped into the darkness of *shahaut*. Sutcay Tay natives refer to the darkness after Gearthot sets as *shahaut*, meaning "thick night." *Shahaut* means safety to a Shardasko Warrior and I prayed my precious darkness would last until the moon Eno broke the horizon, an hour before dawn. As I merged with the sheltering *shahaut*, six hot-white meteorites burst into the atmosphere and illuminated the sky. The meteorites arched gracefully before cascading down like a waterfall. Kyron and I watched, relieved that these incessant fireballs from space incinerated before hitting the ground. "No more fireworks, not tonight," I begged the sky.

Nearer the ground, not a breath of air stirred. Pearly mist hovered like tangled threads above the cavities of rough terrain. My mind snagged fleeting images and attempted to create meaning from something that never was. Contrary to popular belief, memory can travel in infinite directions. That night memory slipped a hand inside me as a thief slips a hand inside a stranger's pocket. Memory's call was seductive and nimble in ways it learned inside me eons ago. Just as I was about to sink into memory's pool, the fluttering wings of a bat swooped near my head. "What was that?" I asked with a start.

"It's a gnosis bat," said Kyron. The crazy bat looped toward the east in exploratory circles until it disappeared into the Great Verdant Abyss. Kyron leaned closer, the rutilated shafts in his Gathosian eyes reflecting the flaming torchlights along the trail. He steered me away from the light and deeper into the shadows, where he placed his hands upon my chest. Like a river of white light his energy coursed through me and when he intimated, "You are the meaning behind the First Adaptation," I assured him that I was ready.

Kyron was many unknowable things, but he was not a premeditated mystery. I trusted what I knew of him and knew what he showed me of himself was authentic. Kyron La Teeair Forma was a Shardasko master whose two greatest virtues were propriety and adaptability. Ageless wisdom framed his physical countenance, while adaptability beamed from his eyes as perennial youth. We walked to the end of the trail, where Kyron removed his wand from its *ackinayon* (sheath). This wand was a gift from Kyron's own master, with a lineage of a hundred phases or more. In the future, it would become a valuable art treasure and inspire children to imagine lives of Shardasko Warriors. The wand was lacquered red and featured an embossed, golden snake that spiraled the length. The snake ended in a zaqurlite crystal carved in the shape of a snake's open mouth. Depending on the energy put into the crystal, it could be shades of red, blue, green, or smoky brown.

Kyron had little need for a wand because he could have picked up a common stick from the ground and made it dance. Born a peasant, he ignored offers of wealth and fame and swooped past heroics to become his authentic self. Kyron taught me the authentic self is capable of being anything it chooses, including a humble teacher of Shardasko truths. His physical appearance was plain; however, no doubt existed in my mind that his plainness was a conscious act of camouflage. His erudite mind could dance circles around mine, and he never allowed his life to drift. When he was ill, he appeared frail and when tired, he was absentminded. Yet this last night together, I knew Kyron was one of the greatest souls who ever existed. It showed in his glorious aura. He was diamond-light and glowed with colors of love impossible to describe. Light beyond the visible range and love beyond the expressible was my hearth and comfort in this extraordinary soul. In Human years, he nearly was impossible at 37 Water phases (147 Earth years); but because Kyron was Gathosian, he could expect another twelve Water phases to fine-tune his incredible life.

Kyron leaned forward and kissed the center of my forehead. The physical contact spot tingled and my eager energy leapt up to join his. His kiss awoke new psychic skills within me and prepared me for the trial all Emblematic Warriors must risk on their way to mastery. Shardasko Warriors call this test the *quarrying*. Kyron assured me, "I have complete faith in you, Élan." As always, Kyron spoke with candor, yet a thousand lives hence, I knew my evolution would fall short of his. "I will leave for Sheebrun in the morning," he assured me, "and when you walk out of the Great Verdant, our energy will again dance as one."

Kyron began believing in me when I was a mere whiff of potential, a beardless fleck of a youth. Seven phases prior, I accepted his unshakable optimism when I knelt at his feet and begged that he accept me as his neophyte at the Sutcay Tay School. "Please stand and accept your destiny," was the first thing Kyron ever said to me. Placing his hands under my chin, he remarked, "You have the most incredible blue-green eyes, I've ever seen."

"That's because I'm Human." Then I quickly assured him, "But my heart is one hundred percent Gathosian."

"Being Human or Gathosian is not the issue. Behind your eyes, you are still a child."

"I'm older than I appear. I'm 4 cycles of Fire (16 years old) and completed my level-twelve studies during the last phase of Fecundity." In my adolescent ignorance, I believed I could deflect the truth and cast myself in a better light. If I realized Kyron could see the dark knots of lust in my groin, the clog of grief in my heart, and the fears of inadequacy in my mind, I would have slunk away in shame.

"Whatever your age, your eyes tell me that you are insincere." I swore in my most resolute tone that I was ready to sacrifice everything to become a Shardasko Warrior, but Kyron was correct. I was a youthful dreamer praying a miracle might manifest my fantasies in a few easy steps. "Do your parents know you've run away from home?"

"My parents died in a meteor storm, the one that destroyed Ravenna. My one blood relative is an older sister, who lives on the big world of Gathos. She is of legal age and signed over my rights as an adult. It's my decision to come here and enter Shardasko training."

My father worked for the Galaxy Council as an attaché for the diplomatic corps, part of the second wave of Humanity to arrive on the Island Worlds of Gathos, several phases before my birth. Born on the headwater planet Ravenna, all my life experiences were Gathosian. My childhood memories brimmed with vibrant images of Gathosian peasants, their chatter and camaraderie, and the colorful spectacles during the Festival of the Elements. To me, Earth was a faraway planet I knew only through media presentations and read about in books. On Ravenna, I attended an exclusive private school with Gathosian boys that fired my imagination with the exploits of Shardasko Warriors. My sister Sophia, several phases my senior, had married and moved to Gathos while I was still a child. I was on holiday with Sophia and her husband, Coreese, when we received word that a meteor barrage had ravished the planet Ravenna.

After my parent's death, I fell into a deep and prolonged depression. Insulating myself, I hoped that if I avoided all attachment to people, places, and circumstances, I could spare myself from ever feeling the agony of loss again. For many moons, Sophia coddled me, allowing me to reject Coreese's suggestions that I resume my education. I never returned to proper schooling. Our parents' estate allowed Sophia to hire private tutors who helped me pass my level-twelve studies. I was neither appreciative nor cooperative and the now pregnant Sophia no longer possessed the time or patience to indulge my escalating rebelliousness, which rose to bouts of insolence. When my fourth birthday of Fire arrived, I barely needed to ask her to sign the documents, giving me my legal rights as an adult.

Standing before Kyron, I entertained no plans beyond my lofty dreams to become a Shardasko Warrior. He stepped back and his expression turned sharp. "Nine hundred planets on the Island Worlds of Gathos to choose from, seventy-seven other Shardasko schools where you might apply, and twenty-one other masters here at the Sutcay Tay school alone that might take pity upon you—out of all these choices, why me?"

The first part of my answer was rehearsed. "I came to Sutcay Tay because Shardasko originated here and I want the knowledge from the source." The second part of my reply was spontaneous, candid, and genuine. "I've been wandering your campus for two days, watching the honorable masters go about their duties. I swear, I approached no one until I saw you."

"Please continue your wandering until you find another master. I retired two days before you arrived." His voice sounded irrefutable and my heart sank.

"You can't retire. I need you. I swear, I will sit outside your door like a stray tujet (a small rodent) until you emerge from your recent retirement and accept me as your neophyte. I will neither eat nor sleep and when you find me unconscious upon your doorstep, you will realize that I'm serious."

"Go home," Kyron said and he walked away. Every morning for nine days he emerged to find me camped on his doorstep. By then, I was ill with intestinal upset from eating nothing but fruits and raw vegetables, which I pilfered from the school's Fecundity Garden. On the ninth morning, Kyron walked out the door of his *tritum* (cabin) to ask, "What's your name, lad?"

"My family name is Cœur; my personal name is Journey."

"And of all the journeys a Cœur might choose, you are intent on the path of a Shardasko Warrior?"

My intuition, already keen, knew my concerted enthusiasm was a critical selling point. "To become a Shardasko Warrior is my one and only desire."

"Your energy is strong. Are you aware that your aura is bright orange?" His expression had an eerie, wise edge as if he could see through walls. "It would be a waste to allow your flame to extinguish here on my doorstep. Tell me Journey Cœur, what are you willing to sacrifice to become a Shardasko Warrior?"

"Does that mean you accept me as your neophyte?"

"It means probationary acceptance at the school." This is the only untrue statement Kyron ever made to me. The one way the Sutcay Tay School accepted a neophyte was through the sponsorship of a master. Once a master accepted a neophyte, the master could never disqualify or abandon his charge. I did not realize this delicate point until several moons later. The only way to break the vow between master and student was if the student rejected the teacher by walking away from the Shardasko life. As long as the student remained under the discipline of a master, attainment of mastery was simply a matter of time.

At school on Ravenna, I had a reputation as a Shardasko aficionado. I knew about the moment of commitment between a master and neophyte and realized what Kyron meant when he asked for my sacrifice. Removing my knife from its scabbard, I loped off my long, blonde braid and presented it to him as my vow of surrender. Then I offered him the knife as well. He refused the knife, but took that recently severed part of me and smacked it lightly against both my cheeks. "This will do for starters. In time, you will need to cut off your entire head."

"My commitment is complete."

Kyron held up a finger for silence. "Time, not promises, will reveal your level of commitment. As a mark of your new beginning, Shardasko tradition suggests that I preface your name with a fresh moniker. Accordingly, from this moment forward, your Shardasko name will be Élan. I will call you Élan and you may call me Kyron, but never use this moniker as your official name or write it as your signature."

"Why, Master Kyron?"

"Lesson one, signatures define us and Shardasko Warriors always outpace definition. Élan is your path and that path is infinitely expandable."

"Does the name Élan have special meaning?"

"Élan means joy and joy will lead your way. I suggest that you begin, this very moment, on an infinite journey to your inner joy."

"Do all Shardasko monikers have meaning?"

"Absolutely! All monikers have meaning and meaning directs the warrior's path."

"In that case, what does Kyron mean?"

"Kyron means The Key."

****

Like all neophytes, my initial duties at the Sutcay Tay School were simple. I worked at the Eternal Waters Sanctuary for two hours each afternoon. From a distance, the Eternal Waters Sanctuary appears ethereal, almost like a pale-blue bubble of water suspended above the ground. Design and construction are engineering wonders. Translucent crystaglass rods frame and stabilize the sphere, which are inset with tiles of aquamarine. The crystaglass conducts and amplifies exterior light, while the aquamarine tiles suffuse the temple interior with diaphanous blue radiance. The sphere sits atop a base of obsidian granite and when a warrior walks into the temple, the sense of moving up and into a space greater than the self, is profound.

A fountain dominates the temple interior that erupts each dawn with dancing water. The angle of the water arches in such a way that the sound creates a calming effect. The pool is home to a school of ancient llexal fish, some hundreds of phases old. My work—what Kyron referred to as my "sacrosanct meditation"—literally began at the bottom of the Eternal Waters Sanctuary. My job was to polish the obsidian base. Later when fresh neophytes arrived, I bumped up to the meditation of polishing the mother-of-pearl tiles on the interior floor. For two full phases, I polished, cleaned, and helped maintain the pool and its graduated feeder-locks, which extended three kilometers up into the Tyburnian Mountains. Following my two-phase stint at the Eternal Waters Sanctuary, I worked as a physical laborer in the Fecundity Garden. Another two phases, I spent at the Celestial Air Palace, where masters encouraged me to overcome my basic shyness. Once I emerged from my shell on the stage of the Air Palace, I enjoyed many types of creative expression. In my seventh phase, I studied at the Fire Circle and learned how to focus my psychic energy to a pinpoint and spark many different kinds of fires. While each temple is exquisite, my heart found its home in the Eternal Waters Sanctuary.

Neophytes have the easiest jobs because they need abundant time to establish a routine of study, rigorous physical conditioning, and to process the deluge of suppressed denial that erupts during the earliest phases of training. The traps for neophytes are predictable, insidious, and many. Invariably impatient to divest the greater mysteries, the temptation to complete everyday tasks in a slipshod manner is enormous. A master anticipates the neophyte's impatience and even assumes impatience to be an inherent flaw that all immature warriors must face. The first gift of service asked of a neophyte is the performance of his temple assignment with

6

scrupulous attention paid to feeling, thought, and deed. Kyron instructed me to, "Go to the library and look up the meaning of the word 'meticulous.' Meditate upon the meaning of the word and live the word's meaning as you go about your chores. When you become the meaning behind 'meticulous,' then you will be ready to help me clean our communal toilets." It would take me several phases to understand the implications of what Kyron meant. I would not glimpse the true meaning of "meticulous," until I recognized the insidious traps of pride.

Sitting meditation began my second morning at the school. "The goal of all meditation is perfect awareness," said Kyron. "You must ask your *Holder* * to emerge until its perspective becomes your own."

"How?"

"In meditation we begin by allowing each interior voice to speak. Trace the source of the slightest interior suggestion and know what it wants from you." Kyron was speaking about internal honesty and making internal honesty the external self. The process is exhausting, an actual retching of the unconscious in an effort to release its suppressed poison.

My first meditations were with Kyron, in his private quarters, rather than in the elemental temples. The saturation of higher energies, attracted to these great temples, was too overwhelming for my initial, unstable state. Kyron began nudging my energy with his and assured me, "Soon, you will be ripe for harvest." With Kyron as my personal gardener, it did not take long for me to ripen. Not even two moons into my training, I dropped from the tree of my assumptions. When I hit the ground, I split open and revealed my emotional pulp. For the next seven moons, I scarcely could fulfill my minimal duties, yet Kyron insisted I "go" and continue to strive for meticulousness in everyday tasks. At night, I felt exhausted, insecure, and gloomy. I regressed and became infant-like, as my denial broke free and erupted into my conscious mind. I sought constant assurance and grew afraid—afraid of the dark, afraid of abandonment, afraid of death, afraid of life, afraid of failing, afraid of succeeding, and especially afraid of the truth. More nights I spent shivering in fear in Kyron's quarters than in my neophyte's quarters because of my nightmares. Occasionally, I thought I was losing my mind and Kyron would smile tenderly and assure me, "You're losing your limited mind."

Kyron escorted me through the minefield of my exploding emotions as if we were two tourists visiting an old war zone. "We're visiting old warriors within you so they can at last rest in peace," he said. My first ghostly warrior to step forward was grief. Kyron helped me cope with the grief over losing my parents, which I addressed only vaguely up to that time. The loss of my

*The *Holder* represents the mind component of the Higher-Self and translates literarally as "Essential Witness."; language orgin, Mescale.

mother seemed unbearable. My feelings of loneliness surfaced at growing up in an alien culture, where I believed my parents abandoned me to the confines of a boarding school. Tuning into my loneliness acted as a catalyst and brought up my confusion over being The Alien amid Gathosians. When I looked in the mirror, my Human skin appeared pale and lifeless compared to the dark beauty of the Gathosian people. I hated my blue-green eyes, my pink tongue, my five-fingered hands, and especially my feet that a Gathosian school-chum once ridiculed and called, "creepy and too big." Kyron made me face the mirror and accept my lanky Human frame that was shooting up like a sprout. "A diamond sits at your core and I will find it," Kyron swore. He helped me release the pangs of jealousy I possessed concerning the intimacy my sister Sophia enjoyed with our mother and the anger I harbored for my father over his indifference to me. Kyron forged a means to access bits of internal information that stamped my immortal soul." Through patience and compassion, Kyron gave me the opportunity to address my past.

I grew to love Kyron as a son loves a good father. Truth gleams brightest in the light of love and Kyron convinced me of his devotion by the quality and depth of his continued concern for my evolution. Kyron taught through the vehicle of his own life—by example. He knew how to approach life's paradoxes and especially the paradoxes within himself. "You're too sober and heavy," he kept reminding me. "Remember, your Shardasko moniker is Élan." My confidence was a flimsy veil and I apologized as I did for everything about myself. Then Kyron confessed, "In my youth, I was neither sober nor serious. In truth, I was a frivolous ass and a thief."

"Impossible!"

"I wasn't even a good thief, but a petty thief stealing half-rotten fruit and shoddy merchandise from vendors in the marketplace."

"What turned you around, Master Kyron?"

He laughed and the fine lines deepened around his dark eyes of boundless wisdom. "The process is a mystery, but I can tell you that a beautiful woman named Belinda had a hand in my transformation." Kyron's eyes turned misty, yet the gold-rutilated shafts in his irises felt like daggers piercing my heart. He seemed to gaze across time as he stared through me. "I come from the city Uhurda on the planet Thetacore. It was late in the phase of Fecundity, harvest time, when farmers bring their crops into local markets. I was not exhibiting much skill at stealing anything that day, so I loitered around the main square, begging for handouts from the passersby. Then I saw her. She picked up a red parishfruit to smell its ripeness and her loveliness stuck me dumb. From that first glimpse, I stopped walking and began to float—to move effortlessly through life. My whole life seemed pointless nonsense up to that instant. Then, without warning, she appeared and my life possessed meaning simply because of that one brief glimpse."

"Did you approach her—try to talk to her?"

"Yes, but she wanted nothing to do with me. She knew I was a rascal." Kyron winked and touched his black tongue to his top lip. The physical gesture was a common Gathosian mannerism that often preceded the telling of a joke or a confidential witticism of some sort. "In a miracle of transformation, I came to terms with my pettiness. The truth is, I became the master thief I was destined to be and stole her heart." Kyron's smile seemed like a casual façade, something he threw over the core of his enlightened self and wore as a cloak. "Eventually I even persuaded her to marry me and then I discovered her physical beauty was merely a reflection of her inner beauty."

"Where's your wife now?"

His tender expression went sterile. "Many phases ago, her *Holder* took her from life." Kyron fell silent while my imagination began constructing an image of his wife's face. "Do you know what Belinda means?" he asked a short time later. "It means 'beautiful sound of being.' Belinda's beauty awoke my heart. Through my love and her compassion, I promise to teach you what I know of this fulfillment. This I do swear."

****

My physical training involved participation in three separate Shardasko classes. One class focused on physical endurance through conscious movement, the second taught proper breathing, and the third encouraged physical flexibility. Conscious movement, proper breathing, and physical flexibility are foundational tools that support the art of shadow dancing. Kyron assigned me to an Emblematic Warrior named Aytinous, a moniker meaning, "perfection will reign," who acted as my shadow-dancing coach. At four Air phases (24 years), Aytinous was a Shardasko legend at the Sutcay Tay School. Rumors among my fellow neophytes suggested that Aytinous had completed his *quarrying* in a brisk five-day walk across the Great Verdant and emerged with nary a scratch, bump, or bruise. When Geiger, my roommate and fellow neophyte, heard that Kyron assigned me to Aytinous, Geiger gibed me with, "It's been nice knowing you, Élan."

Geiger meant the quicker a warrior crossed the Great Verdant, the more awesome his attainment and the less empathy he might show a neophyte. Paranoia came to claim me and made itself at home in my vulnerabilities. I presumed that Kyron meant to cull me from training because I was the only Human at the school, so I assaulted him with my demands to know the truth of his intentions. Waylaying him as he walked out the door of his *tritum*, I demanded, "Is my Humanness an embarrassment to your Gathosian sensibilities?"

"Glad you're here," he said and he dumped his entire stack of books into my arms. "Follow me," and he headed for the library.

I followed him like a dog and said, "I refuse to stay here if you sincerely do not want me as your neophyte."

"Are you searching for an excuse to quit?" and he stopped walking and I nearly ran into him. His expression turned thoughtful as his eyes bore down to my core. "Oh! I see your dilemma. You're concerned about Aytinous. I assure you, Aytinous is a dedicated warrior and it is his honor to mentor you in the shadow-dancing chamber. If he fails to teach you, he will prove himself an ineffective teacher and I do not believe Aytinous would care to wear that shameful label. Listen to me and remember this: Shardasko training is a discipline that, so far, has benefited only Gathosians. If you fail here, it means Shardasko truth is limited and we will have missed our opportunity to present Humanity with the universal merits of Shardasko wisdom. For no other reason than to support an old man's faith in Shardasko principles, please realize your inferiority complex is an illusion. Leave your illusions unchallenged and they will destroy you and our chance to spread these truths to all who need them." Kyron was a genius. He managed to make me feel important and humble all at the same time.

Aytinous and I met the following morning. He was a young demigod, the quintessential image of what I imagined every Shardasko Warrior should look like. His calm demeanor and self-confidence suggested his life never suffered doubt. His Shardasko training was obvious and he exuded an air of adaptable determination that allowed him absolute comfort in all situations. Dressed in a simple *moodarry* (gown made of *soaple* cloth), he managed to look elegant and refined. In different clothing, he could have passed as a Gathosian aristocrat. He seemed to be an effortless balance between perfect economy and finesse and even when standing motionless, his body suggested graceful movement. His black hair, he wore in the classic Shardasko style, with the long bulk of curls pulled to the top of the head, and the length draped to one side. His eyes, like all Gathosian eyes, were a haunting blue-black with rutilated golden irises. For the next five phases, his eyes would pursue and haunt me as we met eye to eye in the shadow-dancing chamber thousands of times.

"I was born on Ravenna too and lost my grandparents in the same meteor storm that took your parents," said Aytinous. "Together we will honor our common Ravenna heritage and you will become the finest shadow dancer at the Sutcay Tay School." I liked when he said that because I felt he honestly considered me his peer and chose to ignore my outsider status. Aytinous offered me inspiration even Kyron could not supply. Gathosians lived longer than Humans and I could not imagine ever equaling Kyron's stature. Aytinous became my icon, someone I could emulate, and grow into with time.

Shadow dancing is a foundational Shardasko skill, similar to a sophisticated game of Hide and Seek that eventually teaches a warrior how to jump dimensions. Consummate stealth is both the means and the goal in shadow dancing. The black *slipfal**  worn by shadow dancers allows them to move soundlessly within the darkness of a reduced-gravity chamber. The objective of the game is for the pursuer to locate and confront the pursued, through psychic intuition. Locating needs to be precise, so when the pursuer calls, "lights on," the two players are in direct eye-to-eye contact and their positioning is a mirrored pose.

Aytinous stripped off his *moodarry* and was dressed in a *slipfal* underneath. "What are you waiting for? Disrobe," he said.

Removing my *moodarry*, I stood there feeling embarrassed in a hand-me-down *slipfal* that drooped in the ass and bagged at my knees. I stared down at, what I considered, my enormous bare feet and hid my hands behind my back as I did most of my life. "Sorry, this *slipfal* belongs to Master Kyron. Mine haven't arrived from the tailor."

"Never apologize for your physical appearance," Aytinous snapped. "Besides, clothing is the first superfluous bit of camouflage to disappear in the fourth dimension. Have you completed your initial homework?"

"I read *An Introduction to Shadow Dancing* by Master Jelud."

"Then assume Position 1," and he gracefully danced into Primal Stance. Aytinous closed his eyes and something began happening inside him that I did not understand. He appeared to be undergoing some kind of physical transformation. He simultaneously stepped back and sideways in a sleek and powerful fashion. As his long Gathosian fingers braided the intangible air, he appeared to have four arms instead of two. I watched and envied his grace, but shadow dancing seemed nothing more than an exercise that allowed Aytinous to display his magnificent arms and beautiful hands. Yet time would reveal his gestures were precise postures, capable of transforming his entire being. In Primal Stance, Aytinous stood on the edge of unfolding time. With a mere tweak of his will, he could have slipped through the doorway to the fourth dimension, but he held his third dimensional space, for my sake.

Aytinous continued to dazzle me with his shadow-dancing skills as he shifted into Position 2. "Razor Shardasko," he announced; and he pirouetted and his pirouette turned into a dizzying spiral. When he stopped, he appeared as a thin, black line intersecting the light. *It's real!* I thought. *All those stories I heard at school are true.*

The thin black line that was Aytinous, again pirouetted until he stood

---

* *slipfal* : A bodysuit coated with *slipfarilic*, a substance that reduces frictional sound to decibels detectable only by sensitive instrumentation; language origin, Mescale.

before me full face. Now he seemed even bigger as his authority filled the room out to its corners. "That was not time jumping," came his stern reminder. "Razor Shardasko is the infinitesimal shadow we must become before we can make the jump." He moved into Position 3, completing a perfect Feint Envelope. Low and behold, two images of Aytinous stood side-by-side. This was the visual effect called "the warble," as the warrior attaches himself to the surrounding gravitons, before slipping through the doorway into the fourth dimension.

Bafflement caused my voice to break and stutter, "Which one—of you—is the real you?" He played an unexpected trick on me with this maneuver and carried Position 3 into Position 4, a Half-Dimensional Waver. I jumped a little myself when he tapped me on the shoulder and I found the physical Aytinous standing behind me.

"The envelope is empty," he informed me. He clapped his hands and the illusional twin standing before me vanished.

"How did you do that?"

"Enough nonsense. We must start at the beginning." Aytinous showed me the proper way to stand and adjusted my body where it fell out of alignment. "Head straight, chin in, shoulders open, arms ready and loose, and knees slightly bent. Lead with your heart and keep your center of concentration here," and he tapped me rather hard in the middle of my forehead. Then he spoke to the gravity controller on the wall. "Lights out and gravity one-quarter." The lights in the chamber flickered off and when the gravity in the room leaked away, my stomach abruptly flip-flopped. Thirty seconds later, Aytinous called, "lights on," and I found myself floating parallel to the floor and perpendicular to Aytinous and wondering how I got into that position. Gravity was still at one quarter, or I would have fallen on my face. Again he pulled me into proper alignment and told me, "Move! Strive to emulate and balance my mood and stance. Never allow the energy bound to this dimension to dominate your position and attitude." He tapped me lightly in the gut. "Engage your essential will and challenge your bound up energy if you are unable to disconnect. Lights out," he said a second time; and after a moment, I sensed Aytinous stalking me as if I were prey. When the lights flashed on the next time, we were nose to nose and he was peering into my eyes with the palms of his hands a scant millimeter from my searching hands. It felt spooky. That night and for several nights hence, I dreamt Aytinous was pursing me with his Gathosian rutilated eyes.

It would take me two full phases to learn to disconnect and foil Aytinous in the shadow-dancing chamber and then it happened only once. Three moons later, not only could I disconnect, but I also managed to baffle him. It was an occasion for celebration. By then, I was four and a half Fire phases (eighteen years old) and that evening Kyron and Aytinous took me to the village of Sheebrun and bought me my first beer. Then Aytinous and I switched roles in the shadow-dancing chamber and he permitted me to act as the pursuer for the first time. Aytinous told me, "Now that you've learned to elude, you must become the master of pursuit, for it is the pursuer who commands in the fourth dimension." It took another three phases for me to become a pursuer. When I could track Aytinous in the darkness, with no fixed reference points, and never lose touch, he declared me his perfect twin. He told me, "Our bond is eternal and unbreakable." Then he leaned forward and whispered a word in my ear that henceforward would be our telepathic contact point. Through that single word, we could call each other and communicate with our psychic minds. By then I was five and a quarter Fire phases (21 years), and I invited Kyron and Aytinous to go to Sheebrun, where I bought the beer.

Only then did I graduate to the master shadow dancer, Kyron. Now, all clothing was superfluous; for all wayfarers who journey into the fourth dimension, take nothing into that eternal void save their essential selves. My days of shadow dancing were over. Our eyes joined in focus and when the lights flashed off, Kyron and I jumped to the fourth dimension for my first foray.

****

Shadow dancing and my physical training are the only areas of my early education that Kyron did not conduct; yet I knew he received daily reports on my progress, especially from Aytinous. Without the guiding wisdom received from a master, the rudiments of physical exercise and the flashy tricks of shadow dancing are meaningless. Kyron certainly was capable of instructing me in these skills for he served as an Emblematic Warrior for seventeen phases before becoming a master. My separate classes at the Sutcay Tay School emphasized community and the fraternity of the Shardasko life. The hope was that each student would grow to appreciate the camaraderie of enlightened men.

Once I established myself at the Sutcay Tay School, it was evident Kyron's peers regarded him as an inimitable master. Despite his extraordinary mastery, I cannot deny my Human differences posed unique challenges for him. While other masters had two and three neophytes under their tutelage, I remained Kyron's one pupil and he told me more than once, "When you graduate to Emblematic Warrior, I will retire."

As the Shardasko Credo suggests, a warrior needs to approach every path with flexibility and kinship. Flexibility and kinship demand that a neophyte relinquish his independence and all his assumptions. Paradoxically, if a warrior surrenders his independence and assumptions, kinship and flexibility lead him into unparalleled freedom. Kyron became my loyal guide and teacher, teaching me the meaning behind each form and that form is the shadow attempting to hide its own meaning. "If you realize nothing else, please realize that meaning is essential," Kyron said. Meaning is essential because a neophyte cannot follow meaningless discipline and expect to become an independent warrior. Kyron taught me the importance of meaning by stripping away superficial dressing until each Shardasko concept made sense. After I began to emerge from my lifetimes of suppression and depression, my real learning began and I became a voracious seeker of meaning behind all forms.

Kyron and I attended most of the group lectures offered at the Celestial Air Palace. Often, the Sutcay Tay School played host to visiting Shardasko luminaries of wisdom on tour from affiliate schools. The enlightened climate was exhilarating and we would examine many theories of reality, for meaning and truth. Less often, was the luxury of pure entertainment. Once a troupe of performing shadow dancers visited from the Lomita School, located on the Gathosian planet, Numidia. Afterward, Kyron and I engaged in a lively discussion concerning the art of shadow dancing and this is the only time I ever came close to winning a debate with him. Kyron defined shadow dancing as a practical exercise, a means to an end that had nothing to do with a stage performance. He is right; but at the time, I suggested shadow dancing could be appreciated as beautiful movement that one could appreciate for itself. Kyron accused me of allowing superficial beauty to seduce me and I countered by reminding him of how Belinda's physical beauty first snagged him.

"But I penetrated her physical beauty to realize her actual beauty," he said.

"But her physical beauty first attracted you and brought you as a beggar to her inner door."

"True," and then his concentration sank inward. A few minutes later he emerged from his reverie to inform me, "Perhaps you came to the Sutcay Tay School to teach me as well as for me to teach you."

Kyron transmitted most Shardasko knowledge to me orally, in a one-to-one setting, so he could ascertain my level of understanding. Learning with Kyron never was a lecture. We indulged in dialogues that seemed as if we were exploring new territory together to find the truth. When he taught, he was never afraid to digress and ramble from one topic to the next. One word from me could take him off on a new tangent and sometimes we would not return to the original topic for days. Many times, his answers were open-ended and spawned floods of new questions. I would make a statement I thought inconsequential, try to skirt it, and he would insist, "Let it go, Élan. Let it go and let's see where it flies." His learning was prodigious, yet he was the subtlest, most unpretentious teacher I ever knew. He indulged my proclivities for writing and encouraged me to record my personal experiences in a collection of journals and to compose papers on

Shardasko thought he always was eager to read. Some of my fondest memories are of the two of us sitting cross-legged, on either side of his eating table, and writing in our journals. I was fluent in English as well as Mescale and one day he surprised me by suggesting, "If you came to the Sutcay Tay School to teach me, could you please teach me to speak English?" I managed to teach him some English words and phrases, but our serious conversations always reverted to Mescale because no concise expressions existed in English to describe the subtleties of Shardasko thought. Through me, Kyron did learn a basic understanding of English and enjoyed greeting me and saying goodbye in, for him, this alien tongue. His favorite English expression was, "See you later."

\*\*\*\*

When the moon Eno rises an hour before dawn, the light on the planet Sutcay Tay is infused with a green radiance. Depending on atmospheric conditions, the light varies between a dark, hunter green and a soft, mossy gray. Sutcay Tay natives call the green light of Eno, "*areé didamé*" meaning "balancing time." Kyron expected me to be at his *tritum* each morning before *areé didamé*, so we could meditate in the green light. At dawn, we would break and prepare a pot of razzleroot tea and two bowls of cooked grains with some kind of fresh, seasonal fruit. Our first morning together, Kyron was elaborate with humble ceremony, getting down on his knees and bowing before me, until his forehead touched the floor. "Thank you for choosing me as your master," he said with complete humility. Amazed that a Shardasko master would bow before a lowly neophyte, I returned his bow before accepting the food. After our simple meal, eaten in silence, he gave me a beautiful cloth-covered notebook and a new pen. He instructed me to write my name and date on the first inside page. Remembering that I should never write my new moniker, I wrote, "Journey Cœur, second of Linral, phase of Fecundity, 8426."

Then Kyron gave me my first conundrum and instructed me to— "Write it down exactly, memorize it, and then forget it. 'The brightest light hides the darkest shadows.'" His statement seemed contradictory, so I presumed to question it. He repeated the conundrum more emphatically the second time. "The brightest light hides the darkest shadows."

"How am I supposed to forget something you just instructed me to memorize?"

He laughed with delight and I felt perplexed by his glib manner. "We always begin in confusion."

"That's for sure."

Kyron slid into the effortless grace of an enlightened master and explained the true meaning of being a warrior. "The only battle a Shardasko Warrior ever engages in is his internal battle. He begins by walking down a light-filled path with proclivities and presumptions casting tall, angular shadows in the bright light of his limited mind. Fools trust these shadows and bow down and bless them as reality. A Shardasko Warrior walks into his darkness and meets his *Holder* with unconditional surrender in his heart. Reaching the stage of Emblematic Warrior, he lives in acute awareness of his fragility on the edge of time and accepts his limitations." Kyron fell silent and went internal while I waited. "I have inadvertently answered my own conundrum," he eventually said.

"I don't understand."

"I know, if you understood I would have nothing left to teach you," and he continued to stare off into space. A few minutes later, he told me, "Run along and attend your exercise classes and remember—meticulous."

**\*\*\*\***

Now it was seven phases later. As we stood at the end of the winding trail, Kyron reminded me, "Our spirit is one."

"Our spirit is one," I echoed. The moment was upon me to make my "time declaration." Shardasko custom dictates that each warrior must predict how long it will take him to cross the Great Verdant Abyss. The prediction determines how well a warrior understands his true abilities. For example, if a warrior declares he will cross the Great Verdant in six days, but it takes him more than six days, he has overestimated his abilities and revealed his conceit. If a warrior predicts his crossing will take him six days and the journey takes him less than six days, he is not living up to his potential. Naturally, the strictest rules of integrity apply to *quarrying*. Within the Verdant Abyss, experiential time and honor must be absolute. If a warrior finishes his journey early, it is dishonorable to linger on the edge of the Abyss until the predicted time of emergence arrives. Likewise, it is dishonorable for a warrior to use the fourth dimension to jump to the predicted time. Each warrior meditates intently before making his time declaration. Most warriors allow themselves a day for every phase of their training. Accordingly, I declared, "I will meet you in Sheebrun in seven days, master."

"Seven days," repeated Kyron. "That is a wise choice." Then he put his wand against my chest as a symbol of his blessing. In those final moments, words danced around us and felt their own inadequacy of expression. Time seemed to bunch up and wait for me. The loving arms of Kyron would be waiting for me in Sheebrun, but first I had to get there. Removing my *moodarry* and sandals, I gave them to Kyron. *The moment is now*, said reality and accordingly, I turned my back upon the vibrant community of my brethren, to face the depths of the Great Verdant Abyss alone.

**\*\*\*\***

Naked, my awareness led the way. My one tool allowed was a brain scribe. A brain scribe is a bionic DNA bit implanted under the skin and usually behind the right ear. Calibrated to the user's brainwaves, brain scribes record thought and are a tool exclusively for the convenience of the wearer. Considered superior to memory, a brain scribe is a way to retain full and accurate recall of personal perspective. My otherwise stark vulnerability was a symbol of surrender—a surrender of my false persona to fate. Despite my nakedness, I was dressed in the resplendent riches of accumulated experience from my seven phases of training.

My psychic mind cleared a path for me through the thorn-filled meadows of fickleberries and wildflowers. Complete balance is impossible, but I teetered from one moment to the next with my heighted awareness. Falling from this precarious balance point, one of two fates awaited me. I could fall to my death in the third dimension where temporal forgetfulness and the certainty of elemental decay would gobble up my physical remains. This fate meant a setback, another lifetime of striving. The other alternative was more painful to my soul. If I became lost in the fourth dimension, I would face a full-blown entanglement with the incalculable powers of free radicals*. Losing my way in the fourth meant I would need to endure until my *Holder* sought my whereabouts and ferried me to safe haven. Lost in illusion, I could linger in the fourth dimension for ten minutes or ten billion eons.

Vigilance became my new master while my attention stayed meditative, delicate, and commensurate to the demands of each moment. Footsteps, I placed thoughtfully and nearly soundlessly. For seven phases, I endeavored to learn how to walk in complete awareness. Any initial signs of trails, broken twigs, bent grasses, minor displacement of stones, any raw abnormality, I avoided with focused intent. The peripheral trails retained the tracings of footsteps created by local farmers and their domesticated herds. I had no intention of picking up their composite essence on the soles

*Soul groups operate on the principle of ubiquitous space and timelessness while the elemental universe operates on the principle of finite space and time. Both systems possess propensities: ubiquitous space can lose or gain energy and finite space can become stagnant, temperamental, and wear down. The development of a soul involves the manipulation of precarious energy between elementals and soul groups and sometimes energy does not mesh properly. Occasionally, elemental spirits pump energy into attractive forms at an immature or unresolved stage. This inappropriate and incomplete meshing between elementals and soul groups produces free radicals. The discussion of free radicals is an extensive topic and information on free radicals fills an entire wing in the Library of All Creation.

of my feet and carrying this smell with me as an extra burden. Stepping where my feet left no impressions, I cut a wider path.

Not twenty minutes had elapsed when I knew a dulcerary panther was stalking me. Breaching its territory, I could smell where the dulcerary had anointed the trees and bushes with its musky scent. I caught my mind projecting assumptions concerning what the cat might do next. Allowing my intuition to uncoil, it cut through my mind and then outward in methodical, concentric waves, snagging the mind of the dulcerary. *Hunger!* returned like a boomerang. Mind, held at bay for only an instant, slipped through with its conclusion, telling me the dulcerary would wait until I approached the edge of the deeper woods before attempting a rush. *Maybe,* returned my internal collective. The degree of hunger driving the panther was impossible to gauge. Veering too close to anticipation, I retracted my projections, as intuition alerted me to what I perceived to be a sleeping, mosaic viper ahead. I stopped and deepened my involvement with all my physical senses. Vision could play tricks and was not to be completely trusted in the *shabaut.* My nose lent its credence to sight and sound and told me the viper was physical. The smell of the snake was distinct, a mixture of rancid oils from its diet of maskits and a fetid rot from the moist places where it crawled to escape the intense heat of Insanio. The sensible, mosaic viper had posted a sensual boundary around its body before curling up to enjoy the warmth of a broad, flat rock.

My bladder tweaked me with a gentle reminder. My level two roommate, Harmony, had cautioned me to drink plenty of water before leaving for my *quarrying.* Now I needed to urinate. Urinating in the dulcerary's territory would be a direct challenge. Kyron's lessons surfaced and spoke in his voice, telling me, *Danger and safety are not objective, diametrical states, but conceptual stutters within the continuum of the self. Sagacious warriors are mindful of the First Adaptation and neither savor nor avoid these conceptual stutters.*

The dulcerary was a *skefit* (a short distance) behind and zigzagging from one firethorn bush to the next. The cat merely needed to execute a short sprint to overcome me. It moved into range and rested on its haunches, beside a fickleberry shrub. Fresh understanding emerged within me as I tuned deeper into the animal's energy mass. The dulcerary possessed integrity and its integrity forced it to show itself in all its primal magnificence, before attacking its victims. Whether this characteristic was specific to this particular dulcerary or inclusive of all dulcerarys was uncertain. Whichever, I knew integrity was an indelible characteristic infusing this animal's soul. The dulcerary continued to show itself and I could see its aura like a brilliant star against the *shabaut.* Its energy mass was three times the size of its physical body. Inside its own field, its body was protected, confident, and authentic and its dark sable fur gleamed like polished glass. It began purring in anticipation and its purr was seductive and sonorously deep. The moment of complete confrontation came and its *Holder* spoke through this magnificent creature, questioning my essential motives for existence. *What greater gift can you bestow upon life than to feed the hungry?* it asked me. *Feed me and I will make you a god in your next life.*

My will stayed firm and I returned a message coded on the energy level, the animal part of it could understand. Assuming Primal Stance, I told the cat, *try to seduce me and you will find I am more trouble than I am worth.* Its purr turned into a whine and a bit of drool formed on the animal's lips. Its hunger brought up my compassion and I spoke with actual words as if speaking to a fellow traveler that stopped me along the trail to ask for directions. "Go to the next bend in the stream, a little deeper into the forest," I shouted in the direction of the dulcerary. "You will find a small herd of siberlene there. One is old, injured, and easy prey."

Then the great shadow of its *Holder* emerged from the beast, loomed over me, and filled me with dread. It was a colossal spirit and my mind was afraid. Courage emerged from my solar plexus and again I moved into Primal Stance. I held firm, ready to jump to the fourth dimension. On the brink, I knew the *Holder* behind the eyes of this beast was a spiritual bulwark. Its eyes could penetrate the deeper mysteries with greater authority than I could ever hope to. The skill of its *Holder* in telepathy was penetrating, commanding, and chilling. *Your vision honors me*, it sent through the instinctive ethers. Then it spoke in those mixed pronouns that lets us know the *Holder* can either swoop down and possess us completely or retreat and regard us as a man regards his fingernails. *My hunger blinded my life to the future and made the near fatal error of seeing the potential as a full stomach. Your vision shows my life that satisfaction waits at the first bend in the stream. In return, I wish to honor you with an equal vision. Your hunger will be satisfied in a son. Name him Dulcerary and inspire him with the song of your instinctive heart and he will remember the music that spun out life from the conservatory of creation.*

"I am a Shardasko Warrior and I create my own destiny."

*You will satisfy your hunger with my vision as my life will satisfy its hunger with your vision.* Then the dulcerary disappeared into the *shahaut* and a short time later, I heard the sharp cry of a siberlene and then complete silence.

My sacred duty was to pray for the fast delivery of the soul of the siberlene. This was not a one-time affair, but would continue until my *Holder* told me the soul of the siberlene had reintegrated with its source. The only reason I knew of the old siberlene and its weakened condition was it was soul closer to me than was readily apparent. In another time or place, we were part of the same energy. The death of any creature, especially a death I was instrumental in provoking was a forfeiture of part of myself, so my prayer circled around and indeed, was a prayer for me.

While the dulcerary satisfied its hunger on siberlene, I felt secure enough to sit on my haunches in a secluded spot. Scraping back the decaying leaves with the end of a short stick, I urinated as soundlessly as possible before covering it over. Afterward, I hesitated to reestablish my directional bearings. Kyron's lessons stamped my soul and again spoke through his voice. *The way out of darkness is not around it, but through it. Accordingly, choose your path by walking deeper into the darkness.*

****

The shortest distance across the Great Verdant Abyss is 322 kilometers. No maps, guideposts, trails, or familiar landmarks point the way, in this caldron of primeval life. Under the thick canopy of trees, even daylight is a dim affair. The only fixed reference points are a physical sense of up and down. Shardasko Warriors have written thousands of volumes on the subject of crossing their separate abysses, yet warriors agree on three things only: crossing is a personal experience, no tricks will ever master it, and *quarrying* is the cosmic final exam, for all Emblematic Warriors.

At the Sutcay Tay School, the loss rate to the Great Verdant is about two percent. The fervent prayer of all warriors is they will cross in their declared time. Time declarations vary between five and nine days with six and seven days being the norm. If a warrior fails to emerge in his declared time, his master uses his psychic skills to guide the Emblematic Warrior to safe haven. At the same time, all activity at the school ceases as the elemental temples fill with warriors who use their energy to guide their lost brother to safety. More than twelve days and a party of masters begin to scour the Abyss for answers. One way or another, masters find every warrior. Whatever the outcome of the search, the master who misjudged his warrior's command will never again accept another neophyte under his tutelage. For six moons, the green and purple banner of the Sutcay Tay School will hang upside down. No Emblematic Warrior will enter the Verdant Abyss while the school banner hangs upside down, because even masters consider it a portent of defeat.

****

The moon Eno peeked out from behind the clouds. The green light filtering through the treetops would last until Gearthot rose and warmed the sky with yellow light. An hour later, Insanio would rise and make the Abyss into a caldron of steaming heat. The rainforest on Sutcay Tay is a noisy place, filled with an abundance of rare and exotic species. That first morning, the birds in the treetops celebrated life with rare and intricate songs, while insects droned through the humid air. Flocks of beautiful scarlet kackrels flew from one sarup tree to the next, helping themselves to a fat-rich breakfast of buttery nuts. I was hungry and wished they would toss a few nuts my way. I spent several minutes searching among the empty shells on the ground, but found no nuts. Farther on, I hesitated at a clear-running stream to drink and bathe. Bathing was a precaution, an effort to keep my body free of odor that would attract hungry insects and beasts. I scrubbed myself with handfuls of fine sand before rinsing in the cool water. When I emerged on the opposite bank, I glanced down and halted dead in my tracks. A constellation of large three-pronged clawprints pressed into the moist sand. "Vaspray!" The clawprints were well defined and a bit of nauseating stink lingered in the air from the copious ornithocopros vaspray leave. Then I spied drops of fresh blood.

Vaspray are carnivores and super-sentient cooperative hunters that are fourth dimensional masters. At the end of the rainy season, when they mate, sometimes their sharp, black razor-wings dominate the skies above the Abyss. Stories abound at the Sutcay Tay School that the two percent who do not make it through their *quarrying* have fallen as victims to the dreaded vaspray.

# TWO

While a Shardasko Warrior searches for meaning behind each form, he never defines himself because he believes that defining is a foolish exercise that will frustrate his evolution. Self-definition rests on the laurels of the past, rather than on the crest of unfolding possibilities. In the same vein, a warrior never defines a situation as an obstacle or another being as his enemy. Instead, he strives to find creative solutions to live in harmony with his physical environment. Despite this accommodation, every warrior concedes that vaspray are a difficult challenge.

Gathosian legends claim that, around thirty thousand phases ago, vaspray learned how to negotiate the fourth dimension from Shardasko Warriors. This fable is familiar to all Gathosians and Shardasko masters tell the story to neophytes to emphasize the importance of personal responsibility. Slight variations exist on the theme, but most versions feature a Shardasko Warrior named Tajáno. On the fifth day of Tajáno's *quarrying*, he confronted a flock of hunting vaspray. Realizing they are capable of relentless ferocity, Tajáno stepped into the fourth dimension to avoid confrontation. When he opened a portal to the fourth, the vaspray attacked, and Tajáno dragged three vaspray with him to the other side. The vaspray quickly formed alliances with fourth dimensional free radicals and learned the art of maneuverability between dimensions. Illuminated thinking now concedes that vaspray always were capable of dimensional jumping, just as all creatures are. Only humanoid arrogance continues to perpetuate the myth that the trick was our original and exclusive trick. The real moral of this ancient tale is a warrior needs to be mindful of what and whom he takes with him from dimension to dimension.

It seems ludicrous to call vaspray birds because they appear more like pterodactyls. Some alpha males weigh as much as 40 kilograms and stand taller than a man. Wingspan can exceed 5 meters. Vaspray bodies are efficient killing machines with wing-barbs capable of slicing off a humanoid arm, leg, or head in one savage swipe. Three-pronged talons on their wingtips and feet are thick, sharp, and deadly, while their beaks curve downward and are efficient at ripping flesh and breaking bone. The head and neck are bald with gray, warty flesh hanging in sagging folds along the jowls, while grizzled down covers the breast and blends into black feathers on the back and wings. Vaspray are hyper-sentient, but their sentience is unlike humanoid sentience. Eyesight and hearing are a thousand times keener than ours and their incomprehensible senses serve as a vehicle for their clairvoyance and clairaudience. Ignoring all humanoid efforts at communication, vaspray guard their intraspecies' secrets in sheltered valleys of thick Gathosian rainforests. What little we know about these creatures is from distant observational science. Rarely do ornithologists get close enough to scrutinize vaspray habitats and behavior.

Every Gathosian planet hosts its indigenous vaspray. Within the species, six sub-species exist, but all vaspray appear identical to chance observers. Females construct rough communal nests in the tops of sturdy trees, where they lay huge, brown-speckled eggs. On the planet Sutcay Tay, their favorite tree is the wingwan, a type of cycad palm, capable of accommodating a large nest in its crown. Males live alone, except during breeding season when a covey of sixty to eighty males invade the female's territory and both sexes indulge in a noisy orgy. Mating season is the only time vaspray are vulnerable. As soon as the mating frenzy ends, males become voracious hunters in an attempt to refuel their energy and to feed pregnant females that will not leave their nests until their eggs hatch. Ten days after a vaspray egg hatches, its mother begins to teach her nestling to fly. Twenty days later, males take fledglings into the fourth dimension and when a young vaspray flies out of the fourth, its mastery is comparable to any adult.

Vaspray do have a few limitations. Their large size makes them unexceptional flyers over long third-dimensional distances and this limits their range. Fire terrifies them and they realize humanoids possess weapons capable of killing them from a distance. Vaspray energy vibrates at a faster rate than ours and their lifespan is not more than a few phases at best. If they lived longer, their cunning would undoubtedly improve. Vaspray have no propensity for radically altering the physical environment and philosophically, I guess that makes them less dangerous than our kind.

****

During *quarrying*, every warrior anticipates a jump to the fourth dimension. A warrior might jump to circumvent physical dangers or to discover if his attitude is creating new shadows he needs to address. No warrior deliberately engages vaspray because it's a foolish game that's impossible to win. Thanks to Kyron, I got a firsthand glimpse of a warrior who decided to provoke vaspray. Kyron took me to the planet Gathos, to see my sister Sophia and her husband Coreese. While there, we took a side trip to a confederate school, Sycottie Shardasko. Kyron said he wanted to visit an old friend that was in hospital for treatment. His friend was a master who, as a neophyte, received the moniker Riyarday (meaning, "anger quelled") from his master. A few days earlier, I foiled Aytinous in the shadow-dancing chamber for the first time and was beaming with heroic pride. That morning Kyron said, "While your victory with Aytinous is impressive, you are not yet ready to help me clean our communal toilets." In retrospect, I realize Kyron contrived this meeting with Riyarday to expose me to an important lesson concerning pride and cure any spurious notions I entertained concerning heroism.

Riyarday's physical appearance was enough to vanquish any notions I harbored regarding fighting vaspray in this dimension or any other. Riyarday's appearance was fierce. At fifty Fire phases (200 years), he still was a mountain of a man with a deep, booming voice capable of projecting lessons in terms of absolutes. He wore some deep and ugly scars from a long ago confrontation with a vaspray. His right ear lobe was missing and so was part of his nose. A scar, from where the wing-barb of a vaspray clipped him, ran across his left cheek and ended on his chin. His old wounds had become re-infected, because a parasite infects vaspray that hosts a fungus that can lead to necrosis. The necrosis eating away Riyarday, so far, was incurable. "Listen to me, boy," he thundered. "Vaspray cut for a reason—so they can pour all their free-radical poison inside you." He moved his head from side to side as if struggling to look around a solid obstacle blocking his view. "I got a blind spot," he roared, "and I'm hard of hearing too, so speak up and tell me your moniker."

"My moniker is Élan, sir."

Riyarday softened as if his armor unintentionally popped open and now he must reveal his big heart. His voice thickened and clogged with emotion. "You are a fine looking lad, with a balanced face. Keep it that way." He snatched my chin and turned my head sideways. "You got a nice straight nose too. Keep your nose pointed toward Shardasko truths and nothing else." He tapped me on the side of my head. "And listen to Master Kyron. He's a fine warrior." Then Riyarday picked up his shirt and showed me his chest where two old wounds intersected. His chest bore an X where the vaspray cut him. The X was turning necrotic and sinking inward as if he were a piece of fruit rotting from the inside out.

All the way back to Sutcay Tay, I pondered Riyarday and his fate. We went to Kyron's *tritum* and prepared a late supper. As I furiously diced up vegetables with a huge cleaver, Kyron interrupted my reverie with, "Let it go, Élan. Let it go and let's see where it flies." The experiences of the day still were unwinding in me and I was unsure about what to say.

Later, while we ate by the light of a single candle, I broke the meditative silence to ask, "Master Kyron, what are your thoughts on Riyarday? Why did he attempt to fight vaspray?"

Kyron laid his *estern* (an eating utensil) across the side of his plate with faultless attention before looking up. He leaned forward until the candlelight caught the rutilates in his eyes. "The path of a Shardasko Warrior is never straight. It is a labyrinth filled with dead ends, energy-draining loops, and trapdoors that spring open with a mere thought. Riyarday is a great warrior who once fell through a trapdoor and found that he was angry about it. He now realizes his freedom, but his battle was long and took its toll. Riyarday has volunteered to stand as a sentinel at that trapdoor, to point to the dangers as other warriors make their way through the labyrinth." Kyron fell silent and with absolute concentration, picked up his *estern* and resumed eating. Before we sat in formal meditation, we lit a candle for Riyarday and Kyron again said, "Riyarday is a great warrior. Others pass him by, but he remains as a sacred icon so we might glimpse the truth." In the days following our visit with Riyarday, Kyron expanded the original lesson, explaining the essential meaning of what it means to be an authentic warrior. "A warrior does not waste his precious energy upon anger or in boastful displays of courage. A warrior moves though life and takes only what he needs and after he is gone, leaves no trace of himself behind." This one statement, I believe, is the distillation of thirty thousands phases of Gathosian wisdom and the essence of what it means to be an authentic Shardasko Warrior.

In the Gathosian mind, the greatest triumph in life is to become an elusive adept, one who knows, yet remains unknown. This is an ancient archetype firmly embedded in the early mythology of the Island Worlds of Gathos. A physical body capable of sensitive interaction with its environment facilitates this art of elusion. Usually, the Gathosian physique is elegant, svelte, and flexible. Merely watching Gathosians walk can be a fascinating distraction, while seeing them dance is a wonder to behold. Their four-toed feet tend to be narrow and their four-fingered hands are thin and long. As they speak, hands and fingers gesticulate and dance through the air. Gathosians joke about their mannerisms and sometimes say, "If you tied the hands of any Gathosian behind his back, he would be unable to speak." Physical elegance and joy of movement seems inborn in these people. Even simple peasants, who do strenuous physical labor, dance at the Festival of the Elements with the supple grace of accomplished dancers. When Gathosians first encountered Human civilizations, Gathosians were alarmed that sentient humanoids, similar to themselves, were enthusiastic carnivores and naturally, they began comparing their history to Human history. Many Gathosians now believe the principle of, "we should take only what we need and after we are gone, leave no trace of ourselves behind," as the singular most important belief that distinguishes them from Humans. In many ways, it's the Gathosian equivalent of the Human Golden Rule.

****

I stood along the stream, squinting at the splatter of vaspray clawprints in the moist sand. I moved into a perspective Shardasko Warriors call *turami savatnani*, which means, "circular awareness." It's a hyper-vigilant state of mind, where a warrior centers himself and senses his complete physical surroundings with all the skills he possesses. It takes personal composure and awareness to do this properly. One must be critical and experience reality without preconceived notions and prepare to adapt to each new situation as it presents itself. For several seconds, I became a holographic plate recording the scene. Not a hair did I move until I had scrutinized the physical reality around me. Then, retreating backward, into the water, I obscured my footprints in the sand with the flat part of a stick. On the original bank, I did the same. With great care, I plucked a few palmara leaves from a nearby stand and lashed the leaves to the bottoms of my feet with strips of soaple vine. Secluding myself deeper in the ocean of green, I macerated additional leaves until they were pliable enough to pierce with a fickleberry thorn. I threaded the leaves onto a length of vine and fashioned two crude skirts. To camouflage the major portions of my pale skin, I tied one skirt around my waist and one around my shoulders. As I was doing this, spontaneous prayers welled up inside me and helped me recoup my locus of concentration.

A half-hour later, I resumed my initial stride. I had penetrated the Great Verdant Abyss to a depth of roughly 32 kilometers. 290 kilometers more and I would walk into the village of Sheebrun where Kyron awaited. Unless I faltered and missed my time declaration, he was honor-bound not to assist me through a direct telepathic link. Nevertheless, when a warrior enters the Great Verdant, his master travels to Sheebrun and waits as a beacon of confidence and strength. Aytinous once confided that the inspiration that carried him briskly across the Abyss was his link to Kyron, who was standing near the edge of the woods when Aytinous emerged.

When Insanio reached its apex, I rested at the edge of a *loosh* (a small opening in the tree canopy, where one can see the sky). At midday, the Great Verdant falls into an intoxicating hush. The air becomes intensely fragrant with the redolence of flowers as nature releases its natural soporifics. Sitting on a flat rock, I slowly sank into the green profusion of the forest. I could taste the perfumed air and intense feelings of bliss swept me away. After a while, I found myself wandering through the rainforest. This is dangerous, yet part of me entertained relaxed notions of spending the rest of my days in this semiconscious state. Lost, I sat down in an effort to get my bearings. Nearby, a pair of furry gray maskits seemed oblivious to the heat and somehow found the energy to chase each other up and down a fallen log. The maskits kept distracting me, pulling me back into a trance, while my mind struggled to find a reference point. I glanced down and spied an empty tortoise shell on the ground. Picking up the shell, I used the point of a rock and carved EJC on its surface. Afterward, I studied my handiwork and told myself, "I am Élan Journey Cœur, a Shardasko Warrior." This managed to break the spell. The shell had a hole in one end made by a borer worm. I took a length of soaple vine and laced it through the hole, so I could wear the shell around my neck.

An hour later, I found fresh water and scrubbed the shell clean with sand. The shell made a handy drinking vessel when I discovered a stand of ripe diskberries. Squeezing juice from a few tender palmara leaves, I mixed the juice with the diskberries and the concoction served as a nutritious and refreshing mint-flavored drink. An hour later, I noticed a bract of small, white phylophenium orchids growing in the crotch of a low tree. I ate a tiny portion of one of the orchid petals. Purple phylopheniums are eatable, but I was unsure about the white ones. Near nightfall, I knew I had penetrated the Verdant Abyss to a depth of roughly 40 kilometers. My strength held and I decided to continue walking as long as possible. This approach to *quarrying* is common practice. While energy remains strong, warriors consider it advantageous to penetrate the Great Verdant as deeply as possible. Nothing is more demoralizing than being four or five days into *quarrying* with 200 kilometers still to walk.

It took the remainder of the night to cover an additional 8 kilometers, but my confidence remained high. I started to believe my walk across the Abyss would be uneventful except for sighting a few vaspray clawprints along a stream. By morning of day two, most of my makeshift clothing was gone. Sensing no vaspray in my vicinity, I discarded the remaining leaves. At half-day, Insanio blazed at the apogee of the sky and the humidity hung like ghostly ectoplasm along the ground. The terrain was steeper now and walking more difficult. I did not stop, as I had the previous day, yet it took until late afternoon to cover a paltry 4 kilometers. As early evening advanced, tiny patches of blue sky, viewable through the treetops, grew dark and a torrential rain began to fall. After a while, water oozed from the ground and made walking treacherous. Once or twice, I missed a step and bruised my barefoot on a sharp rock. Brief periods of inattention seized me, signaling my physical fatigue. Picking some tiny palmara leaves, I mashed them up in my tortoise shell with rainwater. I was bored with the mint taste of palmara, but found no other eatables. For added nutrition, I forced myself to eat the leaves along with drinking the juice.

Huge-rock outcroppings poked up among the dense trees and I discovered a handy refuge where three rocks leaned against one another and formed a simple cave. As I gathered a fresh supply of palmara leaves and blessed them for being my food, clothing, and now my bedding, *shahaut* was upon me. Scattering a few leaves inside the small shelter, I crawled inside and made myself comfortable. I removed my tortoise shell and laid it by my side. Then I entered a state of meditation warriors call *delchow savatnani*, which means, "rekindling awareness."

*Delchow savatnani* is a conscious act of interior fragmentation that restores individual integrity to the major parts of the self. *Delchow savatnani* is the underpinning upon which each warrior constructs his conscious purity and trust in himself. During this state, the *Holder* acts as a guardian while the body reposes and restores, mind floats in tranquility, and feelings are venting. Feelings function as a filter between the *Holder* and the mind and body. So if anything impedes feelings from venting, during *delchow savatnani*, interior functions begin to create greater distortions. Distortions cannot help but encumber communications among our centers of consciousness and while *delchow savatnani* is safe in normal situations, in the middle of *quarrying*, there are risks.

****

All physical creatures possess a body, mind, feelings, and an *Holder* and all physical creatures need reparation, be it as simple as sleep or as sophisticated as *delchow savatnani*. We cannot expect to dam up our feelings because we are in an inconvenient location, anymore than we can expect our hearts to stop beating or our lungs to stop breathing. If anything, facing the Great Verdant demands that this process be working in top form. I already had made three mistakes. I failed to block the entrance to my cave with an additional rock; I backed into a hole with only one way out; and finally, I become preoccupied with the venting of my feelings and went internal for about thirty seconds. This state of inattention is where all accidents happen, where individuals step in front of fast moving vehicles and walk blindly off cliffs.

I felt a tickle along my left ankle and a bolt of realization shot up through my leg. My *Holder* reacted first and put an energetic hand over my mouth to prevent me from making a sound. It took me about three seconds to realize a dulcerary panther had crawled inside my shelter with me. It took me another three seconds to realize the dulcerary was struggling to escape from a flock of vaspray that landed outside our mutual retreat. I expected to die, even thinking, you deserve to die for such incredible laxity. My life did not flash before my eyes, but rather a vision of my incompletion seized me. I strained to glimpse future sunrises yet unseen, longed to savor days I never lived, and grasped for feelings that slipped away like the last rays of Insanio. And all the while, I could hear the arrogant chattering of the vaspray, communicating in an unintelligible language of screeching and gibes, a language I considered the antithesis of all poetry, music, and reason.

If I attempted to jump to the fourth dimension, I would drag the dulcerary with me. Like Tajáno, major parts of me were attempting to execute a leap, but my *Holder* blocked the way with the warning, *the dulcerary is an unknown factor*. It took me another three seconds to decide my *Holder* meant to suck the juice of meaning from my last few breaths of life. I responded by aligning completely with my body and then I knew true fear. My basal instincts were scrambling while my mind became aware that I soon could be dead. Even my Shardasko skills seemed to sputter into absurdity. Outside my training, I knew I lacked the ultimate cunning and wile of the vaspray. Hurled into new chaos, I saw my riddled self and my limitations. I was a flinty little rock hoping my occasional spark might scare the beasts away.

My *Holder* stepped fully into my body and told me my feelings of worthlessness were fanning the flames of my fear. I knew then that my *Holder* was the ultimate warrior, not me. I was prepared to withdraw to the fourth dimension. Yet my *Holder*, which easily could have stepped back— gone anywhere—and watched its incarnation die, did not. My *Holder* was the one component within my hierarchy willing to fulfill the first tenet of all warriors everywhere—it chose to be present and be responsible. Paradoxically, this realization renewed my importance and crumbled my pride at the same time.

My *Holder* dominated my every function and began using my mind as its own. As soon as this happened, I was stone cold with acceptance. Not more than fifteen seconds had elapsed since I first jerked to attention. As my inimitable *Holder* dominated me, I became a junior partner in my life and the apparatus of its greater will. Blind, deaf, and dumb to anything outside my body, I heard only my breathing, the throbbing of my heart, and my *Holder* telling me, *the honorable path is to introduce a sense of absolute serenity inside this small refuge and to burnish it with your complete dominion. This will help calm the dulcerary and establish our authority. Communicate with the beast. Through communication, it will recognize our interdependence and a thread of hope exists that it will not kill you.*

My psychic projections needed to be scrupulous. The vaspray were a short distance away and if they did not realize my proximity, they certainly would if my psychic projections grew too large. A tiny crack opened in my energy mass and I made my communication as precise as a laser beam, in the direction of the dulcerary's ear. My message went out on a frequency just below my heart and I made sure to fill my projection with plenty of camaraderie. *I will not harm you*, I thought

The dulcerary was female and smaller than the one I encountered the first day of my *quarrying*. Testing the waters, attempting to communicate with her *Holder*, I received nothing back. The animal was lying flat on her belly, with her paws crunched up under her stomach. To give her sufficient room, I drew my legs up tighter against my chest. Her long tail twitched in nervous agitation and made gooseflesh prickles up and down my arm. Her tail became an outward expression of her feelings, an attempt to vent her nervous agitation at being stuck in a hole with a creature she considered food. A few more seconds elapsed and I filled our mutual space with thoughts of fraternity. She ignored me. Her tail snapped, emitting bursts of nervous energy. The body of the dulcerary blocked my view, but I could smell the sickening, sweet stink of the vaspray. Whatever they were doing, it was a noisy affair. Chattering, accompanied by a methodical vibration, grew in intensity. "Thump! Thump-bump!" and then, "Thump! Thump-bump!" again, as if the vaspray were hammering out coded messages with their feet against a hollow log.

The dulcerary's rudimentary sentience flickered and I scooped all the way down into my lower energy centers to understand her meaning. *Spit on flying ghosts!* she thought and then her control wavered. A growing portion of her seemed suicidal, for she wanted to leap out of the cave and confront the vaspray face to face before she died. Never had I encountered anything like it before. It reeked of some kind of heroic nonsense—animal martyrdom!

Awaken her *Holder,* I begged my own *Holder*. The scales seemed on the verge of tipping. The dulcerary vacillated and I sent her a new calming message. As ridiculous as it was, I told her, *you are safe with me.*

Miraculously, my physical presence seemed to restrain her and she scrunched backward until her rump pressed against my legs. She put her head down between her paws in frustration. In a barely audible telepathic whisper, she attempted to communicate for the first time, perhaps wanting someone in life to understand her frustration. *Spit on flying ghosts! Eggs born rotten*, she thought.

Her meaning was clearer this time. She was cursing the vaspray, telling me they were involved in some kind of mating ritual that would end with the laying of their eggs. What a lucky break for us both. That meant the vaspray were distracted, and any creature that was distracted was incapable of using its complete psychic skills.

****

The ultimate goal of all Shardasko Warriors is to become a master of options in infinite space. Fooling the self is deadly, so I faced the facts that my space was limited and my options few. Seconds seemed like minutes in that claustrophobic cave. One minute, two minutes, even three minutes and the fact that I was still alive, seemed a miracle. Then the chattering and thumping abruptly halted and it seemed too quiet outside. One vaspray broke the silence—the voice coming from far right. I could hear the caution in its alien, "chawang?" and sense the question it posed in a tone that ended on a higher octave. I could almost hear it asking, *what was that?*

A second vaspray, a little to the left, let go a queer "tayweak!" which I interpreted as *listen!* Yet I knew they were listening with more than ears. Slowly and deliberately, I showed the dulcerary that I meant to touch her. I placed my palm on the scruff of her neck and she allowed the physical connection to happen. Using the opportunity to strengthen the connection, the instant I felt her internal rhythm, I synchronized my breathing to hers.

All at once I heard a loud, dull thump overhead and knew the vaspray were converging, to see what hid beneath those three rocks. My imagination swarmed with nightmares. Beyond our cave, it sounded as if we were greatly outnumbered. Again, I heard chattering, but this time their communications remained subdued, as their plotting outlined an imminent assault. A frightened little gurgle erupted from the dulcerary's throat, and life and death hung on cause and effect, action and reaction. A few more seconds of absolute silence, then in barely audible tones—I heard a "hewuuuu" and the exhalation of a foul-smelling breath poured into our cave. The vaspray made their first mistake. One poked its head a millimeter too close to the opening of the cave. In one fast instinctive response, comparable to the finest Shardasko masters, the dulcerary lashed out. An instant before she struck, I wisely removed my hand from her neck and glued my body to the rear wall. She recoiled and then snapped like a spring. When she snapped, she lashed out at the foul-smelling breath at the entrance to our cave and ripped the face of the vaspray. The injured vaspray shrieked and retreated followed by cries and sounds of sympathetic moaning, mixed with more chatter and angry "caws" and "chuck! Chuck! Chuck!" The smell of blood wafted into our cave and I suppressed a strong urge to vomit.

Mayhem erupted as the vaspray began a frantic thumping and pecking at the rock protection above our heads. The intense pressure I was exerting on my *Holder* to jump dimensions, climaxed at that instant. Sanction exploded inside me and I knew I was clear to go. The dulcerary was bound as my dimensional traveling-companion and whatever reservations existed before, no longer mattered. I approached the Cliff of Time. *Steady,* I communicated. *Trust me,* I thrust her way. She did not understand, but I had no time to explain. I faced the future with a commitment to action. *I will hold nothing back.* I declared. *I will not loose unless I loose completely.*

I was uncertain if the vaspray realized I was in the cave too. As soon as the dulcerary vanished, the vaspray would know something peculiar occurred. Dimensional jumpers can ascertain quickly if a creature facing them is also capable of jumping dimensions. By now, I convinced myself the dulcerary was a simple and innocent animal and her innocence was the only reason my *Holder* allowed me to take her with me. I will not deny I felt a flush of rage concerning the vaspray. A portion of me wanted to jump out of the cave, exactly like the dulcerary. I wanted to scream, why don't you pick on somebody your own size? Thankfully, Riyarday was inside my head too and telling me to be a sagacious warrior. I tucked away my heroism for safekeeping. Besides, the fourth dimension offered me a multitude of options I might explore.

As soon as I jumped to the fourth, the highly psychic vaspray would sense the momentary warble created by my execution of the Envelope Feint. The warble would begin with a dim flash of light and a reverberating swish the unaware rarely, if ever, notice. Yet all dimensional jumpers realize when they see that particular flash and hear that characteristic swish, someone in their vicinity is undertaking a dimensional jump. As far as I know, Shardasko Warriors and vaspray are the only third-dimensional creatures in the geographical locale of the Abyss, capable of jumping dimensions. The predictable course for any jumper is to move forward or backward along the timeline and reemerge in the past or future. I possessed another strategy taught me by Kyron, one that required complete focus and trust in my skills as a Shardasko Warrior.

My will aligned with the intention of my *Holder*, fixed, and a dimensional door opened. I touched the haunch of the dulcerary and made the jump taking her with me into the fourth dimension in one of the cleanest jumps I ever made. When I jumped, I left no trail of myself behind and I leapt directly into the fourth that forever holds the shadow energy of that particular moment.

Perception within the fourth dimension is psychic vision not physical vision, yet what one sees, appears visual and is incredibly vivid. The key to the fourth-dimensional door sits directly between our eyes, but we cannot open that door unless we learn to focus with our complete consciousness. The experience of fourth-dimensional vision is analogous to peering through a microscope at a slide specimen. As a microscope enhances our ability to view cellular reality with greater precision, psychic vision enhances our ability to view the fourth dimension with greater intimacy and clarity. The only difference between the vision afforded by the microscope and the vision of the psychic observer is—the psychic observer is also the specimen upon the slide.

My vision adjusted and the blue-gray strands of lingering time greeted me as they flagged toward eternity. Beyond, lay the black funnel leading into the continuing concentration of all consciousness, and behind lay the third dimension. Below, dimensional doors riddled infinite space; these doors opened into tunnels that emptied into the ever-widening thinness that led to Chaos. I scanned up and down the timeline for indigent residents of the fourth, those free radicals capable of gluing themselves to our denial and making us into monsters. Nothing seemed to be pursing me except a few of my personal elusive shadows that began flitting around me like a whirlwind of tiny gray snowflakes. Then a bigger, snowball-sized apparition appeared that headed straight for the dulcerary. When the apparition made contact, it changed shape and turned into another dulcerary panther. Despite the innocence of the dulcerary, she was meeting one of her prime personal shadows for the first time. As soon as the shadow touched her, it gained strength and began to grow. Then it let go a rumbling earthquake of a roar. Like all novice time jumpers, the dulcerary did not recognize this shadow as her accumulated denial. She viewed it as another dulcerary and roared back, which frightened her shadow and caused it to disburse.

However she interpreted what she saw, she acted admirably considering she did not know what was happening and roaring back at her shadow served as a quick and effective way to vanquish denial. For humanoids, with their layers and layers of suppression, more is involved than a simple roar. Negotiation and understanding need to precede either disbursement or integration of shadows. Gathosians and Humans cannot step into the fourth dimension without extensive preparatory work. I worked for five phases before it was safe for me to make my initial jump.

All creatures that face their shadows, transform themselves in beneficial ways. Many free radicals attached to personal shadows, simple vanish and the jumper feels a sense of release and calm. True to form, as soon as the dulcerary roared away her shadow, she became as tame as a domesticated tabby cat and was content to glue her body to my side for security. I pulled her backward into the undulating time strands, where we crouched and waited for the vaspray to emerge.

Then it happened. Vaspray blasted through the wall between dimensions and appeared along the borderworld of the fourth dimension. There was no sound, but visually, it was an impressive display of illusion. The "warble" split them up and the effect made it appear as if hundreds upon hundreds of vaspray were arriving over a spread of a few seconds' time. When all their fragments emerged in the fourth, I counted thirteen birds. I felt safer from their threats here than I did in the third, for the vaspray acted as shallow travelers in the fourth, never deviating far from the timeline. True to form, like thirteen automatons, six vaspray began flying into the future and seven flew the opposite direction, into the past. Among the seven that flew into the past, I saw the vaspray the dulcerary ripped with her claws. Three deep lacerations raked across its face. Bubbly-looking fat bulged from the wound and blood dripped from its sagging jowl.

I waited an additional ten seconds and then the dulcerary and I slipped back through the opening I created moments before. It definitely was Razor Shardasko. Just as we emerged in our third-dimensional cave, I saw the tail of the last vaspray disappear into the fourth dimension. Only then did déjà vu shutter through my body and leave its wake of realization behind. I remembered the clawprints and blood I observed along the stream the previous day and knew I had experienced a narrow escape. Seven vaspray had just jumped into the third dimension of the previous day. Those seven birds were searching for me along a stream. Lucky for me in the past, the vaspray miscalculated and emerged too early.

From my present third-dimensional perspective, I knew my past was secure unless I jumped to that specific moment when I first saw the vaspray clawprints along the stream. No way would I ever jump to that previous moment, for I was not suicidal. That past moment was now forever off-limits to me. Here in the present, as the future unfolded and then refolded into the past, I enjoyed a tenuous immunity from the vaspray threat. However, six vaspray had disappeared into the future and the present and future continually converged. My fate rested on two factors: my cunning at adaptation and the intention of those six vaspray. Calculating my odds, I knew they were just about even. The hyper-sentient vaspray possessed advantages, if determined to find me. For one, through cooperative efforts they could create a phalanx across the fourth dimension that corresponded to my time and space. This would block me from using the fourth dimension, from my immediate area in the third. The fact that the dulcerary possessed the audacity to injure one of the Vaspray's own might provoke them further, and make them more determined in their pursuit. I still held a few tricks in reserve and my best trick was to adapt quickly to the reality of each new situation. Snatching my tortoise shell from the cave, I looped its vine around my neck. I lied just a little to the dulcerary. "We're safe," I told her. "Run! Run like the wind!"

# THREE

**W**hen the dulcerary and I emerged from the fourth dimension, it was *shahaut* on the third day of my *quarrying*. Following my own advice, I ran like the wind. My strategy remained straightforward and simple—put as many kilometers as possible between the vaspray and myself before first light. By all evidence, the female dulcerary intended to stay with me. She was a fast runner and quickly established a routine of doubling back and waiting for me to catch up. The vaspray could track us more easily if the dulcerary and I remained together, but I had little choice of losing her, unless I again jumped to the fourth dimension. Until the situation calmed, jumping to the fourth was a risky option.

My stamina was dwindling from scant food and little sleep and my short-circuited attempt at *delchow savatnani* was distorting my perceptions. Feelings emerged—and they were surging—anticipating every dark shadow as the vaspray. Then the dulcerary began to growl and shake her head and communicated, *not that way. Your way leads right into flying ghost country.* I stopped dead in my tracks and stared at her. *Don't stop. Hurry! Follow me.*

Holy Fecundity! Her brief foray into the fourth dimension had expanded her consciousness to the point of telepathy. My internal confusion broke loose and it was screaming, *I don't want this.* My Shardasko training had only two things to say about the matter—*you must accept each new situation* and *truth is your responsibility and karmic legacy.* This was my first inkling that my journey across the Great Verdant Abyss was going to take a little longer than I originally planned. I thought then of poor Tajáno. At least I wasn't responsible for three treacherous vaspray. My charge was a wily Dulcerary panther.

****

The dulcerary proved to be a psychically adept communicator. With minimal referential information, she possessed the ability to comprehend meaning behind language and project meaning so I could understand. Naturally, she couldn't speak Mescale, but her telepathic skills were excellent. She could have presented herself as a citizen in-good-standing in any super-conscious realm.

People plug into clairaudience, sometimes by accident and sometimes because they leap into the fourth dimension where greater reality shatters their single-minded perspective. Communication requires an input of information on one end and a recipient on the other. Psychic projections emerge from the transmitter and the recipient senses only the meaning in a flood of symbols and disordered cognition. The recipient must wrap his personal words around the deluge and interpret the message using the constructs of his or her own language. It takes lifetimes of practiced skill to hear and interpret without distortion; however, the longer one practices with a single partner, the clearer and more precise communications become. Between two Shardasko Warriors, it's a simple exercise; but between a dulcerary panther and a humanoid, communication is hampered by genetic differences. Despite the distinctions between the dulcerary and me, the longer we remained together, the easier it was for me to understand her. Her early projections were warnings, such as, *watch! It's a slithering stick* (a snake). Beyond that, her intelligence was lively and confident, although her logic was tinged with provincialism and made me smile.

I trusted her as a physical guide. The Abyss was her natural habitat and she knew the safest route around vaspray territory. She cut a wide arch to the south for 30 kilometers, before turning east. After a while, the forest grew so dense, walking became difficult. We climbed a dozen moss-covered ledges, ducked under thorny trees, and waded through swamps filled with exotic and colorful epiphytes. We seemed to be moving upland and by degrees, the terrain grew drier and cooler. We walked through a region where terrestrial orchids grew so abundantly that we seemed to be wading through wave after wave of purple translucency. I plucked a few orchids petals and ate them as I walked. Up and then down we went, but mostly up. The slow and steady climbing allowed me time to calm from my adrenaline rush with the vaspray. The new pace found its own natural and soothing rhythm. The dulcerary's butt and swinging tail became familiar sights as her body cut a temporary path through the thick vegetation.

The slower pace also gave me a chance to reconsider my situation. My journey through the Abyss involved more than living up to a time declaration. Kyron once said, "No relationship is ever one way. No one is always the teacher or always the student." I knew the dulcerary had something to teach me. We walked and climbed and greater patience descended upon me, until I felt at peace. As far as I knew, no warrior ever jumped to the fourth dimension with a dulcerary panther, only to discover the panther had attained sentience. Each *quarrying* is different, but I was the first Human crossing the Great Verdant Abyss and I thought, *perhaps the journey across is going to be a little different for me.*

\*\*\*\*

Eno seemed to rise slower than usual that morning. Gradually the green light bathed us in the blessings of full *areé didamé*. The dulcerary and I paused in a misty little *loosh* to rest. While she sauntered off to urinate, I decided to bathe in a nearby waterfall. The icy water was pure and came from high above in the Tyburnian Mountains, so it felt exhilarating to stand in the cold spray. I attempted to relax my fatigued muscles and briskly massaged my legs and feet. Then, just for a fraction of a moment, I thought, *I wish I had a simple bar of soap.*

The dulcerary returned and asked, *why are you soaking yourself in that wet?*

"I'm bathing so I don't smell," I said.

*Wetness can't wash away your smell. I could find you anywhere. You smell of crushed sweetness* (forest plants) *under my feet.*

I knew it was a compliment. "You are equally agreeable to me. I can see you give your fur attention because it is very shiny."

A private thought passed through her mind. I glimpsed a memory of her mother and she brushed the painful thought away. I saw an iceberg of unresolved grief in her then and she thought, *My-ma taught me how to care for my fur.* She shook her head and made a blubbery sound like a forced sneeze. *I feel so strange,* she thought. *What has happened to me? Am I really communicating with this balancing backlegger* (she meant me) *or am I having a sleeping experience?*

To reinforce the reality that we truly were communicating and she was awake, I continued to speak aloud. She started transmitting her thoughts more spontaneously and we got a real conversation going. She became so involved in her projections that she could not help punctuating them with growls, purrs, grawruffs, and a few gurgles. All her audible sounds were archaic, a type of sub-language she used to communicate with other members of her species. Now that she was an evolving sentient, she no longer needed to grunt, but she could not suppress her verbal diphthongs. Not all the conscious enlightenment in creation could stop either of us from being our habitual selves with millenniums of genetic predisposition defining our behavior.

I used sweeping hand gestures and simple terms when attempting to explain what happened to her. "When we left the cave together, I took you to a faraway place and the experience helped you see better and farther than ever before." I pointed to my eyes. "Balancing backleggers call it greater perspective." Then I pointed to my head. "Greater perspective has awakened your larger consciousness and now you can talk with me through the means of telepathy."

She emerged from her reverie concerning her mother and pushed a question in my direction. *Telepathy?* she grawruffed.

"A conversation that bypasses spoken words is called telepathy."

She flicked an ear when an insect buzzed around her a moment too long. *Telepathy,* she repeated a few times. *Telepathy feels strange. It's a soundless voice.* She turned alert and sat upon her haunches. *When we came out of faraway place, I heard Wind speak in the way of telepathy. Wind told me the flying ghosts were gone. Then you said, 'Run like the Wind.'* She admonished me. *It's boastful to think we can run like Wind. My Troubler* (doubt) *asked me if it was possible for a balancing backlegger really to hear Wind.*

Stepping away from the waterfall, I shook water off my body. "Sometimes I hear the wind when it blows through treetops and often I can feel the wind tickle my face. Even when I cannot hear the wind, I know it is around me because it helps dry my body when I'm wet."

She peered at me and I swear I could see curiosity forming as she cocked her head to one side. *Wind travels fast and seems to run away, but Wind is forever.* The red pupils of her huge, golden eyes dilated. *What did Wind once name you besides balancing backlegger?*

Dancing around to dry my body, I ran fingers through my hair as I would a comb. "I'm unsure what you mean, but my master named me Élan."

*Does Élan claim meaning?*

"Élan means fire, passion, and freedom."

*Are you all those things?*

"I try to be."

*Then it's a fine name. Tell me, why do you call Wind my-master?*

"My master is not the wind, but another balancing backlegger similar to me." I touched my penis and crossed the forefingers on both my hands to demonstrate opposites and said, "opposite of you and your ma." She understood.

*Master heard your name from Wind because you couldn't. Before I learned to hear Wind, my-ma told me Wind chose Cerebow for my name.* She began to purr. *It's difficult to translate into actual words, the emphasis Cerebow put on her name. The sound in my head was so lovely, like the deep-rolling vibrations of conference drums or distant thunder, still a long way off.*

"Does Cerebow claim meaning?"

"Cerebow means 'gusting of Wind' like when it comes as a surprise.'"

I laughed. "Well, little surprise, do you think we've eluded the flying ghosts for a while?"

She abruptly glanced around to assure herself that we were safe. As she sniffed the air, her long tail twitched in agitation. *They can't fly here because the sweetness* (forest) *is everywhere. Flying ghosts get crunched in sweetness.* She meant the trees were so dense that the vaspray would not have ample wing clearance. Scanning the scene through *turami savatnani*, allowing my psychic senses to reach farther and farther away, physical reality did seem safe. If the vaspray wanted to land in the small clearing, they would need to pop in via the fourth dimension. Then I understood a truth Cerebow knew through instinct. The densest part of the forest was safer for me, just as the darkest dark was safer.

\*\*\*\*

I decided to rest, but took practical precautions before I did. Searching the immediate area, I found a straight, sturdy stick that I could use for emergency protection. That's when a second wish came tumbling out of my mind. *It would be nice if I had my knife, so I could hone the tip of this stick to a point?* Improvising, from a nearby firethorn bush, I found a thorn, the size of my thumb, and lashed it to the end of the stick with *soaple* vine. To make my weapon more menacing, I crushed a red-hot fickleberry on the thorn-tip. The capsicum in fickleberries has a well-deserved reputation for burning like fire on skin contact. I said to Cerebow, "Let's climb up that short outcropping above and sit in the shade of those rocks."

Above, I picked a few large palmara leaves to sit on and leaned my back against a smooth rock. From my new perspective, I felt secure. I possessed a full view of the *loosh* below and a weapon if I needed it. Fresh water for drinking and bathing were nearby and all the palmara leaves and orchids I could eat. I also enjoyed the companionship of a sweet, sentient female who wanted to be my friend and guide. Naturally, our separate species were irreconcilably different, but my feelings used the opportunity to slip a third wish my way. This thought I dismissed, just as I had for the last seven phases. However, when this thought left me, it went directly into the fourth dimension where the thought joined my other shadows in a macabre dance of denied sexual desire.

Sitting on that rocky outcropping, I understood for the first time that I had struck a few precarious bargains over the past seven phases. I knew the sex urge never goes away, yet my will and mind were in total agreement. My proper destiny was to fulfill myself as a Shardasko Warrior. Shardasko precepts are explicit concerning abstinence. Soon after entering training, I stood on the stage of the Air Palace, with other neophytes, and swore, "Upon my sacred integrity, I accept and will uphold the guidelines of the abstinence precepts." This vow did nothing to ease my typical adolescent yearnings. As I advanced through the levels of training, I learned how to unite my energy centers toward my goal. The process of alignment opens a warrior to increased energy. Need for sexual release does not lessen, the need becomes more intense. When Kyron and I traveled off-campus or to other planets for conferences, I would see Gathosian women, who are some of the most exquisite beauties in creation. Seeing them, even from a distance, made my heart feel fluttery and I would get lightheaded and silly as my energy drained into my groin. Sometimes I would attempt to memorize their faces and remember the way their bodies moved, so I could think about them later. Human women were nearly unknown to me because I had seen only a few in the flesh.

With no women involved in Shardasko life, men were in the strict and intimate fraternity of other men. Neophytes rarely, if ever, indulged in sexual activity because their masters would know and challenge the neophyte's singularity of purpose. Despite these precautions, even as a neophyte, I knew a hidden underbelly existed at the Sutcay Tay School. Sexual liaisons did exist between a few Emblematic Warriors. Always discreet, yet common knowledge, warriors mentioned this practice only through innuendo. Like most adolescents, I longed to believe in absolutes. Role models with impeccable virtues were important to me. Because I wanted to believe Shardasko Warriors were irreproachable, I learned to ignore this duplicity and gloss over the double standard of the few.

I, along with eighty-three other neophytes, entered the Sutcay Tay School, during the phase of Fecundity, 8425. Only six of the eighty-four survived First Cut. Because I was one of the six, Sophia and Coreese finally realized my intention to become a Shardasko Warrior was serious. My brother-in-law, Coreese, is a self-assured person and his confidence serves him well. He is a successful investment manager who inherited a chair from his father on the Gathosian stock exchange. As a child, Coreese received a blueprint of his life from his father and the one outrageous act of rebellion he indulged was to marry a Human woman. During my first two years at the Sutcay Tay School, Coreese and Sophia pressured me to change my mind about becoming a Shardasko Warrior. Shamefully, they even undertook to bribe Kyron with money, in an effort to make me quit. On one of our visits to Gathos, Coreese said to Kyron, "Let me be perfectly candid with you, Master Kyron. Sophia and I hoped a short hiatus on Sutcay Tay would cure this Shardasko fever in Journey (they refused to call me Élan). Now he has squandered two phases of his life and seems more intent than ever on this harsh lifestyle. I understand the trauma of losing his parents was traumatic, but now he is approaching manhood and should be considering his higher education. Isolating himself, on a backward planet such as Sutcay Tay, will do nothing to secure his future in the real world. It makes no sense to live as an ascetic, when Sophie and I can provide him with all he needs. What can he hope to gain by excluding himself from the pleasures of life and more importantly, from the love and companionship of women? Besides, abstinence practiced in a strict male community is unnatural and breeds deviant behavior."

Out of respect for my family, that day Kyron called me Journey too. "I'm sorry you feel that way. I hoped your opinions concerning Journey's decision to continue his training would have softened by now. As a Shardasko master, I'm aware that abstinence in an all-male setting has its difficulties, but abstinence is the fastest way to concentrate our energy inward. If we become one with our *Holder*, then we are secure in our unique purpose and our virtue is unimpeachable. As a Shardasko master, I make a personal pledge to each my warriors to protect them from harm until they become independent Emblematic Warriors. Honoring this duty, I continue to be explicit with Journey concerning sexual matters and he understands what he is forfeiting and what he can expect in exchange, if he continues with training. He has decided to continue and I plan to be his champion."

Coreese was unmoved. "I'm sorry Master Kyron, but Sophia and I don't believe in or support abstinence. Shardasko emphasis is otherworldly and lopsided."

Up to that point, Kyron spoke softly like an obsequious old man. Now his complete mastery emerged. He had lived ten thousand lives—been an innocent, a consummate sinner, a king, a saint, and finally the complete sage. Now, wherever he sat, he accepted the situation as home. With lifetimes of experiential wisdom as his foundation, he was unafraid to raise the stakes and he took the question of my future to the highest levels with Coreese. Kyron's voice held incredible authority, yet he did not raise his voice, if anything, he spoke more quietly. "It's inconsequential whether you or I believe or approve of abstinence because belief and approval always are a subjective affair. Each of us travels an objective path, but our reactions and beliefs in the virtue of each path, remain personal. This is Journey's life; and his life is an affair between him and his *Holder* and neither you nor I have the right to dictate his decisions or approve his goals. When he finishes with Shardasko training, he will know he is finished because absolute awareness is the goal of Shardasko training. I want you to understand that I once enjoyed the pleasures of marriage with an incredibly lovely woman. I know the fulfillment this life holds. I've also been a Shardasko Warrior for over one hundred twenty phases and realize its flaws as well as its virtues. No equity exists in any life without commitment to it; and one life is never superior to another, no matter how much we attempt to convince ourselves of the righteousness of any one choice. Journey wants to be a Shardasko Warrior and my intention is to acquaint him with as many Shardasko virtues as possible and help him avoid the pitfalls when they appear. I respect his freewill because my interest is the education of his immortal soul. My commitment to him is complete, for if I fail to bring Journey to spiritual maturity, then I fail too. Tell me, can your commitment to Journey's evolution compare with mine?"

Coreese had no interest in becoming my mentor. The truth was, Sophia felt guilty about cutting me lose at a tender age and now she was pressuring Coreese to help her extricate me from the Shardasko life. It was too late, for I already loved Kyron beyond question. My total awe for him actually prevented me from telling him, "My love for you equals your commitment to me." It's difficult to explain in actual words the authority any master exercises over his warriors, but it always is an intense two-way focus. Kyron possessed many noble virtues, but of all his virtues, his total commitment to me was the most seductive of all.

How did I handle my sexual urges? The usual enigmatic Kyron turned explicit as a cohort when discussing my sexual urges. "You are a man born during a phase of Fire, when Ravenna was in close conjunction with Insanio," he explained. "You cannot distance yourself from sexuality as someone who was born in a phase of Air or Water because you're too hot. Your challenge is to transform your obvious propensity into your greatest virtue. Take charge of your powerful sex drive and funnel it into your *Holder*." Kyron was specific about how I should accomplish this funneling and it was through, "sacred masturbation." I followed his advice and thought of my *Holder* primarily as feminine and my masturbation as an act of sacred communion. Since meditation never afforded me a clear image of my *Holder*, sometimes I superimposed the faces of the few Gathosian women I saw upon my *Holder*. When I did this, I felt confused and ended up feeling guilty. Confessions to Kyron only made him laugh. "It makes no difference," he said. "Your *Holder* wears many faces and feels comfortable behind them all. Look closer, Élan. Look closer at your *Holder* and you will discover that it balances both feminine and masculine with ease. Learn to respond to the masculine or the feminine as your *Holder* requires." Now after seven phases of entertaining both the feminine and masculine perspective, in response to the needs of my *Holder*, I can play either role.

****

The sun Gearthot climbed higher and *areé didamé*, which began that morning as a deep emerald green, slowly morphed into a soft mossy gray. Languid with fatigue, the singing repetition of faraway birds made me sleepy. Cerebow sat facing the clearing with her paws dangling over a rock. She was a natural Shardasko Warrior and I asked her, "You think of my kind as a balancing backlegger, but what do you call others such as yourself?"

She glanced over her shoulder and told me, *Wind calls my kind, "chosen special." Wind tells us we are her favored and select kind.*

Why the wind was involved in so many of Cerebow's thoughts was puzzling. Then, I realized she was not really talking about wind, but talking about Wind as an elemental deity. I wondered how a dulcerary panther could develop an abstract spiritual concept, comparable to an evolved humanoid? *Did a pandemic link exist among the 900 Gathosian planets that made all its indigent creatures think in elemental terms?* All Gathosian religions essentially were some form of elemental worship. My questing turned further inward, where I had to admit that even I was not completely free of elemental idolatry. Elemental worship affected, or infected, me too. After all, I felt a great affinity with the Eternal Waters Sanctuary. I was as close to being Gathosian as any Human might be. Born and bred on these worlds, Gathosian language and mythology saturated my thinking. Back on Ravenna, natives—at least sentient humanoid natives—all were elemental worshipers. Thousands of cults thrived on the nine hundred planets of Gathos, but every one focused on an elemental spirit. And worship was not confined to Water, Air, Fire, and Fecundity, for there were Cloud followers, Crystal gazers, Star and Moon devotees, and Rainbow spiritualists, to name a few. The great Gathosian masses worshiped nature and many claimed a particular element chose them and spoke to them in intimate ways. Elemental worship was so entrenched in the Gathosian mind that even in the illuminated ambience of the Sutcay Tay School, four elemental temples literally defined the cornerstones of the campus.

My mind jumped and questioned my limited beliefs. *Could elemental spirits be more than symbolic icons?* I longed to communicate with a variety of other species to understand their views on elemental worship. *What, or who, did vaspray worship?* I became lost in my personal projections and concluded, with no evidence whatsoever, that vaspray were air worshipers. I knew I still entertained too many assumptions and some of my assumptions were as ingrained as Cerebow's genetic predilection to accompany her telepathy with archaic grunts. Up to now, I presumed elements were symbols that contained energy, but no consciousness. When I traced this belief backward through my memory, I could see I inherited this belief from my snobby boarding-school education and my parents who considered elemental worship superstitious Gathosian nonsense.

Cerebow interrupted my drifting mind with her own musings. *I sit in this place looking out from above. Wind comes and talks to me, and teaches me the names of things. It named your kind balancing backlegger, and another kind, flying ghost. That body part* (she meant my tortoise shell) *once was part of a wisdom walker.* A wisdom walker, I loved it! Never again could I think of a tortoise in any other way than as a wisdom walker. Wind calls each kind by its true name, she explained to me with great confidence.

I tried to show her that my appearance was unlike the balancing backleggers she usually saw. I stuck out my tongue and showed her my hands. "I have a pink tongue and ten fingers and toes."

*To me, you look like every other balancing backlegger.*

"My specific kind of balancing backlegger comes from a faraway place, a planet called Earth."

*Did we go to Earth when we escaped from the flying ghosts?*

"No," and I pointed toward the sky. "Earth is lost in the points of light that appear in the nighttime sky. We cannot see Earth with our physical eyes. We would need to travel in a spaceship to get there." I resorted to hand gestures again, showing that if my right hand were a spaceship and my left hand were a flying ghost, the spaceship would fly above the flying ghost.

Cerebow called spaceships, "shiny flyers." *Once my-ma led me to the edge of the sweetness and we watched as a shiny flyer perched upon land. When the shiny flyer opened, my-ma said a great my-ma was giving birth to many balancing back-leggers. Now I know this cannot be true. The huge shiny flyer, of which you speak, is a thing-put-together, like a nest in a tree.* She looked over her right shoulder and stared at me again. *Is that why you balance on your back legs, so you can put shiny flyers together?*

"That's very observant of you."

*Tell me more about the things you put together.*

"First, tell me about Wind and what it tells you."

She gazed into the distance before telling me, *Wind speaks truth. Wind sometimes brings special smells and then I know flying ghosts soon will follow. I can smell flying ghosts before they arrive, if they fly with honor like most lovely sweetness flyers* (birds), *but usually they do not. Now, thanks to you, I understand how flying ghosts appear from faraway place. They watch and then they swoop down and kill. They have no honor and I spit on all flying ghosts! They took my-ma for food without her permission and ate her very last bone.*

The image of the voracious vaspray killing another creature made me shutter. "I'm sorry you lost your my-ma. I lost my ma in a meteor storm."

*Meteor storm?*

Again pointing toward the sky, I explained, "When the points of light seem to fall from the sky."

*I've watched the falling lights, but I'm unafraid. I no longer fear flying ghosts either, since you took me to faraway place. Tell me about faraway place so I can go there again. It interests me because it seems to be home to a large chosen special. I want to get to know that large chosen special, because all chosen specials are one and through our combined power, I will learn to defeat all flying ghosts.*

My own amazement silenced me. Her statement was literal, but the meaning behind her declaration was a signal that her *Holder* was on the verge of sweeping away the last tacky vestiges of her simplicity. Cerebow could not go back. She would make jump after jump in consciousness until she could jump anywhere at will. A part of me mourned her innocence, for she was the vanguard of her species and her journey would be lonely. "We call that faraway place the fourth dimension," I said.

*Fourth dimension. What is the purpose of fourth dimension?*

"Telling you means you must take responsibility for all your actions."

She blinked and jerked back her head as if startled. *The chosen special always take responsibility. We cooperate with Wind and it sends our scent out to our food. We show ourselves to our food before we eat. We take responsibility for the things we eat and never take the life of what we cannot eat. Often, our food waits for us and considers itself privileged that it is feeding the hunger of the chosen special. I did not take your life in the cave because it would have been cowardly to trap you, although you smelled good and I was hungry. This is my pride and the pride of all chosen specials. Now, tell me about fourth dimension,* she said again.

Attempting to use her language, I told her, "The fourth dimension is a snag zone filled with thorns and briars, similar to the thorns and briars which grow on the edge of the sweetness and catch bits of your fur as you walk past. The fourth dimension is outside time, a place of no aging. It functions as a separation between what we consider physical reality and the remainder, about which we know very little."

*Once I stepped on a thorn and it hurt.*

"You've got the right idea. Sometimes thorns do more than catch bits of fur; sometimes thorns hurt. That huge chosen special you met in the fourth dimension was like a piece of your fur caught by a thorn."

She glanced over her shoulder toward her tail and then at her front paws. *I seem to be all here.*

"When we were trapped in the cave, you created that chosen special with the feelings you could nor express. When you roared at the chosen special, you reclaimed the original energy you put into it. Sometimes balancing backleggers call what you saw, a shadow."

Dawn was arriving and the sun Gearthot sill sat low in the sky. Shadows were long and it was easy to demonstrate what I meant. I pointed to each our shadows upon the ground and she understood. *The chosen special call shadows little selves; but a little self cannot come loose from the thing that made it.*

"True, but the farther away from the light one gets, the longer the little self appears. Sometimes, when the energy we put into a little self grows powerful, it appears to break away, but it really cannot break. Instead, the umbilical"—I pointed to my navel—"grows long and thin as one blade of grass. When this happens, the little self feels lost and seeks refuge in the fourth dimension, but it's impossible for the little self, or shadow, to come loose from the thing that made it. You can attest to that truth because when we arrived in the fourth dimension, your shadow knew you as its own."

*Why didn't you encounter your shadow in fourth dimension?*

"Because balancing backleggers possess a learning we call Shardasko training that teaches us how to negotiate fourth dimensional space. I'm a Shardasko Warrior and have learned to integrate most of my little selves."

*Do you take pride in reclaiming your little selves?*

"A Shardasko Warrior regards pride as vanity."

*Pride is good. I can see you have pride and pride makes you one of the few chosen special, just like me.*

"I'm unsure what you mean. It's true many balancing backleggers believe they are chosen specials, just as you believe you are a chosen special."

She looked confused and I guess we were mirroring each other. *But I am a chosen special. My kind is select, the favorite of Wind.*

My empathy went out to her. I remember when Kyron began shredding my childish assumptions like a head of cabbage. The old saying is true, "When the student is ready, the teacher arrives." As this moment's teacher, I decided to push Cerebow a bit further because I thought it important that she expand her consciousness to include the specialty of life everywhere. "I have visited other worlds, other dimensions, and I remember other times," I told her. "I know many kinds of chosen specials exist. A chosen special does not always look as we do. For instance, a chosen special can even look like a flying ghost."

*No!* she said and her no came tagged with an annoying growl. *My-ma told me chosen special were few and must be noble in appearance.*

"You're my-ma was wrong about shiny flyers giving birth to balancing backleggers, perhaps she also was wrong about the appearance of chosen specials."

Cerebow jumped up and stared at me with a precise flick of the tail. *Mistaking a shiny flyer as a my-ma giving birth, rather than as a-thing-put-together, is a small mistake. Being wrong about being a chosen special is much bigger.*

The beautiful castle built upon her illusions, began to crumble. Her provincialism and innocence were endearing and I had mixed emotions about destroying her assumptions. Still, the door to higher consciousness was open. This couldn't happen unless Cerebow accepted the consequences. I do not wish to belittle any lifeform, but if I accidentally transported a few paramecia with me into the fourth dimension, they could not attain sentient consciousness. A foundational sophistication needs to exist in the body/mind/feelings to support the evolutionary jump. Cerebow courageously claimed her shadow and when she did, her *Holder* began paying closer attention. Her *Holder* knew she was potential within itself and responded with a greater influx of energy. It was a kiss met with a greater kiss. It would be fascinating to watch her evolution from this point forward. Once she understood the principle that she was the pursued as well as the pursuer, her *Holder* would allow her to dance with it on greater terms. Right now, I was a handy teacher, another physical being she could relate to under the auspice of her *Holder*. If I disappeared from her life, other teachers would follow. "Do you doubt my integrity or, as you call it, pride?" I asked.

*I can see your pride is honest,* she thought.

"Okay then, we both have integrity or honor in our pride. Honor speaks the truth it knows. Honor is the virtue that makes any creature into a chosen special, no matter what he or she looks like. Each of us has favored connections. For me, water speaks and tells me I am a chosen special. For someone else, it might be clouds in the sky or a distant star."

*But if my kind is not the chosen special, then why does food offer itself to me?*

"How does food offer itself to you?"

*Old brown-spotted jumpers* (siberlene), *horned kickers* (a type of wild goat Gathosians call watikiki), *slow-climbing tails* (Tyburnian sloth) *all wait for me when I am hungry. I go out to them and sooth their pain with my songs.* Cerebow showed me what she meant by songs. It was purring. *Then I stop their life and eat my fill.*

"How do you stop the life of your food?"

She opened her mouth and showed me four, big, white fangs along with some other large, impressive teeth. Then I noticed her tongue was black like the Gathosians. *I could show you how I do it on the long part where your voice comes up. It's painless. I do not taste my food until all the spirit leaves* (meaning she suffocated her prey before eating it).

Managing to open my eyes wider, I told her, "no thanks!"

*I only meant to show you, not chase your spirit away.*

"If I fall sleep in the next couple minutes, will you try to chase my spirit away?"

*I have pride, you have pride; we are in pride together and pride is greater than hunger. Besides the stinking breath of the flying ghosts ruined my appetite.*

"Now that your pride has greater perspective, perhaps you might try tuning into the minds of old brown-spotted jumpers, horned kickers, and slow-climbing tails. You might gain fresh perspective on whether they truly are honored about offering their bodies as your food."

*What is your food?*

"I eat the sweetness all around us. Balancing backleggers call the sweetness fruits and vegetables."

*I cannot eat the sweetness. Besides, the sweetness is always new. The chosen special eat what is old and injured when they are seeking release from their bodies. We do not take a body that needs to live and grow.*

My eyelids began to flicker from exhaustion. "The sweetness has less consciousness than brown-spotted jumpers and horned kickers and slow-climbing tails," I argued with little enthusiasm. "The sweetness does not feel pain as we do."

*Untrue! The sweetness feels too, it just doesn't have a voice as loud as ours.*

Her absolute truth startled me and I woke up, just a little. "Perhaps you're right, Cerebow. Did you ever take a life of a flying ghost?"

Lying down again, she put her head on her paws and thought about my question. *No,* she thought; *but I would like to.* She half-closed her eyes and attempted to build a new fortress of reason she could hide behind. *If I knew how to go to fourth dimension then I would wait for the right moment to pounce. While I was waiting, I would learn to balance on my back legs. Then I would figure out how to put things together like shiny flyers, and then I would ride down in my shiny flyer and take the life of every last flying ghost.*

"If you did, you would lose your pride because you would no longer be showing yourself to your food before you took its life."

*I would show myself, just so they would know it was Cerebow who was doing the taking.*

"Would you eat a flying ghost?"

*Never!*

"If you killed a flying ghost, you would need to eat it to maintain your pride because you told me you eat everything you kill."

Cerebow picked up her head and stared menacingly at me. *You're tricking me.*

This was partially true. I learned how to "trick" from Kyron who always manipulated me into accepting my illogical conclusions. Only Kyron was an expert compared to me. He never forgot anything I ever said and he had thirty-seven water phases (147 years), just in this life, to fine-tune his skills. Once he got started, he could be relentless. Sometimes he would grind away on me for hours, making me take responsibility for my every utterance and thought. When he finished, sometimes only a tiny seed remained and no words at all.

*I am in pride, Cerebow reasserted with greater conviction. You are in pride and we are in pride together. That is enough. If I ask Wind—and I intent to—I am certain it will say that you are a chosen special. But Wind would never say flying ghosts are chosen specials. I'm sure Wind will say, take their lives and cover them over like stink-filled droppings.*

"If Wind says you can take the life of honed kickers and brown-spotted jumpers, perhaps Wind is telling flying ghosts that they can take the lives of the chosen special."

*No! Flying ghosts cannot hear Wind and if they could, they would not understand, because they have no pride.*

I decided to push Cerebow one final time before slipping into *delchow savatnani.* "The Wind gives flying ghosts powers it has not given you. Perhaps Wind loves flying ghosts more than it loves you. Did you ever consider that Wind might be lying to you? Perhaps flying ghosts are the real chosen special. Besides, did you see any shadows waiting for the flying ghosts when we entered the fourth dimension?"

*We didn't stay long enough for me to get a good look.*

"Maybe we should return, then you could get a closer look."

*You let me know when and I will be ready.*

"Right now, I need to go into a state of meditation Shardasko Warriors call *delchow savatnani* to restore myself for a few hours."

*Go ahead, I will watch for flying ghosts and rouse you if I smell them near. I will rest too. I need time to think about all we shared and maybe I will talk with Wind.*

"Good idea," I said and I felt my mind split off and sit to my right. My feelings split off and sat to my left. My *Holder* sat directly in front of me and promised, *I will watch too.*

*Do you mind if I sit a little closer?* Cerebow asked.

"The honor is mine." She scooted closer and rested her huge warm head next to my left knee. Her fur was soft, silky, and comfortable. She began to purr and I felt peaceful as I began my *delchow savatnani* with a prayer for the siberlene that died in my stead.

# FOUR

*Delchow savatnani* took five hours plus and it was mid-afternoon when I arose to resume my *quarrying*. After drinking palmara juice from my tortoise shell, I offered some to Cerebow. *I eat sweetness only if I need to*—and she made a gagging sound and stuck out her long, black tongue. Twenty minutes later, I experienced an episode of diarrhea from eating nothing but palmara leaves and orchids for the last four days. Digging a shallow hole, I squatted over it, while holding my cramping guts. Cerebow declared, *freshness is the wrong diet for you. I will go find food.*

"I can't eat meat, so please fulfill your hunger a safe distance away from me." She began to walk away. "I must continue my journey as soon as darkness comes," I called after her. "If you return then, I will be gone."

Two hours later, Cerebow returned and claimed, *no food was waiting for me*. She blamed the lack of game on the vaspray, saying, *flying ghosts, long ago, gobbled up all waiting food and now they've gone elsewhere to gobble up more food.* Maybe Cerebow was right. In spite of the abundance of wingwan trees, not one foul whiff of vaspray did we smell anywhere.

Wondering if Cerebow could tell me more about our geographical location, I decided to see if she was capable of abstract thinking. With the tip of a stick, I drew a rough map of the Abyss on the ground. "Think of yourself in a shiny flyer peering down on the whole sweetness," I said. "The area inside these marks represents the sweetness." I placed a pebble on the western edge of my rough map. "This is where my Shardasko School is located." Positioning a second pebble on the opposite side of the map, I said, "This is Sheebrun, where I need to go." Pointing to the center of the map, I asked, "Is this where we now stand?"

*Closer to Sheebrun*, she said. If Cerebow was correct, the rugged country she led me through brought me closer to my goal than I anticipated. Then Cerebow warned me, *many more flying ghosts live between here and Sheebrun, than between here and your school.* Her statement lent credence to my theory that the preferred habitat of vaspray was border space.

"From here, what's the best direction to walk to reach Sheebrun?"

*It's too dangerous to walk through the sweetness from here to Sheebrun. It's better to return to your school. Besides, more food is available on that side of the sweetness. Closer to the backlegger place, you call Sheebrun, is where the flying ghosts killed my-ma.*

"I'm supposed to meet my master in Sheebrun in three days."

*Then you will need to walk through the most dangerous sweetness and walk faster if you want to get there in time.*

"Does the sweetness get easier to walk through closer to Sheebrun?"

*Yes, but the flying ghosts beyond there are always hungry. Why don't you go to fourth dimension and travel to Sheebrun that way?*

I didn't explain that I could jump only time, not third-dimensional space. Even if I possessed that ability, the greater issue was personal integrity. "It's a matter of pride," I said instead. "Pride means friendship in my Mescale language."

*Friendship*, she repeated, just as she repeated the word telepathy. *I will help you across this next dangerous sweetness. Then, together, in my pride and your friendship, you will teach me how to travel to the fourth dimension.*

"You'll need to become a Shardasko Warrior to do that."

*Then I will become a Shardasko Warrior*, she assured me.

****

My mind and feelings felt refreshed from *delchow savatnani*, but my digestive tract was still upset. I communicated with my body by using the highest praises within my being, telling my body that it was doing a marvelous job at the physical crossing of the Verdant. My body was my outer link to experience, the soft flesh absorbing the shocks of the rough terra firma and doing its job on little food. If my body continued to carry me to my goal, I promised to give it extra attention at the conclusion of the experience. My guts growled in response, *no more palmara juice.*

When Cerebow and I quit our little *loosh*, the moon Enola was mid-heaven and heading northwest toward the Tyburnian Mountains. We walked directly east through the entire night and covered another 35 kilometers. I drank no more palmara juice and ate no more orchids. We made our best time after Eno rose and I used the energy of *areé didamé* to bolster my physical stamina. That morning, I was a strict Light worshiper, breakfasting on the green light of harmony and tranquility. I felt nearly weightless by the time Gearthot diluted the green light to full day.

As Cerebow predicted, the ground gradually leveled and walking became easier. The farther east we advanced, the larger the wingwan trees grew. The air grew hot and humid and we ran into a swamp-pocket of fierce, biting mosquitoes. My only protection was to slather my body with mud. Covered this way, I lost the weightless sensation I absorbed during *areé didamé* and felt all my aches and pains. As full daylight arrived, the noisy exchange of birds reached a din. I hoped they were not telling the vaspray that a mud-covered balancing-backlegger and a dulcerary panther were below. An hour later, we found ourselves on the crest of a high ridge. The ridge swooped down into a valley of dense wingwan trees. "See anything unusual?" I asked Cerebow.

*There*, she said with an upward tilt to her nose. I looked where she pointed and saw one black dot circling in the distant sky. *My-ma told me that for every flying ghost we see in the air, ten are hiding in the freshness.*

"Let's hope you're my-ma was wrong about this one too."

*My-ma was right. I've seen them. One flying ghost stays in the air, as a watcher.*

For certain, we were on the border of a vaspray concentration. The distance across the valley was difficult to determine from where we stood. The situation was tantalizing. Sheebrun was approximately 115 kilometers due east. My feelings acted as an impatient child, urging me to keep going and run toward Sheebrun at full tilt. My *Holder* held council in every part of me and no chance existed that impatience would rule the day. I had come too far to allow impatience to cause my failure. I decided to wait until dark to cross the valley.

Vaspray are most active at dawn and sunset. Like most forest creatures, vaspray are quieter during early afternoon when Insanio reaches its apex. Because vaspray are birds first, they take to their nests near dusk. One exception to this rule is if they are mating. Mating is an all-night affair.

We had no water, food, or comfort as we did in the *loosh* the day before and we had nothing to do but watch and wait. When the day grew brighter, I estimated the valley was 40 kilometers across. Straightforward walking, with no interference, I could transverse the valley by *areé didamé* the following morning. I planned to cut sharper to the southeast, where the wingwan trees were less dense.

When Insanio reached its apex, the day was blisteringly hot. An hour later, blue-black thunderheads emerged along the eastern horizon. For over an hour, thunder kept edging closer. Just as we felt the cool rush before the storm, Cerebow said, *I know this kind of day in the sweetness. This wet will last all day.*

This was an unexpected opportunity. "If you're right, the storm will give us excellent cover." I pondered the opportunity for five more minutes before deciding, "We need to go now." Without further ado, I made my way down the slope, toward the valley. This time Cerebow tagged behind me. The storm would baffle sound and the rain would quickly wash away our footprints. Because vaspray are afraid of fire, I hoped they also were wary of lighting. Looking up, toward the foreboding blue-black clouds, a little prayer slipped out toward the elements. *Congress of Mothers: Air, Water, and Fire, nursing all Fecundity. I am your child. Speed me on my journey, in this my last few hours, of my greatest trial.*

The first few raindrops pelted the top of my head with stinging blows. The storm front was dangerous and lightning struck a nearby tree. I kept glancing up and pleading, "Please be careful." Seconds later, the rain turned into a veritable downpour and the air smelled sweet, clean, and cool. Just as I hoped, rain beating against the canopy became a masking roar. The ground turned slippery and I needed to use my makeshift weapon, as a walking stick.

Cerebow continually sniffed the air, checking for what she called *flying ghost stink* and I used my *turami savatnani* like a psychic flashlight, poking a hole into the unknown forest ahead. Cerebow and I kept flashing between us—*no sign of vaspray anywhere.*

Rain came down so hard that the gullies quickly filled with water and became gushing streamlets that plummeted over the edge of rises as waterfalls. The deeper we descended into the valley, the wider and more rapid the streamlets became. On the valley floor, the accumulating water turned into a small river we needed to forge. If my calculations were correct, this stream was an authentic stream, and we were standing at the headwaters of the Tartha River. Tartha River is an important landmark because it cuts through the village of Sheebrun. The surest approach was to follow the stream, but it would force my journey radically south, taking me on what I considered a needless detour of an additional forty kilometers. I still had time to walk the longer distance, but whether my journey coincided with my time declaration, had lost its urgency to me. Weighing my options, I knew that without food, my body could not endure the stark rigors of the Verdant Abyss for much longer. Honor was as important to my body as honor was to all my other parts. If my body failed before I reached my goal, my body would assume the full brunt of my failure. Knowing this, I decided to cross the river and continue my journey east, in the most direct way I could find.

Cerebow and I traced the edge of the stream along its meandering southeastern bank. We hoped to discover a fallen log across the water that we could use as a footbridge. We found no fortuitous fallen logs and the farther southeast we trudged, the wider the stream grew and the more loudly it roared. "This definitely is the Tartha River," I said.

*It's impossible to jump*, Cerebow thought. I decided to backtrack to a place I spotted earlier and when Cerebow saw it, she thought, *it's still too wide to jump.*

I gazed hungrily at the opposite bank and told her, "We will need to get a lot wetter before we get any drier." She didn't understand and I resorted to hand gestures again. "We'll swim like fish," and I dipped my hand in the water and wiggled my fingers back and forth.

*Chosen specials do not swim.*

"Then I will carry you across to the opposite side."

*I'm too heavy.*

Because she was wet, I could see she was thin and I swore, "I can do it."

She huffed and gave the stream a menacing glare for impeding our progress. *Go across the river and meet your master in Sheebrun and I will return the way we came and meet you on the opposite side of the sweetness in a few days.*

"No way am I deserting you in the middle of vaspray territory. If I prove I can lift you, then will you trust me to take you across the river?"

She hesitated before giving me a shaky, *maybe.* After some jockeying between us, she allowed me to pick her up under her belly. She weighed approximately fifty kilograms and I managed to get her to the height of my shoulders. She did not enjoy being picked up. *I believe you; now put me down,* she grawruffed. I set her down and she shook her body to regain her composure. *You're strong for a balancing backlegger,* she communicated with a few sputters. *Now prove you can carry yourself across this wetness, and we will have a bargain.*

Wading into the stream, I immediately realized the water was moving faster than I anticipated. Its strong current tore my leg sideways and I nearly toppled over and went under. Fear loomed up within me. This was not false fear. It was real and informing me that I was pushing my luck against a powerful force I was underestimating. I heard Kyron inside my head coaching me to see the situation as it is. *Adapt! Use your ingenuity. What are the tools available to reach your goal?*

I asked my *Holder* to, *help my body realize its potential.* A sudden adrenaline surge arose within me and I began swimming for the opposite bank.

Cerebow called out several times, *are you okay?* The swift current nearly swept me away, but I made it across. I dragged myself up the muddy slope and fell as Cerebow continued to call.

I managed to lift my arm and let her know that I was alive. Then I began to pray. *I am a Shardasko Warrior. I accept each new situation. My disposition cooperates with me. I am at peace with myself.* On the verge of admitting defeat— that I certainly could not carry Cerebow across the Tartha River—I noticed the *soaple* vines dangling from the wingwan trees and a flash of inspiration hit me. I got up and started yanking *soaple* vine off the surrounding trees. My consciousness seemed split into several different spheres of attention, each doing what it did best. My *Holder* was putting ideas in my head; psychic self was scanning the area, alert for signs of danger; and feelings danced around with enthusiasm telling me, *you can do this.*

By now, Cerebow's psychic projections were turning into psychic shouts and she demanded, *what are you doing?*

Our indiscreet antics along the stream would have drawn the attention of any creature in our vicinity with a modicum of curiosity. My communications switched to telepathy because it was unwise to shout the distance across the stream. *Wait, you will see.*

Cerebow sat on her haunches at full alert with her little triangular chin lifted high in the air. *I understand!* she triumphantly declared. *You are using your hands to put things together.*

It took my hands a full hour to fashion a braided rope long enough to bridge the stream. When I finished, I looped the major portion of the rope around my shoulder and prepared to toss the remainder across to Cerebow. *I'll need your help to put this idea together,* I signaled her. *I'm going to toss this rope across to you and I want you to take your end and wrap it around the tree behind you.*

She turned and stared at the tree in question. *How?*

*When I toss the rope, you catch the end in your mouth.* I put one end of the vine in my mouth to demonstrate what I meant.

*I'm not sure I can do that.*

*Certainly you can. If you want to become a Shardasko Warrior, you will need to adapt to each new situation and use the tools at hand. Get ready. Here comes the rope.* I tossed one end of the rope across the stream, and damn! She caught the rope on her first attempt. *Excellent eye and mouth coordination,* I communicated. *Now walk around the tree with the rope until it holds tight.*

*Which way should I go?*

*Either way, the choice makes no difference.* She thought for a second and then chose to go clockwise. *Make it tighter,* and I pulled a short length taunt between my hands to show what I meant. She backed up and pulled the rope tighter and I kept up a profusion of encouraging praise to keep her moving. *Great! Great work!* When she finished wrapping the vine around the tree several times, I secured my end to the closest wingwan tree on my side of the bank. I took a new length of vine and tied it to my left wrist before looping it around the vine that bridged the river. Even with my new safety line, it took all my nerve to wade into the water a second time. When I reached the middle, where the current churned, the vine around my wrist twisted and chaffed my arm raw. As I struggled to free myself, I swallowed a huge gulp of water. Crawling up the original bank, like a half-drown *tujet,* I collapsed facedown in the mud.

*You look sick,* Cerebow noticed, and she came over and nudged my head with her nose several times.

"Give me a chance to breathe," I begged through my spitting, huffing, and puffing.

When I managed to crawl to my hands and knees, Cerebow peered at me with careful consideration. *I feel like a real Shardasko Warrior,* she informed me. *For the first time in my life, I helped put something together.* Then she appeared confused. *I can see how you used what we put together, but what am I supposed to do with it?*

"You will use the rope exactly as I did," I managed to say.

*Aren't you going to carry me across the wetness?*

"I'm sorry, the current is stronger than I imagined and I will not be able to carry you as I promised." It took me several more minutes to recover enough to perform the next waiting task. I told her, "I'm going to make a harness to fit around your body. I'll attach a few loops to the harness and then tie the loops to the line across the river so you can float across in safety." She did not understand the concept of "harness" or "float," so I said, "Wait, you will see." To demonstrate the strength of *soaple*, I attempted to sit on my braided rope near the tree, and promptly fell backward on my ass. "It has stretched," I explained. Tightening the rope around the tree, I attempted to sit on the suspended rope a second time. "See!" I said as I swung back and forth. *Soaple* vine is strong.

Cerebow was a trusting soul. If someone presented me with a shaky plan such as mine, telling me, *believe me, it will work,* I don't know if I would have trusted that person. I trussed Cerebow with one vine looped behind her front legs and a second vine just in front of her back legs. I joined both loops with a length of vine running down her back and one under her belly. Then I secured this makeshift harness loosely to the lifeline so she could slip along to the opposite shore. I checked all knots one last time and Cerebow assured me, *I'm comfortable.* It took me another five minutes to coax her to wade into the water, which she complained was cold. Stepping into the water, in front of her, I again tied my raw wrist to the lifeline, and then eased her in by pulling gently on the harness. *My feet aren't touching anything,* she announced a moment later.

"Good! That means you're swimming like a real Shardasko Warrior. Move your paws like this and kick your back legs," I said, showing her how to paddle.

She looked excited and scared, but began paddling with her paws. *I'm doing it,* and her mouth made a blubbering sound. *I'm swimming.* Out in the center, where the current was swiftest, her fear made her thrash more than swim and her thrashing made her inadvertently scratch my forearm with her claws. By the time we reached safety on the opposite bank, my arm was bleeding profusely and my wrist was bloody from the safety loop. I snatched a palmara leaf and tied it around my arm to stop the bleeding. *I'm sorry I hurt you,* she whimpered in empathy. It was difficult to tell if real tears were rolling down her face, because we both seemed soaked to our souls.

Untying Cerebow and the vine from the tree, I tossed the harness and the braided vine into the water. The swift current whipped everything downstream and the only visible anomaly was the vine tied to the tree on the opposite bank. My sloppy cover-up was the best I could do under the circumstances. Cerebow sniffed the air and announced, *no flying ghost stink on this side either.*

I scanned with my *turami savatnani,* searching for clues to the absent vaspray. Then, something unusual happened. A shield—that I did not realize existed—shattered, and fell away from my physical vision. I had no notion what caused my abrupt visual shift, but now the world appeared clearer and more vibrantly alive than I believed possible. Exhaustion was causing distortions throughout my being; yet, I honestly felt as if I could see more clearly than at any instant in my life. My fragile existence questioned, *am I alive? Perhaps I drowned in the river and only now realize my fate.* I studied the Tartha River and peered back over the forest for visual clues of my death. The scene was perfectly normal, except for the rope tied around the tree on the opposite bank. *What changed?* I vowed not to move until I received an answer and sat down cross-legged on the very spot. I did not probe for answers, but opened myself to all possibilities and waited for understanding to embrace me.

In a matter of seconds, understanding came, but it did not flow through me as understanding usually does. This time, understanding struck like a thunderbolt. The answer came from a source greater than my *Holder* for it was exposing itself to greater understanding, along with me. The Tartha River spoke, telling me, *you've been anointed through your triple immersion into me. You crossed me first with your total physical commitment; second with your mind's ingenuity; and finally, with your love for another creature. Each part died its own small death to accomplish this goal. Now I give these three energies greater consciousness to continue on your journey through life.*

*The rain is slowing,* thought Cerebow.

I stood up. "Then we should get going. All the noise we made crossing the river is bound to attract the attention of vaspray."

*What are you looking for?* she asked.

"I lost my wisdom walker shell."

****

My trial with the Tartha River consumed more than three hours of my time and early evening was near when we climbed the eastern ridge. A gentle breeze rustled through the trees, as the last fiery rays of Insanio dried my skin. My goal was near and I felt an irresistible attraction pulling me toward Kyron.

Cerebow and I were three-quarters the way up the ridge when the first dim flash of light and characteristic swishing, shattered the innocence of sundown. The warble phenomenon of a door opening between dimensions cued my senses and I instinctively sank to the ground to camouflage my physical presence. Pulling Cerebow down with me, the last thing I communicated was, *vaspray.* Seconds later, father up the ridge, a vaspray appeared in the sky. Huddling and crouching together into two small mounds, Cerebow and tried to appear as two common rocks among the dead leaves and forest floor plants. I held my breath. The vaspray was a huge alpha male. The powerful sound of its black wings seemed so close that chills prickled my back. The giant bird flew directly overhead, leaving that lingering, sweet stink in the air. Exactly ten seconds later, on the heels of the initial flash and swish, another vaspray came through the same dimensional door. The vaspray had passed the storm in the fourth dimension and now were returning home en masse. Cerebow was correct in her claim that more vaspray lived between the heart of the Abyss and Sheebrun. For the next ten minutes, I felt as if I was witnessing peak time at the Gathos Spaceport. In total, I counted one hundred seventy-six vaspray as they emerged from the fourth dimension.

The scene was awesome, an amazing display of cooperative genius. The vaspray were using a technique Shardasko Warriors call, "Interlude Shading." Shardasko Warriors use Interlude Shading when they jump dimensions in larger groups and inexperienced jumpers are involved. The intricacies involved are many and can involve the construction of elaborate energy grids inside the fourth. However, basic Interlude Shading takes only three experienced warriors capable of synchronizing their energy to each other. One warrior opens a door and jumps to the fourth dimension; another warrior follows, but remains in the corridor between dimensions as a guide; and the third warrior stays in the third dimension, where he cues the inexperienced warriors when to jump. This exercise may sound straightforward, yet the logistical coordination necessary in Interlude Shading is overwhelming because time warps as it moves out through the fourth. The critical factor allowing Interlude Shading to succeed is the psychic trust the three guiding warriors maintain throughout the exercise.

Cerebow and I waited in our crouched position, although I could feel the tension in her body and again she wanted to bolt—this time for the top of the ridge. I was afraid to breathe, despite the cacophonous chatter of vaspray. Piercing cries of *curee* filled the air. Hearing their *curees*, a desire again seized me to understand vaspray language. Putting my clairaudient abilities to work on a translation, I decided *curee* was a happy exultation from the emphasis vaspray placed upon the word. *Curee!* In other words, *we are home, safe, and free. Praise the day!*

Most vaspray went to their nests, while a few slipped through the trees presumably to land on the ground below. *So much for the absurd notion that vaspray could not penetrate the thick tree cover.* Three large males acted as watchers and remained aloft, riding the air currents. I knew with intuitive certainty that these three were the experienced masters responsible for actualizing the Interlude Shading. The *curees* faded and the chattering grew subdued and seemed more like intimate conversation. A short time later, that now familiar rhythmic thumping began. This time the foot thumping began with one "thump-bump," which was answered with thumping from halfway across the valley. Soon, the thumping and bumping was coming from a half dozen different locations below. The thumping did not cease until Gearthot sank behind the Tyburnian Mountains. A moment before *shahaut*, the three males careening over the valley flew down and disappeared in the darkness of the trees and the night turned quiet. The breeze slowly shifted and began blowing out of the northwest. The direction of the wind hid our smell from the vaspray, but we certainly continued to smell them.

Why the vaspray failed to detect our presence remained a mystery. Logic told me their psychic abilities combined with the clearing of the storm would make us as obvious as two red flags. Were the vaspray careless that night? Were they exhausted from dodging the storm? Cerebow thought, *maybe they've already eaten.*

As soon as the situation seemed safe, I picked up my stiff, weary bones and Cerebow and I finished scaling the ridge. In doing so, I used every one of my Shardasko skills. It took over four hours to reach the crest at that calculated pace. At the top, the breeze was stronger and I wondered if another storm was brewing beyond the horizon. For the first time, the view was expansive. The forest below seemed surreal from our elevated perspective, a mass of indistinct wingwan trees daunted by a vast star-studded sky. My clear vision held; and as I gazed over the Great Verdant Abyss, I knew its apparent immutability was an illusion. Physical reality was not a place, but rather a conjunction of elements that danced intimately before moving on. Then, through the grace of Cerebow, I heard Wind singing for the first time. It hummed sweetly and told me, *nothing ever changes but personal perspective.*

# FIVE

If I continued at my present pace I would undercut my time declaration by a full day. After first convincing myself that I was going to be a day late, I was going to be a day early. This seemed incredible to me. If I decided to rest and contemplate my *quarrying*, Kyron would not have faulted me; nevertheless, I knew that stopping for another day would be procrastination, a dishonest delay. *Was any facet of my* quarrying *still eluding me?* I checked with Cerebow. "Are you tired?"

*I'm more hungry than tired*, she thought.

Sheebrun was 55 kilometers due east through an increasingly civilized area. I gazed into the darkness, knowing Kyron was a sentinel of attention. "Then I'm going to continue straight for Sheebrun."

*Okay, but if I smell waiting food, I may take a detour. I'm not as crazy as you are. You think you can live on green light alone.*

We walked through *areé didamé* and it renewed my strength. Later we found fresh water, nuts, and delicious fruits. Because of my queasy stomach, I indulged sparingly. Eventually we happened upon a deserted, ramshackle cabin. Behind the cabin was an abandoned garden with gramlick tubers, yellow tie beans, and fresh rainberries. I ate a few berries and a couple of beans and decided to bypass the tubers because I felt full. While exploring, I noticed a trailing pattern of cloven tracks in the moist earth and knew siberlene frequented the garden too. A moment later, Cerebow caught the scent of, what she called, *waiting food*. Ferocity loomed up in her yellow eyes and in an instant, her blood-red pupils dilated with hungry anticipation.

"It's okay," I said, and the sound of my voice broke her instinctive concentration. She glanced my way and the savagery vanished from her eyes. "I understand that we each take what we need to survive." I could no longer deny that my food meant the death of something or someone. I had felt the same eager feelings of delight over a plate of *grash* that Cerebow showed over a siberlene.

*I must go*, Cerebow explained; and I could sense her physical hunger, a compulsion a thousand times stronger than any other compulsion, save one. This one compulsion, a compulsion for intimacy, compelled her to ask, *will you wait for me, Élan?*

Waiting for Cerebow would be against the rules of the *quarrying*; however no rules existed about how fast I had to walk. "I'll walk slowly for the next couple of hours and when you finish eating, you can pick up my trail or meet me at my school in the Sutcay Valley in a few days time. If you're intent on becoming a Shardasko Warrior, you will need to come to my school and petition a master to accept you as a neophyte."

Her head cocked in a questioning way. *I thought you were going to teach me how to become a Shardasko Warrior.*

"Only a master can teach you and I am not yet a master."

*If you are not a master, then what are you?*

"I'm called an Emblematic Warrior. In the language of Shardasko, it is a way of saying, I am displaying all outward characteristics of a real warrior, but not yet a complete internal master."

*You may not be a master, but you certainly are a complete chosen special.*

I laughed. "Thank you, that's a lovely compliment." I touched her front shoulders sending a gift of my energy to her and then kissed her between her two yellow eyes. She was purring as she bounded away.

**✳✳✳✳**

Approaching Sheebrun, I was increasingly aware of my physical nakedness. In the past, fully clothed and appearing my normal self, situations arose where my Human appearance provoked Gathosian children to stares and whispers. They did not mean to be impolite, but Humans still were a rarity on Gathosian worlds, especially undeveloped worlds such as Sutcay Tay. Now naked, with my hair in a tangled mess and my face sprouting a scruffy beard, I knew my appearance would be startling to anyone in a chance encounter. Groups of foragers were in the woods, searching for mushrooms, and I heard their excited voices in the distance. The heavy rain the day before caused several varieties of eatable fungi to appear during the night. I stopped to drink at a stream and noticed someone had lopped off a bounty of numidian deliciousos with a sharp knife.

Sheebrun was a short four-hour walk to the east. I did not relish the notion of emerging from the Abyss in broad daylight with my nakedness in full view. A delay of three or so hours made no difference to my time declaration, so I decided to avoid the crowd and wait until Insanio set. I discovered a secluded spot to rest where a flat rock jutted out over the edge of a shallow ravine. The storm had created a tiny meandering streamlet that trickled down the center of the breach. I climbed down and untied the palmara leaves wrapped around my injured arm. Golden streams of light filtered through the trees and warmed my face. In the brighter light, I examined my wound carefully. The chaffing around my wrist was healing, but the gash Cerebow inflicted on my arm appeared ugly and ragged. The laceration began at my elbow and extended nearly to my wrist. In normal circumstances, I would have sought medical attention. As I gazed at my wound, a vision of the wounded vaspray with its bloody, sagging jowl jolted my memory. The gash on my arm was pale gray and the edges of flesh blubbery white. *It's because the wound is damp*, a tiny voice inside me rationalized. *But which of Cerebow's paws scratched the vaspray and which paw scratched me?* I could not remember, but if the paw in question was the same paw that scratched the vaspray, a chance existed that Cerebow had contaminated me with the fugus the vaspray carried that could lead to necrosis.

*Stay calm*, I thought. *Nothing can be done until I get to Sheebrun. Cerebow will return and she will remember which paw was the culprit*, yet I feared that I would not see her again. Unsure if the palmara leaves were helping or hurting, I decide to leave the wound exposed. I missed Cerebow's companionship, but she did not return. Two hours later, I headed straight for Sheebrun, knowing I would reach my destination a full day ahead of my time declaration. Kyron and I planned to meet on the outskirts of the village, near an old well. We had discovered the place together on a pleasant morning's walk and I had said, "If I ever become an Emblematic Warrior and succeed through my *quarrying*, let's meet at this well."

"No question about it," Kyron promised. "We will meet at this exact spot in the future."

****

I emerged from the Great Verdant Abyss a moment before *shahaut*, on the sixth day of my *quarrying*. A few meteorites shot across the sky, just as they had when I entered the Abyss. I did not presume my presence attracted these meteorites, but recognized the meteorite display and my emergence as coincidental. The meteorites were a cosmic symbol, an important marker placed at the crossroads of time. Standing at the peak of the present moment, I tuned into the night, became one with it. My arms reached up and starlight embraced me and together, we danced, creating spiral bands of light across the sky. The dance reset my inner cadence for the new Journey ahead, and I again felt a shift in consciousness, an adjustment like the resetting of a watch when arriving in a new time zone.

Placing my hand across my physical heart, I thanked my *Holder* for bringing me safely through my *quarrying*.

\*\*\*\*

The well where Kyron and I planned to meet was a *skefit* away. I skirted along the edge of the woods, hiding in the shadow of the trees, while attempting to avoid the dim light of the nearby street lamps. I spied the well and then the shadow of a man. The shadow abruptly stood up straighter, peered into the darkness, and began running straight toward me. When Kyron's energy met mine, a resounding clap, like thunder, exploded inside my ears. I fell to my knees just as I had seven phases earlier. Now Kyron fell down too and we embraced with complete abandon. "My precious child," he said several times. "Did you see the six meteorites? The sky celebrates our humble success." Tears of joy, relief, and indescribable feelings of love passed between us.

Kyron appeared radiant. His beauty was ancient beauty that only inner divinity can create. A fresh, red parish flower dangled from the end of his neat braid and he was wearing his best *moodarry,* the one with embroidered triangles around the neck and sleeves. He inspected me and declared, "You are the most beautiful mess I've ever seen." He examined my injured arm and said, "this needs medical attention." His incredible piercing eyes glanced up from his intent scrutiny of me to ask, "Did the vaspray—?"

"They did not touch me. I will tell you later how my injury happened. And if you agree, I would like you to review my entire mind scribe, so you can help me wrap meaning around my *quarrying*."

"I am forever at your disposal," he promised and I expected nothing less.

"As I am forever at yours," I vowed in return.

Kyron handed me a clean *moodarry* and my sandals. It seemed a shame to put on clean clothing when I felt so dirty, but I dressed for modesty sake. My feet were too sore to wear sandals, so I continued barefoot.

"I have a gift for you," he said and he plucked a velvet box from the side pocket of his *moodarry* and opened it. The box contained a string of jade prayer beads. Every master gives his Emblematic Warrior prayer beads when he completes his *quarrying* and each warrior considers this gift a precious possession. "This jade is not any jade. This is sacred jade from the moon Guile," and he ceremoniously placed the prayer beads in my two hands.

"I thought Hectarian authorities would not allow any more jade to be mined on Guile."

"This is old jade that came from the leftover bits when they constructed the San Delphi Monastery at the foot of the New Delphi Crystal."

Guile is one of three moons orbiting the planet Delphi. Delphi sits 1.5

light years beyond Sutcay Tay and Delphi is not part of the Island Worlds of Gathos system. New Delphi is an important spiritual center because of the New Delphi Crystal. The New Delphi Crystal is a huge energy vortex that acts as a cosmic substation or a conductor of energy from Source. From New Delphi, sub-atomic particles stream out to different worlds. Trinity Witches and Hectarian Mystics call these particles "aurora lights" and claim their energy brings the power of self-illumination. The prime recipients of Delphic light are the headwater planets of the Island Worlds of Gathos and the reason Gathosians feel such a strong affinity with Delphi.

Legend claims that Trinity Witches and Hectarian Mystics, from the headwater planets of Gathos, knew of and guarded the location of the planet Delphi eons before its actual physical discovery. Then, two hundred fifty phases ago, when Human explorers discovered Delphi, the difficulties for the Gathosian headwater planets began. Delphi and its moons were rich sources of precious opal, fire opal, and jade. Opal was a valuable commodity in the production of Gathosian multidex chips and these gems were accessibly close to the surface on Guile. Guile took the brunt of the environmental assault from the mining entrepreneurs that cared solely about getting rich as quickly as possible. A plethora of Hectarian publications now claim the plundering of Guile for opals is the main reason many Gathosian headwater planets are being devastated by meteorite barrages. The Galaxy Council, which established itself as the ubiquitous political voice for Gathosians and Human worlds, continues to argue that this is superstitious nonsense, but just in case the Galaxy Council is wrong, all mining operations on Delphi and its three moons have ceased. For the last two hundred phases, Hectarian Mystics and Trinity Witches have kept scrupulous guard over Delphi and her three moons. Environmental controls are so strict that Delphi law prohibits the use of powered vessels in the waters within a three-hundred-kilometer radius around New Delphi Island. In order to reach the New Delphi Crystal, one needs to undertake a veritable pilgrimage in a windship that involves several days of travel.

"The prayer beads are exquisite," I told Kyron. "Even in the dim light of the street lamps, I could see the strand was not a casual work of art. The jade was translucent green with orange marbled veins. Each bead threaded to the next bead by an intricate series of silver loops and hooks. The string was finished on both ends with two silver triangles inlaid with bars of opal and fire opal. On one triangle was the inscription, "I am The Chalice of All Understanding," a space, then the words, "The essence of Love therein." On the other triangle was the inscription, "I drink of my *Emayre* and to The Elements who fuse my life with Life."

"These beads once belonged to Belinda," said Kyron.

I stared at him in amazement and he offered me nothing but a quiet and steady smile. "They're too precious to give to me," I finally said.

"What's the matter, my fiery prince?"

"As always, your generosity makes me feel—inadequate."

"If you feel inadequate in accepting this simple talismanic tool between us, how will you ever accept my entire kingdom, which I am eagerly waiting to give you? Now hush and accept your own divine glory," and Kyron wrapped the beads around my waist and hooked them by their silver clasp. As soon as the beads wrapped around me, I felt a new and protective energy and I no longer worried about  the vaspray infecting me. I knew I was safe.

We walked the short distance to the Sheebrun campus, where Kyron had accommodations for us in a guest *tritum*. I felt like a savage interloper trudging through those ordered streets. We entered the campus through the northeast gateway, where groups of irrepressible neophytes were spilling out of the temples from evening prayers. My ragged appearance caught their attention and they grew quiet and followed me with their eyes. "*Afen* (peace) brother!" they called out and touched their foreheads in greeting as we passed by."

Kyron left me at our guest *tritum,* while he went to the administration office to send a message to the Sutcay Tay School that I was safe. After he left, I stood unmoving inside that simple room for several minutes. Everything I ever took for granted, I now saw through new eyes. The sparsely decorated room was typical of all rooms created by Shardasko brothers and similar to Kyron's *tritum* on the Sutcay Tay campus. The stone blocks, that formed the walls, adjoined perfectly, without use of mortar. The floor was a construct of tongue-and-groove conference wood. Huge wooden beams formed a tray ceiling and supported a thatched roof of *soaple* vine. The rear wall had wide cantilever windows and double doors that led out to the garden. Along one sidewall sat a sink, a small cooker, and a washer/dryer for clothes. Above the appliances, three simple shelves held dishes, pans and utensils, and a few staples. The only furniture was a low eating table, two bed pallets with folded bed linen on top, and a simple chest with three drawers. Everything a warrior owned fit in these three drawers. Down a short hall to the left, I knew I would find a bathroom with a tub, and a sink with a mirror above. The room would contain a plain wooden stool and two shelves for towels and toiletries. In the far-left corner, would be another door, leading to the toilet. I marveled over all these simple amenities, marveled that it took eons of conscious evolution to refine these simple conveniences to their present state.

I walked down the short hall to the bathroom and spoke to the light. "I am a Shardasko Warrior," I said and the lights turned on as a nameless Shardasko wonder programmed them to do. The arrangement of the space was as expected, but the room felt peculiar. The artificial light generated a harsh glare against the mirror, highlighting the angular lines of the room. I used the toilet and it felt odd to sit instead of squat. Afterward, I stared in the mirror and saw a madman staring back at me. The environmental elements had burnished my nose and forehead to a reddish tan. My eyes were red-rimmed from lack of sleep and my hair was a tangled mess. A scraggly six-day beard covered my chin and upper lip, my fingernails were broken and stained, and my feet bruised and sore. My injured arm appeared ghastly in the stark light. Other than that, I felt wonderful and was ecstatically happy.

After shaving, I climbed into the bathtub and washed without plugging the drain because I did not want to sit in the sweat and grime rolling off my body. The mere act of bathing seemed an incredible luxury. Picking up a bar of soap was a sacred act. I noticed the slick feel of the bar and the sensuous way it slipped through my hands. During my *quarrying*, I wished for soap and now soap was real and creating webby bubbles between my fingers. I was overwhelmed with gratitude and tears rolled down my cheeks. I scrubbed my feet, but neither they nor my fingernails would come completely clean. Washing my hair with shampoo seemed like an amazing indulgence.

I climbed out of the tub, dried myself, and was careful with my injured arm. Indulging, I put on another clean *moodarry* and while I was combing my hair, I heard Kyron returning. He had brought a master named Arithmarur Das (*arith* means alloy, *mar* means gold, *ur* means silver, and *das* means healer) to examine my arm. Arithmarur was old—somewhere in the neighborhood of two hundred phases old—and a respected healer on both Sutcay Tay campuses. Neophytes usually recognized Arithmarur before they knew his name, referring to him as, "The funny old master that always carries a reed basket." He was a hands-on healer who was also a great teacher. During my level-two training, I attended several of his lectures pertaining to the pharmacology of native plants on Sutcay Tay. He taught, among other helpful facts, that a palmara leave makes a wonderful antiseptic for wounds. Arithmarur was a combination of modern thought and ancient healing techniques that he claimed he learned in another life as a Trinity Witch. Whoever Arithmarur was in another life, in this life, he was a true Shardasko master. He took delight in outpacing descriptions and the face he showed the world, kept everyone guessing. Sometimes he was candid and at other times, evasive. He could be abrupt or patient, serious and often funny. His humor was uniquely his and some of his humor was raw. Warriors taking his classes invariably attempted to imitate him, but no one could be Arithmarur except the authentic Arithmarur. His stature was short for a Gathosian and he reminded me of a mischievous elf or gnome. Most Shardasko Warriors were clean-shaven because the climate was hot and humid, but Arithmarur wore a beard that hung down like a bib on his barrel-shaped chest. Like most other masters, he treated his physical appearance as incidental, something he wore like an old, comfortable *moodarry*.

On the eating table, he placed the reed basket that contained an assortment of amber-colored bottles, jars, and a variety of surgical paraphernalia. Arithmarur's movements, like all Shardasko masters, were conscious and he waltzed over to the sink to wash his hands. "Does your arm hurt?" he asked.

"Not anymore."

"Take a seat at the table. I'll need to clean the top tissue away or it will not heal properly. Do you want a pain killer or do you trust me to be quick?"

"Be quick," I decided.

"Go get a towel from the bathroom," he told Kyron. Kyron returned with the towel and draped it over the table. "Lay your arm on the towel, take a deep breath, and let it all out." By the time I was finished with my deep breath, Arithmarur had trimmed the raw edges of the laceration with a laser tool. Fresh blood poured from the wound, just as when the injury first occurred. He pulled an aerosol bottle from his basket and, after giving the bottle a quick shake, sprayed my arm with the contents.

"That burns," I said. "What is it?"

"Just a little concoction I learned to make when I was a Trinity Witch. It works too." He shook the bottle again and sprayed my arm a second time.

This time I squawked, "That's worse than the laser bite!"

He ignored my complaining and told me more about the "concoction" then I wanted to hear, considering my arm was on fire. "It's a balanced suspension of neutrophils, lymphocytes, and platelets from the blood of llexal fish. Llexal fish possess fantastic healing capabilities. Never will you catch an llexal dying from a little snag such as yours. By the way, the sting you're experiencing is from its weak acidic nature."

Kyron joked, "Is Élan going to grow fish scales on his arm?"

Arithmarur chuckled. "That would be pretty!" Then he used a smaller laser tool to cauterize the wound. "How did you injure yourself?" he asked.

"A dulcerary panther accidentally scratched me."

He whistled. "Accidentally?"

"Quite accidentally!"

"Sorry, but you will have a scar. See me after the wound heals and I can use a laser tool to abrade the skin surface so it will be barely noticeable."

I decided to quiz Arithmarur concerning his opinion on the transmission of fungus from Cerebow's claws. "What's the probability of being infected with the vaspray fungus if the dulcerary in question, used the same claws to scratch a vaspray two days before?"

"Élan!" Kyron gasped.

Arithmarur played with his beard. "Can't say." He reached into his reed basket, pulled out a silver-wrapped cube and tossed it to me with a casual, "Here. Burn this *tartan ratu* and inhale the fumes. If you experience a shred of anger while under its influence, deal with it. If the vaspray infected you and you fail to deal with your anger, then you will die a slow and agonizing death." He patted me on the shoulder. "Try to sleep before you do it, but do it soon. If the fugus establishes a foothold in your system, even inhaling *tartan ratu* will not save you."

I held the cube between my thumb and forefinger and stared at it. "And how do you formulate *tartan ratu*?"

"Never mind!" Arithmarur barked. "I'm not giving away all my secrets. As far as you are concerned, *tartan ratu* might be made from the piss of Shardasko masters that I've scraped off our communal toilets." He rubbed his stubby fingers together and chuckled as if he were insane. He leaned closer and told me in a stage whisper, "Confidentially, the piss of masters needs just a drop of elemental magic and poof—new batch of *tartan ratu*. Now give me that towel, so I can get a blood sample. I will need to run a few tests and will let you know as soon as I get the results. Now I am an old man, it is way past *shahaut*, and I'm tired. You need anything else before I go to bed?"

Kyron asked, "Can you remove the mind scribe from behind Élan's ear?"

Arithmarur seemed to have everything in his reed basket even a scribe extractor. He felt for the spot behind my ear with his fingertips until he located the subtle pulsing sensation of the mind scribe. He pressed the extractor against the spot and said, "Got it!"

Arithmarur appeared serious for the first time. He instructed Kyron to, "Leave the scribe in this extractor for at least eight hours, to sterilize the program, before inserting it under your skin. Just in case Élan is infected." Then he again turned glib and patted me on the shoulder a second time. "Don't worry, Élan. We don't call Kyron The Key for nothing."

After Arithmarur departed, Kyron carefully stored my mind scribe in the top drawer of his chest. "The vaspray did not infect me," I insisted.

"Even if you are, it is merely an opportunity for you to experience a little side trip. I've been down that twisted trail with a few other warriors. The illusions are always bigger than the actual problem. Forget it until tomorrow. Are you hungry?"

"Just tired."

"I want you to eat before you go to sleep."

"Yes, master. Do you want me to help you prepare food?"

"It would be my pleasure to serve you tonight."

Kyron went outside to the little garden behind the *tritum* and collected a few vegetables. Countless times, I saw him go to the garden behind his own *tritum* to collect vegetables. On this night all movement was special and I watched through the open doors as if he were performing a special ceremony. "Please leave the palmara leaves out of the mix tonight," I called to him. He collected spicy green *mala* pods, a handful of wonderful mealy spiral beans, and a few herbs and brought them inside. He rinsed the vegetables and let them drain while he put a pan of *grash*, which is a type of rice, on one of the burners to cook.

"Guess what Aytinous gave me for this special evening with you?" and Kyron went to the chest at the end of his pallet and pulled out a bottle of *lume* wine.

Kyron filled two small cups with the inky black wine and set them inside the heater for a few seconds. When he handed me my cup, I was amazed how hot to the touch the cup became in a few seconds time. When I attempted to drink the wine, the alcoholic fumes caused me to feel lightheaded. "I drank *lume* only once before," I said.

As he continued to prepare our dinner, he said, "Tell me about it."

"I was only eight phases old."

"It must have been a special occasion if your parents allowed you to drink alcoholic spirits."

Memory of a long-ago night drifted through me and I felt an uncomfortable resistance. "I don't want to talk about it tonight. I'm too happy to think about the past."

"Let it go and let's see where it flies," Kyron urged.

Suddenly the memory loomed up with greater authority and I saw all the lights burning in our big stone house on Ravenna and heard noise filling the common rooms. The sound of escalating conversation and loud laughter, which always comes when people are drinking too much, was drowning out the music from a three-piece band. Sophia and I were home from our separate schools, so my father could display his happy family to colleagues. "It was a different type of night than this," I told Kyron. "My mother allowed Sophia and me to drink a thimble of *lume* at a special dinner party she and my father hosted to celebrate Ravenna endorsing the alliance with the Galaxy Council. It was a formal celebration—a bunch of self-serving diplomats congratulating themselves over dividing the Gathosian spoils."

"Your memory sounds bitter."

"My father was seduced by a superficial dream and that makes me sad."

"Was your mother seduced by this superficial dream too?"

"My mother was seduced by her feelings of responsibility to my father and to her children. Her will was not strong enough to carve out a place for herself in life. She was a midnight poet that ended up writing only for herself."

"Aren't you being judgmental concerning your parents' choices in life?"

Kyron and I stared at each other. "I guess I could use a cure for judgmental impudence rather than anger."

Kyron amazed me. He loved me unconditionally, yet his love never clouded his vision of my faults. "My dear child, judgmental impudence is the part of us that exclaims, 'I know better,' while it projects our impatience onto others. That is a form of anger."

"Maybe I am infected with the vaspray fungus."

His voice softened. "Let's wait until Arithmarur gets back to us on your blood test. Tonight, let's be happy and drink to your complete mastery, which is close at hand."

"Perhaps you should review my mind scribe before we drink to my complete mastery."

He turned serious and it was a glimpse of his ability to adapt at a moment's notice. "Whatever your mind scribe reveals, my commitment to you stands." He immediately balanced his seriousness with a tender smile. "Élan, let's be in this precious moment with respect for where we are now." He lifted his glass to me. "I drink to the first Human Emblematic Shardasko Warrior in the history of this universe. I drink to a man who finished his *quarrying* a full day ahead of his time declaration; therefore, I drink to a man not yet living up to his potential. But, by the power of all that's holy, I swear, he will." Kyron put his hand under my chin and forced me to look into his piercing eyes. "Élan, I know you want complete fusion with your *Holder* and I swear it is an attainable dream. Do you love yourself enough and trust your *Holder* enough to meld with it completely?"

"I know beyond all doubt that you are my key to this fusion."

"Then put your Emblematic days behind you and reach for your mastery." He pointed to my cup. "Drink it down." The wine stimulated my appetite. Afterward, I felt pleasantly tired. Parts of my conscious mind kept wandering off and I felt strung out through several dimensions. Kyron insisted that I submit to some intensive energy work. I reclined on my bed and he worked on me for over two hours as I kept drifting deeper and deeper into recuperative slumber. The energy work was more physical than usual. He said this was necessary because my physical body needed the extra attention. I loved the physical part, especially when he rubbed my feet with perfumed oil.

****

Life is lived differently when one is a Shardasko Warrior. When two people marry, first comes the wedding, the honeymoon, and finally the couple attempt to face the frank realizations of life together. For a Shardasko Warrior, the honeymoon comes when the marriage is about to end. My time with Kyron, at Sheebrun Shardasko, was my "honeymoon." When we returned to the Sutcay Tay School, we would enjoy a "wedding" to celebrate our triumph. Afterward, we were supposed to sever day-to-day connections for a period of six moons, so I could establish myself as an independent Emblematic Warrior. With a continued emphasis on self-sufficiency, I would work at the temples, teach a class to neophytes, and take greater part in running the school. Eventually, I would leave Sutcay Tay and assume duties at Shardasko schools, on other worlds, which would broaden my education. Naturally, I had no experience concerning what a real honeymoon entailed. However, all my instincts informed me that a honeymoon was a time to be with one's beloved. For me, this is what the next six days were like with Kyron.

That night I slept without consciousness and this was unusual for me. Habit abruptly awoke me as the green light of Eno peeked through our windows and Kyron said, "Go back to sleep, my prince." I nodded and went back to sleep. When I awoke the next time, my body was soaked in sweat. It was mid-morning and the day hot.

That first glorious day, we drank cooled razzleroot tea as we sat behind our *tritum* in the shade of a parishfuit tree. The tree was abloom with scarlet flowers that oozed their spicy scent and the bees were buzzing their familiar songs as they made love to each pollen soaked stamen. While we were sitting and soaking in total bliss, Arithmarur came by and told me, "Élan, you are clean." Arithmarur stayed for tea. I tried to return the cube of *tartan ratu* and he told me, "Keep it. *Tartan ratu* is wide-spectrum. You might need it in the future to root out another unacknowledged emotion."

Later that afternoon, Kyron inserted my mind scribe behind his ear and began reviewing my thoughts during my *quarrying*. It would take him the next three days to review my entire file. Some parts he skipped over quickly while others he listened to three and four times. The first incident we discussed was my encounter with the male dulcerary as soon as I entered the Great Verdant. "This is extremely important," Kyron insisted. He cued the mind scribe to, "regress," and then recited the dulcerary's words as he heard them from the mind scribe and the way I heard them from the dulcerary. "'I wish to honor you with an equal vision. Your hunger will be satisfied in a son. Name him Dulcerary and inspire him with the song of your instinctive heart and he will remember the music that first spun out life from the conservatory of creation.'"

"It was a projection, a mere possibility," I insisted. "It's my freewill not to take that path."

"It's too late; you've already embarked upon it."

"How?"

"Did you lie to the dulcerary about the existence of a weakened siberlene?"

"No, I spoke true."

"That's why the dulcerary said, 'I wish to honor you with an equal vision.' The truth of the dulcerary's vision promised that it would equal the purity of your vision. If you lied to escape, then the dulcerary's vision might have evaporated as an illusion, but you strengthened the dulcerary's vision and made it equal to yours through your integrity."

"How—can that be?"

"You mean how will it be," corrected Kyron. "I could waste my time and jump to the fourth dimension and root around in the infinite possibilities of the future. You and I both know that before I got far along any of your future timelines, the snowflakes of your desire would be expecting their due. Fire Élan! You have not dealt with your creative fire. The evidence sits right here in your mind scribe pumping its information into my brain. Your need is as obvious as Mount Tyburnian when Insanio shines upon it. The *Holder* that incarnated that dulcerary recognized your need as clearly as it recognized its own hunger. Cosmic law is a mirror. Like attracts like and desire attracts desire."

"You know that my first desire is to become a Shardasko master."

"Why do you presume Shardasko mastery and dealing with your creative desire are incompatible? You cannot become a master until you address every speck of yourself in the fourth dimension. Deal with your fluttering specks of denial and you will not need anyone, including me, to proclaim your complete mastery. Deal with your specks and your *Holder* will kneel down and worship you."

The creative fire Kyron was talking about was my suppressed sexual desires. I struggled to take the focus off myself through generalizations. Finally, I said aloud what I long knew was true. "Is that why other masters overlook the sexual intimacy between Emblematic Warriors? Are those Emblematic Warriors dealing with their specks of desire on their way to mastery?"

"It's not for me to judge what other masters overlook or how their Emblematic Warriors behave. I've learned through experience that double standards do not work for me and I would bluntly confront any of my warriors that attempt to compromise their integrity. You know I enjoyed a life with Belinda and, believe me, it was a lusty affair from beginning to end. After she died, I wanted no other physical lover. Now I'm an old man, but I still burn with creative fire. In her name and through her image, I kindle my fire and it burns brightly for my *Holder*. The embers and ashes, which remain, are mine to do with as I wish. These I stir with you and a few others and together we try to make sense of life. This arrangement fulfills me; yet for others, it's not enough. Some of us need physical intimacy. What can I do but respect those who honor their true desires?"

"I do not know how to deal with my specks under these present circumstances."

"Circumstances change," Kyron warned. "Respect your true desires and they will emerge and change your circumstances and put you on your true course."

I felt uneasy then. Perhaps it was my initial realization that the path of Shardasko training could not carry me through to my journey's end.

****

We sat in meditation through twilight and into the dark. Again I prayed for the siberlene that died in my stead. Afterward, we ate, but I couldn't sleep. My anticipation that our honeymoon soon would end was enough to keep me awake. A big part of me was content to remain in Sheebrun, to putter away my days in intimate dialogue with Kyron. I knew he had participated in other honeymoons with other warriors. He rarely mentioned these other men. I knew the facts only because I researched Kyron in the library, under the topic, "Shardasko Heraldry." Kyron fostered the careers of fifty-six Emblematic Warriors—twenty-two of which became masters. While most masters gave simultaneous instruction to two and three students, Kyron concentrated his efforts on one student at a time. His meticulous one-to-one approach paid off. Only four other masters, in the history of Shardasko tutelage, had graduated twenty-two masters and only three of Kyron's neophytes ever left his training. Aytinous and I were Kyron's last two warriors at the Sutcay Tay School. Why Aytinous remained at Sutcay Tay, after seven phases as an Emblematic Warrior, was a mystery to me. He refused prestigious offers from other schools, and one time even used me as his excuse. "I want to see you through your training in shadow dancing," he said. Yet, when I finished shadow-dancing training, Aytinous continued to stay on at the Sutcay Tay School. I knew he was uniquely special to Kyron, but was unsure why. Kyron gave Aytinous the challenging moniker of, "perfection will reign," for an important reason. Regardless, the times Kyron mentioned the name Aytinous in my presence, I could count on one Human hand.

****

The following morning we meditated through *areé didamé* and after breakfast, we plunged into the topic of my encounter with Cerebow in the small cave. "I made an error trapping myself in a cave with no way out," I said.

"You made no error," Kyron insisted. "You knew a way out; it merely took a little time to see your way clear. Besides, potential traps are everywhere and traps are dead ends, only if we believe they are." I thought I fell short in denying my Shardasko training and Kyron said, "You proved Shardasko training really works. You understood during those critical moments that nothing is capable of preparing us for every contingence. When we realize that fundamental truth, panic sets in. The inflexible can spend lifetimes experiencing reactionary panic to this truth, bewailing,

'Where did I go wrong?' while a Shardasko Warrior adapts and breezes through his panic in the blink of an eye. All physical life stands poised on the edge of unfolding time, but only a Shardasko Warrior fully acknowledges his fragility and, like a thief in the night, steals what he needs and runs into the arms of his enlightenment."

Kyron's reaction to Cerebow reaching sentient consciousness came as a total shock to me. In discussing Cerebow, Kyron graciously bestowed some of the most profound insights on the nature of reality that I've ever heard. "Cerebow's consciousness emerged because you attracted the attention of her *Holder*," said Kyron. "You are a prince of fire. Greater spirits enjoy playing rather strange games with our fire energy for reasons not always obvious to mortals. In your case, I believe, Cerebow's *Holder* was attracted to your fire and was playing games with your unresolved desire for female companionship."

"Then you don't think my encounter with Cerebow was an accident."

"I certainly do not."

"You make the encounter sound—well, sexual."

"You see!" laughed Kyron. "We are back to the subject of your creative desire again. This subject is not going to go away for you, Élan. Fire energy is sexual energy and sexual energy is creative energy. What pleases me, concerning your involvement with Cerebow, is your integrity never wavered. Your integrity taught her *Holder* something it needed to know, as well as giving you an opportunity to learn more about yourself."

"What about Cerebow's *Holder*? Was it my *Holder* in disguise?"

"Hum!" was his open-ended reply. "Explore that possibility the next time you sit in meditation. I'd love to hear what you come up with."

I was concerned about the physical Cerebow and wanted Kyron's opinion on what might happen to her. Kyron said, "When a seed first breaks open, it does not produce a flower its first day and consciousness does not surge forward in one long leap to enlightenment. Sentient consciousness develops gradually, as we develop a deeper relationship with our *Holder*. I may be wrong, but I believe Cerebow will slowly slip back into her instinctive state. Her initial exposure to you probably was not sufficient to sustain higher awareness." Kyron smiled and touched his tongue to his upper lip. "Besides, can you imagine a dulcerary panther arriving on campus and making the round of masters, to ask for acceptance as a neophyte?" He slapped his thigh in amusement and chuckled softly. "Now that would be a completely humorous sight. I'd love to see it!" He looked up, as if asking for absolution from the sky. "Forgive me, but it would be such a pleasure to see my brothers squirm as their assumptions dissolve."

What did he mean? An admission slipped out of Kyron that he never before shared. "When you first came to Sutcay Tay as a neophyte, a few masters believed you would be gone in a flash. They believed a Human could never accept the philosophical underpinnings or endure the rigors of Shardasko training. Now as you grow toward mastery, your endurance challenges our Gathosian presumptions and humbles us before truth." Kyron held up his right hand and twisted it from side to side. "Our bodies are essentially the same, except for a few superficial differences. Our brains are masterpieces the elemental universe has been fine-tuning for eons. Cerebow is different. Every soul group channels energy from Source and has the freewill and ability to use that energy to maintain physical reality through forms such as flowers, siberlene, and dulcerary panthers."

"That explanation sounds as if you believe flowers, siberlene, and dulcerary panthers are merely backdrops for sentient consciousness."

"Not at all! Flowers and siberlene are divine, but are missing a critical factor they need to support higher consciousness. They lack an ego memory. They have no nagging voice, telling them that they are separate, alone, and will die. It's a protection for their benefit. They exist in a blessed state of grace and as soon as they die, their life's spirit loops back from whence it came."

"Are you absolutely sure?"

He laughed in amusement. "May the heavens descend upon me if I am ever arrogant enough to declare that I am absolutely sure of anything. I am absolutely sure of nothing, only experientially sure from what I have observed."

"But if the siberlene that died for me returned to my soul group— doesn't that mean I can stop praying for the animal's soul?"

"Pray for the siberlene," Kyron urged. "And pray for the vaspray too. Pray for every living creature until your *Holder* tells you to stop." After this conversation, I felt a sense of grief concerning Cerebow, similar to a person who looses a beloved pet. I was disappointed because I identified with her and thought it would be gratifying to have another alien challenger appear at the Sutcay Tay School. Kyron and I went for several walks during our six-day honeymoon. We walked into Sheebrun village the night before returning to the Sutcay Tay campus. We ate dinner at an ancient tavern called *The Dog and Duck* and drank beer again. On the walk back to the Sheebrun campus, I kept glancing toward the edge of the forest for signs of Cerebow. I hoped to see her big, yellow eyes shining from between the dark trees, but the night was silent and the woods dark.

# SIX

It took less than fifteen minutes to fly from Sheebrun to the Sutcay Valley. As we whisked over the green blur of the Great Verdant, I sensed a subtle but growing uneasiness, a yearning to turn around and rush right back to that cozy little guest *tritum* on the Sheebrun campus. My shift was so gradual and wily, I didn't understand what was happening until a new mood paralyzed my mind and trapped me into running around, in a morning of spastic nonsense. Kyron sensed my shifting mood, so when we landed, he leaned closer and gave me the clue I needed, to recoup my balance. "Mind finds truth through greater perspective, while feelings find truth through greater intimacy," he said. By now, I should have realized Kyron never spoke in an off-handed manner; but instead of asking for clarification, superficial assumptions sidetracked me. I presumed Kyron was referring to my reluctance to return to the Sutcay Tay campus, but as usual, Kyron meant so much more.

Higher consciousness is neither a destination nor a conclusion; if anything, higher consciousness is a momentary gasp of wonder. When wonder subsides, sometimes we find our assumptive ruts still waiting to trip us up. Limited mind is stuck in linear time, with a memory as conditioned as any trained dog. Indulging our limited mind causes internal stagnation, which stymies imagination and evolution. Mind stagnation is what we commonly refer to as, "nostalgia." Nostalgia creeps out of our assumptive ruts and distracts us with its claptrap, while searching our pockets for our energetic wealth. When "nostalgia" first springs into awareness, mind identifies the yearning as emotion and dispatches the yearning to feelings for proper expression. Feelings cannot express vague yearnings, because feelings need to experience life through the sensual dance of intimacy. With no hope for resolution, nostalgia ricochets back and forth between the limited mind and feelings, leaving a residue of free-floating anxieties in our feelings and confusion in our mind.

This was my exact predicament. The future was waiting, but I couldn't embrace it because my yearning for what just ended was sucking me dry. As I wallowed in the backwaters of nostalgia, no chance existed that Kyron would stick around and indulge my nonsense. As we disembarked, just a *skefit* southeast of where I walked into the Great Verdant, Kyron wished me his English, "See you later," and briskly walked away. Our honeymoon was over. Now all that remained was the wedding before our divorce.

Several practical chores awaited my attention. I was supposed to move out of level two housing, where I lived for the past five phases. My stubbornness decided that it was too difficult to move and now my stark little room, in level two housing, took on a rosy glow. My mind supplied plenty of rationalizations to support my resistance to change. Level two housing was closer to the Fire Circle, where I was committed to work for another phase. Despite the fact that I walked 322 kilometers across the Great Verdant, a ten-minute stroll across campus now seemed too far to go. Groping for justification, I discovered brand new reasons to appreciate my good-old roommate Harmony. He was quiet, respectful of my private space, and never left toothpaste in our sink.

A round of procrastination seized me. I went to the Eternal Waters Sanctuary to pray for resolution and stayed for less than twenty minutes because a vague post-breakfast hunger overtook me. Bouncing across campus to the central eating area, I chatted with a few brothers about various and sundry Shardasko topics, but forgot to eat. By midmorning, I decide to go to the administration office and pick up my messages.

At administration, no one was waiting to use the multidex. Our communal multidex is the only means of indirect communication among the brothers and to the outside world, so this usually is a busy location, but this morning everyone was attending classes. Sitting in the chair, I placed my head against the eyelets, and requested, "correspondence?" Our multidex is old and slow, so it took nearly a minute to identify my eye patterns and display a list of thirty-four messages. When "ready" flashed on the screen, I assumed my automatic mode of, "delete." Three items managed to catch my attention, a memo from the housing office, a messaged signed, "Brother Noveil," and a video from my sister Sophia. The memo from the housing office was a reminder to vacate level two housing by the following afternoon, and to move into a *tritum,* along Queen of Crystal Trail. After reading the first few words, I took my revenge with a resounding, "delete!"

The correspondence from Brother Noveil intrigued me because the letter was written in English. "Hi!" it said. "I just transferred to Sutcay Tay from Lomita School on Numidia. The housing office informed me that we are supposed to share a *tritum* somewhere along Queen of Crystal Trail. I'm in temporary housing now, but must vacate the space by this afternoon because a master has reserved it for visiting family. The housing office suggested I locate you and you would know exactly where our *tritum* is located. Looking forward to meeting you. Noveil Epay ESW (Emblematic Shardasko Warrior)." My mood was so strange that I barely questioned why my new roommate spoke English. All I thought was, *he probably snores.*

Opening the video from Sophia, I saw her standing in her library on Gathos with her arm around her son Valent. As usual, the initial shock of seeing another pale Human face, after looking at golden-brown Gathosian faces for so many moons, gave me a minor jolt. Valent was a smaller version of Coreese except Valent possessed Human hands and feet. As more Gathosians and Humans mate, it's apparent that Gathosian eyes are dominant over Human eyes, but their children usually have five-fingered hands and toes if no genetic manipulation is used.

Sophia further startled me by also speaking English. We usually spoke Mescale out of courtesy for Coreese and our act of courtesy had evolved into habit. "Say hello to Uncle Journey," said Sophia to her son and she enunciated each English word carefully so Valent could understand.

"Hello, Uncle Journey," Valent said like a mime. He dangled his little Human hand toward me and then dashed off screen to an unknown location that held greater interest.

"He's getting really energetic," Sophia apologized. "He can't stay in one place for more than a minute or two." She struggled to refocus and then I noticed she was distracted. "It's difficult to talk when I can't see your face. Anyway, I'm leaving this video because when I called the administration office they had your friend Aytinous call me back. He told me you were off *quarrying*. I remembered you told me your *quarrying* was coming up. Aytinous told me not to worry because you are an excellent warrior and he is sure you will be okay. I know this *quarrying* business is important to you and I'm certain you'll do fine, just as Aytinous expects. You're a determined person just as Dad always was. You know, once Dad made up his mind to accomplish a task, he never let anything get in his way. Just the same, I've been worrying, especially when I think of my little brother out in the middle of a jungle full of wild animals. I don't know much about prayer, the way you do; but since I talked to Aytinous, you've been on my mind, and my every thought is kinda like a prayer for your safety." Her eyes turned glassy before she said, "The real reason I called, was to ask you to come to Gathos. Big changes have happened around here since we last spoke. I'm delighted to say all the changes are wonderful; although I feel hassled because, as usual, everything is moving too quickly." Her expression flashed brighter. "First, I'm pregnant again and second we're moving to Earth—not permanently, but we will be staying on Earth for at least two Earth years because of Coreese's business." She looked even brighter. "I'm practicing my English. How do I sound? I hope I haven't forgotten too much because Coreese is expecting me to help him. I really want to see you before we leave; besides, Coreese says he needs to talk to you, in person, because he wants to explain the details of your trust fund. So tell Master Kyron that you need a holiday and grab the first flight for Gathos and we will have a wonderful fling before I go."

Was nostalgia targeting the Cœurs of creation? Sophia's tired-and-hassled look glazed over her bright facade giving her a patina of nostalgia. "Please Journey, I love you so much; please come." She sniffed and apologized with a, "sorry. Being pregnant is making me emotional." She put on a grin to hide her sentiment. "Coreese says I am sensitive this time because we are having a girl." The screen flickered and went black.

"Save correspondences six and twenty-two and eject," I said. As I sat waiting for my copy to pop out of the multidex, I thought, *it's an inconvenient time to go to Gathos*, but I knew I must go.

Right outside the administration building, a voice called, "Wait up, brother!" Stunned because someone again was addressing me in English, I turned around and saw a Shardasko brother rushing toward me. "Brother Élan?" he asked breathlessly.

"*Afen*" I greeted him.

"I'm Noveil Epay, your new *tritum* mate. I've been chasing you all over campus this morning."

"Where did you learn to speak such perfect English?"

He laughed. "My mom works for the Galaxy Council. I was born on Earth and lived there until entering training at Lomita School on Numida."

"My father worked for the Galaxy Council on Ravenna."

"No kidding! What's his name?"

"His name was Simon Cœur. He and my mother died in that meteor storm that ravished Ravenna, nine phases ago."

"I'm so sorry. When I talk to my mom, I will ask if she knew him. Wow! This is weird—us meeting like this—don't you think? When I arrived yesterday, I was surprised to learn a Human was in training here and then totally freaked when the housing authority said we were going to be *tritum* mates. Now I discover my mom and your dad were Galaxy Council cohorts. Means something—don't you think?" He laughed and pointed up toward the sky. "Whatever the scheme up there, it seems you and I are destined to be roomies down here."

As I stood, impotent within my nostalgia, it seemed as if a giant hook emerged from the future, snagged me, and now I was helplessly spinning forward in a whirlwind of inevitabilities. I dug deeper into my yearning, as I searched for that indefinable thing I could not find. I was stiff, unresponsive, and needed to blame somebody for my sniveling and obvious confusion.

His Shardasko moniker was Stellium and my nostalgia-tainted mind fabricated a pile of vague excuses to dislike him. His initial effusiveness allowed me to decide that he was not a quiet person and I loathed the notion of a *tritum* mate who was an incessant talker. His demeanor, I decided, lacked proper Shardasko humility, *a typical product of Lomita School and their artsy-crafty approach to Shardasko training*. My limited mind helped by reminding me, *it's a fact that the Celestial Air Palace on the Lomita campus is twice the size of their other temples*. Stellium was dressed in a red smock and white baggy trousers, which is the official dress of Lomita School. At that critical moment, his clothing appeared ostentatious to me, as if he were a member of a moronic marching band instead of a serious Shardasko Warrior. He was an exceptionally handsome person too and this made me feel uneasy and embarrassed. In a secular setting, one might say Stellium possessed style, but I decided style for a Shardasko Warrior was misplaced emphasis. He wore his black hair in the classic Shardasko manner, on top of his head and draped to the left side, but Stellium's hair appeared a tad too arranged. His hair was shorter over his forehead and around his ears. His sideburns were works of art and curved out in front of his ears like two sharp sickles. He wore a small wedge of beard cut into a diamond shape right under his bottom lip. *He's vain*, I thought.

My behavior turned taciturn and I showed Stellium that I was bored and disinterested in our moving dilemma. Together, we went and borrowed the small electric transport and I accompanied him to guest quarters so he could collect his belongings. He had a suitcase and three large boxes filled with possessions and I thought, *this vain twit is bringing his personal clutter along with his cluttered mind*.

To top it off, he said, "The rest of my stuff will be here in a few days." I was aghast. We stopped at level two housing, and he seemed too cheerful when he asked, "Do you need help bringing down your belongings?"

"Wait here," was my curt reply. Just in case Harmony was upstairs, I did not want my new stylish *tritum* mate to embarrass me. At that moment, I owned thirty-three items in the universe and I knew exactly where each item was located. I went upstairs and got a brown cardboard box that always sat next to my bed. From the bottom drawer of my chest, I took my five handwritten journals, my pen, and a small box of memory capsules that I had downloaded from the multidex. From the top drawer, I retrieved my knife and scabbard, which was a birthday gift from my father when I was twelve, and my three quartz crystals, which were gifts from Kyron. From the middle drawer, I took my two extra *moodarrys* and one *slipfal*. I went into the bathroom and packed my ever-sharp razor, comb, ultrasonic toothbrush, and a half-empty bottle of shampoo and two towels. I left my bar of soap because it was sticky, but did think about taking it. Soap still seemed precious to me. Leaving the soap meant I now owned thirty-two items. I took the mind scribe, the cube of *tartan ratu* from my right pocket, and the green velvet box from my left pocket and put these items in the cardboard box along with the other items. I collected my two sheets, one pillowcase, blanket, and pillow from the bed. All these items fit into one box except for the pillow and blanket. I owned only three more items, the *moodarry* I wore, my new prayer beads, and the sandals on my feet. I took one last glance around the room before picking up the box and bedding. "Goodbye," I said to my dear old room. The future was dragging me forward, but I was kicking and screaming the entire way.

****

All the way out to our *tritum,* Stellium chattered away in English. By the time we arrived, I knew more about him than I thought possible. I drove the electric transport because I knew exactly where Queen of Crystal Trail was located and which *tritum* was ours.

His family name was Esay. The word *"esay"* is one of the most intimate expressions for love in the Mescale language, a word I never spoke aloud to anyone. Now my new *tritum* mate openly sported Esay as his family name. His Shardasko moniker, Stellium, meant "a favorable conjunction of stars." The moniker suggested his master believed the elemental universe blessed Stellium with powerful gifts. Born, an only child, his parents had "split up" when he was three. He was twenty-seven Earth years old and an accomplished Emblematic Warrior, who walked across the Numidian Abyss, approximately nine moons earlier. He told me, "As a child, my mom and I lived in an Earth city called San Diego, where the weather is always fabulous and the people always laid back. It was a great place to grow up—water surfing and trips into the desert. As a kid, I loved karate and holographic art. Now my absolute passion is transpersonal art. What interests you?"

"I'm a Shardasko Warrior."

"Sure thing!" he replied and he finally turned quiet.

Our *tritum* was the last one on Queen of Crystal Trail and no one had occupied this *tritum* for two phases. Weeds clogged the small rear garden that sloped up toward the Tyburnian Mountains. "Too much shade and too many rocks," I declared. We were responsible for maintenance of the grounds around our *tritum*. Like most Gathosians, we wanted to grow our vegetables and fruits so we could eat them immediately for optimum flavor.

"No problem!" Stellium chirped with enthusiasm. "Let's situate our garden in front." We went inside. The interior was similar to the *tritum* Kyron and I occupied on Sheebrun campus, except this one was dusty and full of spiders and cobwebs. Stellium said, "Wow! This place is a real fixer-upper." The only furniture consisted of two bed pallets. I wanted to return to the housing authority to complain, to tell them I had to stay in level two housing until the *tritum* was livable. Instead, Stellium said, "We should get started cleaning if we want a decent place to lay our heads tonight."

"Okay," I reluctantly agreed. My work in the temples taught me how to get whatever I needed in a flash. My nostalgia kept a grip on my enthusiasm, and I allowed Stellium to believe that getting cleaning supplies and furniture was going to be a hassle. We unloaded our belongings, leaving them outside the front door before driving back to the housing authority. The office was deserted, but this was not a problem. Supplies at the Sutcay Tay School always were available and apportioning was a matter of trust. We let ourselves inside and strolled back to the area where supplies were stored. Stellium was impressed with my knowledge concerning these mundane details and he kept up a steady stream of praise that annoyed me. We picked up furniture, two mattresses, pillows, cleaning supplies, cooking utensils and food staples, and hauled everything back to our *tritum*. For a person who, a short time before, owned thirty-three items in the universe, I felt overburdened with all these new possessions. "I need to return the transport," I mumbled. I deserted Stellium, leaving him in front of our *tritum* with our old and new belongings strewn around him on the ground.

"Wait," he called after me. "How do we get water and electricity?"

"Valves are on the outside wall," I yelled over my shoulder. As I drove off, I added, "Any neophyte would know that much." I parked the electric transport at the housing office along with a note, explaining we needed to use the transport for two trips instead of one.

****

No matter my mood, I intended to return to the *tritum* and help Stellium clean, but as I passed the Fecundity Garden, the secret connection word between Aytinous and me popped into my head. Aytinous was calling me and I knew where to find him. Taking a detour, past the huge bronze bull that sits in the epicenter of the garden, through the fruit orchard and rose garden, I discovered Aytinous on his knees in the vegetable garden. Since I embarked on my *quarrying* and Kyron departed for Sheebrun, Aytinous had performed both our chores, as well as his own. On top of these chores, he taught a two-hour course on flexibility to neophytes.

Aytinous was now eight Air phases (31 years). His physical appearance had not changed a jot, since we first met. He still was elegant and commanding. Nothing he did suggested jerky movement or disorganization. All morning, I had been misbehaving, but now it was critical to focus and I became appropriately serious. Kneeling down before Aytinous, I kissed his hands. "Thank you," I said. My thank you went back seven phases, for his patience in teaching me shadow dancing and being a par-excellent example of a Shardasko Warrior. Aytinous was a pivotal person in my life and what he taught me was critical to my development as a Shardasko Warrior.

He seemed to understand the depth of my thank you and replied, "I remain forever at your disposal, my dear brother." He stood up and brushed the dirt off the front of his *moodarry,* until it was perfectly clean. "Let's go sit in the shade."

I knew then that he wanted to dance. As always, our conversation began slowly and gracefully and was as ritualized as a minuet. He offered his arm to me and we walked to a stone bench under a nearby tree. Arm linking is a deliberate gesture among warriors, a way to synchronize energy and facilitate the art of conversation. It would be presumptuous for a neophyte to initiate this gesture with his master or older teacher. The rules of etiquette were fuzzy between Aytinous and me because we shared the same master and had cemented our intimacy in the shadow-dancing chamber many phases earlier. Now that I was an Emblematic Warrior, no barriers existed between us, but I held Aytinous in such awe, I would not have taken his arm without explicit invitation. He noticed the injury on my arm and asked about it. I avoided his eyes and minimized the story by telling him, "I had a minor mishap when attempting to swim across the Tartha River. He accepted my explanation without question.

His small glass bottle of water sat on a nearby stone bench. Three quartz crystals floated around at the bottom of the water. Kyron gave these crystals to Aytinous, one by one, as he cleared the blocks, first in his body, then mind, and finally his feelings. These three crystals need to be in the possession of a warrior by level two training when his master begins imparting the greater truths of the Shardasko brotherhood. The crystals represent the purity of a warrior's consciousness in these three concentrations of his being. Putting the crystals into drinking water, symbolize that we drink of an infusion of our essential three selves. On that basis, the crystals act as a constant reminder that the body, mind, and feelings need to stay as pristine as three crystals sitting in perfectly clear water. Aytinous drank from the bottle and then offered it to me. His gesture was more than a courtesy; Shardasko tradition considers the act a sacrament. When a warrior offers to share his crystal water, it is an unthinkable insult to refuse. Accepting his gift, I made sure my lips touched the exact spot where his lips touched. I drank and returned the bottle to him with proper attention to Shardasko etiquette.

"Master Kyron and I took a late breakfast this morning," he said. Aytinous' hand made a delicate movement, as if trying to scrape a substance from an inverted bowl. I had observed other brothers employing similar gestures, when approaching topics they were uncomfortable discussing. "I hope you don't consider what I am about to say as an invasion of your private relationship with our master, but Master Kyron was candid with me, concerning your *quarrying*. He told me you undercut your time declaration by a full day." Aytinous fell silent, allowing that seed to sprout up between us.

"I planned to tell you as soon as we had time to sit and indulge in unhurried conversation."

Aytinous nodded as if to say, okay, so far so good. "While I am impressed with your achievement, at the same time I'm concerned that you are not living up to your potential." Aytinous went silent again and I realized he wanted me to offer an explanation concerning why I miscalculated my time declaration.

"Perhaps my journey across the Great Verdant was an anomaly. It did take me seven phases to become an Emblematic Warrior and I chose seven days to reflect my seven phases of training. My situation changed once my *quarrying* began and I adapted to those changes in the best way I knew how."

"I understand the basic logic behind your time declaration," and he folded his hands and pressed them against his solar plexus. I knew then that anything coming from his mouth would be coming from his *Holder*. If Aytinous was a demigod then his *Holder* was—something more. "A warrior can lie to himself, but the Great Verdant will never lie to the warrior," declared that perfect voice coming from Aytinous. "Your six-day crossing means you could have finished your training in six phases instead of seven. Master Kyron insinuated that you could have crossed the Verdant in less than six days, perhaps in five or even four."

"I consider that suggestion pure flattery."

My use of the word "flattery" troubled the awesome voice behind Aytinous and he said, "I would slap your face before flattering you."

The thought of Aytinous slapping my face was absurd and I felt like laughing to ease the tension, but to laugh would have been an inexcusable insult. "I did not mean to be glib," I replied instead.

"Flattery is a game played between two people who have false barriers between them. Are you interested in knowing my opinion concerning the discrepancy between your projection and your performance?"

"I respect and look forward to all your insights."

He nodded again. "It's my opinion—and I do emphasis the two words *my opinion*—that you have always felt uncertain among Gathosians because your Humanity is unexplored." I began to object and he stopped me with one delicate flick of the wrist. "Your Humanity is your genetic and karmic foundation. When we do not understand our foundations, our uncertainty encourages us to build a *tritum* on a foundation meant to support a temple."

"Are you suggesting I've built a mere *tritum* on the foundation of my Shardasko training?"

"I am. As your secondary mentor, I'm attempting to comprehend why, after seven phases of Shardasko training, that you still do not comprehend your hidden potential. I see your structure and it is quite beautiful, but I want to know your hidden foundation and what you are capable of supporting."

"Hiding my foundation or potential was never my intention. If anything, I am inside out with surrender before you and Kyron."

Aytinous smiled for the first time since I kissed his hands. That scary *Holder* of his sunk down and allowed Aytinous a modicum of control. "As usual, your verbal eloquence is extravagant." This statement definitely was not flattery; it was an accusation.

"If you could offer me a few clues as to how I am falling short, some specific instruction, then perhaps I could set new goals."

Aytinous wrapped his long Gathosian fingers around my hands in a deliberate way and I felt trapped. My hands rested gently in his, but I felt his incredible potency, his focus holding my focus and I could not escape. His will was absolute, a beacon as unwavering as a laser. "Look at me," he demanded; and my eyes looked up from our entwined hands to his blue-black and gold eyes of perfect resolution. "I can hint that an intrinsic link exists between us that surpasses our training. That link makes your evolution as important to me as my own. I personally cannot go forward without your fullest surrender to your potential. Do you understand what I'm suggesting?"

I really understood the briefest smattering of what he meant. My first impulse was to say he was flattering me again, but if I did, I think he might have slapped my face. "I feel unworthy compared to you and, especially to Master Kyron."

"I know you do and that's why we are having this exact discussion." Aytinous reclaimed his hands and they began to move through the air with typical Gathosian expressiveness. "Established convention dictates that a master must distance himself from his warrior after the *quarrying*. The reasons for this distancing are prudent. A warrior never plumbs the depths of his essential worth, if he remains tied to his master's energy. I understand the difficulty of separating from Master Kyron because I appreciate his enlightened energy as much as you do."

"Except my appreciation goes all the way to love."

"Yes, I suppose love is a better word than appreciation." His hands moved off on another expressive journey as if they were capable of constructing objects from thin air. "I understand about the sudden sense of abandonment you may be feeling, so I am offering you my conscious attention during your transition into independence."

"Are you suggesting that we become better friends?"

"I would prefer to call what I am suggesting, a mutuality of purpose."

"Mutuality of purpose? Did Master Kyron suggest this mutuality of purpose to you?"

Aytinous became even more formal, yet he asked, "May I speak more candidly?"

"Please do, because I'm still confused."

"Master Kyron implied that I might learn more about the energy of the heart from you, as you might learn more about the energy of the will from me."

"I see." Now I understood why our conversation was difficult. He was asking someone he once taught as a neophyte for help. "I apologize, Brother Aytinous. This morning I'm rather confused concerning my heart energy. In truth, my heart is breaking at the moment. All I can think about is getting up tomorrow morning and not seeing Master Kyron's face during *areé didamé*."

Aytinous immediately suggested, "We should meditate together until you get used to the idea."

I felt uncomfortable committing to a schedule of meditating with Aytinous before trying to meditate alone. A flat-out no was ungracious, so instead of being honest, I conveniently decided to remember my sister Sophia and I thanked him for talking to her while I was away. "She and her husband and child are moving to Earth for an extended period," I explained.

"Certainly, you must see her before she leaves," he agreed. "If you are concerned about your chores at the Fire Circle, I will continue your work until you return. And since you have evaded my question on meditating together, I understand you do not wish to pursue it."

Now embarrassed with my stinginess, I said, "No, let's do meet and give it a try."

We both were tentative upon parting—trying to protect what we knew and afraid of what the other might need. "I will meet you at the Eternal Waters Sanctuary tomorrow morning before *areé didamé*," he said because he knew this was my favorite place to meditate.

"No, let's meet at the Fire Circle," I returned. "It is a better place for initiation."

\*\*\*\*

When I returned to my new *tritum*, I found Stellium up to his elbows in a bucket of soapy water. He was shirtless and barefoot and had rolled his white pants up to his knees. His chest gleamed with sweat and black ringlets of damp hair framed his face. He had just finished mopping the floor. The first thing I let him know was, "I'm sorry I acted so brusquely with you earlier today. My first day back feels confusing and I feel like a neophyte again."

"No problem," he assured me. "When I returned from my *quarrying*, I felt confused for months. I even felt as if my master had abandoned me."

Stellium was so much on target concerning my current state of mind that I sought a quick evasion with, "What can I do to help clean?"

He leaned the mop against the wall and made a typical Gathosian hand gesture that meant the cleaning could wait. "I would like to add that I understand your uneasiness concerning me. The First Adaptation comes under definite strain when we are expected to move in with strangers." His eyes glanced like darts around the room before coming to rest upon me. Stellium owned a set of those piercing blue-black Gathosian eyes. His eyes could have melted the coldest heart and I felt further shame over my selfish behavior with him. Laughing to myself over my moronic conduct, I felt a strange urge to march Stellium over to Aytinous, at the Fecundity Garden, and say, look into these eyes and you will know everything about heart energy there is to know.

It was time to get serious with my new *tritum* mate too. Shardasko tradition dictates that Emblematic Warriors must share a *tritum*, but how we accomplished our sharing, was our choice. We could section off particular areas of our physical space with metaphorical ropes or we could use the space as an honest refuge, where we felt comfortable and respected the rights and privacy of the other. "If you have time, perhaps we should talk and clear up the confusion between us," I offered.

He was instantly happy and said, "Great idea!" We went outside. The mid-afternoon heat from Insanio made it intensely hot, so we sat in the rear of the *tritum* in the shade. "I'm sorry I was chattering so much when we first met," he said. "After all my training, I still talk too much when I am in new situations."

His confession made me smile and I admitted, "When I'm in new situations, I clam up." I pointed to the sky, as he had earlier. "Maybe there's a reason fate put us together."

Our conversation easily slipped into English. My mother preferred English to Mescale. She and I spoke English as our secret language. Out in public, we frequently indulged in English exchanges, knowing that chances were excellent that no one could understand us. Now I felt a small bit of that confidentiality with Stellium too.

Mescale is a vivid language containing endless feeling metaphors, while English is comprehensively graphic and technically precise. Mescale has at least two hundred different verbs meaning, "To love," which Gathosians use in different situations with different individuals, while English has only a handful of verbs to express this special elevated feeling. The musical cadence of Mescale makes it a harmonious sounding language, which appeals to poets and writers who refer to Mescale as, "the language of love." Now I felt safer resorting to the territory of English, as I proceeded to confess my feelings for Kyron. "I haven't even begun my six moon separation and I already miss him. To top it off, my shadow-dancing mentor just challenged me concerning my time declaration."

"I guess you undercut your time," said Stellium. I glanced up and again he snagged me with his piercing eyes. "I undercut my time declaration too. My projection was for six days and I made it in five."

"Five? I'm impressed. Talk about shadows!"

He smiled and moved his head from side to side in a mock of shadow dancing. "Yeah, but which one of us is the shadow here?"

"So how did you resolve the dilemma when your mentors said you were not living up to your potential?"

He dropped his gaze. "So far, I've found no resolution. Truth is, I'm on the verge of resigning from Shardasko training. My master suggested I come to Sutcay Tay for a few moons before I make my final decision and I agreed only because I want to repay a little of what I took from the brotherhood. The Sutcay Tay School needed someone to refresh the frescos on the outside walls of the Celestial Air Palace and I plan to work on that project and teach an elective art class before resigning. Besides, the masters here are legends at the other schools. I would love to do some sketches of them, if they agree." He looked up at me again and sincerity filled his eyes. "It's difficult to face the stark realities of our potential with the tiny quotient of our lonely minds—don't you agree?" I said nothing and an awkward silence arose between us. I felt as if his statement undressed me and I felt particularly obtuse. Then he asked, "Have you felt pressured because you are the first and only Human enrolled here?"

"I never thought of myself as a Human representative among Gathosians—if that's what you mean. I watched my father play that role and don't intend to repeat his mistakes. I became a Shardasko Warrior for myself. As a neophyte, I felt like an outsider, but if I now fail to live up to my potential, I blame only myself."

"That's noble, but you must realize your master will also fall short, if you do not live up to your potential."

"Not in this case. Master Kyron has been a flawless guide."

"I believe that mastery boils down to the proper interface between master and student. If the interface is askew, then the warrior misses his potential. My master confessed that he felt partly responsible for me not living up to my potential. He said that if I would stay within the brotherhood, he would find me a master that would offer me perfect interface."

"What did you tell him?"

"I told him that I no longer believed in perfect interface."

"That's somewhat cynical."

Stellium shrugged. "Cynicism is my biggest challenge. The truth is, I don't have much faith that divine fusion with my *Holder* is a real possibility either."

"What? How did you manage to become an accomplished Emblematic Warrior with so little faith?"

"I've done my work and crossed the Numidian Abyss. Nothing in Shardasko precepts requires that I believe in divine fusion or that I must live up to my fullest potential—whatever that means."

"But why did you go through all the training if you don't believe in it?"

"At the outset, I didn't know that I would not believe in it."

"In my opinion, you missed something important along the way."

"What, my full potential? Sorry, in Mescale, I might label both divine fusion and my full potential as *le sistil payrel\**. In English, I would call both concepts, impossibilities. My full potential is nothing more than a vague expression in both languages that ends up making me feel inadequate."

"I'm unsure what you mean."

"Look at it this way: our full potential is everything we have not experienced or might become. Most of the time, I sit right here in my subjective little life and in my subjective little moment, and my full potential is the infinite all around me. Tell me, which direction do I go first to fulfill my infinite potential? I am a man, not an omnipresent god. As a man, I don't know how to swallow the whole universe." He smiled and assured me, "Despite my obvious cynicism, I have no regrets about my time in training. Shardasko has helped me find inner peace and I have faith in myself for the first time in my life. And I can jump to the fourth dimension. I know it's real because I've been there. My training helped me see myself more clearly and other people as well. People can no longer fool me, as I once allowed them to do. Five minutes with a person is enough time for me to see right through their projected façades."

"You must have psychic abilities."

"I always possessed good psychic abilities, but Shardasko training has sharpened them. That's why I can say, as far as the pressure coming from your shadow-dancing mentor is concerned, he's playing games with you. It's similar to the games played with neophytes during First Cut, only a hell of a lot more consequential."

Games played with, or rather, on neophytes, I understood. These games are extensive yet neophytes never realize the truth of the situation unless they progress into secondary training. Eight moons after a neophyte enters training he must go to the edge of the Great Verdant, where he spends three days and two nights alone. He takes water, food, a blanket, and

*"black dream" but refers to something wanted with all one's heart, but cannot be realized even through one's wildest imagination; language origin, Mescale

nothing else. Each neophyte believes he goes alone and must remain alone, but an accomplished Emblematic Warrior always trails the neophyte and watches over him the entire time. It's frightening to sit on the edge of the Abyss, surrounded with fears of vaspray and the like, especially when exhaustion takes hold. Stories circulated around campus that a few Emblematic Warriors were not quite so altruistic and might execute certain pranks, to turn the situation into an adrenaline-pumping affair for the neophyte. Sometimes a mere rustle of a few leaves, a strange animalistic grunt, or a mere flicker of light is enough to scare the neophyte straight back to the campus and out of Shardasko training. However, the thought that Aytinous could be playing nasty games of this sort was more than I was prepared to believe.

****

As I sat in the afternoon shade with Stellium, I found he was a wealth of insider information, which he generously offered to share. "The reason you are not supposed to see your master for the next six moons is not for the reason everyone believes," he said. "Yes, warriors are supposed to be gaining greater independence, but at the same time your master is distancing himself from you, he is getting more intimate with your *Holder* to gain its confidence."

The scene on the airfloat that morning, when Kyron told me, "Mind finds truth through greater perspective while feelings finds truth through greater intimacy," flared up in my mind. It was the last thing he said before, "See you later."

Stellium explained. "Your *Holder* knows your Achilles' heel, your fatal weaknesses. Even as we speak, a little dance is going on between Kyron and your *Holder*, for those final secrets."

"How can a master get through to another person's *Holder*?"

"Are you kidding? Why do you think we call them masters? A master can flash over to the fourth dimension and tickle your denial with the feather of his will until you squirm. He can run up and down the timeline and create little gullies for you to fall into or nudge you in new directions. A master knows how to talk to your *Holder* better than you do."

"How come you know so many secrets when you've been an Emblematic Warrior for only nine moons?"

Stellium gave me a candid nod. "Artists are a sub-culture at Lomita School. Neophytes, secondary and Emblematic Warriors, and masters come together at the Celestial Air Palace, just because they enjoyed creating. Air is light, facilitates conversation, and highlights personal truth. Confessions sometimes would slip from masters, especially late at night when the barriers came down. Let me show you, something." We walked through the *tritum* and out the front door to where our possessions sat. He opened one of his boxes and pulled out a large brown folder shaped like an oversized envelope. Inside were dozens of incredible sketches of Shardasko Warriors and their interactions within the fourth dimension. "This is why I became a Shardasko Warrior, so I could experienced what only a few have been blessed to receive. My sole purpose, I believe, is to translate my experiences into pictures, so others might know the fourth dimension is real."

When I looked through his drawings, their visual authority stuck me like a thunderbolt and a lump lodged in my throat. His artistic style was both subtle and frank, and considering the subject matter that's saying a lot. The fact that he needed to work from memory, the detail and refinement of each drawing was amazing. He had created dozens of sketches of warriors in the breach and warriors performing the Feint Envelope. Several illustrations showed the process of Interlude Shading, of warriors opening dimensional doors, and the actual vision of the fourth dimension. "That's my master," he said pointing to a figure half-crouching along the blue and gray threads of the fourth dimension. The picture showed an obvious master, his long, dark hair blowing around his body and hiding most of his nudity.

"I love your drawings. They have power, grace, and movement. Do you have anything else to show me?"

"A couple of my paintings will be here in a few days. Don't get me wrong. I don't plan to inundate our *tritum* with my art." He gestured around the room. "I understand you prefer the sparse look. It's just one of my favorites and a painting I'm working on now."

Two hours earlier, I hated this stranger and now he felt familiar and comfortable. "Feel free to inundate me as much as you want."

My first day back was turning out to be a synchronistic rocket ride, but the day was just beginning. Stellium and I attempted to get practical. In case it rained, we carried our belongings inside. By then, it was late afternoon and I needed to think about my final moments of glory before I could not see Kyron for six full moons. My frustrated smelly body needed a relaxing bath, but I possessed no soap because I left my only bar in my old quarters. Stellium found a new bar of soap among his belongings and gave it to me. In exchange, I loaned him my extra *moodarry* for the evening because I told him, "Your red smock might be obvious in a sea of *moodarry* white." The bathroom was still dirty, so I scrubbed the sink before shaving and Stellium cleaned the tub and we switched back and forth and managed to bathe and shave. I dressed, putting on my one other clean *moodarry*, my new jade prayer beads, sandals, and then decided to wear the knife my father gave me for my twelfth birthday. The knife was the only token I possessed from my father. Everything tangible, my father gave me, the meteor storm on Ravenna consumed with fire.

Stellium put on my *moodarry* and it was long on him. "It sure feels breezy under here, minus undershorts," and he shrugged his shoulders up and down in a silly gesture.

He made me smile. "That's the whole idea, brother."

"Well, what Sutcay Tay considers tropical-weight attire, my mother would consider scandalous."

Stellium had shaved off his elaborate sideburns and the little diamond under his lip. "How come you shaved clean?"

He reminded me as Kyron often did, "After I'm gone, no one should remember I was here."

****

Kyron was expecting me, but before I went to his *tritum* to pick him up for our "wedding ceremony," I stopped by the Fecundity Garden and used my knife to cut the most beautiful red rose I could fine. I knocked on his door a few minutes later and when he answered, I presented him with the rose. "I stole this for you in the garden," I said. "I know only a master thief could appreciate the perfection of my crime."

He roared with laughter and was quick to say, "So glad you extricated yourself from this morning's funk. A soggy prince of fire inspires no one. Come in; before we go we need to discuss an important matter."

As I walked into this familiar space, my eyes collected images and my feelings overlaid the images with nostalgic memories. The ancient bookshelf with Kyron's private journals and favorite books went through a holographic stutter. Memory saw Kyron walk to that bookshelf and remove a book, as he so often did. My eyes feasted on the *ackinayon*, containing his wand, which sat in the corner by the door. The old, battered pan and spoon resting on the cooker, each familiar knot in the floor, and Kyron himself filled me with heartache. For seven phases, I considered my level-two housing as a place to sleep. This *tritum* was my home. The layout was similar to all other Shardasko *tritums*, yet this place held unique memories. Kyron worshiped, slept, ate, and defecated here, sanctifying this space with his physical presence. This simple dwelling was a shrine, proof that consciousness could live in a physical body and regain the perfection of its divine soul.

Kyron put the rose in a glass of water and set it on the eating table. We chatted while he made tea. In all likelihood he would make some comments concerning our past seven phases together. It was a given that he would say it beautifully, and it would be full of wisdom and likely be profound. In order to say it, he would not dilute his attention by making tea and talking at the same time. Complete focus was the usual approach for any Shardasko master and this was especially true for Kyron. I sat down on, what I thought of as, my cushion and waited, staring through the open doors into the rear garden. Many dawns we spent sitting in that garden meditating through *areé didamé*. Nostalgia had used and abused me all day long and now I was limp with yearning and a hopeless case. Plucking myself up, for the evening ahead, I, again, conveniently used dear Sophia as my excuse. "Sophia called while we were away."

"What was on her mind?" asked Kyron as he poured me a cup of razzleroot tea. After I went through the story, he said, "You must go," just as Aytinous said. However, Kyron added, "Actually, it's perfect that you are going. It coincides with what I want you to do for me—that is, if you agree."

"I am forever at your disposal, master."

Kyron walked over to his bookcase and began removing his journals from the shelves. These were his personal journals that I saw him write in many times over the past seven phases. "You'll find a box in the bathroom that you can use." Barely could I contain my curiosity concerning what he intended. Returning with the box, he explained. "There are twenty-one journals here. I have one more journal to give you, but it's incomplete. Do you have access to some money?"

"I have a trust fund from my parents that Coreese is tending for me."

"Good! Now this is what I want you to do. When you arrive on Gathos, go to a bank and lease a safety deposit box large enough to hold these journals. By the way, make sure the bank is reliable. Find out which bank Coreese deals with because we both know he uses only the best."

Unable to contain my curiosity any longer, I asked, "What's going on, master?"

Kyron returned with the ambiguous retort, "Many things are always going on, my prince. Are you asking my specific reasons for sending these journals to Gathos with you?"

"That's exactly what I'm asking."

"My reasons are many. To begin with, please understand that once you take possession of these journals, they belong to you. I have etched the contents of each journal upon my heart, so the actual paper no longer is of use to me. I merely ask that you not read them until I give you the final one, which I will finish in a few moons."

"You have my word."

"We are one in complete trust," he said and he kissed the palm of his hand and glued the kiss on my forehead with a slight pat. Then he opened his heart to me and his golden essence came pouring out as never before. As ever, he was capable of astounding me. "In my career as a Shardasko master, I have mentored many different men. Each man comes to me with unique problems and special gifts; however none ever showed an interest in writing and journal keeping. You and I have that in common and that's the first reason I am giving these journals to you. The second reason is you are the first Human Shardasko Warrior. The knowledge is here on Gathosian worlds and Gathosians who want Shardasko teachings know where to come, but Humans scarcely realize we Gathosians exist. Now you are an accomplished Emblematic Warrior, which means you are your own man. I know you will find your focus and purpose because a Shardasko Warrior can go anywhere and do anything, because his life is flexibility itself. From the first time you knelt at my feet and looked up at me with your incredible blue-green eyes, I hoped you might, someday, consider taking Shardasko truth to your people. We've spoken of this a few times, in an off-handed manner, over the past seven phases, but for me, it remains a dream I hope you will consider. If you decide to go to Earth to teach Shardasko truths to Humanity, these journals will give you a foundation."

"Master, I feel unworthy of such an honor."

"Hush, I'm not finished. My final reason for giving you the journals is difficult to explain, because I must touch the quick of my soul to expose my reasons. As you know, once Belinda left this physical plane, I dedicated my passion to becoming a Shardasko Warrior. When I became a master, many men came my way—believing I held the secret to their lives. Yet the truth is, each man must create his own mastery, for mastery is different for each man. Now that I am old, I believe I possess a spectrum of understanding concerning what it takes to bring many different types of men into their own mastery. With that knowledge, I can tell you that you are the kind of man I relate to best. You have inspired me and I consider you a gift from my divine *Holder*. My prince, the instant I first saw you, you filled my heart with warmth and joy and you have never ceased to be my lively flame. I always look forward to seeing you and miss you as soon as you are gone." He stopped speaking and deliberately pierced my heart with his Gathosian eyes as I began to weep. "My precious child, your tears only feed my fire."

"Words cannot express my love for you," I confessed.

He laid a warm hand on my shoulder and said, "That's why we must never speak of our love. Now dry your eyes because we do not want to miss a celebration being held in our honor."

I went over to the small sink and splashed my face with cold water before asking him. "Are my eyes blue-green or red?"

"You are Human perfection," he said; "and it was my privilege to watch you grow into your spiritual manhood. Now, how do I look dressed in my old-man Gathosian body?"

"You are the most beautiful person in this universe." He plucked the rose from the glass and I expected him to fasten it at the end of his long braid where he usually put his flowers for celebrations. But Kyron was a true Shardasko master who survived by doing the unexpected. That night he tucked the rose behind his right ear.

Since the earliest beginnings at the Sutcay Tay School, masters and

Emblematic Warriors have celebrated crossing the Great Verdant in the same manner. Kyron and I did not vary this tradition one iota, yet this evening was wholly unique to me. Kyron had preformed this particular ceremony seventy-nine times before, once when he reached mastery, twenty-two times with his graduating masters, and fifty-six times with his Emblematic Warriors. If this was a real wedding night, Kyron's chastity would have been in question, but Kyron was a master and performed the ceremony like an eternal virgin.

We walked to the exact center of the campus where the circular slab of New Delphi jade lies. We took our places upon the stone and sat cross-legged, facing each other with our knees touching, while brothers filled in the space around us. By the time everyone positions themselves in a tight circle around the master and Emblematic Warrior, the bodies form a network of energy around the two centered individuals. The ceremony starts nine minutes before sunset as nine drummers begin their rhythmic drumming on the steps of the Fire Circle. The assembled warriors are hushed throughout as the echo of the drumming eventually fills the Sutcay Valley.

Kyron and I sat staring into each other's eyes for the full nine minutes. What he saw in my eyes, I do not know, but I saw someone I adored in his. It did not matter that he was thirty-seven water phases old or was an alien lifeform with a black tongue. It did not matter that we both lived in male bodies or never kissed as real lovers do. If Kyron looked like one of my sandals, I would love him the same. When Insanio sank below the horizon and the drumming stopped, Kyron rose to his feet to pronounce these words in full and confident voice: "I, Master Kyron La Teeair Forma, do solemnly swear that on this night, the seventeenth day of Natva, phase of Air, 8433 that Élan Journey Cœur has fulfilled all provisions to become an accomplished Emblematic Warrior. Let no one deny his worth!" Then it was okay to cheer and shout.

I focused all my attention on Kyron that evening. After the ceremony, many people chatted with me. I recall introducing Stellium to Kyron and Aytinous, and my good-old roommate Harmony. Afterwards, I walked Kyron back to his *tritum* so I could claim the box, with his journals. The wedding was over and now it felt like our first and last date. "I will take care of these journals, exactly as you requested," I assured him. We went inside and I picked up the box and prepared to slip away into the *shahaut* to nurse my nostalgia.

"Write me," he said and he lightly touched my arm.

"Won't we get in trouble?"

He smiled my favorite wisdom smile. "Who is going to tell on us, the Eternal Waters?" Then he gave me a conspiratorial grin and kissed me on the forehead. "See you later," he said in English.

# SEVEN

That night I experienced a vivid dream. *I'm driving along a serpentine road on the planet Ravenna. It's twilight and the sky is turning a soft, mousy gray. To my right lay dark mountains and to my left was a barren desert of rolling dunes. The road sits as a depression between the mountains and dunes and is the only flat surface in the dream. I've promised to meet my mother for dinner, but now it's dark and I feel anxious because I'm running late. I sense a commotion ahead on the road and stop to investigate. When I emerge from my vehicle, I discover a crowd of people blocking the road. They tell me, "After dark, it's impossible to negotiate this section of road." I explain that I promised to meet my mother and several people say, "Then you should have begun your journey earlier." In a quandary, I return to my vehicle and ponder what I should do next. Chiding myself for not starting earlier, I convince myself that my "roadblock people" are authorities on what's possible and impossible. I drive home and telephone my mother to offer my excuses. When we speak, she asks, "Why did you listen to those ninnies? You can drive that road after dark. I do it all the time."*

My mind woke up a little and the truthful witness inside me said that I was wandering a path between my spiritual aspirations and my languishing physical desires and I was depressed about it. My witness pulled me into its greater perspective, suggesting my roadblock people symbolized my fear of exploring either reality adequately. I felt stuck and believed it was too late to change. My limited mind was allowing outside authority figures to influence me, while my nurturing mother urged me to complete my journey.

Thunder growled in the distance and I woke even more. My mind drifted to Cerebow out in the wilds of the Verdant Abyss. Even if her greater consciousness had retreated, I still felt a twinge of protective love for Cerebow, the life.

The sound of the wind brought me to full consciousness and I heard the first raindrops as they splattered against the windowpanes of the *tritum*. My promise to meet Aytinous for *areé didamé* and our "mutuality of purpose" came to mind and I remembered that I did not have a clean *moodarry* to wear. Again, Shardasko tradition dictates that it's unthinkable to go to a temple for formal meditation without bathing and putting on fresh clothing, as a sign of respect. Never before had I questioned this tradition, which I honored for the past seven years. Eventually, I would realize I could meditate as well in my honest filth as I could in my *moodarry* white. It was the middle of the night, but I crawled out of bed and prepared to wash my clothing. Stellium picked himself up on his elbows and asked, "What in creation are you doing?" I apologized for waking him and explained my dilemma. He got out of bed and twisted his top sheet around his waist before heading off to the toilet. I did not question his careful covering gesture. As our intimacy grew, he would explain why he felt self-conscious about his nakedness, but that night I barely noticed as I stood there in my naked virginal innocence. My unexamined rational was I simply was adhering to more Shardasko tradition. It was unspoken etiquette to overlook physical nudity in all situations. If a warrior wanted the power to jump dimensions, he needed to leave his clothing behind—the fourth dimension was the great leveler in that regard. Even in the third dimension, a warrior owned three precious *moodarry*s and did not squander their freshness by sleeping in one. When Stellium returned, he handed me the *moodarry* I loaned him. "Thanks, I should be getting mine later today," he said. As I put it into the washer/dryer, with my two other garments, I noticed it held traces of perfume.

****

That morning *areé didamé* remained a sulking gray. Rain came down by bucketsful and it was obvious monsoon season had arrived. Outside our *tritum*, I picked a large palmara leaf and, ridiculously, held it over my head all the way to the Fire Circle. My world appeared deserted and I did not see a soul the entire way.

The Fire Circle sits at the southeast corner of the campus. The temple is painted black with a bright-orange spiral that begins at its foundation and ends at the tip of its flame-shaped spire. The six meter-high walls of the temple soar straight up. Mica tiles cover the interior floor and walls and the tiles glitter with reflected light from the inside fire. Near the top of the wall sit three rows of eyelet windows for ventilation. The roof is conical and at its apex is an opening to create the proper draft. The interior of the roof is black with soot from the constant fire kept burning in the heart of the temple. The Fire Circle is always hot. This is not to its detriment; in fact, this is the whole purpose of a fire temple, the experience of incredible heat.

The proper way to meditate at the Fire Circle is to stop below, pick up a log, and reverently carry it up into the temple. Inside, a warrior places his log on the existing fire that burns in the center pit. Then he prepares to sit facing his burning donation and meditates upon it until the fire consumes his log. As the log burns, patterns within the fire create meaningful suggestions and images. Many brothers feel an exclusive affinity with the Fire Circle and meditate there constantly while others go only when they need to gain insight into their confusion or, metaphorically, burn their confusion away. Attuning personal energy to the energy of fire is essential when beginning any new venture or project. For example, an Emblematic Warrior would not enter the Great Verdant for his *quarrying*, before spending several moons of intense meditation in the Fire Circle.

My personal chore at this temple was to clean the fire pit of excessive ashes and to stoke the fire for the coming night. I had several neophyte assistants and as usual, their chores were easier than mine. For example, the fresh neophyte, Cerman, drove the electric transport to deliver the ashes to the Fecundity gardeners. Nord, a recent First Cut survivor, chopped and stacked firewood. Shardasko brothers plant all the trees harvested for wood at the Fire Circle and I, along with eight other Emblematic Warriors, and two masters, kept track of the exact location of these trees. As the need for firewood arose, we'd venture into the woods, meditate before these trees, then harvest and replant seedlings for future demand. My scheduled time in the Fire Circle was late afternoon and I found this a low point, when the fire would be simmering down to mere suggestive embers. Many nuances emerge from smoldering embers and I enjoyed this time of day, despite my chores being messy and dirty. I learned to love my fire meditations, because Kyron had convinced me that I carried abundant fire energy.

That morning, I stopped at the outside wood box and decided my first meditation with Aytinous was worth one log. Like a good Shardasko Warrior, I chose my log carefully. Going upstairs, I found the temple empty except for my fellow pyromaniac, Brother Daymin, whose scheduled time was early morning. The thick humid air was not allowing the fire enough draft and the place smelled of smoke. *I am not going to ignite and burn up this potential until Aytinous arrives,* I thought, and I set my log down on the mica floor. While I waited, Brother Daymin and I chatted about the humid environmental conditions and its impact on fire. Our conversation was so boring, I yawned in his soot-stained face. "Looks as if we could all use extra sleep after your big night last night," he yawned back.

I waited until past sunrise, but Aytinous never came. I took my log downstairs and returned it to the wood box. By then, the rain was so heavy, the logs looked like huddling siberlene waiting to offer up their bodies for food. Rain sheeted off the roof of the temple and I gave up the notion of attempting to stay dry under a palmara leaf. I dashed over to the administration building and sent a message to Sophia asking her to purchase a ticket for my trip to Gathos. While there, I wrote a note to Aytinous saying, "I missed you at the Fire Circle. Tomorrow morning, I leave for Gathos for a ten-day visit with my sister Sophia. Let's try to get together when I return." I also wrote to Kyron. "Dear Master, I miss you," I began, and then I sat staring at my silly confession as water dripped off my body and made a pool on the floor. "I love you," I added. *I can't send this pathetic little note,* yet I did. My world was wet and I was soggy with love. I sloshed over to the housing office, my sandals squishing and squeaking as I walked, and helped myself to food supplies—bread, tea, grash, oil, and a few pieces of fresh fruit. A large wheel of yellow cheese was available, which a clever brother obtained through barter with a local farmer, and I helped myself to a wedge. I put all the food in a large bag and mucked my way back to the *tritum*, where I found Stellium still asleep. "I brought food," I said.

Wet and muddy, I went to bathe for the second time that day. More modest the second time, I wrapped one of my towels around my waist before emerging from the bathroom. I found Stellium standing by the cooktop with his baggy Lomita pants hanging low on his hips. His chest was bare and he was making tea. He said nothing and I was thankful for the silence. He automatically handed me a cup of hot tea when it was ready and we sat down and broke off bits of cheese and bread, nibbling on them while we sipped our tea. After a while, he informed me, "I'm not a morning person."

"No problem," I said, returning one of his expressions.

We did not pray before we ate, nor did we eat consciously. I was thankful that I was dry and had something tasty to eat. "How'd your meditation go with Aytinous?" he asked a few minutes later.

"He didn't show up. What's your five minute analysis of him from last evening?"

"Other than the fact that he has a gorgeous ass?" I abruptly stopped eating and went into full-alert *turami savatnani*, wondering what Stellium might say to top that curious statement. I did not have long to wait. "Aytinous is a stalactite," he declared. "And he's hard." He sipped his tea until he added, "Brother Stalactite knows he's dripping away, but like a typical stalactite, does not realize he is evaporating to do it." Stellium nibbled at his piece of cheese. "My guess is he wants to make you into his stalagmite—drip, drip, dripping away on you, hoping someday you will meet and then he will understand himself."

"No way! Aytinous is a perfect saint."

Stellium laughed in a suggestive manner. "He's a calendar saint—that's for sure! On Earth, he definitely would be Mr. January—cold, hard, and proud. I guarantee stalagmites would change caves so he could drip away on them."

"I have no clue to what you are talking about."

Stellium ignored my ignorance and went back to eating cheese. "Who told Brother Stalactite that you undercut your time declaration?"

"Master Kyron."

"Aytinous really got to you—didn't he?"

This suggestion annoyed me. "Aytinous did not get to me. Although he did suggest I was not living up to my potential. Aytinous told me, 'A warrior can lie to himself, but the Great Verdant Abyss never lies to the warrior.'"

"That's absolute stalactite drivel!"

"Somehow Aytinous got the notion from Kyron that I could have accomplished my *quarrying* in four or five days. I accused Aytinous of flattery, which really annoyed him."

"Games!"

"Tell me Stellium, do you usually see intrigue wherever you look?"

"We all play games. In a few games we are lucky enough to realize our parts, but most games we do not even realize we are playing or even whom we are playing with."

"What game could Aytinous possibly be playing with me?"

"My guess is Kyron suggested to Mr. Perfect Stalactite that you were really hot—just enough to goad him a little."

"Kyron does not play warriors against each other. Anyway, no way could I walk across the Verdant Abyss in four days and Aytinous knows it."

"It doesn't matter what's possible. Brother Stalactite sees the fissure in himself. His ego is in an uproar. He believes you are capable of surpassing him—competitive aggression. It's a curse. Kyron might be nudging Aytinous in the way he needs to be nudged to face his inadequacies in the same way Kyron is nudging you."

"If you think Aytinous is a stalactite, how do you see Master Kyron?"

Stellium rolled his eyes. "Kyron is an awesome fox dressed in sheep's clothing."

"And what game is he playing?"

"Kyron is a Shardasko master. He invents his own games."

"If you believe so many people are playing games, you must be playing a few yourself."

He shrugged. "True, sometimes I convince myself that I'm an artist struggling to create and trying to live up to my potential, but when I'm honest, I know nothing can define me."

"Interesting, and how do you see me?"

Stellium glanced around the room before staring intently at me. "At the moment, you seem like an innocent child."

"That's funny. Yesterday, I thought you were the innocent child." We were dancing and Stellium was about to sweep me off my feet.

"Yesterday, when I first saw you, I thought, this man is critical to my evolution."

He made me feel dizzy and I could not stop myself from saying, "This morning I know you are critical to mine."

He laughed and glanced around the room before hacking me to the ground. "You really are a barbarian—you know that? It's not your fault, it's the consequence of living in an all-male environment for most of your life." I felt my face go red. "Maybe the real reason I came to the Sutcay Tay School is to teach you a few social graces and you—what do you want to teach me, Brother Élan? I'm ready to learn."

"What could I possibly teach you? Obviously, you're smarter than me."

"Not smarter, merely more cynical."

"Why are you cynical? Your master named you Stellium, a favorable conjunction of stars. You're talented, smart, handsome—"

"Since you do not know what you are supposed to teach me, let me start by teaching you a few things about interior design. Let's start with our fixer-upper of a *tritum*."

Puzzled about what he meant, I glanced around the room for a clue. "We cleaned, aren't we finished?"

"Trust me, there's more." My level one education, Esthetics for Barbarians, began a short time later. Stellium possessed a flair for organizing everyday objects in attractive ways. All his cynicism disappeared when he was involved in what he called, "creating livable space."

Stellium entertained me with many suggestions concerning how we might accomplish the goal of "livable space" and my input was limited to an unsure, "yes," or "no." My major concern was our *tritum* would end up resembling a room my sister Sophia might put together. "Please, no flowered curtains," I begged.

"No flowered curtains," Stellium agreed. "However, we must paint." He danced around the room and his Gathosian hands went wild as he explained his ideas. "Let's paint that shabby rear wall around the windows and doors peridot green and we will stain the dingy furniture white."

"I know white, but what's peridot green?"

He peered at me closely. "Peridot green is the color of the inner oceans of your eyes; however, those rings around your oceans are *shahaut* blue." We spent all morning moving our furniture around into every conceivable configuration. By early afternoon, we began discussing the disposition of smaller items and moved into Level Two Esthetics for Barbarians. Stellium dashed outside in the pouring rain, returned with a handful of common pebbles, and showed me that an uneven number of pebbles were more visually appealing than an even number. My barbarian self allowed a little light into the cave and I saw what he meant. He owned a blue vase that he pulled out of one of his three boxes. He ran outside again and this time he picked a handful of weeds. He brought them inside and arranged them in the blue vase, showing me that weeds really were flowers.

That rainy day with Stellium was a refreshing change of pace. I never met anyone like him. He was lively, irreverent, insightful, talented, cynical, and handsome and that was just his surface. I didn't realize how Human, Stellium truly was. He was as much a Human as I was a Gathosian and I was in denial of how attracted I was to him. Because he was able to command the space around him, my attention focused on what he was creating, instead of the impact he was having on me. Beauty fascinated me, but I was afraid to get too close to beauty because it arouses sensuality. Stellium began to help me touch that unexplored part of myself, and with him, it felt comfortable and natural. As I fell asleep that night, I remembered one of the few debates I won with Kyron and it was over the appreciation of beauty for its own sake. It happened after the shadow dancers from Lomita School gave their performance at our school. Had those shadow dancers from Lomita School cleared the way so Stellium could bring beauty into my life?

The following morning, I decided to take my four completed journals and the mind scribe from my *quarrying* and include them with Kyron's journals. The notion that an intimate part of me might snuggle up with Kyron's journals in a safe place, such as a bank vault, comforted me. Just in case the sky decided to let loose again, I took the food bag, from the day before, and wrapped it around the box. Stellium decided to go to the Celestial Air Palace to work on the frescos and he walked with me to the airfloat pad nearby. He offered to carry the box, but never asked about the contents. The airfloat landed and I said, "See you later," just like Kyron.

Stellium laughed and moved his head from side to side in a mock of shadow dancing. "Not unless I see you first," he returned. "Hey!" and I turned back toward him at the top of the airfloat stairs. "Beware of those stalactites," he yelled. I did not get his joke until I was halfway to Gathos and then I sat in the space shuttle and laughed myself silly.

I took the airfloat to Sheebrun and waited for my connection to Tacings, which is a larger city about a hundred kilometers east of Sheebrun. From Tacings, I made my space connection holding the box on my lap the entire way. As usual, Sophia bought me a first class ticket on the space shuttle. To sit in first class while people sipped champagne and ate chocolate mints embarrassed me in the past. My complaining to her about the extravagance did no good. This time I was happy I was going first class, because it meant I did not have to check my box.

****

Gathos is the largest planet in the Island Worlds of Gathos system. Gathos is farther away from Insanio and Gearthot than Sutcay Tay. Nine moons orbit Gathos and when they conjunct in various ways and eclipse parts of Gearthot and Insanio, the weather can be cold.

Sophia and Coreese lived in the Southern Hemisphere in the city of Wacar. It was early spring in Wacar and chilly. I felt the temperature difference as soon as I disembarked from the ship. Sophia came alone to pick me up because it was midday. Valent was in school, and Coreese was tending his business. Her gravid belly was a little round knob sticking out in front of her and I was surprised that her pregnancy was so far along. We stood in the space terminal and hugged and as usual, she told me I was, "too thin." We had not seen each other in eight moons. She eyed the box, but did not mention it. Instead she said, "I'll go get the vehicle, because it's too cold for you to go outside in your nightgown."

I waited inside by the terminal doors for Sophia to pick me up. As I stood waiting, I slipped into my *turami savatnani* to get my bearings. As usual, circular awareness in public places begins with memory asking, *what do you remember of this place?* Going to Gathos is different each time I go. Wacar is a large tumultuous city and workers are always constructing thoroughfares, demolishing or amending structures in drastic ways. *What do you observe on the physical level?* Clashing smells, noise, and the visual overload of information are vying for my attention. People move faster and take shelter in their anonymity. *Conclusions?* The anonymity is not like a Shardasko Warrior who, "Takes only what he needs and after he is gone no one knows he was there." Here, a warrior is not the clever thief, but a barterer. The *turami savatnani* recoiled inward and then burst outward in concentric circles until I could see with my psychic vision into the private lives of passing strangers. *What is seen?* People draw their consciousness in around themselves like skintight *slipfals*. In some, consciousness has retreated to two tiny flames. One flame burns in the groin and the other in the head. Everywhere else, their flames have burned down to embers. Seeing so many, gray-tinged auras, I pulled my aura in too, for depression is as contagious as the flu.

Sophia and Coreese owned a beautiful home. Their kitchen was bigger than my whole *tritum* on Sutcay Tay. One drawer in their kitchen held more items that I owned two days earlier. On the surface, the house was spotless, because house cleaners kept it that way. However, the kitchen drawers and pantry frequently were in chaos. I would ask, "Where can I find a sauté pan?"

Sophia would say, "Look around, I'm unsure." When we arrived at their home, Sophia loaned me a sweater belonging to Coreese. As I put it on, she grabbed my arm and asked, "How did you injure your arm?"

"I was helping a dulcerary panther cross a stream and she accidentally scratched me."

Sophia laughed and accused me of having a "fanciful imagination. Now tell me the truth—how did you really injure yourself?"

"I scratched myself on a fickleberry thorn while chopping wood for the

Fire Circle."

She shook her head in dismay. "You should be more careful when you are in the woods."

"Thank you, I'll remember that." Coreese's sweater was too short on me, but I told Sophia, "It serves the purpose and is warm." She replied that I looked ridiculous and immediately wanted to go shopping. She had bought me clothing in the past, which I always left behind. When I visited the next time, the clothing had disappeared and again she would want to buy me more new things.

We sat in the kitchen and she asked, "I can't remember if you are allowed to drink wine or not." She asked me about wine before, along with dozens of other imagined austerities that she attributed to Shardasko Warriors. "Are you allowed to do this?" or "Are you allowed to do that?" She never remembered asking me before and each time we met, I would need to start from ground zero.

"I can drink whatever I want," I told her as usual. "If you don't mind, I would like a cup of hot tea."

She said, "I'll see if I can find the teapot."

Pointing to a particular cabinet, I said, "The teapot is on the second shelf."

When she found the teapot, she said, "You are such a smart-aleck. Did you put that damn teapot up there with one of your Shardasko tricks?"

"I put the teapot there after I finished using it, the last time I visited."

We chatted for over two hours. Sophia was a conversational skimmer and this was the mode where she felt most comfortable. She was worried about Valent adjusting to the changes on Earth. Sophia and I both remembered being the alien outcasts when we were children. "I'm going to put our furniture and belongings into storage and buy everything new when I get to Earth."

The notion of all those belongings seemed daunting to me. "How are you going to keep your life straight?"

"Haven't you ever noticed that the moment you create order, life starts to tear things apart? Valent taught me that simple lesson when he was a toddler." Sophia abruptly went quiet and internal. I waited because I did not want to disturb whatever was going on inside her. She put the flat of her hand on her round knob of a belly. "She's kicking," she said in awe.

I acknowledged to myself that Sophia was the only female in the physical universe I was on speaking terms with and her unborn daughter the only continuation of Cœur femininity ahead. Sophia's life held no appeal for me. If anything, I felt sorry for her because she never took time to understand what was happening to her. As Kyron said, "Meaning is everything," and skimmers miss the deeper meaning. I did envy her ability to take bits of her potential, and the potential within Coreese, and create an authentic body for a soul. In our subjective little lives and goals, if any possibility exists that we may live up to our potential, the creation of a body for a soul certainly is high on the list. On the Sutcay Tay campus, four elemental temples exist, which were created by original Shardasko masters. When warriors meditate in these temples, their energy attracts spirits that come to commune, but spirits do not commit to temples as they do to bodies. Feminine bodies come equipped with biological temples dedicated to the alchemy of creation. As I sat watching Sophia, with that thrilled expression on her face, I called out to my *Holder* to help me explore my potential. While I wanted my spiritual desires to feel free to aspire to every height, I still wanted to cast a few seeds over the barren dunes of my physical life and bring that part of me to full bloom.

"Do you want to feel?" asked Sophia.

"Certainly, I want to feel" and she took my hand and gently placed it on her solar plexus.

"Right here," she said.

I closed my eyes and tuned into the body growing within her, feeling its rapid heartbeat. "The fetus is healthy," I told Sophia. Beyond, in the Jumping-Off Place, I could hear the murmuring of consciousness casting forth their lures. "You and your fetus are popular. Souls are jockeying to see who is going to get to live in the new body you're creating."

"You're teasing me."

"I'm not. If you want, I can listen and tell you what they are saying."

She leaned closer. "Okay, tell me, but don't tell Coreese we are playing this crazy game."

"My lips are sealed," and we touched the tips of our index fingers in a promise as we did when we were children. Placing my head close to her tummy, I listened. Behind the heartbeat of the fetus was a language of meaning before words. As I understood Cerebow communicating with me in the Great Verdant, I understood the language of the souls wooing this body. "Three souls want to live through the body you are creating. Their consciousness is advanced and they've lived many lives before. All are resolved that their next life will bring them creative fulfillment. One wants to be a musician, another wants to be a poet, and the last one—the last one has more confusion."

Sophia quietly ask, "How will it be decided which soul wins?"

"Like attracts like. Each one will meditate on the fetus and the one that displays the greatest affinity and love with the potential within that waiting life, will win." I listened again. "The poet is singing a lullaby."

"What's she singing?"

"Let me listen. 'I've closed my sea-indigo eye far too long, but with the strength of this new bond, I will teach with tender grace. Together, we will meet as innocent lovers and dance upon life's beaches, with the infinite sands of fortune between our toes. We will swim in the space between moon and tide, where life meets spirit in open embrace. Sacred child of Light, my growing potential, come—play naked in the sea with me. Your beating heart is my cipher, telling me that love is forever within you.'"

Sophia said, "Sounds like a poem Mom might write. By the way, do I have any say about which soul will win?"

"Absolutely! After all, your body is creating the new body. Your will is strong and just a little shoulder nudge can determine the whole matter."

"In that case, I'm rooting for the poet." Her eyes glazed over with tears. "Just think! Wouldn't it be great to have mom here again?"

****

Sophia and Coreese wanted to take me out to dinner, but I owned no appropriate clothing. Then the strap broke on my right sandal. The strap had rotted from getting wet and never drying properly. Sophia began teasing me, calling me, "an anal-retentive holy man," and telling me, "Your saintly bad habit—that soaple cloth nightgown and sandals—are ridiculous." It made me realize my tropical-weight *moodarry* was impractical on chilly Gathos. I was ridiculous because I was ignoring the First Adaptation principle, which states a Shardasko Warrior accepts, "each new situation." Clinging to my old habits, I was a cold, pathetic martyr and could not go out in public without sticking out like a sore thumb.

Instead of dining out, Coreese went out to a restaurant, bought food, and brought it home. We ate the food from little disposable containers sitting around the dining room table. While we were eating, Coreese mentioned that he wanted to discuss my trust fund along with the reminder, "You will need to take more responsibility for your investments now that I'm going to Earth."

"Truth is my responsibility and karmic legacy," I said. He gave me a quick, but questioning stare. "It's Shardasko philosophy."

"Well the truth here is—you're a man and your karmic legacy is you need to take responsibility concerning your inheritance."

Sophia interrupted Coreese. "Please dear, don't get into one of your lecturing modes. Just tell Journey what he needs to know."

Coreese softened. "Of course, I always will be available to advise you."

After we ate, we gravitated into the library. It was Valent's bedtime and Sophia excused herself to go see him off. The library primarily belonged to Coreese. The walls were dark and the furniture large and manly. They called this room a library, but the room held no books. Coreese's collection of silver statuettes of men playing strikeball lined the shelves. The room was chilly and I offered to start a fire. "That would be nice," Coreese agreed. "We don't use the fireplace often enough." I went outside to where they stored wood, chose my logs carefully, along with a handful of tinder that

107

the gardener conveniently left in a pile. That night, I felt as if I was the only one capable of chasing the chill from the library. Coreese offered me matches, but I was showing off and he watched me light the fire with the concentration of my energetic will. He suspected a trick and admitted, "I still do not understand many things."

"There's nothing to it," I returned. "It's as natural as having sex."

He laughed. "You have a wild imagination for a, supposedly, abstinent Shardasko Warrior."

Sophia walked into the room and asked, "What's so funny?"

Coreese said, "Your brother has been a Shardasko Warrior for seven phases and all he's learned to do is start fires with his will."

My *Holder* materialized like a swami over my head and declared, *the unaware belittle even the jewels of gods. That's why real gods never display their wealth in public.*

Sophia attempted to defend me by challenging Coreese. "Let's see you start a fire with your will."

"I don't need to," he returned. "I can afford to buy matches."

When the conversation turned to the trust-fund topic, it was the first time I paid attention to money. My parents left a substantial estate. When they died on Ravenna, an accident clause in their policies doubled the amount of insurance payment. Coreese managed and invested my estate, which I had ignored for the past seven phases. Coreese worried about my financial future and he mentioned it often. He knew very little about Shardasko philosophy and believed that without my trust fund, I would perish. Coreese lived in a world alienated from his greater consciousness, where he trusted external forms more than his instincts. Many times he told me, "You have plenty of money," but money seemed superficial and embarrassing to me. That night, Coreese said, "You can draw on the interest from your estate, for anything you need."

"Right now?" I asked.

"Right now," said Coreese.

"Thank you for handling my finances for all these years. Do you know of a bank where I can rent a secure safety deposit box?" Both he and Sophia were curious and I explained briefly about Kyron's journals.

"So that's what you were clutching like a precious toy box at the spaceport," Sophia said.

"What's so important in those journals that Kyron wants them in a safety deposit box?" asked Coreese.

"I don't know. Master Kyron asked me not to read them until he finishes the final volume."

"You must have taken a peek," said Sophia. "How can you stand the suspense?"

"I honor my word."

"Honor be damned!" Sophia exclaimed. "Let's take a peek. Kyron will never know the difference. I want to know the secret behind that obsequious little smile of his." It was amazing that a little female dulcerary understood more about honor and pride than Sophia.

That night I slept in one of their six guestrooms. The bed felt squishy and I thought about sleeping on the floor, but reminded myself of the First Adaptation principle. I placed the box beside me on top of the covers. That night, I sat for a long time in meditation. I did not try to initiate anything in the Fire Circle sense. My mood mirrored the Eternal Waters and I floated in the watery silence of peaceful nothingness.

Afterward, I opened the box and stared at the neat row of journals side by side. Each cloth-covered book was a different color and they looked like a rainbow of waiting mysteries. I took out the bluish-green journal and pressed it against my chest. The cover smelled of Kyron's favorite amber incense. *Kyron?* I called out, using one of the many secret words between us. *Can you hear me you old master thief?* I knew he could. *I miss you. Are you tickling my passion merely to bring me to completion as Stellium suggests? Do not tell me lies. If this passion is mine alone, then cast me off as the fool. Tell me you are finished* with me, but do not kiss me and tell me to write.

I waited. His image sat crystal clear within me and I saw him sit down before his altar and link his mind to mine. A profound silence followed and then the strangest and truest words he ever spoke echoed inside my ears. *We will meet in other lives, on other worlds, and you will not remember me. You will pass me by and call me stranger. You will ignore me when all I want is for you to recognize that I am alive. All these insults will not extinguish my eternal love for you, for we are one.*

I did not argue or try to defend myself for I knew this was entirely possible. What he was asking was clear enough; he wanted me to surrender to the knowledge that we were one.

**\*\*\*\***

Eno is not visible from Gathos and therefore no *areé didamé* exists. Because I was a creature of habit, I was up before dawn and meditating. That morning my meditation left me with the realization that I needed to adjust to my present situation. Still not ready to address my anal-retentive disposition, I funneled my resolute behavior into an urgent need to get Kyron's journals into a bank vault. Sophia proved her Cœur stamina that whole day. Considering she was pregnant, she held up splendidly under all my pressure.

At breakfast, Coreese suggested two or three banks that provided safety deposit boxes and I researched all three. I dragged Sophia to the three banks, embarrassing her by asking questions about security, whether they were earthquake proof, fireproof, flood proof, meteor proof, and so on. It further embarrassed her that I was traipsing around in my white *moodarry*, Coreese's too-small sweater, and my broken sandal that I temporally fixed with plumber's tape, which I found on Coreese's workbench. By midday, I still had not decided on a bank. We stopped for lunch at a small café and Sophia said, "Even if you put those journals in a bank vault, what makes you think the paper and ink will hold up? People store books and papers in what they consider secure vaults, only to return in a few phases to find nothing but dust."

"What can I do to prevent such a thing from happening?"

"I suppose you could contact a paper specialist, a person who knows how to preserve important documents." I saw Kyron's journals disintegrating before my eyes and my resolve, to get the journals into a bank vault, by the end of the day, evaporated. We returned home and I forced Sophia to help me locate a document curator. She called her friends over the multidex and by late afternoon, we discovered a woman named Lissa Tayover who specialized in the obscure art of paper and ink preservation. We made an appointment and Sophia swore, "I'm not going unless you wear normal clothing and decent shoes. It's difficult enough being an alien minority on this planet without calling attention to ourselves wherever we go."

Ignoring her demands, I said, "First we'll take what we need and then we'll hide." She did not understand and this time I didn't try to explain.

The minute I saw Lissa Tayover, I knew she was one of those Gathosian beauties that would haunt me after she was gone. Her hands were elegant and her wrists long. She possessed the most beautiful ankles and my methodical self wanted to follow through on my impulse to lift her skirts and see if she also had lovely thighs. Traveling upward, her eyes were pure Gathosian. However, when she opened her mouth to speak, she had a peculiar lisp. The Mescale language sounds lyrical in comparison to English and is slightly nasal. Pronunciation of words begin higher in the throat and some words whip off the end of the tongue with a little click. To hear Mescale spoken with a lisp, sounded like affectation.

Because I trusted no one concerning Kyron's journals, I became just as fanatical with Lissa Tayover. I watched as she examined the books to determine their durability. Squaring my body between the open journal on her lap and Sophia's prying eyes, I was certain neither of them could be trusted. The end of my two-day whirlwind of worry came when Lissa Tayover assured me, "I believe theses journals are quite secure. The soaple paper is acid free and the ink will last indefinitely." She recommended that I discard the box and store the journals in an acid-free bag that would maintain the proper moisture level and prevent dust mites from using the paper or bindings for food. Naturally, she sold these bags and they were expensive. I paid the price because I wanted the best for Kyron's journals.

By then, I remembered that Kyron had told me, "Find out which bank Coreese deals with, because we both know he uses only the best."

On the way to Coreese's bank, I told Sophia, "Master Kyron would never write important information on anything less than the finest quality paper."

Sophia remained caustic and unimpressed. "He could have spared us the inconvenience and put the information in a memory capsule."

As I was tucking the twenty-one journals into their safety deposit box, I relaxed for the first time. I felt certain I connected with the proper bank because my safety deposit number was twenty-two, the same number as the completed journals. Making a connection between Sophia and her unborn child and me and my journals, I told them, *I love you my precious journal children. Go to sleep. I will return for you when the last journal is complete and then we'll all be together.* How did the greater configuration of my mother's spirit put it? "Life's flow, the beating of your heart, this murmuring spirit, the silent mystery behind my prayer, is you."

****

The next day, Sophia and I went shopping to buy "a few things." She was as happy shopping as Stellium was "creating livable space." The problem of shoes for Humans on any Gathosian world is a special consideration. Gathosian feet are narrower than Human feet, so Humans must purchase their shoes from a company on Earth or have shoes custom-made. Our first stop was at a foot tracer or cobbler. A foot tracer makes an outline of the person's foot and creates shoes to match. Having shoes created by a foot tracer is more expensive than buying shoes readymade, but I had made my peace with this situation years earlier.

One essential difference emerged between this shopping expedition and all the others we took. After Coreese spoke to me about my finances, I promised myself that I would be responsible for my money and possessions. And when I returned to Sutcay Tay, whatever I bought, I would take with me. That did not mean Sophia did not have plenty of opinions about what she thought I should buy. She talked me into buying three pairs of shoes—sandals, loafers, and a pair of boots. As usual, it would take the foot tracer several days to finish my new footwear and I was grateful he was able to repair my sandal strap immediately.

At the clothing store, Sophia insisted that I buy socks, because now I owned shoes and boots. Our conversation eventually drifted into the esthetics of underwear. As a neophyte, I was keen on the notion of discarding my underwear, which I had trouble keeping clean. Now I asked Sophia her opinion. "Do you think I am a barbarian because I don't wear underwear?"

"You don't wear underwear?"

"Better get some—huh?"

"While you're at it, buy some deodorant?"

"You think I smell? I wash several times a day."

"Let's say, you could smell better."

"For your information, a sweet little dulcerary panther told me I smelled of the sweetness of the Great Verdant Abyss."

Sophia snickered. "Your imagination is better than your smell."

I bought three shirts, two pairs of pants, socks, underwear, a lightweight raincoat, an umbrella, and deodorant. At a jewelry store, I bought a sturdy silver chain to thread the safety deposit keys onto, so I could wear them around my neck. Finally I bought a backpack because Sophia insisted that packing my new clothing in the now empty box would be, "tacky."

****

That night, I dream I am attending a gathering of masters at the Sutcay Tay School. *Kyron is weaving in and out of the crowd and talking to people. Feeling as if I do not belong, I leave the gathering early. Again, I remember that I am supposed to meet my mother. "Journey, we should spend more time together, I hear her say. The scene shifts and now I find myself at my mother's house, but I still can't find her. I wander into her sleeproom and finally into her walk-in closet. Unlike my mother's actual closet, this wardrobe holds sequined ball gowns, silk and satin robes, all in the most vibrant of colors. On the floor are hundreds of pairs of shoes, not sensible shoes as my mother wore, but extravagant shoes. Again, the scene shifts and it's late at night. I'm walking on a familiar street that I knew as a child. I stop and ask a streetguard about connections on public transportation, telling him, "I need to get home."*

*The guard asks, "Do you live in North Ravenna?"*

*I cannot remember where I live and I feel stupid. "I live in West Ravenna," I tell him, but still I'm unsure.*

*The guard replies, "Then you are out of luck. No public transportation goes into West Ravenna this late at night."*

*I walk away, toward the heart of the city, and feel the inner turmoil of loss and loneliness. Someone walking beside me says, "The streetguard is wrong. I know an infinite number of ways to get home."*

*Then someone else comes up behind me and suggests, "This situation is your fault. You've relied on Master Kyron to navigate for you and never learned the lay of the land."*

When I awoke in the morning, I arose and completed my usual ablutions. I used deodorant for the first time in my life and put on new clothing. The clothes seemed constricting and I felt like one of the cylindrical pillows on the end of Sophia's sofa—rolled and stuffed. By the time I sat down to breakfast, I had yanked my shirttail out of my pants and rolled up my shirtsleeves. I continued to feel uncomfortable in my new clothing and Sophia reminded me several times that it was impolite to adjust my "package" no matter how snug my new underwear felt. I

112

reminded myself of the First Adaptation and apologized for being a barbarian. While we were enjoying our second cup of tea, a message arrived from Sutcay Tay. Assuming, or rather hoping, the message was from Kyron, I rushed to the multidex between the kitchen and dining room to see what he had to say. Initially, I was disappointed because the message was a video from Stellium that he sent late the previous night. Then I realized that seeing him from this distanced perspective, it was okay to admit that I found him sexually attractive.

"Hi!" he said. "I hope you are having a good time on Gathos. It's still raining here and even the Air Temple is beginning to smell moldy. I envy you being in a dry place. I did not call to give you a weather report, but wanted to tell you what happened here a short time ago. You know that intuitive hunch you get when you enter *turami savatnani* and your senses tells you there's more to a situation than meets the eye? Well my intuition is in an uproar. This morning, a few brothers strolled past me while I was working on the frescos; I overheard one say that a group of neophytes spotted a dulcerary panther near the Fecundity Garden last night. This did not concern me because I realize Sutcay Valley is a tiny pocket between the rainforest and mountains. I glanced up from my work and asked, 'What do you do when a wild animal wanders out of the Great Verdant?' One brothers said, 'the masters handle the situation. They use their powers to return the creature to where it belongs.' I went back to work on the frescos until my back was aching and it was so dark, I could scarcely see. It was *shahaut* when I reached our *tritum*. It was dark and rainy, but I noticed a large rip in the front screen. Something about seeing the ripped screen catapulted me into *turami savatnani*. I looked through the screen and saw a dulcerary panther sitting on your bed. Scared, I backed away until I could run and then I ran down to administration for help. Luckily, somebody offered to rouse a few masters. Twenty minutes later, Kyron showed up and informed me, 'It's okay Stellium. The dulcerary was confused. She has returned to the Great Verdant so you may go home now and go to bed.' I couldn't shake the feeling that I had a narrow escape. I patched the window screen and then meditated, ate, but didn't notice until a short time ago that a length of soaple vine was hanging out, from under your pillow. I lifted the pillow and that's when I found a tortoise shell attached to the vine. When I picked up the shell and held it to the light, I noticed your initials carved on the surface. Intuitive hunches began exploding like a fountain in my head, telling me this dulcerary was more than just a wild animal that wandered out of the Great Verdant Abyss. I'm not sure what any of this means, but felt you should know a dulcerary was sitting on your bed and left you a present under your pillow. I love a good mystery, but this mystery is a tad too close. Would you mind giving me a callback when you get a chance, so we can talk?"

I immediately told Sophia. "I must return to Sutcay Tay,"

"What's wrong? Don't tell me. It's Kyron again—isn't it? He cannot allow you out of his sight even for a few days. Why does he always act like a possessive tyrant with you? Our visit is only halfway though and your shoes will not be ready for another three days. Besides, I was hoping I might talk you into coming to see us on Earth. Aren't you even interested in your Human roots?"

"Please Sophia, the message was from my new roommate, Stellium. He needs my help."

She put up her hands as if to say stop. "Okay, have it your way. I'll mail your new shoes when they're ready."

I walked outside to breathe the cool morning air while Sophia changed my reservation. I paced up and down with impatience realizing my body was shaking and my mind confused. Valent was outside with me and he was striking blows with a short stick along the metal railing around the patio. He owned a bedroom full of expensive and exotic toys, yet he was playing with a stick he found in the woods. I asked him, "What are you playing?"

His voice elevated to the voice of The Announcer when he exclaimed, "I am master of this universe!"

"Really? What does a master of this universe do?"

"Shoo! Shoo!" he shouted making a sound like a laser gun. He hit the railing again and this time his voice went into a falsetto manly tenor. "I, Valent, the master of this universe, will vanquish all vaspray. I will rule with might and make us safe through truth, cunning, and the Gathosian way."

"Do you know what vanquish means?"

"Sure!" he said in his little man's voice. "It means to kill."

"Not really, vanquish means to overcome and conquer, as in to conquer our fear."

Valent did not acknowledge that he heard me. Then he hit the railing a couple of more times and the stick split in two. "Dammit!" he said in English.

"I must go back to Sutcay Tay today. I'm sorry we did not get to spend more time together." He shrugged and I hunched down so we were the same height. "I love you."

"I love you too," he said automatically.

"Let me show you how to be a master in any universe," I offered. I took his small Human hands in mine and showed him how to hold them in Primal Stance. "Allow your hands to move together in braided spirals. Concentrate all your energy into your braiding and you will be able to vanquish all vaspray with your thoughts. I swear!"

# EIGHT

Logic stood to reason, and as usual, logic caused me internal frustration. Logic suggested that Cerebow had traced me to my *tritum* by my scent. Thinking that Kyron dismissed her out of hand, or worse, that he whisked away her new seeds of consciousness, was a damning thought. No doubt existed in my mind that Kyron possessed the power to accomplish such a deed. *Please prove me wrong,* I prayed. I loved Kyron too much for him to fall that far in my esteem.

When I reached the Sutcay Tay campus, it was early evening. Using my new umbrella and raincoat, I stayed dry despite the deluge pouring forth from the water-laden sky. An umbrella and raincoat seemed so much better than a palmara leaf that I questioned why I avoided these simple conveniences in the past. Later, I realized even these simple questions were leading me away from the Shardasko brotherhood and toward independence. I felt caught between my loyalty to Shardasko principles and the process of questioning that Kyron taught me. The death of tradition and ritual come hard when tradition and ritual are the things that once saved us. No matter my feeling, the truth remained clear. No ritual or tradition is worth the gesture we put into it, unless we can infuse the gesture with our own sacred meaning. Along these lines, I was prepared to question even my master. His meaning and intent needed to ring true and match his form, which, to me, still appeared as pristine as a white orchid.

I did not go to my *tritum,* but went to the administration office to arrange an interview with Kyron. My suspicions aroused my cunning and I composed a message in Mescale typescript, so he could not read my eyes. "Dear Master," I wrote. "I cut my holiday short and just arrived on campus.

Despite the six-moon rule of separation, I need to see you so we may look into each other's eyes. If I may, it is my preference to come to your *tritum* for a few minutes, on this same day, for that purpose only. Please leave a message on the multidex if I may come ahead. I miss you and love you. As always, Journey. Alias, The Prince of Fire."

All eyes are special, but Gathosians eyes possess powers most Humans do not comprehend. Gathosians can pierce through another person merely by peering into that person's eyes. Humans can hide in many ways, but rarely can they hide when a Gathosian faces them directly and stares into that person with direct intent. Shadow dancing ameliorates this power to perceive and a Shardasko master helps his warrior hone this skill to a laser point when they begin jumping between the third and fourth dimensions. My request to look into Kyron's eyes was code, a request for his naked honesty and a guarantee of my naked honesty in return.

"Print," I told the multidex. My message oozed from the printer two seconds later. Folding the letter into thirds, I tucked it inside a plastic envelope I retrieved from a nearby trashcan. I walked outside and waylaid the first neophyte to pass. "Brother Passel?"

"*Afen*," he greeted me and touched his forehead while rain dripped off his chin. His soaked *moodarry* allowed his private parts to hint through the fabric, but his eyes were innocent as a babe's. Brother Passel had not yet jumped dimensions, but when he did, his hair would be long enough to cover most of his nudity. Long hair was the only shield a Shardasko Warrior owned.

I held the open umbrella over us while asking, "Will you do me a favor, please?"

We were almost the same age, but I was an Emblematic Warrior and Passel was a neophyte, so tradition dictated that he must show me proper respect. "I am forever at your disposal," was his automatic reply.

"You do not need to be forever at my disposal," I barked at him. "Just do me this one simple favor, tonight. Do you know which *tritum* belongs to Master Kyron?" My sharp tone startled Passel and he nervously nodded yes. "Take this note to his door and make certain you hand it to him personally."

"I'm already halfway there."

"And don't allow it to get wet," I yelled after him.

I had set the wheel in motion, now came the difficult part. I had to wait and see where the wheel stopped. I went to my *tritum* and found Stellium sitting cross-legged at our eating table. He was working on a sketch, a scene of a boy reminiscent of Passel, a young seeker about to sacrifice his hair to his master. "You've changed!" he greeted me. "You're wearing secular clothing. You look—commanding. Must be because you're so tall."

My compulsion concerning Cerebow was equal to my concern for

Kyron's journals and now nothing mattered except the truth. "Where's the tortoise shell?" I asked.

Stellium forced me to wait by putting down his drawing pencil with typical Shardasko consciousness. "The shell is still on your bed." I strode over to my bed and found my lucky tortoise shell that I lost along the headwaters of the Tartha River. "What's up?" he asked.

"It's too early to say." Examining the screen where Stellium patched it, the tear was odd. It was not three-cornered as I imagined, but a mere slit about thirty centimeters long. *How could Cerebow slip through such a tiny opening?* "Did you mention to Master Kyron that you intended to call me?"

"Not one word did I say to anyone. My curiosity is choking me, Élan. What's going on?"

"I would rather not say until I speak to Kyron."

"Why?"

"Because I don't want your insights clouding mine before I face him."

"Can I give you some advice?"

"I wish you wouldn't."

He waited for almost a minute before saying, "Élan, please listen."

I sighed with impatience. "Make it brief."

"It's obvious you're involved in a whirlwind of conclusions. Remember, we are always partially right and partially wrong. Don't wed yourself to complete assumptions or bog yourself down in the obvious conclusions of physical reality and miss the subtler view. When we leave our enlightened surroundings and interact with worldly dunderheads, sometimes we begin acting like dunderheads ourselves. You might say superficiality is a contagious disease." Stellium repeated part of the Shardasko Credo, the part I needed to hear most. "'My disposition cooperates with me. I am at peace with myself. I am moderation, loving kindness, constancy, and kinship.' Remember, you are the embodiment of these virtues."

After thanking my ears that they still knew how to listen, I settled right down. "You're amazing," I told him. "In fact, you're so amazing, I think I love you. Now I need to go and bathe before I go see Kyron."

On walking into our *tritum*, our new peridot-green wall had greeted me. *So that is peridot green*, I thought. The floor was extraordinary shiny too. I did not mention to Stellium that I appreciated these changes until I emerged from my bath. "How did you do all this redecorating in such a short time?"

"Remember, paint is my specialty."

"How did you get the floor so shiny?"

"Two coats of crystathane. It's practical too. We won't get splinters in our bare feet anymore."

"I love the improvements you've made to our fixer-upper."

He slyly returned, "Thanks, Brother Élan; I love you too."

Stellium had put his blue vase on our altar, which held a spray of white orchids and the bowl of fresh fruit on our eating table, appeared as living art. As I glanced around the room, it amazed me the beauty Stellium was able to create from a few simple items and a bucket of paint.

One of his paintings hung on the east wall. The canvas was large, about three and a half meters long and about half that high. From a distance, the painting appeared as a scintillating rainbow, capable of rupturing the eyes with intense colors. I went over to the painting and stared at it for several minutes. The focal point was a warrior clearing the timeline in the fourth dimension. Behind him, his physical life was rooted in the wine-colored chaos of reality. Behind the physical chaos was another and another reality all ending in an emery-colored corundum point, too remote to define. The warrior gave me the impression that he was a time traveler, full of cosmic intent. If one can fall in love with a face in a painting, I fell in love with this fabulous face. His eyes were incredible and they shadow danced with me as I shifted my head back and forth. As all Gathosian eyes are capable of doing, his eyes pierced through me and brought me into my feelings. His long hair gleamed with fiery light and blew up and away from his face. His left knee was deeply bent and his right a little less so, while his arms spread wide. The positioning of his arms was important. At first glance, I thought he was seeking to regain his balance, as so many warriors do when they land in the fourth dimension. Then I knew his arms were wide open with humble surrender to all that he was or could ever be. His own denial fluttered around him like silver fireflies; and in a moment, he and his denial would become one. I surrendered to this warrior and knew him as my *Holder*.

Stellium said, "You've been staring at that painting for ten minutes. Does that mean you like it?"

"I want it. Is it for sale?"

"It's not cheap."

I turned and gazed at Stellium with my complete powers of observation. The rain had stopped and the early evening light was managing to pierce through the gloom. One shaft of warm yellow light came through the rear window and sat upon his head, making him into an authentic saint with a halo. "I didn't expect it to be cheap. I don't have much money, but I'm willing to make a trade."

"What kind of trade do you have in mind?"

"You give me the painting and I'll give you my eternal devotion."

"Seems like a huge decision. Let me think about it for a while."

Love began to shadow dance with us, flickering around inside the destiny of our lives. As a neophyte lover, I did not realize Love was sentient and knew when each beating heart needed to dance. That night, I only knew I felt Love's rhythm inside me, singing sweet words of romance.

\*\*\*\*

The second time I went to the administration office, four brothers were ahead of me, and I had to wait. Impatient, I questioned why the Sutcay Tay School owned only one multidex, while Sophia and Coreese had a multidex in each room of their home. When my turn came, I sat down and faced the viewer forcing myself to take a deep breath. "Communications?" I said. The multidex could not recognize my tension-filled voice and I had to repeat "communications," three times. Then the all-critical message flashed onto the screen, telling me in simple Kyron fashion, "Come ahead my incredible blue-green eyes and we will dance in complete honesty."

My first impulse was to race to Kyron's *tritum* so I could see him sooner, but I walked slowly and consciously to steady my concentration. By doing this, I realized a few new things, by the time I knocked on his door. I knew my prince-of-fire days were over. I was ready to become a king of fire. I could not do this unless I was willing to burn away my ignorance and become the essence of fire, one steady flame. I was committed to dealing with my specks in the fourth dimension and anything else wrong in my life. *My commitment is total and I will not lose unless I lose completely*, I swore.

Kyron answered the door and his radiance was as obvious as ever. I walked into his *tritum* and up loomed two hungry warriors inside me that were prepared to fight The Ultimate Battle. One was my potency that wanted to vanquish Kyron's control over me and the other was my tenderness that wanted to surrender completely to his enlightened love.

"A new umbrella and raincoat!" he exclaimed in a mocking tone. "Did you think this little downpour might extinguish your fire, my prince?"

Closing the dripping umbrella, I handed it to him. "You never allowed me to give you anything material before, but would you accept this umbrella as a gift? It would give me pleasure to know that something I gave you was able to make your life a bit more comfortable."

"Thank you," he said. He examined the umbrella as if it were grand and I felt embarrassed that I so little to offer him. As usual, I knelt before him and attempted to kiss his hands, but this night he stole his hands away and said, "This is nonsense, Élan. You are an accomplished Emblematic Warrior. Get up! Sit or stand if you wish, but please do not kneel before me, ever again."

*As you wish*, I thought, but I said, "Okay, let's sit as equals."

"Would you like tea?"

"No thank you," and I took off my raincoat and placed it by the door.

He let me know that he was on the edge of my thoughts and replied, "As you wish."

"Your journals are now safe in a Gathos bank vault and the keys to the safety box, I'm wearing on a chain around my neck." I pulled the chain from under my *moodarry* to show him the keys. I took the liberty of placing the journals in an acid-free bag to give them further protection. My sister Sophia suggested a problem might arise with the paper disintegrating or the ink disappearing."

These words were no more out of my mouth than Kyron was ready to use them to take us to the deepest levels of our relationship. "Everything I ever gave you, if not quite eternal, was the best I could give," he said. "After all these years, why do you still doubt me?"

"My doubt is my responsibility."

"Don't be cold with me. It's against your essential nature."

"Then let's leave my doubt behind and cut to the truth between us."

He bowed his head toward me before saying, "Would you care to dance, my prince?" We sat down face to face as two Shardasko Warriors. Now I had no choice. The situation demanded that I assume the role of the aggressor for the challenge came from me. Our eyes met and his were so submissive, I felt like a goat in a rose garden. My psychic vision stopped short with self-consciousness and he beckoned me forward with a, *come ahead*. Cautiously, I went into him deeper and knew the vitality of his genius, deeper still the absolute peace of his will. Beyond, I saw his love, a steady and eternal blue flame of heartbreaking purity. Teetering on the edge of his love, I knew nothing foul was in him except my shortcomings. I pulled back into my mind and offered my eyes in return. The Key, also a master locksmith, knew how to open my inner doors. He slipped into my mind, as if he forgot an item inside me, which he now decided to retrieve. He snatched my conscious memory—knew it and owned it. "Thank you," he said as he was leaving, and he broke the psychic link between us and shut the door. "Now we may speak."

His internal purity so startled me, I told him, "Innocence is omnipresent within you and since I was the crass invader into your solitude, I will not ask you to explain your actions with Cerebow."

"This time my innocence is tinged with perplexity," he admitted. "If you will listen, I will explain what happened between Cerebow and me and perhaps together we can crack open the door to greater understanding. I will skip the synchronistic details of how I was in the right place at the right time to learn a dulcerary panther was in your *tritum*. As soon as I heard, I knew it was Cerebow. I thought, I was wrong and Élan was right. I even experienced an interior giggle as I remembered our conversation in Sheebrun about a dulcerary making the rounds of the masters and the befuddlement it might cause here on campus. I reasoned that you shared more consciousness with her than either of us imagined. Straightaway, I went to your *tritum* and found her sitting on your bed with her huge paws dangling over the edge. However the instant I came into in her presence, I knew I was not standing before a simple dulcerary, but a colossus of consciousness. She communicated telepathically with me, demanding, *what name do you wear?*

"I told her my Shardasko moniker was Kyron and asked her in return, 'What name are you wearing this evening?' She said, 'I wear the name Cerebow every evening and I came here to find my friend that wears the name Élan.' I remembered her term for spaceship from the mind scribe and said, 'Élan is not here. He has gone off in a shiny flyer for a few days to visit his sister.' At that point, she jumped off the bed and it seemed her intention was to leave without further ado. 'Wait!' I begged her. 'Didn't you come here to become a Shardasko Warrior?' She stepped back, exactly like a Shardasko Warrior and I knew she was playing with me. 'Are you a master?' she questioned. 'I am a Shardasko master,' I returned. 'And do you believe you possess the mastery to teach me to jump to the fourth dimension?' I told her, 'If you're willing to learn, I can teach you to become a Shardasko Warrior and then through your own will, you will master your energy and jump to the fourth dimension. However, before I consider accepting you, I must know your intentions. What are you willing to sacrifice for this sacred knowledge?' Cerebow then astounded me by saying, 'Why should I sacrifice anything for this sacred knowledge, for I am complete as I am? My question to you in return, Master Kyron, is—what are you willing to sacrifice to have the privilege to teach me this sacred knowledge?' For several seconds I stood there in total shock and amazement. I was unable to speak and knew with complete certainty that this colossus of consciousness had taken my key and was unlocking me."

"Why?"

"Because Cerebow is the only soul who ever approached me that possessed the right answer to my question of sacrifice. She forced me to understand with those few simple words that when we sacrifice any part of ourselves, we put that part of ourselves into denial and are rejecting our full potential."

"What about sacrificing our misconceptions?"

"Misconceptions are not parts of the greater self. Misconceptions are hindrances that dissolve, as the illusions they are, once they are revealed." Kyron shook his head in astonishment. "Cerebow made me realize the journey into wholeness should never begin with sacrifice and I will never expect another neophyte to kneel before me or allow him to cut off his hair. Never will I ask another soul what he is willing to sacrifice to become a Shardasko Warrior."

"What happened next?"

"When I recovered enough to speak, I said, 'Enlightenment is yours, daughter of the universe. You are now a Shardasko master. Would you care to jump to the fourth dimension with me for a short spin?' She said, 'No thank you, Master Kyron. I jump only with my friend Élan.' Then she leapt toward the window and disappeared out through a long split in the screen. I ran outside to see where she went, but she had vanished."

Flabbergasted, I exclaimed, "You made Cerebow a master after one interview?"

"I did, but you must realize mastery already was hers. Naturally, I wanted to jump with her, so I might collect a few more clues about who she is and what she wants."

"What clues do you have so far?"

"I suspect the male dulcerary, you encountered the first day of your *quarrying*, and Cerebow are of one consciousness. Their power must come from a consciousness, at least fifth or sixth dimensional in nature, because they can project their consciousness into receptive forms. I felt incredible love coming from Cerebow. It was compassionate love and an intense personal love for you. I think I owe you an apology for steering your thinking in the wrong direction when we were in Sheebrun. These greater spirits are not merely amusing themselves with your fire energy. Their intent is serious and you are important to them."

"Me?"

Kyron put his hand on my shoulder and after a moment gave it a gentle pat. "Each one of us is greater than our personal destiny, but rarely do we get an opportunity to glimpse what part we play. These spirits might be offering you a chance to participate in more than your own evolution. When your time comes to stand before them, remember, you are a Shardasko Warrior, not a stick lying alongside the road. Greater consciousness is yours. Use it! Guard your internal integrity for it is the one virtue truly your own. External circumstances always attempts to impeach freewill, but nothing can touch our internal integrity unless we lie to ourselves. Guard your honor and you can stand even before a god without shame. Other than that, wait. This consciousness will return. Of that I am certain."

"I can't believe Cerebow is now a master."

Kyron smiled. "It's a mistake to think of this consciousness as exclusively Cerebow."

"You're right. I'm confused and that's a terrible state for a warrior."

"Even warriors get confused, but warriors never lie to themselves regarding their confusion. Now you are troubled because you don't understand the nature of this consciousness or why it is challenging you. Continue to clear your specks of denial in the fourth dimension, so when this consciousness returns to face you, you will be able to separate its intent from your own."

"Then you definitely think it's returning?"

"I do. Don't look so distraught, Élan. Everything happens for a reason, we merely need to be patient and put the clues together as they present themselves. Aside from this challenging mystery, another matter jumped out at me like a signal flag when I read you through your eyes. I'm mentioning it now because I don't want the matter to distort your judgment or distract you from the challenges ahead."

"I cannot help my intense love for you. Sometimes I think I am terminally ill with it."

"This is not about the love between us. This is about the tension between you and Aytinous."

"Aytinous? I don't understand."

"Please find it in your heart to forgive him. I saw what happened between you two in the Fecundity Garden and Aytinous told you a falsehood. I didn't tell him you finished your *quarrying* a day early. Never would I divulge confidential information between us to Aytinous or anyone else. Aytinous figured it out for himself, which is not difficult since I called the school as soon as you reached Sheebrun to let the other masters know that you were safe. Neither did I suggest to Aytinous that you two should indulge in energy-sharing meditations. I have no objections if you want to meditate with Aytinous. You're both Emblematic Warriors and may do whatever you wish; but I will not allow anyone to use my influence with another person without my permission."

"Why would Aytinous tell me a lie?"

"I will not discuss this matter further with you because it would violate my privacy with Aytinous. You are your own man and you must decide how to handle this situation. As ever, I would nudge you toward compassion. Now, is there anything else we need to peer into or discuss this evening?"

"Only that I wish never to leave you."

"Go!" he advised. "Wherever you are, I am with you." He smiled one of his wise smiles and flicked his hands as if brushing me out the door. "Right now, I feel old and tired; still, I must work on the final journal before going to bed. Write me and please say more than I miss you and love you, although if you cannot think of anything else to say, then I am delighted to hear at least that. I did hear your plea from Gathos and my eternal pledge stands. Nothing can extinguish my love for you, for we are one in more ways than you currently understand."

As I walked back to my *tritum*, I sensed the approach of my mastery. The night I emerged from the Great Verdant and danced with my *Holder*, I had stood at a crossroad. Crossroads are conjunction points where choices offer themselves, not as burdens, but as seductive lures. The new road chosen is not a conscious choice, but a union of intuitive insights, that nudges the traveler along, until he commits to the new road ahead. Only now, did I feel the snap of commitment to my new journey. I was one with the road and the challenges ahead.

Two mornings after my interview with Kyron, I spotted him with

Aytinous. They were walking arm in arm, under Kyron's new umbrella. They were headed toward the Fecundity Garden. My intuition suggested that Kyron was about to confront Aytinous and Kyron would help Aytinous toward mastery over the problem he was experiencing. I decided not to challenge Aytinous concerning his behavior with me and figured he would come to me when he was ready. His lie had diluted his influence over me. He would need to repair my loss of respect through honest confrontation. It would be difficult for us both, but especially for Aytinous because he would need to confront his denial and share it with me. I possessed pity for Aytinous and the problem he was experiencing; after all, I was wrangling with my sexual denial. Over the next two moons, I saw Aytinous several times and he always was in a rush. One morning we met at the administration office and I told him, "If you're still interested, I'm willing to meet for our mutuality of purpose."

"Let me check my schedule and I'll be in touch," he said. That morning, he appeared clumsy to me for the first time and I realized an internal earthquake was rearranging the tectonic plates of his outer control.

The mystery of Cerebow seemed unsolvable, unless she returned. My only strategy was to use my training and flexibility to maintain my honor and integrity in whatever game I was forced to play with her. My focus became dealing with my denial in the fourth dimension. Kyron was right. I could not face this colossus of consciousness with authority unless I dealt with my remaining denial. Since I dragged my sexual repression along from the first leg of my journey, I knew its power over me. I faced the fact that I could not live without a physical intimate—someone to love and someone who might love me in return. I wanted a safe confidant, where our intimacy offered no chance to call new life into form. I was uncertain how I could bridge my sexual need into my existing life of sworn abstinence. If I broke my abstinence vow within the context of my Shardasko life, I would abrogate my integrity. Still, my personal truth cornered me. I needed a physical intimate and the identity of that physical intimate was as obvious to me as a blooming tree in the desert.

When I opened the door of the *tritum* Stellium asked, "What happened?"

"This talk might take an entire pot of tea," I said. Instead, our talk took the next three moons.

****

Stellium and I did not sleep that night. We talked across our eating table over several pots of razzleroot tea. I began telling him about my life and he did the same with me. Our mutual confessions went backwards and mine began with my last visit with Kyron. I attempted to be completely candid and even confided about the twenty-one journals sitting in a Gathos bank vault.

"It's a great honor that he would trust the distillation of his life's work to you," said Stellium. "How do you feel about being the bearer of Shardasko truths to Humanity?"

"Inadequate; the only thing I know about Humanity is I am inside a Human body."

"I might be able to help you understand Humanity." Stellium held strong opinions concerning Humans and he doubted that they would be receptive to Shardasko truths. "Human societies are extremely disassociated," he said.

"In what way?"

"I believe Earthlings will view Shardasko knowledge as alien and claim it's irrelevant to their lives. Humans value confrontation, display, and often reprisal. Stealth and cunning, of the Gathosian variety, are not traits Human admire. Most humans segregate their spiritual, cultural, and physical worlds and define themselves as their professions. Most of their spiritual leaders build their reputations on exoteric authority within their particular cult or religion, while remaining ignorant of authentic mystical experience."

"Sounds like the blind leading the blind."

"It's worse. If you talk to a Human scientist, he or she probably will deny their greater consciousness. Most Human scientists believe consciousness is brain chemistry and will not be happy until they can see consciousness spread out on a slide. Talk to a Human businessperson and out pour quotas, salesmanship, and the belief in the holy profit margin; talk to a professional athlete, and he will be a slave to his body and tell you life is a game. Humans love symbols, to the point where their symbols are more important than the symbol's underlying meaning. Many Humans refuse to look beneath their symbols and view greater truth as a loss of their little worlds. Perhaps you could present Shardasko truths through an amalgam with one of their more refined disciplines. Shadow dancing might be taught through something such as karate." Stellium stood up and demonstrated a couple different karate stances that appeared similar to Primal Stance. Stellium was a skilled and graceful shadow dancer and we experienced no trouble following each other as we danced around our *tritum*. His karate moves were beautiful until he showed me how deadly they could be. He explained, "My training in karate helped me when I began shadow dancing as a neophyte; but as you can see, Human karate has nothing to do with jumping dimensions." The dilution of Shardasko principles with Human karate did not appeal to me and I believed Shardasko was strong enough to stand on its own merits. That night I decided that if I took Shardasko to Humans, I would not dilute its basic philosophy, to make it more palatable.

The next morning, I sat in meditation through *areé didamé* and entertained many questions and feelings of inadequacy concerning my ability to take Shardasko truths to Earth. It was amazing that I felt so strong and positive a few hours earlier and now doubts filled me again.

That evening, Stellium mentioned his master's name—Lumenet—for the first time (*lumenetic* from the Mescale word *lumetsay* meaning, "lamplighter"). The name Lumenet sounded familiar and I asked, "What was the name of Lumenet's master?"

Stellium admitted, "Lumenet didn't share his Shardasko lineage with me. He referred to his master as simply, 'my master.' Why do you ask?"

"Because if memory serves me correctly, Lumenet reached mastery through Kyron." I remembered an incident and told Stellium about it. "I was in the library about three phases ago and my *Holder* began whispering in my ear, *read this!* Then a book flew off a shelf and dropped at my feet. It was a book on Shardasko heraldry and I'm certain the name Lumenet appeared on the list of Kyron's warriors." The Sutcay Tay library was the oldest and most extensive library on any Shardasko campus. It contained information on high shelves and in back rooms forgotten by time. I told Stellium, "*Holders* cruise through this library all the time. It's as popular as the Celestial Air Palace is with dead philosophers."

"Tomorrow morning, I'm going to cruise through the library myself and look for that information," said Stellium. That evening, he could not wait to tell me, "You're right! Master Lumenet reached mastery through Kyron." More suspicions arose in us and Stellium asked, "Do you think Kyron and Lumenet shared a hand in getting us together?"

"If they did, I'm enjoying the setup to no end."

Over another pot of razzleroot tea, Stellium told me, "Despite the lack of total interface between Master Lumenet and me, he is the first man I met that held my total respect. He helped me uncover my rage and it was big, because all my masculinity was hiding inside my rage. Lumenet opened my anger with his energy and my pain flew out like a flock of wounded birds. I had convinced myself that my sexual orientation was resolved, but nothing was further from the truth. Lumenet showed me I was living in only half my consciousness. Despite the fact that I lived inside a masculine body, my masculinity terrified me. Sure, I felt liberated enough to have sex with a woman or a man, but the truth is, no matter whom I was with, I assumed the submissive role. Now my six phases of abstinence has allowed me a respite and been positive in every way. Before, I was struggling to find my balance through dominant lovers. Now, my balance is within myself."

We talked all night and near morning, Stellium confided, "After I emerged from the Numidian Abyss, I went through an intense period of longing because I could not see Master Lumenet. I used to cut off locks of my hair and send the locks to him with notes saying things like, 'I surrender to you with each snip.'"

"When I first saw you, I thought you styled your hair that way because of vanity."

He imitated scissors with his open fingers and made a scissor sound with his tongue. "No, they were all cuts of longing for Master Lumenet. My shadow-dancing mentor, Brother Oronetsu, tried to explain my feelings to me—saying, 'It's impossible not to love an enlightened master when they are pouring their personal energy into you on a daily basis.' Oronetsu made me face the truth when he asked, 'Do you honestly want to have sex with a man a hundred phases old?' At first, I decided I might be willing to overlook the age difference, but the more I thought about it, the more absurd my passion seemed. After the six-moon period of forced separation, Lumenet saw me again, but I did not feel the same way. Now I believe that if we truly embrace the First Adaptation, our Shardasko training will free us."

The following morning, I wrote to Kyron asking him if he and Lumenet shared a hand in getting Stellium and I together. Kyron wrote me a long letter saying, "Lumenet came to me as a neophyte, eighty-seven phases ago, and was my ninth master. He and I now communicate infrequently, but we maintain a psychic link. Six moons ago, he contacted me to tell me that under his charge was an Emblematic Warrior named Stellium who was seeking a temporary position at Sutcay Tay. In the course of our conversation, Lumenet revealed that Stellium was born on Earth. I responded that I had a Human warrior preparing to cross the Great Verdant. I did not hear from Lumenet after that and believed Stellium changed his mind or preparations for his transfer were stalled somewhere. On a literal level, warriors that work in the Housing Authority make these decisions, not me. However, we both know that under the literal is a universe of subtle pressures. The fact that you and Stellium are now roommates, I can only say is one of those synchronistic puzzles that I find intriguing.

As far as I consciously know, I did nothing to get you two together; but unconsciously, my energy is indubitably involved. The more we move into personal mastery, the more energy becomes available to influence physical reality. This influence is beyond consciousness and is more in the realm of subliminal thought. It's like the mind skipping over a wish and suddenly that subliminal thought or wish becomes manifest reality. I cannot deny that you probably can learn much from a Gathosian brother that has lived on Earth. He would be invaluable in helping you understand how to approach the task of sharing Shardasko knowledge with Humanity. Whether the psychic energy between Lumenet and me has leaned on reality to allow this to happen, I do not know. I merely can say, "Holy Elements! Another fortuitous synchronicity has occurred, which I cannot explain. Remember, what I've taught you. The relationship between actual events and the recognition of the patterns that litter the trail of reality, suggest that we pay close attention to what is happening. I love you my princely fire! La

Teeair."

That night I asked Stellium through the darkness from our separate beds, "Do you believe your potential and my potential has a future together?"

After a few seconds he said, "To me you are a very tempting potential."

Under protection of darkness, I felt brave enough to admit, "I enjoy playing games with you, Stellium, but I need to know if you are as serious about me as I am about you."

There seemed an interminable pause before he asked, "You want candor?" Before I could answer, he said, "For me, you are definitely Mr. July. My physical attraction for you began the moment we met outside the administration building. You dazzled me with your beautiful eyes that I've attempted to pay homage to, in painting this humble room. Still, I don't want to break my vow of abstinence as long as I am committed to the Shardasko life. It took me six phases to establish my sense of balance and I am not sacrificing it for anyone. Beyond that, I'm aware of your sexual innocence. You might say your virginity etches your aura. Your innocence is a challenge for my masculine side. If anything happens between us, we need to decide together, with total respect for each other on all levels of our being. I want no seducer nor do I wish to seduce you. That is as serious as it gets for me."

I was relieved with his reply. I reasoned that our physical attraction for each other did not need to end in a sexual relationship. Perhaps I could fulfill my need for intimacy with another person through a deep spiritual friendship. "I respect you," I assured him. "Do not break your vow of abstinence for me, break it only for yourself, if and when you are ready. I'm merely happy to know someone I can talk to with complete candor."

****

We did not break our vows of abstinence, but I increasingly wanted to. I possessed new pity for those Emblematic Warriors with their secret sexual liaisons that I criticized in the past. It seemed that every judgmental thought I ever entertained was returning to challenge me, demanding, *how does it feel to suffer the judgment of yourself?* Self-forgiveness was the only cure and I vowed greater compassion for the dilemma of suffering brothers too.

Stellium and I continued to talk. Our conversations were ongoing and through conversation, we realized our lives were emotional reflections of each other. The impact life made upon us was similar and our understanding and resolution to problems focused on our Shardasko skills. When we spoke, we were on common ground. I had more in common with this Gathosian brother than anyone I had ever known. As children, our lives had shadowed each other. Stellium grew up on Earth as a minority feeling like a dark outsider among, what he called, "the blondes of

California," while I grew up on Ravenna feeling like a pale, ten-fingered freak.

We rushed nothing between us nor did we run away. We both knew that running away was a neophyte trick. We were accomplished Emblematic Warriors who had crossed our abysses. We were committed to mutual exploration and as the days piled one upon another, we became deep spiritual friends. Sometimes we would lie in our respective beds and talk until we fell asleep. When it was not raining, we worked outside our *tritum* establishing our garden. We took walks arm in arm and drank from each other's crystal water bottles, with full attention to consciousness. We possessed plenty of time to do whatever we wanted. Stellium's work on the frescos came to a standstill because of the continued wet weather. I accepted a senior position at the Fire Circle and volunteered to work at the library for four additional hours each day. Stellium would drop by the library and help me re-shelve books, disks, and memory capsules and our conversations would continue as if our time apart was a complete illusion.

Our shared feeling of early abandonment emerged and we wanted to comfort each other. He told me, "After my dad and mom divorced, I rarely saw Dad." His father now worked as an architectural engineer on Mars and Stellium said, "Every time we spend time together, we both feel the strain. I'm a nervous talker, but when I'm around Dad, my chest feels tight and words stick in my throat. When I was seventeen, I finally found the courage to tell him that I loved him. Do you know what he told me in return, 'It's better to be strong than to be loved, son.'"

One rainy and intimate afternoon, Stellium and I sat on the floor between the narrow stacks in the library. As our feet touched opposite shelves, he told me about the last time he saw his father on Mars. "Dad and I were standing at the spaceport, saying our usual uptight goodbye. All during my visit, I struggled to explain how important art was to me, trying to reach him through our mutual artistic expression, which we funneled into our respective crafts. I told him I wanted to become a Shardasko Warrior and he said, 'It's not a paying job.' Then he said something so strange that it's still difficult to believe I heard him correctly. He said, 'Follow your heart and you will end up with another man's hands in your pants, without a coin to call your own.' He never heard his own slip. He meant pants pocket." Maybe it was his nasty way of projecting his opinions about me in an unflattering way. Everything I suspected and suppressed about him, turned obvious at that moment. An avalanche of understanding, and compassion, came over me concerning his repugnance of intimacy. Dad was alienated from women, other men, his own child, and even himself." Stellium gazed up at me and his eyes glittered with tears. "My dad's loneliness is absolute."

Over dinner the next evening, he told me more about his mother. When he spoke of her, his eyes seemed to sink inward and he glanced to the right. "Mom worked since my earliest memories. For a long time I blamed her for leaving me with a string of strangers, while she worked. A few were kind, but most were distracted as you describe your sister Sophia. These strangers always were women, because Mom was suspicious of men. For a long time, this put me into a critical bind. I presumed I was falling short in her eyes or was a 'loser' as she called dear old Dad."

The next morning in the garden, Stellium picked a small blue skyflower and held it between his long delicate fingers. He said, "Mom and I lived in a cute little yellow stucco house, just north of San Diego. The houses were close together with clumps of blue African Lilies and yellow daisies growing between. I cannot think of my childhood without feeling the emotional wash of intense blues and lively yellows around me. The sky along the California coast is a shade of blue I've never seen anywhere in the universe, except there. As a kid, I spent hours at the beach with my two best friends, Yancy and Pearl. We would lie in the warm sand and imagine castles in the wandering clouds that spouted up from the Pacific Ocean."

I took the flower from his hand and tucked it in his hair. "*Ejesay epay*," slipped out of my mouth so easily, the words were out before I realized I spoke them. *Ejesay epay* is not a casual I love you, but is personal tense Mescale meaning, "My love is fulfilled only in you." Never had I uttered these words aloud to another living being. Up to that time, *ejesay epay* were words I reserved only for my *Holder*.

That night, Stellium awoke during the night, and told me, "My sexuality was aroused too early. When I was eight, one day I wandered down to the beach and a vagrant—we called them beach bums in California—molested me. He lured me to a deserted area of the beach. I knew it was wrong, but was scared and enjoyed the sensation at the same time. He kept telling me, 'I bet you lost those missing fingers by playing with yourself.' A beautiful blonde woman seemed to come from nowhere and saved me. They never caught the man and I never saw the woman again. I swore she was my guardian angel. It took Mom years before she would allow me to go down to the beach by myself again. She mistrusted men and that incident gave her fuel for her angry fire. After that, I spent my free time alone—sitting in my bedroom drawing." I got up from my bed and went to Stellium and he allowed me to hold him in my arms for the first time. "That was my India Ink period," he laughed. "I drew many indelible pictures of that beach bum."

Over breakfast the next morning, he was brighter about his life. He said, "Mom has softened in the past few years. She even has a boyfriend, which I think is a strange term for a fifty-five year old lover. She calls him, "Chris, my Human boyfriend."

****

For three moons, Stellium and I continued to dance. During this period, my concern for my personal appearance grew all out of proportion. The self-conscious problems most adolescents experience concerning their hair, skin, and teeth, I postponed until adulthood. My sister made me aware that I had body odor and now I scrupulously bathed, used deodorant, and brushed my teeth several times a day. I shaved with extra attention so I did not to nick my neck and chin. I tried wearing my hair in different ways other than my usual braid. I wore it pulled up and to the left side like other Shardasko Warriors, but Stellium said he liked my hair down and around my face and from then on, that's how I wore my hair. I obtained a new journal from the library and dedicated it, "to Stellium." We picked flowers and put them in each other's hair with the conscious attention we learned in our training. When each flower faded, I would press it inside my new journal, journal number six.

Neither of us was the pursuer in this unusual love affair; rather, love continued to pursue us. Our hands would touch and linger longer than necessary. We spent time in private gazing into each other's eyes. We meditated in our *tritum* facing each other. During these meditations, my energy would shoot up into my heart and I would know with utter certainty that I loved him. He was teaching a two-hour elective course on transpersonal art, which I decided to take. I would sit in his class and love him from a distance. Between the frequent rainstorms, we would take hikes because he wanted to sketch the countryside. I would allow him to walk ahead and enjoyed watching his Gathosian gait and the way the breeze splayed and tousled his thick mop of black hair. We would stop and linger in idyllic places; and instead of sketching the countryside, he would fill his sketchpad with drawings of me.

Then one day we decided to go swimming up in the Tyburnian Mountains between the graduated feeder locks. That was the day! It was hot, but not as humid and over the past few days it seemed the rainy season was waning. White clouds bubbled up from the horizon and filled the blue sky for the first time in three moons. When we arrived, the water appeared an inviting translucent green. Stellium turned his head away as I stripped off my *moodarry* and leapt into the tepid water. I swam around a little before yelling, "The water is warm."

"Okay," he said reluctantly. He slipped off his *moodarry* and slid into the water. After a moment he relaxed saying, "You're right. The water feels wonderful."

I was breathless over my own excitement and asked him, "Are men only handsome or can they be beautiful too?"

"Some men are handsome and some are beautiful, just as some women are beautiful and some are handsome."

"Then you are handsomely beautiful." The bright white light of Insanio sat upon the surface of the water and reflected off his golden brown skin. His long dark hair glistened like slick feathers and the gold in his eyes was Insanio itself. He swam over to me and we kissed for the first time. His lips were soft and moist and his black tongue was smooth as an orchid petal as it slid into my mouth. Our kiss was a confession of mutual feminine lips and our tongues equal male pursuers. Never had I kissed anyone in that way before, someone I wanted to penetrate completely and that I wanted to penetrate me. Then he said, "I can't live this way anymore. What are we waiting for? Let's resign so we can be together in total honesty." After our kiss, I would have broken my vow of abstinence in an instant, for I already had broken it in my heart. Yet hearing Stellium say these words, made the dream real. Thoughts of living without seeing Kyron still seemed inconceivable; yet, as always, the moment of decision had arrived. Reluctantly, I said, "All right. I will go see Master Kyron tomorrow morning and tell him that I am resigning."

****

That night I experienced a frightening nightmare. *I glance down at my ankle and see a worm sticking out of my flesh. Horrified, I believe necrosis is eating me away. I look up and see Arithmarur Das standing by my right knee and he hands me a pair of tweezers as if he is my surgical aide. Methodically, I extract the worm from my flesh with the tweezers, afraid that if I break the worm's body, necrosis will be forever stuck inside me. I manage to get the whole worm out, but when I glance at my ankle, a huge gaping hole remains in my flesh. I worry about disease and remember my cube of tartan ratu. I stare at the worm pinched in the tweezers and notice it has the head of a vaspray. Suddenly, the vaspray worm begins to fight like a viper, recoiling and attempting to bite my fingers. I'm on the verge of killing it when Arithmarur Das warns, "Don't kill it!"*

Awakening with a start, I heard myself make a sharp noise. It was enough to awaken Stellium. "Did you have a disturbing dream?" he asked. I told him the dream and we tried to interpret it together. Stellium pointed out the Achilles heel analogy and that felt uncomfortably on target to me. This dream-worm was attacking my vulnerability. What was my greatest vulnerability? At first, I thought it was my defenseless spiritual side that was under attack by my sexual urgency. Stellium got up and sat on the edge of his bed before asking me, "Are you afraid of losing your virginity to another man?"

"At this point, I think I may be more afraid that I will never lose my virginity. You know my fears, which are letting go of this proscribed monastic life and my thoughts of not seeing Kyron, seem impossible."

"What else?"

"The prediction from this greater consciousness that wants me to father a child keeps emerging within me, just like the worm. When I was sitting in that cave in the Great Verdant, with vaspray coming at me from every direction, I knew I was not in complete control of my destiny. Even the path that brought me to loving you seems littered with synchronistic perfume. Why has this intense love happened between us if I am destined to father a child? The last time I saw Kyron, he told me, circumstances can compromise our freewill, but nothing can compromise our internal integrity unless we lie to ourselves. Right now, I'm struggling to hold onto my integrity in the face of knowing my freewill is compromised each way I turn."

"I do not have the same commitment to Master Lumenet that you have to Kyron. Perhaps you are supposed to stay here and become a Shardasko master."

"Why does this decision need to be an either/or choice? Why do warriors need to be abstinent? As a neophyte, I was willing to sacrifice what I thought I did not need; but now, with you, my abstinence is draining the life out of me."

"What about your attraction for women?"

"The one woman I know is my sister Sophia."

"Are you worried that you might meet a woman that could be irresistible to you and she will come between us?"

"I can't answer that."

"Maybe the dream is a mirror," suggested Stellium. "Perhaps the worm or wo-man has assumed the dominant role of pursuer in this dream and is attacking your vulnerability, which is your fragile passion. You want to extract this wo-man from your life without touching it, ergo the tweezers. The contamination you fear is not from the vaspray fungus, but from your unexplored connection to the feminine. You extract your passion for the feminine from your vulnerability, but the gaping hole or question remains. Arithmarur is warning you not to kill your passion for the feminine because this wo-man is critical. If you kill it before you know what it is, you will never understand its meaning."

That seemed so close to my truth, it felt frightening. I told Stellium about Arithmarur giving me the silver-wrapped cube of *tartan ratu* that could help me root out my unacknowledged emotions. "The dream does seem to be advising you to burn the *tartan ratu*," said Stellium.

"I'm going to do it. Would you sit with me in case I need someone to talk to afterward?"

"Sure thing! Do you think there might be enough for me? That way, if I have any unacknowledged fears about us being together, we both will know the truth before we get in any deeper."

When I got up from bed, I wrapped my top sheet around my waist. Now we both covered our bodies in front of each other. I took the *tartan ratu* from the top drawer of my chest, peeled back the foil, and set the cube in the incense burner. We placed the burner between us and I lit the *ratu* with the concentration of my energy. The incense began to smolder and release its lazy spiral of smoke. I could smell its rose carrier, but knew something potent was under the rose perfume. About five seconds after my first whiff of *tartan ratu*, I became a cauldron of burning sexual desire and got an erection that could have challenged even the King of Fire. Stellium said, "Forget this foolish abstinence. Let's make love."

"*Snystellium opti*," ("shoot for the stars") I returned, which seemed like the quintessential response to a man named Stellium. We stood up, dropped our sheets, and braided our hands into Primal Stance. On the way to the bed, we made a short detour and jumped to the fourth dimension where I collected all my eager specks of sexual desire. Then, we returned to the exact instant we left for I did not want to miss one precious moment of what would follow.

My sexual exuberance made me unsure and my inexperience made me nervous about what Stellium might think was appropriate lovemaking. I thought I knew what men and women did together, but had only vague notions on how to approach making love with another man. My need to caress and taste whipped up inside me and I was on the verge of instant orgasm. My heart was beating so wildly, I felt like a runaway colt. Trembling inside my private need, I struggled to contain my lust, so Stellium could show me what to do. I tried to stop kissing him and breathed more deeply; but the more I breathed, the more *tartan ratu* I took into my lungs. The more *tartan ratu* I breathed in, the more I felt an urgency to reach climax.

Stellium was as fragile as a moment in time. Despite his six phases of abstinence, his love for me made him too compliant and he was on the verge of giving away his satisfaction to satisfy me. Knowing that, internal integrity demanded that I make a choice. I knew I could fall from grace if I took the slightest wrong turn. "This passion is more than mine; it is ours," I said.

My Shardasko training that taught me how to harness my energy, allowed me to bridle the lust I felt coursing through me. The instant we were able to merge our desire, absolute trust blossomed between us and the experience was both physical and metaphysical, a sacred ritual of true love. Our *Holders* got so close that they compressed our minds and feelings, until we were one orgy of intent. Then my lover's naked feelings came out to play and they were not passive, but active and one of the most powerful spirits in the room. Total wonder lifted me as Stellium's *Holder* plunged into the waters of my soul. We gasped and sighed and our bodies made silly noises I didn't know were possible. Happy was I as love's total fool. Love skipped down a path inside me, celebrating the greatest Festival of the Elements in the universe. A moment came inside me similar to the state in *turami savatnani* when the psychic consciousness recoils and gets very large inside the self. Then I surrendered my will to his love and my body could not help but do the same. The one thing left was to accept his love in return. He was a wondrous flame, a taste of the primal fires of all life. What could quench the passion of my fire, but more fire? Yet when it was over, I was a calm worshiper in the Eternal Waters of Love. What a paradox! Never before did I feel so calm, clear, or sure with another person. The *tartan ratu* still was burning and the orgasm only stripped away our desperation and my denial. Then we became even more conscious with each other and the real lovemaking began. We did not sleep until *areé didamé* faded into dawn.

After a late breakfast, we went to the library to look up information on *tartan ratu*. A nervous little laugh erupted from Stellium when he read aloud, "*Tartan ratu* is a powerful aphrodisiac." Arithmarur suggested *tartan ratu* was the only antidote to anger. When I told Stellium this, he said, "What else could be an antidote for anger but love?"

My daylight guilt grew and I had no idea what I could say to Kyron to justify my behavior? Merely writing him a letter, to ask that I might see him, seemed difficult enough. Stellium went with me to the administration office to give me moral support in posting the message. When my turn came to use the multidex, I noticed on a list of my communications that Kyron sent me a note early that morning. It said, "Dear Journey, as soon as you receive this message, please come to my *tritum*. It's a matter of critical importance. La Teeair." Many questions raced through my head, all beginning with notions of manipulation and me wondering where I stood in the management of my life.

Stellium was my greatest ally and I thanked my *Holder* who continually urged me to be candid with Stellium concerning all facets of my life. Now I possessed no last minute secrets that needed to jump out of the truth box to scare him. Stellium knew how much I loved Kyron and now Stellium demanded nothing of me and promised his unconditional support. We planned to meet later at our *tritum*. Right there in the administration office, in front of the multidex, we discreetly kissed goodbye.

# NINE

I went to the Eternal Waters Sanctuary to meditate before going to see Kyron. As I sat drenched in the pale blue light, truth soaked me like monsoon rain. *I accept it*, I thought and my emotions broke through and I cried. Considering my revelation and the critical importance of what lay ahead, I was calm two hours later, as I took the final footstep and knocked on his door.

"Come in," I heard him say. Opening the door, I stepped inside. Kyron was sitting cross-legged in front of his altar with his back toward me. His creamy-white hair spilled down his back and crinkled into subtle waves while the hair-ends made curlicue question marks upon the floor. He was naked. "Come and sit, so we may speak in as much privacy as we may fool ourselves into believing we possess," he said.

Picking up a floor cushion, I placed it to his right and sat in my usual cross-legged fashion before him. A thick stick of amber incense was burning itself away and tingeing the air with a scent that seemed inseparable from Kyron. He said nothing so I interrupted the silence by asking, "Are you suggesting privacy is as elusive as freewill?" He glanced at me before nodding his head with an affirmative jerk.

"Then for the benefit of eavesdropping angels, I missed you and love you as much as ever."

His face showed no expression when he replied, "My love might equal yours if I could find it. Now my love is only strong enough to let you go."

That Kyron had premonitions into what I wanted to say came as no surprise, the shock would be if he possessed none. His premonitions did not make this moment easier. In some ways, it made it harder because truth sat like two jagged mountain-peaks between us. Now we needed to cut through our differences and our mountain-peaks needed to match. I felt breathless, as if my love for him was sucking the life out of me. "Dear master, may I give you an affectionate kiss this morning?"

"My eyes, please kiss my eyes," he begged. The request was unusual, but I did not hesitate. I rose to my knees and kissed each of his eyelids deliberately with full tenderness. "My eyes are so weary," he sighed. "I spent the night in the fourth dimension searching for you in the future. Now I am exhausted with acceptance." He decided to stand, but struggled when he attempted to straighten his legs. "My legs hurt from my body sitting in the same position through the night." I helped him stand and then he seemed to notice that he was naked. Clasping his arms, sprinkles of gooseflesh dancing across his chest. He brushed back his hair along his temples before telling me, "I made several jumps last night. Only one jump was to the fourth dimension." He retrieved his *moodarry* from the end of the bed and slipped it over his head.

"I'm sorry to be a problem for you."

"As always, I'm my own worst problem."

"What's wrong, master?"

He shrugged a little and waved his hands around in the air in frustration. "Complainers are bores to those who must listen to their complaints; therefore, I do not wish to fuss about my mundane particulars."

"Even your complaining is wisdom to my ears." He smirked and it was such a bizarre mood for Kyron that it threw me into further confusion.

"Okay, physically, I'm exhausted and a headache is throbbing in my temples. Mentally, I feel like a fool, and spiritually, my *Holder* has decided to allow me to stew in the truth for a while. This morning, I feel quite alone except for my little self, my little mind, and my pervasive feelings. Other than that, I'm a Shardasko Warrior and prepared to adjust to this new situation, no matter how high the stakes."

"I'm sorry you do not feel well." I showed him my open hands and offered to adjust his energy with mine. We sat on his bed with my back resting against the wall and he laid his precious head in my lap. His hair fanned out around his paradoxical ancient-youthful face and I consciously touched the energy around his head until my hands rested on his forehead that I loved so dearly. He was receptive as ever to me, but more fragile than I ever thought possible. He was a rose petal poised to drop away from its stem. As I mingled his energy with mine, I knew he was a mighty and eternal flame. After a while, he said, "I feel better now." When I questioned when he last ate, he said, "I honestly don't remember." I fixed him tea and a bowl of hot *grash* and insisted he eat, despite his equal insistence that he was not hungry. After his second cup of tea, he seemed more his usual self, but the tension within the inevitable, lurked like a spring-loaded trap between us. Finally, he asked, "Did you come here, this morning, to stare into my eyes?"

"No, merely to put final words around our denial," and now I knew my moment had arrived. An hour before in the Eternal Waters Sanctuary, I realized it would be impossible to plan what I would say. The best way to speak was from my heart and hope heart-words found their way to say what needed to be expressed. "I'm selfish compared with you," I began.

My beginning was feeble and he interrupted with, "You took what you needed and I think I'm honest enough to admit that I was more than eager to give you what I thought you needed."

I reached across the table and held his hands so I could get out the words sticking in my throat. "Seven phases ago when I first knelt at your feet, I possessed no idea of the sacrifices I was asking you to make. I was foolish enough to believe my mastery was right around the corner and now, I realize my fragile limitations. I know you are a greater consciousness than I could ever hope to be. If you had not picked me up from my ignorance and told me, 'Accept your destiny,' my soul would be lost. Only now, do I understand the immeasurable energy you expended to bring me to this point where I can say—I take full responsibility for my life. What recompense I could ever offer you, that would equal your initial pity for me, remains an unanswerable question in my mind."

"No recompense is necessary between those who love each other as we do. Besides, when you seduced me out of retirement, you revitalized my life."

"The seduction was rather mutual—don't you agree?" Quiet ebbed between us for an interminable moment. "My sweet master, this morning in meditation, I came to realize that while my commitment to the Shardasko life is great, it is less than my commitment to you. Squinting into my distance future, I cannot imagine wanting to be with another soul, so much, that I would sacrifice my sexual zeal for seven phases to do it. The last time we were together, you told me, 'External circumstances can impeach our freewill, but nothing can touch our internal integrity unless we lie to ourselves.' Your words have been doing their work inside me and now I must speak of the denial between us or jeopardize my internal integrity." His quiet was absolute, so I continued. "Not even a million social conventions can alter my complete love for you. We have shared energy on many levels and know each other shamelessly well. That's why I can say to you with complete authority that the denial I claimed last night, in the fourth dimension, was partly yours."

Kyron took his hands away from me and touched his forehead as if his headache was returning. His voice cracked and came out as a mere whisper. "I searched into the past for seven phases for my love. I looked into the future until my eyes grew weary and there, I saw our love covering a rolling desert with the sacred flowers of possibility. Now we sit in this moment, yet we are trapped between the unrequited past and a future possibility.

Between these two, you taught me the true meaning of yearning."

"Your yearning continues because last night I claimed your denied love and my denied love and expressed it with another soul. I broke my vow of abstinence, but you already knew that—didn't you? Foolish me! Last night, I believed those fluttering snowflakes of fourth dimensional passion belonged only to me. Not until this morning's meditation was I aware that our mutual denial was cohabiting in the fourth dimension to torment us both. Master, I was unaware such an energy confluence possible, but now the truth is stronger than my denial. Last night I was an innocent, so what can I do except forgive myself? This morning, I forgive you too, because I love you and understand your yearning, but this morning, I also know that abstinence is foolish and I will no longer support anything I consider foolish, with my conscious loyalty."

He nodded in acceptance.

"I'm resigning from the Sutcay Tay School. If, as a free agent, you want me to carry Shardasko truths to Humanity, then I am prepared to dedicate myself to this purpose. However, if you consider abstinence a prerequisite for carrying the Shardasko banner, then we must go our separate ways." My words were harsh and silence sat like a widening gap between us. While I waited for him to say something—actually anything—my thoughts ran right down into my heart and reminded me of Stellium. "I would like to add, the person with whom I broke my abstinence oath is a fine individual and our commitment is deep and not a casual affair. Three moons ago, my physical attraction for him seized most of my attention. Yesterday afternoon, I decided it was impossible to continue here the way I felt. That brings me to the topic of *tartan ratu*. I take full responsibility for not doing my homework on this chemical substance, but I must ask if you realized *tartan ratu* is a powerful aphrodisiac. Furthermore, what would have happened if we burned that *tartan ratu* cube in Sheebrun when we were in intimate contact with our mutual denial between us? Anyway, the naïve me of last evening decided to burn this substance to see if I possessed any unresolved emotions concerning my decision to leave this life. No sooner did I ignite that cube of *tartan ratu* than our penned up sexual denial came to claim me." I fell silent again and then decided to add, "If you would care to peer into my eyes, to verify my truth the way I understand it, I am willing to surrender to such an inspection."

"Your integrity is unimpeachable with me," said Kyron. Despite his insistence that no need existed for him to look into my eyes, there was eye contact between us. This eye contact was not invasive, but tended more toward bridge building for mutual support. "First, you need to understand that if we burned that cube in Sheebrun, nothing sexual would have happened between us. My vow is to protect you and that includes protecting you from me. If you inhaled that aphrodisiac in Sheebrun, true, your sexual repression would have emerged, but it would have been an artificial and premature emergence, and your passion unsatisfied. Drugs are useful only to clear entrenched blocks within us and your blocks never were entrenched. If anything, your sexual denial has been worming its way to your conscious surface over the past few moons."

"Worming its way to the surface? Yes, you are quite right about that."

"I hear you. You want to know how I can know these intimate details of your dream? I know because last night while you were making physical love, I was meditating. During meditation, my fourth dimensional denial came to interrupt my peace and shame me by showing me how it must seek expression through you. I do not deny that since I reviewed the information on your mind scribe, I have been nudging you to face your denial. I have nudged all my warriors in the areas they hold within denial, thinking it is my duty to do this. However, last night, I saw for the first time that's its impossible for me to separate my energy from others, especially when the other is as precious to me as you are. Last night, truth made me see that under the guise of helping any other soul, any nudging I ever did was a greater benefit to me. To state it plainly, my mastery I have built upon the denial of each man I helped. Your devotion to your internal integrity is as strong as any warrior I ever mentored. You broke your abstinence vow because you were burdened with my denial, along with your own." Kyron showed me his open palms as a sign of total surrender. "My complicity is evident to us both." He smiled weakly, showing me that he was coming to terms with this new truth between us. "It's amazing. Despite our mutual twisting and turning, and incredible ignorance, we've ended up in a better position than when we started. This is because the emotion propelling us along this particular journey is love. If our motivation was any other emotion, besides love, we might have gotten away with our crime of denial. You see, love blinds denial with its absolute truthfulness. True love exposes all liars unequivocally, and love's true love is the naked truth."

\*\*\*\*

One can be going toward a destination for eons, yet an instant comes when one knows the journey is complete. My time at the Sutcay Tay School was over, but the fusion between Kyron and me was as strong as ever. Where I ended and he began, I no longer knew. "I love you in every way I know how to love," I confessed.

"That's because love is more tenacious than a common garden weed."

"Is that the extent of your revelation—love is as tenacious as a garden weed?"

Then, Kyron truly did surprise me. "No, that's not the extent of my revelation. I need to tell you about the greater consciousness that again paid me a surprise visit late last evening."

A thousand synchronistic needles pierced through me. "Was it Cerebow?" I asked.

"Not exactly." Kyron put his hands to his forehead. "My head still hurts," he complained. "And my eyesight is fuzzy." He stood, but his body teetered a little and I helped him sit on the edge of his bed. His body felt cool to the touch and I draped the blanket from the end of his bed around his shoulders. I asked if he wanted another cup of hot tea and he said, "No, but I still feel cold. Would you sit close to me and put your arm around my shoulder." I sat down next to him and embraced his shoulder to steady him.

"When I finished meditating, it was a couple of hours past *shahaut*," he said. "I wanted to get a breath of fresh air before going to bed. I went outside and was admiring this lovely night-blooming orchid when two yellow eyes appeared from the darkness and burned up the night. This time, it was not Cerebow, but it definitely was the same consciousness. This time, there was less sham about the form, as if the consciousness wanted me to know its true sovereignty. The beast held savage intelligence and I thought for an instant that death came to claim me; but after a moment, I realized this was my projection. I dared to ask, 'What is your purpose here?' It spoke telepathically, just as Cerebow did—telling me, 'I'm a chosen special and I am here to claim Élan.' I asked, 'Are you the dulcerary that met Élan the first day of his *quarrying*?' It replied, 'I am.' My psychic senses felt like a nervous wire, bunched up inside me, so I carefully extended my attention toward the beast in hopes of detecting a few clues. The instant I did that, it seized me by the throat and I felt unable to breathe. Then it forced me back—down deep into my core—where it unmasked me before my truth and told me, 'Two hours ago, when you began meditating, my *Holder* suggested to your *Holder* that together they might raise your evolved consciousness a bit. Your *Holder* recognized an excellent opportunity for you to make an evolutionary jump and decided to cooperate. For your greater glory, together, they nudged you to the edge of your denial.' Then the dulcerary released me, so I could humbly reply, 'Thank you. I accept both your gift and your challenge.' The beast nodded its head in encouragement and I admitted that I understood, more clearly, from the evening's meditation, that I had mingled my denial with every warrior I trained. The dulcerary offered me congratulations, saying, 'Excellent, Master Kyron. Then we are in understanding together. Our intent was to demonstrate as clearly as possible the true communal nature of reality.' Then I quickly slipped a question forward, before it could bear down on me a second time. I asked, 'What is the greater meaning behind your demonstration?' It must have been the right question because the dulcerary cut to the bottom line saying, 'Master Kyron, your plan to have your Human protégé carry Shardasko truth to Humanity is only part of his destiny. In truth, if he continues along his present path, without intervention from higher consciousness, Humans will pervert Shardasko truth into a tool to perpetuate violence across this universe. Allow Élan to come under the tutelage of my master and a chance exists that this time the song of creation will sound more harmonious.'"

"The dulcerary's use of the words, 'this time' made me suspicious and I wondered if you were involved in some kind of time alteration. I admit my fumbling here. I attempted to explain that as much as I loved you, I possessed no claim upon your life. This definitely was the wrong assertion and the dulcerary again seized me and forced me down into my core. This time I nearly died." Before my own truth, I realized that no matter how much I proclaimed my detachment from you, it would always be a lie. I knew then that my love for you was holding you here—and falsely holding you, since Shardasko life denies your need for a physical intimate. As the greater consciousness brought me up into my mind for a few gulps of air, I managed to whisper, 'I understand. Tell me how to extinguish my love for Élan, then our problem is solved.' The dulcerary sat on its haunches and rested for the first time. It looked me squarely in the eyes before declaring, 'Foolish soul, the love between you and Élan is inextinguishable. How can it be otherwise, for you are each a finger on the same hand? Élan cannot leave you anymore than he can leave the hand that moves you both. Your *Holder* has accepted this challenge and it is our intention to facilitate both your physical realities and make it easier for you and Élan to accept this short illusion of separation. Our intention is to give each of you a clear-cut physical incentive that will pull you out of the rut of your persistent ignorance. Understand Master Kyron, your twenty-second journal is gone from your library shelf. It's gone because, as of this moment, you do not possess the proper ending for this volume. The ending is different than you imagine it to be. It's different because my greater configuration has, is, and will explore the infinite possibilities and see a better ending than what your consciousness now holds. My greater configuration plans to write not only a new ending, but also plans to amend reality wherever its greater influence takes hold. We want to make this situation easy for you both, so we offer you even more incentive to cooperate with our developing plan. After I depart, go to your *ackinayon* and open it. Inside, you will find your wand of authority broken in half. Give the *ackinayon* and wand to Élan and ask him to deliver it to a Trinity Witch named Iosobell. She is a teacher at the *Emayre* School, located a short distance past the village of Pointilla. She will repair your wand and through Iosobell and Élan, we will harmonize time.'"

I interrupted Kyron's story to utter her name for the first time. "Iosobell?" Then I got up, walked over to the *ackinayon*, and unscrewed its cap. I carefully dumped out the wand. It was shattered, as if a person took it and deliberately broke it over a knee. The zaqurlite head of the snake had turned deadly white.

"Attempting to run away from this greater consciousness is futile," Kyron reminded me.

"I'm past running away. Besides, whoever this greater consciousness is, it has gone through considerable finagling to bring us to this juncture. I'm cautiously curious to try to understand as much as I can."

"You indeed are a Shardasko Warrior. You might even enjoy this new adventure." The concept of enjoying this challenge seemed impossible, as I considered the audacity of this super-conscious force that directed my life. "Its best not to linger, but to act with courage and verve," Kyron reminded me.

"The most auspicious time to leave would be tomorrow at *areé didamé*," I said.

"That sounds like a sensible choice. Tonight I will pray over the wand and bring it to you tomorrow before *areé didamé,* so I can be present to bless you before you leave. If either of us has any new insights between now and then, we should call out to the other with one of our contact words and meet forthwith."

Not all his protests could then stop me from kneeling before him and kissing his hands. "I swear master, this witch, Iosobell, will repair your wand and I will return it to you."

Kyron shook his head no. "The wand means nothing to me, but you must get the twenty-second journal. It's critical that you possess the complete story."

****

I found Stellium behind our *tritum,* in the shady part of the garden. As I approached, his back was toward me and he was standing in a way that was uniquely Stellium. He turned to greet me and, to me, he was more beautiful than the orchids growing out of the nooks and crannies in our garden. *Don't move,* I wanted to tell him. *Let me be forever in this moment, where I can see light filtering through the trees and freckling your fabulous face.* My compulsion was to jump to the fourth dimension and arrive endlessly at this tender moment.

"You were gone so long," he said. The golden rutilates in his blue-black eyes held the same look as the night before, a look that told me, *I'm as fragile as a moment in time.* The moment was over and I mourned its passing. Like any careless lover, I would have committed to another lifetime simply to recapture that one precious instant with him.

"Please?" I asked and I led him inside.

Making tea or love would prolong his pain and I did not want to put him through any more anxiety than necessary. We sat cross-legged on his bed facing each other and held hands while I plunged into what Kyron told me from beginning to end. After a while, Stellium stared down at our joined hands because he no longer could look into my eyes. The usually effusive

Stellium said nothing—asked no questions or pleaded for dispensations—and, for me, this made the situation more difficult. He already felt like my anchor in physical reality. After a while, tears trickled down his cheeks, but he still made no sound. "We knew this greater consciousness might return to claim you, just not the instant we began to make physical love," he finally said. He looked up and showed me his eyes and I wilted with shame over the pain I was causing him.

"Maybe I really am a barbarian for only a barbarian could inflict pain on another person and not know how to stop it."

"Do you want me to wait for you, Journey, or are you traveling on with this Trinity Witch named Iosobell?"

"Journey would say, 'wait!' and 'think of me every moment I am away.'"

"And what does Élan say?"

"Élan says he cannot ask you to wait because he does not know what is going to happen."

"Then I release you, so you can fly unfettered. However, I refuse to believe that reality is a treacherous killer of our love. Fate would not have brought us together with such intensity, only to rip us apart a few hours later. Our *Holders* blessed our union. Who are we to question their wisdom?"

"I will return to you, if and when I can. You must know I want to spend at least one full lifetime with you," yet I realized one lifetime was not sufficient time to do Stellium justice. His face remained expressionless with stoicism and it was a side of him I never saw before. His voice remained so quiet that I put my head against his and listened intently, so as not to miss his words.

"I will not be pessimistic concerning this twist of fate," he murmured as softly as a prayer. "Don't you remember, Élan? Artists stick together. This greater consciousness must be an artist too. It's a master, working on a masterpiece, which merely needs more refinement. At the moment, we are its subjects and lost in a few shadows. Let me tell you a secret about the art of painting," he said with a burst of spastic energy. "Sometimes artists find that when they are approaching the final stage of a painting, the details have become lost in shadows. An inexperienced artist might try to paint over these darker areas with white, but doing that produces an artificial and stark effect. Do you know right way to correct a dark diffusion?"

"Tell me, Stellium, how is it done?"

"The painter returns to his palette and mixes fresh paint of the proper color and uses it to both refine and soften the edges. This brings the picture into proper perspective. When the painting is complete, everything appears in its true form and color. I believe the unknown artist creating this new painting is not a novice and will know the proper way to correct shadows. We will survive this crisis."

****

Stellium and I clung to each other and our clinging led directly into lovemaking. Afterward, I remembered the first day we met. He smiled, moved his head from side to side in a mock of shadow dancing and teased me by asking, "Which one of us is the shadow?" With Kyron, I knew he was a grand emanation of a super-conscious force that owned my soul; however, with Stellium, I felt differently. In the fullness of mutual surrender, no doubt existed in my mind that we were equally one. We fell into a half-sleep of sexual fulfillment and not until it was too late, did I remember I was supposed to go the library for my usual job. Not going to the library was excusable, but not going to the Fire Circle for my late afternoon shift, was inexcusable. Still, I could not drag myself away from Stellium to do this final chore, no matter how I tried, so he finally went with me. If I could not leave him even to go to the Fire Circle, I could not imagine leaving him the following morning and perhaps never seeing him again.

Late in the day, I decided I might need cash for my journey and we went to the administration office and I drew on my line of credit for a few thousand bank notes. I thought about Sophia and Coreese who were now on Earth and asked Stellium to contact them, if I did not return in a reasonable amount of time. "You might need to make up a plausible lie because they will not accept the unadulterated truth." He promised that he would. Then I wrote a letter to Sophia telling her, "If you are reading this letter, it means I have left this physical plane. I ask you to honor my last request. All and any monies in my trust fund I wish to leave to Stellium Noveil Esay whom I have taken as my lawful mate on the last day of Wendar, phase of Air, 8433." Sealing the letter in an envelope, I gave it to Stellium. "This is my will," I told him. "If I die, Kyron will know instantly and will help you substantiate your claim to my estate."

"I will know instantly too," he assured me.

****

Stellium fed me his precious energy as we rested on the edge of *delchow savatnani*. I felt as ready as I could be, considering I was walking into a blind situation created by a super-conscious force. I performed all my morning ablutions before dressing in my civilian clothing and new boots. I wore socks and even underwear and left my three *moodarrys* and *slipfal* behind. From my chest, I took my journal and pen, knife, lucky tortoise shell, three crystals, and prayer beads. I wanted to give something precious to Stellium and remembered the keys to the safety deposit box. "I want to give you something important to me besides my virginity." I took one of the keys and gave it to Stellium. "If I do not return, my wish is that you might consider taking Shardasko truths to Humanity. After all, you know more about Humans than I do. If I return, then we will make a lifetime of it together."

"Only if Kyron agrees," he stipulated. Then he gave me a small sketch of us jumping to the fourth dimension together that I tucked inside my journal, journal number six, the one I dedicate always to my sacred love, Stellium.

Kyron arrived a few minutes later. "You did not call out to me during the night," I said. "Am I to assume you gleaned no new insights since our meeting yesterday?"

"Let's leave this morning clean between us," he said and he handed me the broken wand inside its *ackinayon*. "Again, I want to stress that the reparation of this wand is not as important as retrieving the journal."

"The journal I will get for myself and the wand I will get for you," I promised again.

I wanted to give Kyron something precious too. I knelt before him and offered to cut off a lock of my hair, but he said, "absolutely not.

This time I will take your knife."

I kissed the blade of the knife and handed it over to him. "It's yours. Use it as your wand until I return your wand of authority to you." I untied the scabbard from around my waist and gave him this as well.

He smiled one of his wise smiles. "Maybe I will use the umbrella you gave me instead. It seems a little less intimidating than a blade."

One more detail remained before leaving. On my knees before Kyron, I said, "Today, this first day of Aeon, phase of Air, 8433, I reclaim my personal authority and in so doing, resign my allegiance to the Sutcay Tay School. May the Elements that created my body, grant mercy upon my free and wandering soul."

"So be it," Kyron replied and he pulled me up as he had seven phases earlier and gazed into my eyes. "All revelation is in your beautiful blue-green eyes," and he kissed me on both cheeks, in a conscious way. "See you later, my prince of fire."

Outside, I watched as he walked away and I called after him, "Hey you old thief! You've not seen the last of me yet."

My goodbye with Stellium was subdued and without grand gestures. "All I can promise is—I'll return when I can."

"That's enough," said Stellium.

We kissed as we stood in our garden and I told him, "Please take care of my new painting."

Seeing Stellium standing among the fecund greenery, I almost lost my courage to go. Walking to the foothills, I allowed myself the comfort of looking back over the valley and the Sutcay Tay campus. The light of *areé didamé* was fading into dawn. Crossing the Great Verdant was easy compared to this. This morning I faced a situation for which I had no training. I thought about a time declaration concerning my new journey, but owed no explanation to any master. I decided to take five days to walk to Pointilla, even though it was an easy day-and-a-half walk. Arrogance and living up to my potential no longer mattered to me. Arrogance and living up to my potential was a game, the meaning somebody else put on time declarations. Now I was going to take five days to savor my journey, whatever that journey might offer.

About an hour later, I saw a dulcerary panther ahead of me. It was Cerebow. Calling out to her, I even sprinted to catch up with her, but she continued to outpace me. Then I realized she was attempting to lead me and hurry me along, just as she had in the Great Verdant. This time I refused to pick up her pace. "Five days," I vowed. "I claim five days for myself."

# TEN

## Part II: THE TRINITY WITCH

I am a Trinity Witch
A chalice of Understanding
I am the Truth holding the cup
And the essence of Love therein
I drink of my *Emayre* and
The Elements that fuse my soul with life

The past sits with me. We often drink tea together. Before the past departs, it always leaves its impressions in the bottom of my teacup. I scry these leaves for guidance, but the message always is simple and straightforward, a reminder of where I began this life and how far I've come. I swirled the residue in the bottom of my cup and this time I saw myself, not as I am now, but as a child.

I was born Follie Lanai-Trunn, on the planet Oceania. My mother named me Follie, after the follie flowers that bloom on the hillsides of the headwater planets. My early years I spent with my mother in a fishing village on Noer Island. She and my father were estranged and I had met him only once. When I was 2 water phases (8 years old), my mother died of necrosis, after being scratched by a vaspray during an autumnal invasion. A few weeks later, my life changed dramatically, but not for the better.

My father's name was Captain Loy Trunn and he skippered a windship that hauled cargo and commuters among the many islands in the Noer Island locale. A few weeks after my mother's death, my father sold our small cottage, which overlooked the sea, and took charge of me. My new life became windshipping. At first, the prospect of living on a ship seemed exciting. I dreamt of seeing new places and yearned to make new friends; however, none of these dreams came to pass. The reality of living on a commuter ship meant limited space and scheduled routine. The ship never docked long enough for me to go ashore and, after a while, I could identify any town or hamlet along the northern coast, simply by its port. When I turned my attention inward, toward what was happening aboard, I found myself living in a rough man's world, where no one had time or patience for a curious little girl. Worst of all, it was a dangerous world, filled with chains and cables, a place where an untethered sail could snap like a whip and fling a sailor into the sea. Below deck, the atmosphere was dark and grimy. Its smell was a toxic perfume where mold and the smell of cooking oil from the galley, mingled with the musk of sweating men and stale beer.

By the time I was an adolescent, the raunchy laughter of seamen was as familiar to me as their off-color jokes. I no longer was interested in windshipping and happy to attend a land-based school where I reveled in my newfound freedom. My father reacted to my new streak of independence, by becoming authoritarian and suspicious of most of my activities. On holiday from school, I came on deck at an inopportune time, and he went into a rage and told me, "You're confined to quarters."

Quarrels erupted between us and once he slapped my face when he accused me of flirting with a seaman. I told him, "You couldn't imprison my mother and you can't imprison me either." During this period, my sense of estrangement from the feminine deepened into feelings of abandonment by the masculine.

During my last year of formal studies, three Trinity Witches visited my school and talked about the opportunities for witches in education and the healing arts. At first, I felt enamored with the notion of becoming a witch, but when my father swore, "By Fecundity, you will never join those brazen whores," I become determined. The day I left for induction, he told me, "Walk off this ship and you are as dead to me as your mother." I never saw him again. For two years, I continued to write, but every letter he returned unopened.

When I became a Trinity Witch, my mentor gave me the moniker, Iosobell. I earned a music scholarship to the Celestial Queen Air Palace, on the planet Numida and my personal ambition was to become a music teacher. That does not mean my metaphysical education suffered from inattention. In fact, with time, metaphysics would become the motivating force of my life.

My mentor was a witch, named Sister Viobella. Her moniker meant, "Live wire." Viobella had a green lightning bolt tattooed on her left cheek that she said was a reminder of her "live wire," status. She was 49 phases old (196 years) when we first met. She had fostered the metaphysical education of hundreds of witches and yet her interactions with me always remained fresh, lively, and engaging. Her greatest virtue was her ability to make other people feel special. She was interested in everything I did and everything I thought. She introduced me to other witches, her colleagues and taught me the virtues of community. "I am so honored to serve as your mentor," she told me often. At this early stage of my development, I was fearful. I could not understand what qualities Viobella saw in me, because I could not see these qualities in myself. My father taught me that feelings were sharp as pins and needles and the only strategy I knew for survival was avoidance. I had learned to sidestep any issue dealing with feelings, nuance, or dreams. In my entire life, I never met anyone I could talk to about my feelings, until I met Sister Viobella.

Right after Viobella agreed to mentor me, she asked me to come to her cottage for what she called, "an interview." That morning, she had her green thunderbolt tattoo outlined in blue and wore a green caftan and large earrings that looked like spider webs. "Come in!" she exclaimed. She seems so happy to see me, but I did not know why. The room was practically empty of furniture, but pillows and mats were stacked in one corner, "Grab a mat and few pillows and make yourself comfortable here in the heart of my humble cottage," she said and she kicked off her shoes. "How do you like your tea?"

"I don't know," I said. "I usually don't drink tea."

"If you want to become a Trinity Witch, you must drink tea. It can be any blend you choose, but you must drink tea."

"Okay then, I'll take whatever you're having."

"Good choice," and she went over to her food area, where a kettle already was spouting steam. She pulled some bottles off a shelf and dumped some green herbs from each bottle into a wire basket. When she poured boiling water over the herbs, the steam rose off the tea and circled above the cup, in pink milky spirals. She brought the tray, with the tea and accouterments, to where I sat and asked, "Do you know how to scry?"

"I don't even know what you mean by scry."

"Then take the cream and honey sitting in front of you and add each one to your tea, to your own taste. Careful! Don't stir. Now look into the depths of your tea and tell me what you see. And don't forget to inhale deeply—very good for the sinuses, I hear."

I'm unsure what happened next, but in retrospect it seems our conversation continued without my conscious involvement. I went somewhere else and the next thing I remembered saying was, "I always knew I was different."

"How are you different?" asked Viobella.

"I notice things other people go to great lengths to ignore. My father instilled the idea within me that being different was bad. When I tried to tell him about my visions, he'd say, 'Ignore them! They're a damn curse!'"

"Your father was sadly misinformed. What he labeled your curse is your greatest gift. Now that you are a Trinity Witch, you will learn a new vocabulary that you can use to understand the mechanics of your gift. You will learn how to set ethical boundaries and protect your gift as you would your own child. Through this exercise, you will learn who you are and your purpose in life."

Viobella was right. I would learn much about myself over the next four years. I had innate psychic skills and I was an intuitive healer and knew how to commune with the elemental world of nature. Viobella used my inborn gifts as my doorway into the metaphysical world. Through her efforts, I would learn to scry, the art of psychokinesis and telepathy, the use of crystals and herbs, and most importantly, how to jump dimensions.

When my time came to make my first jumped to the fourth dimension, Viobella jumped with me. There, among the lingering time threads of the third dimension, I experienced an emotional breakdown of a magnitude I had never experienced before. My personal boundaries vanished, along with my sense of time and space. All my pretenses vanished and then, for the first time ever, I was capable of seeing the truth as never before. No past or future existed in the third dimension. I had been born into a universe of persistent reality held together with patchwork after patchwork of endless possibilities. So shattered was I by this truth, it took me months to make peace with this new knowledge and accept the gift of divine fusion offered by my *Emayre* (Foothote: The *Emayre* represents the feeling component of the Higher-Self and translates literally as "Creative Heart, language origin, Mescale.) Six months before my graduation from the Celestial Queen Air Palace, Viobella fell ill and soon would die. My psychic reputation was growing and I had offers from several witches who wanted to sponsor my career. In many of their minds, it was a forgone conclusion that I would go directly to New Delphi and study to become a high priestess. I still was an innocent virgin and had no notion how deep or lascivious the corruption on New Delphi ran, but I did know Viobella. Though she was gone when it was time to make my final decision, I knew in my heart how she felt about New Delphi and the New Delphi Order of Trinity Witches. New Delphi was the wrong place for me.

After graduation, I accepted a modest position at the *Emayre* School, on the planet Sutcay Tay. On the surface, I led the simple life of a music teacher. Beneath the surface, I knew my power and I knew why I was on Sutcay Tay. My own karma had drawn me here and my goal was clear. I would attempt to repair persistent reality with my own patch across this lifetime.

I sat in my room at the Emayre School and stared into the residue in the bottom of my teacup. Then I said his name aloud for the first time, "Élan

Journey Cœur. I knew the next few months of my live would be pivotal. I was ready to gamble everything on this new reality because I refused to accept the persistent reality of the past.

****

The night before Élan entered the Abyss, my *Emayre* stirred me from a light sleep. I rose from my bed and quickly pulled a shawl around my shoulders before slipping outside. A wide path meanders past the *Emayre* School. Beyond, the path narrows and elbows its way around to a spot where the path begins to climb up toward the summit of Mount Tyburnian. An enormous conference tree grows to the right of the elbow that has become my friend.

It was several moons earlier, at the height of the dry season, when many woodland spirits drift in recuperative slumber, that the conference tree first startled me. Her gnarly roots, which snake above the ground, support an interactive network of eyes that function as watchful sentinels to the world. These never-sleeping eyes espied me and sent a message up through The Mother's slumbering limbs. Leaves shuttered as if the tree awoke from a restless dream. Then, like tiny tuning forks, the leaves angled into the breeze and spoke with plaintive reverberations. *Black daughter? Black daughter?* called The Mother.

I felt a faint gust of wind catch the loose tendrils of my hair. Breathing deeply, my nostrils filled with the earthy scent of the nighttime woods. "Who speaks?" asked I.

*I do, said the tree. I am The Mother of The Forest. Come—come closer, under my sheltering branches, but step lightly around my roots. Touch me, and I will tell you the story of this exact place throughout all seasons of my life. Come—come and sit beneath my outstretched limbs, for charity is our common path, our journey home. Know—know, as do I, that all heartwood rings with trust. High—high above, we peer out toward freedom, the freedom that is Source.*

That evening, it took me ten minutes to hike to The Mother of The Forest, where I stood beneath her branches. Embracing her trunk, I attuned my spirit to hers. As usual, she called me *black daughter* and assured me, *I am your open channel.* I stood apart for a moment and mimicked the sonic high-pitched screech of a gnosis bat. This is my come-hither signal to the two dulcerary panthers helping me reweave events across this timeline. Taro and Cerebow were prowling the nighttime forest; but within seconds of hearing my beckoning call, they scurried down Mount Tyburnian to sit by my side. As usual, they hoped my pockets held a treat. This night I cautioned, "Only when you return, my chosen specials." Kneeling between them, I rested a hand on each of their magnificent sable heads.

The raw energy for their transformation was coming through Élan's soul group. My *Emayre* transmuted this energy into a gentle stream the dulcerarys could absorb and understand. Into the male, Taro, my *Emayre* directed a large stream of communicative talent. The mission of the female, Cerebow, was subtler, so my *Emayre* directed a larger stream of intuitive insight into her. She needed to guide Élan through the portal connecting the persistent stream to the realm of fresh possibility. Taro spoke telepathically with his new burst of language skills, telling me, *I will watch over Cerebow to make sure she is safe, even when my part is complete.*

"Don't try to jump into the fourth dimension with Cerebow," I cautioned. "We need your physical presence in the persistent stream, to augment the vigor of the situation here."

*I am your humble servant,* Taro swore.

"As I am yours," I assured him, for his new voice resonated with the bass *forzando* that often was the voice of my *Emayre*. No metaphysics were involved in Taro and Cerebow's initial encounter with Élan. The quick and cagy disposition of dulcerarys and their well-muscled bodies meant that it would take them only a few hours to reach the Great Verdant Abyss.

****

Returning to my room, I spotted a dark slinking form on the walkway between the schoolrooms and teachers' quarters. It was my tormentor, Brother Remette, a Hectarian Mystic, and the new assistant administrator at our school. Remette's frequent interference in my life is that of an annoying mosquito. "Sister Iosobell," he scolded me. "Why are you out so late? Aren't you afraid of the beasts of the night?"

"Only the beasts that disguise themselves in Hectarian robes," I replied and I picked up my pace. As usual, he snickered, for Remette, at this stage of his evolution, seemed incapable of unguarded laughter.

"Wait!" he called and he caught up with me and impudently placed a hand on my shoulder. I could feel the heat of his breath on the side of my face and I turned toward him and said, "Remove your hand from my shoulder or I will turn you into a toad."

His lurid smile appeared presumptuous as the night cast angular shadows across his face. He might have been handsome, but his personal denial contorted his face. Remette possessed dank places inside him that gave people the chills. He practiced a weird physical intrusion into other people's space. It was his clumsy way of suggesting he possessed personal power. His attempts at intimidation were futile because his eyes were feeble. His rutilates resembled shattered glass, and possessed no power to pierce through another for truth. Despite his weak eyes, every child at the school feared Brother Remette because of his eyes.

He removed his hand as if I had shocked him and said, "Ouch!" in a sarcastic way. "Yesterday, when I was walking along the trail to Pointilla, I met a local farmer who told me that wild animals are able to smell a woman when she resonates with Eno. Do you think there is any truth to that claim, Sister Iosobell?"

"I have no idea."

"The farmer suggested I keep a close watch on all the sisters here at the school because a couple of dulcerary panthers were spotted in this vicinity."

"Why don't you retire to your bed before you succeed in frightening yourself?"

"Come with me, to my bed. A friend of mine, on Namor, just sent me some Harvest Cream." Trinity Witches and Hectarian Mystics on the Gathosian planet of Namor produce the finest strains of *tartan ratu*. Harvest Cream is considered the best of the best.

Remette possessed no clue of the authority I was capable of wielding. Neither did he possess any concept of his true nature or personal authority; for the only authority he honored, was superficial and emanated from his status as a Hectarian Mystic. Remette arrived at the *Emayre* School with an assumption already in place—that his position as assistant administrator would fill his bed with a long line of admirers. Instead, Remette slept alone. On the conscious level, he declared himself a pious Hectarian Mystic, but Remette was entrenched in exterior structures and ignored his spiritual opportunities for growth. His life dangled from his soul like a frayed thread—obvious, annoying, and capable of unraveling the essential patterns of his heart. From the dark pit of his warped opinions, he spilled out secondhand rumors and dark projections with regularity. Barely hidden beneath his conscious mind was a compulsion to pull others down into his confusion. My compassion went out for the despair of his *Emayre*; but Remette's armor remained rigid, as he continued to buzz around the school and annoy others with his intrusions and speculations.

A garden of mind-altering herbs grows in a star formation in the center of the courtyard. I stepped into the herb garden and Remette shouted, "You can't go in there." I was super quick—stepping backward in time—hoping Remette would not awaken anyone capable of questioning my authority. I quickly picked a sprig of bitter rue and rofteg. "Bless your generosity," I whispered to them in gratitude. I skipped over the border of low-growing scented geraniums and again forward in time, where I wafted the rue and rofteg in Remette's general direction. "Go in peace," I commanded him. Remette walked away as if programmed to do so. Unfortunately, the rue and rofteg would stall him for only a short time. Negative karma sat between us, which demanded my attention. I could not deal with Remette and Élan at the same time. My only hope was to approach Remette in a different lifetime, where I would attempt to dissolve the negative karma between us.

\*\*\*\*

The following night was the Fifth of Natva. My *Emayre* alerted me a few minutes before *shahaut* that Élan and Kyron stood near the edge of the Great Verdant Abyss. I hurried outside because I, personally, wanted to witness the miracle about to unfold. This night I chose my path with deliberate caution and walked the longer way, behind the row of schoolrooms. Gearthot was dipping below the horizon and *shahaut* was commandeered all lingering light from the sky. A remarkable hush slowly settled over the elemental universe. Taking my cues from creation, I settled into my inner stillness. Then, mesmerized, I watched as the youthful grace of fresh reality crept out of the eternal *shahaut* and sunk a hook deep into the persistent stream. Suddenly, the elemental universe reacted and six meteorites appeared in the sky. These meteorites performed a few spectacular gymnastics. They traveled southeast until they were directly over the Great Verdant, where they began to fall. They were so bright that for almost ten seconds, the Sutcay Valley glowed with an eerie silver luminescence. Then, as abruptly as the breach opened, it squeezed shut, leaving only the ordinary dark to replenish the night. The unaware mind in its ruthless self-trickery would dismiss these fleeting images as happenstance. Only the *Emayre* would nudge the body and cause the hairs on the back of the neck to prickle—a clue to the incredible truth. Through a wee hole in persistent reality, the refined energy of Élan's soul group had just dropped an anchor. Now a real opportunity existed for change to take hold.

****

Cerebow is an extraordinary soul. She returned from her mission full of telepathic chatter and enthralled with Élan, calling him, *my new balancing backlegger friend.* Attempting to extract the intuitive gifts my Emayre bestowed upon Cerebow, her telepathic skills held firm. The truth was becoming increasing clear. Her encounter with Élan had spiked her rate of evolution. How great was Élan's potency if his mere presence could inspire higher consciousness to fuse within the body of a dulcerary panther?

Through the days and nights, I continued to scry for favorable signs of change, but nothing seemed to be happening down in the Sutcay Valley. While waiting, I came down with a severe case of impatience. Impatience is an annoying inner jiggle, a phenomenal malady of the third dimension that gets inside us and causes distortions within time. My particular jiggle compelled me to skip the moment and jump into the land of supposition, where I ended up in the byways of impossibility. Warnings from my *Emayre* came at every turn, telling me, *jumping is easy. Staying in each moment is harder, no matter what evolutionary state we entertain. Be patient. If you leap over any moment, that moment will not stick to the persistent timeline and we will miss our opportunity for change.*

During my time of waiting, Cerebow initiated a crisis with the potential to destroy my fragile plan. One evening, Taro raced down the mountain with a distraught cast in his yellow eyes. When my *Emayre* restored his communication skills, he informed me, *Cerebow went to seek out Élan at the Sutcay Tay School. She informed me that she was considering a new life as a Shardasko Warrior.* Cerebow is growing more independent with the power of her new consciousness. Concerned over what she might prematurely reveal to Élan, I sent her a strong telepathic message to rendezvous with me at Mother of the Forest. Upon her return, she was neither contrite nor even meek. Instead, her attitude remained breezy and confident while I grew fussy and annoyed. She failed to locate Élan; but unfortunately, she encountered Kyron and impudently challenged his Shardasko authority. Provoking Kyron was extremely risky. Praying for Kyron's complete illumination, I fueled only the prospect that the challenge Cerebow offered might push Kyron toward greater truth.

I sat in meditative union with my *Emayre* and brought Cerebow into our space. She began asking many questions and some questions revealed that her early plateau of confidence was eroding. We sat drenched in the green light of *areé didamé* and told me, *my Troubler is arguing with the Wind. My experiences with Élan brought up memories of my-ma and the way the flying ghosts ate her. Élan suggested that flying ghosts might be the true chosen specials because they can jump to the fourth dimension and dulcerarys cannot. I'm not sure what to believe anymore, except I still hate flying ghosts. On top of that, I'm certain many things my-ma once believed are untrue. What's real and what's not real, Iosobell? I'm not even sure I'm a chosen special anymore. Who am I if I'm not a chosen special and why am I here?* Despite Cerebow's new confusion, she fearlessly found the courage to pose the first two questions of higher consciousness, "Who am I?" and "Why am I here?"

I honored Cerebow's new enlightenment and I told her the truth, the way I understood it. "No mystery surrounds our true identity or divine goals. The dogmatic insistence of spiritual regimes, which claim the secrets are many and the paths always difficult, are ploys that encourage us to abandon our unique spiritual connections. The knowing, some call "divine illumination," is nothing more than remembering our original perfection, which is the nucleus of all consciousness. When we begin to remember our perfection, then we begin a journey toward recreating what was, is, and forever will be our true self. This path home to perfection is not narrow, but infinitely wide with possibility. In truth, this path is so wide, that without the guidance from our own *Emayre*, our unique perfection might elude us for eternity."

As Cerebow pondered this information, she paced up and down like a caged animal. *Is this Emayre, which you refer to, another name for Wind?*

"Wind, as all consciousness once was, is the longing potential within the

Source. Once Source exploded with its own longing and created Wind, the *Emayres* and so much more. Now we, like Wind, and the *Emayres*, exist as movement, the infinite potential caught up in the dance of creation."

*So if I hear Wind speaking, then I hear the voice of Source?*

"One might say every whisper of Wind across infinite space and time correlates to Source. But I must caution you, Cerebow. Your ears might be muffled by your distortions and you might not hear Wind as clearly as you believe."

She pulled her head back and looked imperious and confident. *Well, what I hear sounds clear enough to me.*

"What does Wind say to you?"

*Wind tells me I need to follow the path of a Shardasko Warrior.*

"Each one of us is an experiential warrior for our *Emayre*."

Not an experiential warrior, but a Shardasko Warrior, she suggested right back.

Cerebow claimed that Kyron made her a Shardasko master, but I thought she still had a few blind spots. She was oblivious to the opportunity for further illumination right before her eyes, and like a typical new seeker, believed she needed to embark on a quest into foreign territory to find her true path. Afraid that she was on the verge of making a second attempt to return to the Sutcay Valley, I dissuaded her by confiding, "I know you miss Élan. Soon he will be joining us here. When he arrives, I'm sure he will be delighted to assist you in becoming a full-fledged Shardasko Warrior."

*Élan said he couldn't teach me because he's an Emblematic Warrior. I need the atmosphere of other masters, such as myself.*

"Then rejoice, Cerebow. Élan's mastery is close at hand."

*It is? I love Élan!*

"You do?"

*For sure! Wait until you get a whiff of him. He smells like forest sweetness.* Cerebow relaxed and gracefully eased her belly down to the ground with her feet sticking straight out in front of her. After a moment her impatience resurfaced and she gingerly rolled over on her side and peered at me sideways. *Will Élan be here by tomorrow?*

"He'll be here within the next three moons."

She thumped her long, thick tail on the ground in agitation. *That's a long time.*

"If you meditate with me, the time will not seem so long." Reluctantly, Cerebow promised to wait. We continued to meditate together, but she continued to exercise a peculiar verve and unique independence.

****

Élan's mastery was forthcoming, but certainly was in slow gear. At times, I felt as anxious as Cerebow. I was certain Kyron would budge first and he did not disappoint me. Meanwhile, Élan surfed along the rim of his obstinate rut, as he agonized over each new possibility. This time around, he did not align with Aytinous and this was an auspicious sign. History proved that when Aytinous and Élan joined forces, their will consciousness magnified to obsessive proportions. An excess of will consciousness distorts truth by squeezing it through a narrow definition of intent. Truth defies narrow definition as much as it defies liars. Truth can be the most illusive bit of consciousness within the light.

Élan's *Emayre* was doing some powerful wheeling and dealing across space and time, to discourage the union with Aytinous. The new plan was to nudge Stellium, a gentler and more adaptive incarnation, toward Élan. Stellium favored his feeling-self that channeled the creative inspiration of his art. Stellium's greatest virtue was his ability to feel authentic empathy and compassion. This alone indicated his feeling-self was a positive nexus in his life. Exposure to this kind of soul would be a powerful influence on Élan. The *Emayre* fueling Stellium was cooperating with our new agenda because it could observe for itself that Élan's soul was fearless, truthful, and committed.

Élan's potential, even without my current intervention, was awesome. If the persistent stream remained unaltered, in his next life he would die a true martyr. My primary focus was Dulce, the infant we would coax into creation. Beyond that, my desire was to support Élan in his efforts to evolve. Without my intervention, his present life soon would end. If I could help Élan, a strong possibility existed that he could elude the destiny of an early death and live to a ripe old age. Much depended on our interactions in the near future. If Élan lived and participated in his own evolvement, the finest consciousness of his soul group was prepared to manifest through his life. Then, no one could predict what might happen next.

****

The time came when I knew Élan and Stellium had actualized their love for each other. Dressing quickly, I hurried up the trail to meet Taro and Cerebow. My behavior remained circumspect as I acted as a conduit for the higher consciousness that slipped into Taro and Cerebow. Once the gifts were in place, we meditated together to calm the energy. My *Emayre* gave the assignment of confronting Kyron to my stalwart rock, Taro. Thanks to Élan, Cerebow had learned to be dexterous with her paws and she frequently bragged how Élan taught her to put things together. The critical task of pilfering Kyron's twenty-second journal from his bookshelf was given to Cerebow. Before they departed, I admonished Taro with added verbal warnings, reminding him to be prudent and alert, when speaking with Kyron. Over the past three moons, my frequent bouts with doubt have allowed me to explore one scenario, where Kyron simply ignores me and writes the twenty-second journal without my input. To prevent this from happening, and to give Élan further incentive to hurry to my doorstep, I returned to my room and preformed a simple bit of Trinity Witch alchemy in the area of psychokinesis. Lighting an orange candle, I sat before it, and focused my complete attention upon my *Emayre*. Submitting myself to its power, I humbly asked it to break Kyron's wand of authority into two pieces.

Toward morning, my *Emayre* awoke me with, *Taro and Cerebow are returning from their mission.* I rushed outside and down the trail to my motherly tree. The morning was damp and cool and I drew my shawl tighter around my shoulders as I peered into the dull light. It was several minutes until I heard the distant sound of scuffling leaves and caught sight of Taro breaking through the dark profusion of underbrush. Cerebow ran right behind him with Kyron's journal between her teeth, carrying the book as she might carry a cub. "I was concerned," I told them. "What took so long?"

Cerebow spit the journal on the ground and made a blubbering sound with her tongue against the roof of her mouth. *Journals taste horrid!* she said in disgust. *You try running with an awful-tasting journal in your mouth and see how fast you can run.* She stretched by extending her front legs and then her back legs and teetering back and forth.

"I'm sorry for your discomfort, but this journal is a critical part of our new plan."

As usual, Taro remained serious, alert, and full of dignity. He flicked his ears a little to draw attention to himself. *The full message was delivered to Master Kyron. May we now enjoy our treat?*

"Certainly," I said. "Sit nicely." Cerebow jumped up and sat on her haunches next to Taro. "Do you promise to stick together?"

*We do*, promised Cerebow.

"Taro, you wouldn't wander off and mate with that cute little female that's been stalking you for the last few days—would you?"

*The one in heat?* he asked.

"Yes, the one in heat."

*I promise not even to sniff in her direction.*

"Fair enough, now don't kill anything to eat, unless it offers itself to you. You know the rules—what's approved and what's not."

*We honor enlightened pride*, Cerebow casually tossed my way.

I was so pleased, I decided to skip the lecture on enlightened pride and removed two cubes of *tartan ratu* from my pocket and tossed a cube to each of them. "Have fun!" They trotted off together into the deeper woods, to enjoy a bit of sex and forget, at least for a while, that they were sentient panthers. Picking the journal up from the ground, I brushed dirt off the cover. Cerebow had slobbered on it and punctured the edge with her teeth, but it was completely intact.

In my room, I switched on the lamp by my bed to enjoy my first peek at Kyron's twenty-second journal. The utmost care went into the physical construction of the book. The sturdy cover was made of *soaple* cloth. The symbols for Fire, Air, Water, and Fecundity stamped separate corners, while the focal point was a brilliant golden ovum in the center.

To Kyron, the creation of these journals—which explore the developmental levels of conscious enlightenment—is the major focus of his present life. Both our purposes entwine. If Kyron is able to remember our pre-incarnate pledge that we made in the Library of All Creation, a new door will open in his conscious mind and he will remember me. Pre-incarnate pledges are agreements recorded as indelible promises in the Library of All Creation. These pledges can be made between souls, *Emayres*, and even soul groups. *Emayres* attempt to fulfill these agreements, through prodding the unconscious minds of their incarnate children. To each life, the agreement expresses itself as an unconscious compulsion to act in certain ways. Yet the unpredictability of freewill is strong enough that the life can anesthetize these compulsions with myriad distractions.

The agreement between Kyron and me involves the pivotal life, Élan Journey Cœur. Kyron pledged to nurture Élan to spiritual manhood; and in loving exchange, I swore to help Kyron fine-tune his twenty-second journal. Kyron has fulfilled his part of the bargain and now it's my turn to do my part. The business of fine-tuning journal twenty-two requires incredible skill and that's why Viobella has accepted the challenge.

Opening Kyron's journal to the first page, I read, "*The Universe,* by Master La Teeair Forma." I adored Kyron's handwriting. It revealed his humor, wisdom, and his vibrant sexuality, and I flashed to a previous life where parts of my consciousness improvised with parts of his, for a time. The loops of his letters swooped freely above and way below the forward thrust of his words. Upon turning the page, shock set in. The page was blank except for the words, "The universe is the beginning and the end of the journey." I leafed through the remaining pages and found every one blank. Had Cerebow absconded with the wrong journal?

I cried out for help and in a heartbeat, Viobella appeared as a half-form and perched on the edge of my bed. Viobella balances perfectly upon a universe of receptive and active energy and is flexible between these two inner polarities. The opposites are identical, and when one looks into Viobella's receptive energy, his/her core is capable of projecting layer upon infinite layer of active energy. What one sees in Viobella often depended upon the viewer's perspective or Viobella's playful whims. Now Viobella wore a tall and svelte appearance. He/she was an unheard of genetic combination—at least in this archaic time—of fiery Gathosian eyes and pale blonde hair, like an archetypal Human angel. "You are not going to believe those crystalline eyes you're wearing this evening," I said.

Viobella leafed through the journal and began to chuckle, declaring that Kyron was afflicted with "cosmic writer's block."

"Do you think Cerebow snatched the wrong journal?"

She flashed the cover in my direction. "It's the right journal. Don't worry; it will be easier this way."

"But this was supposed to be a collaborative effort so all journals matched in style."

"You always worry too much about details."

"That's because details can be the difference between success and failure."

"I know; you're a committed player, just like Élan. Just tell me how you want it written and leave the rest to me."

"What are my choices?"

She raised her eyebrows and assured me, "They're almost infinite."

"Then write it as simple facts."

"No poetry?"

"I doubt Kyron wrote the other twenty-one journals as poetry. It's not his style. Kyron is concise and says what he means—that is, as close as language can explain such things."

"What about the perspective? Should it be yours, his *Emayre* or mine?"

"I believe the perspective should be from the core of our *Emayre*. It would be much closer to the truth that way." That afternoon, when I returned from classes, I found Kyron's journal hidden under the loose floorboard beneath my bed. Opening the book, I found that Viobella left a separate note between the front cover and first page. The note said, "So far, this is an introduction to *The Universe*. I wrote with a no-nonsense style and hope it fits with Kyron's other journals. Élan will have questions when he reads this. Please suggest to him that it would be a fascinating project to complete the body of *The Universe* in conjunction with his input. We could write an additional volume using the format of a dialogue to complement the first twenty-two volumes. This would allow us to answer any ambiguities and fine-tune the message for a Human audience." I wrapped the twenty-second journal in my green shawl and again hid it beneath the loose floorboard. This secret space is where I keep my tapestry valise. Inside the valise is a small portrait of my mother, a packet of unopened letters returned by my father, and my writing journal, in which I am recording these words.

I must be cautious because, when I'm away, Brother Remette frequents my room and searches through my personal possessions for *keylics\**. In the past, Remette has stolen hair from my hairbrush and even my underwear. He has attempted to use these items to charm me, but his limited mind is incapable of reaching my soul.

*A *keylic* is anything stolen from another that one might use to gain knowledge or power over that person. The more intimate the item, the more powerful its value is as a *keylic*. Strands of hair, bits of fingernails or skin, bodily fluids, especially blood and sexual secretions, all are considered superior *keylics*; language origin, Mescale.

# ELEVEN

If any chance exists to amend the persistent stream, then the critical factor that needs to change is Élan's death. As his fate hangs in the balance—in fact, is a mere eight days hence—I'm concerned that not enough time remains to make the necessary adjustments. Experience has taught me that we cannot force change into the margins of the persistent stream. Anytime greater consciousness attempts to create marginal change, results can be confusing in third-dimensional reality and in the worst-case scenarios, a backsliding into inertia.

Élan was on his way to my door, but that's all I knew for sure. Part of me wanted to run out halfway and meet him, but my *Emayre* advised—*wait*. I summoned Taro and Cerebow to Mother of the Forest to ask them to act as protective escorts for Élan's journey. Cerebow is bored again, but she managed to perk up when she heard Élan was on his way. My focus is bringing Élan to my doorstep as quickly as possible, so Cerebow startled me when she began teasing Taro and me. She has learned to use her unique mix of instinct and sentience to poke fun at Taro and me, whenever the mood strikes her fancy. Not exactly sure how it started, I found myself entangled in one of Cerebow's conversational traps that seem to be part of her growing genius. *Guess what?* she asked Taro. *Élan said my fur was shiny.*

*Did you want to mate with him?* Taro asked.

*If I'm hungry, it is only sensible to eat*, she replied.

The bait wiggled a bit more and now I swallowed it. "Just because Élan said your fur was shiny, doesn't mean he wanted to mate with you."

*I knew the truth beyond words. While we were meditating in the Great Verdant, Élan's urge merged with mine. He wondered what it would be like to mate with a chosen special.*

Taro pointed out the truth in his typical dignified manner. If Élan's urge

163

merged with yours, it sounds as if you wanted to mate with him too.

*Maybe I was thinking about it, just as you were thinking about that female chosen special that's been hanging around in our territory.*

The intimate details of Élan's face still eluded me. I knew he was a Human male and his complexion was fair and his hair blond, but not much beyond that was clear. Cerebow ignited my curiosity and I asked, "Can you describe Élan's physical appearance to me?"

*He's smooth*, she said.

"You mean he was without clothing while walking through the Great Verdant?"

*That's true, but he also was very smooth.* Cerebow demonstrated exactly what she meant by "smooth" by prancing around and exaggerating the swinging of her rump and flipping the tip of her tail in the air.

*The proper word is slinky*, Taro interjected.

"Do you mean Élan walks with stealth and grace because he is a Shardasko Warrior?"

*All those things*, agreed Cerebow. *Élan is slinky, graceful, full of stealth, but he also is very smooth.*

Attempting to redirect the conversation, I again asked, "But can you describe his physical appearance?"

Cerebow wrinkled her nose. He mentioned something about his fingers and toes being different. Her face lit up with realization. His smell is what hooked me. He smells of the afternoon sweetness in the Great Verdant and an urge came over me to—"

"Never mind," I interrupted. "Get going before I forget where I stashed the *tartan ratu*. One last thing, don't try to communicate with him. Let him know you're present, but keep ahead of him, so he gets here quickly."

*Consider it done*, Taro promised.

****

Lilla is four Fecundity phases (15 years old) and one of my favorite students at the school. She is musically gifted and possesses a robust appreciation for physical beauty of the masculine sort. She happened to be in the reception area when Élan arrived. She rushed to my quarters, full of breathless excitement, to tell me, "Sister Iosobell, a really handsome Human man is asking for you at reception."

Élan had stretched an easy day-and-a-half walk, into five days. His skittish reluctance was a strong resistance to my energy pulling him forward. The moment I caught a glimpse of Élan's profile, my vital energy became so excited, I almost fainted under an enthusiastic rush. Then the intimate details of our one night together, in the persistent stream, came to claim me. Again, I felt the rasp of his beard, the taste of his tongue, and the fire of his explosive sex inside me. Hope and reverence sat on the doorstep of my previous memories, for I could see, with more than my physical eyes, that this Élan was far more evolved. In the persistent stream, he was a confused virgin who spent one night with a Trinity Witch named Iosobell and fled before *areé didamé*. This Élan had reclaimed his natural passion and his energy burned bright and clean around his body. I dared to believe. *The changes are working*! His energetic body prevented him from really sitting and he was half-poised on the edge of a big overstuffed chair, as if prepared to vault into the fourth dimension at the slightest provocation. His physical body was a glowing example of the Anglo-Human. He was tall and wide-shouldered with a narrow waist. His obvious grace exclaimed Shardasko Warrior on every level of his being. Now I realized Cerebow had described him perfectly, for he had no rough edges. Élan was smooth with perfection. Blondish hair skirted the top of his hips. His features were flawlessly symmetrical with masculine beauty and I could not memorize his face as I could an irregular face. Beauty of his sort was a paradox, beyond definition, an attraction that keeps admirers returning for one more soul-soaking and addictive glimpse. He glanced up at me and his eyes reminded me of lush forests and sapphire-colored oceans. Deep within his eyes, I saw the angelic light of his *Emayre* gazing out upon me. His soul group had stamped him at the instant of his creation with its iconic symbol—a single red rose. Somehow, he managed to remember that symbol and presented me with a red rose. "You are more beautiful in the flesh than I envisioned you," were the first words out of his mouth. He was smooth, so very smooth.

Accepting his red rose with a, "Thank you, Élan," I told him, "It's lovely and perfect as you are."

"Seeing you face to face, I realize I've entertained visions of you for many phases. Some of my visions were quite—sensual. Are these visions mine or did you long ago cast a lure my way, to bring me to this moment?"

"I'm imprinted on your soul's memory and your visions of me are bubbling up from your *Emayre*, or as the Shardasko tradition calls it, your *Holder*. If you are willing to listen, I'm prepared to tell you everything, but explaining will take your active patience."

"I came for no other purpose than to listen and understand. However, my patience hangs upon your ability to speak truth."

"Fair enough, allow me to preface my explanation with the statement that the destination of the future sleeps with us. Now, let's take a short walk into the nearby woods, so we might enjoy more privacy."

Élan stood, picked up his backpack, the *ackinayon* with its broken wand, and we walked outside. Whom did I espy across the courtyard, but the unrelenting mosquito, Brother Remette. Élan carried himself like a Shardasko Warrior, but was not dressed as one. He wore everyday Gathosian attire. *Remette will miss the subtler clues—the graceful way Élan moves and the clarity of his aura.* A remote possibility existed that Remette might notice the *ackinayon* Élan carried, and wonder why a Human would be in possession of such a valuable Shardasko treasure. Losing no time, I created an illusion that would satisfy the blood-sucking curiosity of Brother Remette. Shaking the hand of an illusional Élan, I told him, "Sorry I can't help. I've lost track of my school friends on Numida. It was nice meeting you though and I hope you find you friend." The illusional me strolled away and into my personal quarters, where I vanished. The illusional Élan walked the opposite direction, up the road, toward Pointilla and disappeared. The confused Brother Remette did not know whether to follow Élan or me, but Remette was a victim of habit and decided to follow the illusional me to my room. He knocked on my door a few times and when I did not answer, he let himself inside and again searched my room for *keylics*.

The genuine Élan said, "You first," allowing me to open a door into a realm of possibility, where we headed up the path toward Mother of the Forest. If Élan were not a Shardasko Warrior, I would have excused his gesture of allowing me to walk ahead, as a simple act of courtesy. However, Viobella once was a Shardasko master in a previous incarnation and still enjoyed potential connections with Kyron because of their common link. Viobella had shared her Shardasko life with me and allowed me to experience it as my own. Through Viobella, I knew Élan would seek to find an immediate advantage. His gesture of allowing me to walk ahead was his first attempt to become the observer, rather than the observed.

****

Arriving at my sacred tree, I perched upon my favorite rock, while Élan stood peering up at Mother of the Forest. His initial shock of recognizing me as the woman of his visions had waned and now he seemed formal and leery. "You have fortified this area with your personal energy," he said.

"I have. The space beneath this tree is hallowed ground, yet no ceremony is necessary to enjoy the sanctity of this outdoor space. Sit, relax, and tell me how much you know. Then, without delay, I will fill in the blanks where I can."

"Assume that I know nothing and understand I will weigh what you say with the complete attention of my *Holder*. Also realize that I can overlook your great physical beauty, if your words are marred with deceit."

"I could impart the entire picture in an instant through energetic meditation." He took a protective step backward and locked himself into Primal Stance. "It was a suggestion not a mandate." He nodded and I realized that despite his Shardasko moniker of Élan, light-hearted he was not. Taking a deep breath, I prepared to take the slower approach. "Let's begin with the bigger picture," and I had his complete attention. "Cosmic intelligence informed me when you were ready to enter the Great Verdant Abyss for your *quarrying*. The instant you stepped into the Abyss, energy from your soul group began creating a patch across persistent reality. Since that night, you have drifted in and out of the persistent stream with regularity."

"What do you mean by the persistent stream?"

"I mean the rut of persistence that feeds our ignorance and impedes evolutionary integration."

"Does your finagling have a purpose or are you playing with me for your own amusement?"

"What you call finagling I call soothing irregularities with fresh intelligence. The process, naturally, is for my evolutionary credit, but the process is for your credit too."

"That remains to be seen. Tell me. If I am torn between two realities, how am I supposed to know which one is real?"

"Your consciousness is the sum of your experiences, no matter where those experiences transpire."

"You tricked me into jumping into the fourth dimension with Cerebow."

"Tricks were involved, but not the ones you believe. You jumped and took Cerebow with you and the vaspray followed. The only difference is, you, Cerebow, and the vaspray did not jump to the border of the fourth dimension, where you usually go. Instead, you entered virgin territory within the fourth dimension, where your physical presence brought strength to this new probability."

He began to pace to alleviate the nervous energy in his body, stopped, and scowled at me. "I should have known something was amiss. When I jumped, I caused no warble phenomena in the breach. My attention was lax. After all my training, which has taught me to question reality, I was presumptuous enough to brush off that particular anomaly as merely making a clean jump into the fourth dimension."

"Why scold yourself? This experience was new for you. Now that I've explained, the next time you will recognize the experience for what it is. Perhaps you'll even be able to explain something about creating these possibilities to me."

Tell me sorceress, what part did the vaspray play in this charade you created?"

"The vaspray pursuing you never realized they entered an alternate realm. We conducted the vaspray along a pseudo timeline where they dropped back into persistent reality unharmed and none the wiser."

"Is that why I never encountered the six vaspray that flew into the future, they flew back into the persistent stream and I was still in this other place?"

"That's correct."

He pushed up the sleeve of his shirt and displayed the back of his left arm. A deep scar ran from his elbow to his wrist. "Why did you do this to me?"

"How could I do that?"

He smirked.

"Cerebow told me she scratched you and I have no reason to doubt that it was an accident. Cerebow and Taro—Taro is the dulcerary you encountered the first day of your *quarrying*—are acting as my helpers. Taro and Cerebow possess personal lives. Their histories are intact and they are liable to the twists and turns from their karmic legacy just as each of us is. Surprisingly, our mutual interactions with Cerebow have infused her with some bizarre intuitive and telepathic skills and she has become a willful problem of late."

"In what way?"

"The idea to show up at your *tritum,* three moons ago, was strictly hers." A smile crept into the corners of his mouth. "Does Cerebow's independence please you?"

His smile dropped away and he became even more formal. "I respect the integrity of her individual soul, but question if you do the same. A Shardasko Warrior concerns himself with ethical boundaries and respect for those boundaries, which means I respect demigods and demigoddesses only as far as they respect me. Experience tells me that some shadow bits of higher consciousness are quite willing to invade a life and revel in its personal pleasure; however, when the confusion arises, higher consciousness flees and the life becomes responsible for facing the crisis alone. I accept my confusion in this situation, but I intend to guard my freedom and share my joy with whomever I choose."

I felt as if I was with a brand-new Élan. "No boundaries exist between us except your fear of me."

Élan turned indignant. "Fear you, witch? Through various trials, you may delay my journey, but I will reach my goal nonetheless. You might even kill me, but then again, death is merely another delay." He gazed down at the ground and then surprised me by looking up sharply and directly into my eyes. "Now I see—and quite clearly too. The truth is—you want something from me."

"I want your cooperation and trust."

"I warn you sorceress—you, as a reality, stand outside my sensual visions of you. My cooperation and trust must be earned."

"Then you possess no past life memories of me?"

"None whatsoever."

"I'm disappointed by that. We have met many times across space and time. Every time we meet, we are a particularly potent combination and it's obvious that even a casual encounter between us can spark new possibilities. Cerebow's new consciousness is a fusion of our consciousness within her."

"That's too fantastic to believe. You are a Trinity Witch capable of metaphysical skullduggery. It's more plausible that you possessed her and I met you inside the Great Verdant disguised as a dulcerary panther." His mind was a quick sorter and he pushed new evidence my way. "Besides, Kyron was impressed with Cerebow. He said she was a completely enlightened soul, capable of challenging him on the highest levels. Certainly, you are capable of dancing with Kyron; but it's impossible that an inexperienced creature, such as Cerebow, could fool a Shardasko master."

"Kyron heard truth and did not disregard it with petty rationalizations by saying—these words come from a simple dulcerary panther and hold no credence. I swear Élan; you encountered Cerebow in the Great Verdant, not me. My *Emayre* gave Cerebow intuition and some elementary telepathic skills—just enough to direct your journey into the realm of new possibilities."

Élan turned quiet and sank deeper into thought before asking, "And you swear my personal conversations with Cerebow remain unknown to you?"

"Cerebow divulged only portions of her interactions with you. Naturally, I can comb her mind for details, but this takes time and energy. My purpose is not the collection of sensational trivia or to pry into the minute interactions between other individuals. My purpose is honorable."

"Honorable? Why can't you simply admit that you're here for selfish reasons?"

"Your judgment of me remains harsh. I'm the first to admit that I am here for personal reasons; however, I would hardly label my reasons selfish. I do not make the fundamental error of seeing myself as an isolated speck of consciousness adrift in the elemental universe. I embrace greater truth and when I do, my truth flashes out, and I affect the whole."

Élan lowered himself to the ground and sat cross-legged before me for the first time. "Okay, goddess, you've won the first round. Cerebow deluded me with your sham. But bear in mind, Kyron never was deluded and Kyron remains my fortress. He knew greater consciousness was pushing for a new agenda." Élan's blue-green eyes were penetrating and he poured his concentration my way. "Tell me, dark and mysterious siren. Why did you bring me here, to sit at your feet? Who are you and what do you honestly want from me?"

"That's a peculiar question coming from a Shardasko Warrior. One might say you are asking me to define myself; nevertheless, I'll attempt to answer you question. My personal vow is to bring peace, healing, and love into this universe. In service of my vow, I live and speak what I believe. We have met at this unique moment so I might offer you a personal invitation, an opportunity to live for a higher purpose."

"That sounds like a mission statement put out by a Trinity high priestess."

"My understanding surpasses that of any incarnate high priestess. My *Emayre* contains the transcendent consciousness of many high priestesses and I can draw upon their wisdom when I need to. Through my *Emayre*, I can experience far-reaching realities, introduce charity, and create refinement where needed."

"How can you be in so many places when you body is here?"

"Consciousness can be in many places apart from its physical threshold."

"You still have not told me why you are tinkering with my life."

"The initial request for my tinkering came from your soul group and their desires dovetailed perfectly with my agenda to create refinement where needed."

"And the adjustments you make, you accomplish through creating a parallel timeline that intersects linear time?"

"Not exactly, what you refer to as linear time is a misnomer. Potential timelines are always moving, loop in and out of the persistent stream throughout all time. If one stands back from the timeline and views realty with greater perspective, one can see the scars over the persistent stream are quite thick. Unfortunately, adjustments are the only way we can save the persistent stream from destruction. As a Shardasko Warrior, you must be aware that incarnate attention is constrained. Perhaps your intuition has alerted you to a few of the more radical conjunction points, but it's unreasonable to expect even your enlightened mind to understand the deeper significance surrounding these adjustments. At times, especially at first, the psychic fireworks surrounding conjunction points can be dramatic. Then, gradually, as change sinks into the persistent stream, what at first seems unfamiliar, begins to seem routine. The changes I'm fostering are in alignment with your soul group and I believe the strength of this new reality, if given a chance, will blend seamlessly into the persistent stream."

"What will happen to the original or persistent reality?"

"The fabric of the third dimension is similar to a sieve. If we put enough pressure on the fabric, the energy within certain aggregates of reality sink below into a realm similar to the fourth dimension, which we might call the Sorting-Out Zone. This space is thinner than the third dimension and, therefore, more malleable. An elite core of group consciousness regularly descends into this space with the express purpose of sorting and retrieving bits of consciousness that fall into that state."

"Does this elite core look anything like vaspray?"

"It's unlikely that this elite core would adopt a threatening form when descending into the skittish space of the Sorting-Out Zone. If any form is taken, my guess is it would appear angelic."

Élan picked up a few pebbles from the ground and cradled them in the palm of his hand. "Are we in the persistent stream or this new reality at this moment?"

"When we walked into the woods, we walked into new reality. Here, it's easier for me to explain and for you to understand."

"This places appears real enough to me," and he squeezed the pebbles tightly inside his fist before tossing them on the ground. Then he showed me his open palm where red marks showed from the sharp edges of the pebbles. "It feels real too." He looked up toward the infinite sky and his eyes reflected longing. "Kyron once told me 'external circumstances can impeach our freewill, but nothing can touch our internal integrity unless we lie to ourselves.' Believe me, goddess, I'm attempting to hold onto my internal integrity in this new space."

"Integrity is critical to me too. Without integrity, even love becomes just another cheap word."

A puzzled expression filtered over his face and lingered like wispy clouds behind his eyes. The clouds were the shadows of his unrequited passion. "Of late, my entanglement with the love-topic seems to permeate my life. Tell me about our persistent connections through time."

I directed some of my energy his way to help him remember me in other lives. He amazed me. His higher mind was so lucid, he saw right through my previous façades, to my essential core. Kyron's spiritual education of Élan was astounding and he was more astute than I expected. I decided— why mince words? My *Emayre* agreed and said, *Élan is ready! Offer him greater truth in a direct manner.*" I gave Élan the full force of my consciousness, the way my *Emayre* arranged truth within me. *We are manifestations from the treasury of our Emayres. We are voracity and its erotic lust for the complete experience. Realize your true masculine, for it is the pinnacle of creation that steps fearlessly into the possibilities of unexplored consciousness. Welcome home your true feminine, for she is the eternal womb of your creative possibility. Conceived by yourself, you gave birth to yourself, in a desire for the complete experience.*

Élan did not speak for several seconds. "You want me to commit to this creation with a zeal equal to your own?"

He was an absolute genius and I gave him a gentle nod as that long ago promise—that trademark of the single red rose—came up to claim his life. "It needs to happen through Creation or all will remain as the imaginings of the *Emayre*."

"And our commitment in this life is through the child that Taro predicted I will sire?"

"Before I answer that, allow me to tell you how it happened in persistent reality. Then, together, we can decide how we can amend the future. Beginning with Kyron, let's begin by dealing with the critical players in your present life. Essentially, your love for Kyron was/is/will be—take your pick—no different in this new reality than it was in the persistent stream. Where you're concerned, the slight but critical difference is—in the persistent stream, Kyron gave his twenty-two volumes to you and Aytinous. Here, the twenty-two volumes belong exclusively to you."

"Aytinous is involved in this too?"

"Let's put it this way. He was deeply involved in your life in the persistent stream, but he's already lost his influence over you here. Do you recall the evening you returned from Gathos ready to accuse Kyron of stripping Cerebow of her consciousness?"

Élan abruptly stared down at the ground. "You even know about that?"

"Your *Holder* pushed the memory of your confrontation with Aytinous, to the edge of your conscious mind. Kyron saw the memory and I cannot be sure, but I pray he recognized the ramifications of what might happen if his great knowledge was funneled through Aytinous."

"It astounds me that a brother I admired as much as Aytinous could tell me a deliberate lie."

"Be compassionate in your judgment of him. He is an exceptional soul who, through his will, expends tremendous energy toward perfection. The nature of the will is linear and directive and anything linear and directive naturally leaves a vortex of depression in its wake."

Élan abruptly leaned closer. "Really? Tell me more about how that works."

"The stronger the will, the stronger the vortex of depression. The will is vulnerable through its depressive vortex, and attractive to free radicals seeking expression. If free radicals penetrate the vortex of the will, the soul may continue to appear pristine, but these forces will direct evolution from inside the will in manipulative ways."

"What happens if the free radical penetrates the will?"

"If free radicals penetrate the will, they will control the soul."

Élan's shoulders rounded and his head dropped into his hands. "Did these free radicals take possession of me in the persistent stream?"

"No, you merely entered an alliance with Aytinous that began as a simple exercise in meditation, but ended in him dominating you in an unhealthy way for your evolution."

Élan glanced up and asked me pointblank, "Does my relationship with Aytinous turn into his sexual domination of me?"

"Quite the contrary. While your passion continues to burn away with sexual frustration, Aytinous steels your energy and reinforces your guilt concerning your sexual zeal." Élan was staring at the ground again. He looked up at me and the beauty in his eyes—that always declares vibrant life—was enough to make me swoon. "Your soul group did not send a creation of your magnitude into life deficient in personal will. That would be absurd. Believe me, Élan, your personal will does not hinge on Aytinous or even Kyron."

"Thank you for explaining that to me."

"I'm glad to act as a verbal affirmation for things you already know."

Élan appeared unexpectedly startled and narrowed his eyes. "Please repeat that last statement."

"What, that I don't not mind affirming things you already know?"

"That statement sounds, well—very familiar."

Élan's energy came up higher and perched like a delicate bird on the edge of his psychic insight, waiting for a seed of truth. He stirred my passion even deeper and I held the seed out to him, wishing he would come and take if from my hand, but he remained cautious. I attempted to explain again. "The persistent stream has lost its linear context at this moment and the past and future can seep through quite easily. As a person stands upon a mountain peak and glances across valleys toward other mountain peaks, you can look into your past and future lives. In some life, a peak moment is now visible, complete with the words 'verbal affirmation' and those words are critical to that life."

At this early time, I did not realize a dangerously thin wall existed between Élan and his future incarnations. Élan actually was seeing himself in his next life. As time rushed forward, his future self would reveal more and demand much of the life of Élan Journey Cœur.

Élan let go a tiny gasp and told me, "I see!" I waited as he stared at the space between us and appeared to follow an action with his eyes. He swallowed a huge lump in his throat. "I see Aytinous taking Kyron's knowledge to Humanity. I die. The truth is—I'm going to die—and soon." His face drained of blood and he appeared pale. "Tell me, how long do I have?"

Praying my voice was soft enough, I told him. "In the reality of the persistent stream, you have three days left to live." His body jerked a little, trying to adjust to this difficult truth. "I'm sorry to tell you so bluntly."

He seemed to turn to stone, not allowing any weakness to pierce his armor. "I'm a Shardasko Warrior and I know I stand on the edge of unfolding time. I accept the possibility of death in each moment." His words were a mantra he learned to bolster his fortitude. The deeper truth was, Élan was unprepared to die.

"Only fulfilled souls die with their hearts filled with joy," I reminded him. "Your *Emayre* wants you to live and we are doing everything possible to change persistent reality. But I must be truthful concerning how difficult it is to weave a patch across the persistent stream. People in this dimension believe that if time travelers moved a pebble in a stream, the action would baffle the natural flow of reality. This is nonsense. Disincarnate consciousness barely can do enough to shepherd change."

Élan held firm in what he knew. "As a Shardasko Warrior, truth is my responsibility and my sworn karmic legacy. I will accept each new situation and my disposition will cooperate with me, because my disposition seeks the truth, just as I do. Through the principle of the First Adaptation, I will cooperate with your new evolutionary agenda, but only if I understand and agree with your reasoning. In other words, goddess, I will not dance with you, unless you give me an opportunity to dance as your equal."

"Somewhere in my evolution, I remember coming to the same conclusion as you. I demanded to play as an equal. I speak from hard-earned experience, Élan. If we demand to play as equals, that means accepting greater responsibility and more knowledge."

"I gladly accept both the responsibility and the challenge," he said.

"Then I'm prepared to surrender every facet of my wisdom, passion, and experiential history to you. Eventually you will know my soul mates and my *Emayre*, as you know your own. Tell me, how much of your essential self are you willing to share with me?"

"Forgive me, but many questions still plague me concerning your agenda."

"What still troubles you?"

"Tell me about Stellium, for I know with utter certainty that you introduced him into my life."

"You're correct. Within the persistent stream, you never meet Stellium because he never comes to the Sutcay Tay School. Instead, he leaves Shardasko training at Lomita School and goes directly to Earth. He's psychic enough that he envisions glimpses of you—a tall, blonde Human that he develops into his leitmotif and expresses through his creative art."

Élan's eyes were glassy with emotion. "I'm almost afraid to ask, but I must. Did you introduce Stellium into my life to highlight my sexual weakness?"

"Do you feel shame over your relationship with Stellium?"

"I broke my vow of abstinence to be with him. If I stood before a board of masters, they would tell me I fractured my integrity by breaking this vow."

"Nonsense, the truth is—you hung onto a ridiculous vow until you could not hold onto it any longer. Your love for Stellium strengthened your ability to respond to your honest need for greater physical communion. That's divine goodness, certainly not weakness."

Élan let go an exasperated gasp of air while his face assumed an ironic expression. "You're amazing; you seem capable of dismissing the foibles of others with a nod of the head and a little smile."

"Only when the foibles are illusions. I suggest you let go of your guilt. It does not serve you. You serve it."

"Tell me, what is the breadth of my relationship with Stellium? I mean, does it now exist merely as a possibility or does our relationship possess a real foothold in the persistent stream?"

"Your feelings for Stellium have secured your love within the persistent stream. Now Stellium will not return to Earth and pine away for a face he never meets. If we cannot prevent your death in three days, his memory of you will be conscious rather than unconscious. Because of you, Stellium now realizes true love is possible with another physical soul and that's a monumental realization for him."

"Why did you bring Stellium and me together with such intensity if you and I are destined to be together?"

"Your soul group merely nudged Stellium in your direction hoping it would curtail your alliance with Aytinous. Any intensity Stellium and you stirred up indicates the energy you both are willing to put into your love."

"Wait! My *Holder* is communicating something that's difficult for me to put into words." Élan went internal and listened before saying, "You and I—we—couldn't happen until I learned to love Stellium—why is that?"

"As it now stands, your receptivity is shallow—"

"That's absurd!" The mere mention of receptivity caused an immediate flare in his temper. "I—truly admire women." His defensiveness was a projection from his limited mind's vulnerability, concerning femininity.

"Your fear has little to do with male and female bodies except for the fact that your external situation of not knowing many women, is a reflection of the fact that you are ignorant of your receptive core."

"I know my receptive core. I've worked long and hard to realize my receptivity."

Élan was so pent-up with clogged energy that he jiggled his body to calm himself. "Please understand, your core defies definition even as Source defies definition; therefore only metaphors can take you closer to the truth. Your core is your place of creative incubation, or as Trinity Witches like to call it, the Chalice of All Understanding."

Élan squeezed his eyes shut as if trying to prevent the surfacing of a memory, but he could not shut out Mother Truth. "In the persistent stream, something went wrong between us—didn't it?"

"One day you walked away from your life as a Shardasko Warrior in complete frustration and with a great deal of simmering fury. Aytinous and you had argued over the meaning of Kyron's journals. Your anger was so intense, you didn't even tell Kyron you were leaving. You told me that you merely decided to take a walk and something compelled you to keep walking."

"The memory of it is like a dark and distant dream, but I do see—wait a minute." Élan went internal again. "Yes! Aytinous is scornful. He knows a deeply rooted—a deeply rooted love exists between Kyron and me. Aytinous and I argue over the meaning of the journals, but the real problem is he believes I've taken his place with Kyron."

"Did you take Aytinous' place with Kyron?"

"No, I swear! I admire Aytinous. His moniker means, "perfection will reign," and I believed he was perfect until he told me a deliberate lie."

"Your passionate swearing suggests that you and Kyron are dealing with a powerful compulsion between you."

"By compulsion, do you mean the unconscious magnetism between Kyron and me?"

"That's one way to put it. I might also call it your mutual attraction for each other's receptive core. You both know each other's active side quite well, but each infinite wellspring seeks to experience the infinite wellspring in the other."

"In the Shardasko tradition, we might call what you're describing as seeking someone's deeper meaning; but I can see this is an intellectualization of what you mean. You are talking about something visceral and erotic—aren't you? Dreams have come to me lately concerning the suppression of my sexual receptivity. The meaning of those dreams now seems clearer with what you just said. Can you tell me more about the attraction between you and me? Did I come to you in the persistent stream because of our past life attachments?"

"Partly, our past life attachments always influence our unconscious journey. You wandered up into the mountains, to the village of Pointilla, where you met a woman named Iosobell at a Festival of the Elements. In the persistent stream, she was a simple Trinity Witch, a music teacher, taken with your physical charms as any woman, with an eye for beauty, might be. Our extremely brief courtship, helped along with the drug *tartan ratu*, lasted a few hours. The following morning, your shame made a dramatic appearance before the receptivity of your soul and opened a gap within you."

"A gap?"

"The difference between who you are and who you were meant to be. You left me a note that said you were returning to the Sutcay Tay School and your intention was to return to me, if you could straighten out the confusion in your life. On your return journey to the Sutcay Valley, a meteor storm occurred that cut short your life. I've spent a great deal of time questioning whether your intentions were honest. To your credit, your integrity remains impeccable across dimensions." I encourage you to examine your shadows and decide for yourself. My personal belief suggests that if your honest intentions were to return, you would not have slipped away while I slept."

"I die in a meteor storm? Was I supposed to die with my parents on Ravenna when I was a child?"

"The meteor storm that took your parents could have served as a warning to you to be cognizant of this type of environmental condition for your own protection. On that morning, you ignored these simple warnings, because of your preoccupied state of mind. Incidentally, this meteor storm will occur in approximately three days time and nothing I know can change it. The meteor storm is under the control of elemental forces."

"Tell me about our child, the child Taro called Dulcerary."

"Your soul group is concerned for Dulce and Dulce is the main reason that I am involved. Higher consciousness is eager to manifest through Dulce's life. Part of the reason is the age of his soul, for Dulce was the first individual soul in your group to seriously approach *latturtimelda** and fulfill his/her original imagining. Dulce's soul is prepared to carry gifts of extraordinary genius into the third dimension. In this universe, the name Dulcerary Lanai Cœur will be immortal and his destiny, even without our conscious intervention, will be forever sublime. Dulce will possess the creative ears to hear Mother Truth and the genius to put her Truth into a piece of music that will allow every soul to experience the direct divinity of its spiritual self. His input will be so great, this truth-music will cause a spontaneous mood of receptive enlightenment to occur throughout third dimensional reality."

One of Élan's hands went up to his temple as if psychic distress was causing him a sudden pain. He put one hand on the ground to steady himself and keep from falling. "Now I see what happened. I deserted my son, perpetuating the abandonment my father lobbied against me. I can't bear this. Every way I look, I'm trapped by my own stupid behavior. This is too painful."

"Together, we can change this."

"You don't understand." He lifted his hands and showed me his palms as a gesture of complete honesty. "Only recently, through Kyron, do I recognize the love, commitment, and absolute raw energy it takes to nurture a child to maturity. Without Kyron's guidance, I would be a lost soul."

"Your realizations are all good. You've learned from Kyron how to be a good father."

"It's not all good! I know I fall short of Kyron's mark. I lack his passion, his wisdom, and even his patience to mentor a child. I've vowed never to father children. In many ways, I'm as alienated from fatherhood as my biological father was. Now you tell me I've already fathered a child. This is worse than me breaking my celibacy oath."

"Please don't despair, Élan. When we despair, persistent reality digs its thorns into our hearts."

"I swear, goddess, I feel the intense pain of those thorns. If anyway exists to alter the damned track of bungling I've left behind, then my advice to you is—find a better man this time around. Choose Kyron's patience and

---

**latturtimelda*: "experience finished" and refers to "the last full extension of the soul" and an end to direct incarnation; language origin, Mescale.

unselfish wisdom or Stellium's incredible beauty and uncompromising love; but do not choose me. This time, choose a man worthy of fathering this extraordinary child. Do not repeat your mistake with me."

"You are worthy; you just don't realize it yet. You're future is not only bright, but ablaze with unique genius. This is an extremely rare opportunity for both of us. We can make conscious choices this time, instead of being buffeted about by our denial. Élan, the wisdom, commitment, and patience, you need to mentor new life, flows from our receptive capacity to nurture. These qualities may be embryonic within you, but your love is waiting to bring them to life and I can prove it. If you and Stellium created a child, I know you would care for this child with the utmost patience and commitment because it would be a product of your mutual love."

"Stellium may be a strong receptive consciousness, but we both are living in male bodies."

"Again you are getting bogged down in biological details. My analogy holds. The critical issue is love and through the vehicle of creative love, all good things come into physical reality. Please understand; our child's life within the persistent stream was harsh despite his divine endowment. Life cruelly battered him for several reasons; chief among these reasons—he carried your karmic predisposition. When Dulce grew to adulthood, he fell in love with a woman who was none other than—guess who, Élan?" Élan let go a little gasp because his psychic vision started dancing with mine. "It will be me."

"Yes. Without this patch across persistent reality, it will take you and Dulce six thousand phases to come to terms with the misery you two cook up in your next lives. My wish is that, now, together, we put the proper effort into this lifetime and raise our child with care. If we succeed, it will help you and Dulce avoid a six-thousand-phase side trip."

"Can you explain my soul's relationship to Dulce?"

"Your soul and the soul that will live the life of Dulce Cœur are one in divine fusion. Each time you die, you merge in ecstatic bliss with him/her."

"Then we are soul mates?"

"Dulce is a soul you swore your complete allegiance to in a ceremony I can only call a divine marriage. Words equivalent to *ejesay epay* were spoken in unison."

Élan squeezed his eyes shut. "We said, "I am facing you fully and forever and my fulfillment is only in you."

"That's right. You spoke the words on the steps of the Library of All Creation. Many souls cheered and proclaimed, 'So be it!'"

Élan's face took on an expression of intense emotional pain and I thought he might be on the verge of tears. "What if I feign ignorance and simply walk away from this whole mess?"

"Walk away and the fragile web of possibility will disintegrate and you will sink back into the persistent stream. You still will father this child, but you will die in approximately three days. You will not remember this opportunity because the fragile web of this new reality will no longer exist. My job will be difficult. I will need to jump forward in time and attempt to alleviate some of the misery dumped upon our child."

His eyes were red with unexpressed tears. "I mean this with all respect, but you are indeed a rascal of higher consciousness. You have descended upon me like a dark angel and in record time, exposed my greatest weaknesses and flaws. If I could be like Kyron, I might smile and tell you, thank you, goddess, I accept and will adapt to this new truth; but admittedly, I lack Kyron's tenacity and grit. I still feel trapped."

"You feel trapped because your intuitive instincts are informing you that you need to make a critical jump. The ruts of limited perspective always suggest manipulation while offering nothing in return. If you find the courage to step fully into this new reality and bless it with your complete attention, then you will find infinite choices available for the first time in your many lives. Please allow me to be as direct as possible. The facts are as follows: within persistent reality, you helped me create a body for Dulce. Now, my fondest wish is you help me create this body with your complete conscious love and stick around to help me mentor Dulce's life."

"And Stellium?"

"I will send Cerebow to fetch him and together we will explain the entire situation to him."

"I would rather die in three days than tell Stellium I have no place for him in my life."

"You're still misunderstanding me. My intention is to explain our situation with the hope that Stellium will enter a loving and committed relationship with me, as well as you."

Élan managed to appear startled. Then he started to squirm and offer up a new round of prudish excuses, which was amazing, considering his only alternative was death. "Your suggestion might be acceptable behavior for the Trinity and Hectarian orders, but I am a Shardasko Warrior barely out of my abstinence shell. Besides, I'm Human."

"What's that supposed to mean?"

"Humans have a strong predisposition to bond only with one other person."

"Nonsense! Human are as promiscuous as fleas."

"Perhaps you're right about Humans, but Stellium is not a Human. He's a sensitive Gathosian. You and your *Emayre* must realize the depth of his vulnerability. He easily slips into cynicism when under stress. Our mutual love has rendered his cynicism nearly extinct. I will not put him under the kind of duress that will throw him into a relapse. Stellium knows I am predominately heterosexual and he'll regard himself as a needless indulgence between us."

"Before we proceed any further, you might want to reconsider the assumption that you are predominately heterosexual. Besides, do you honestly think I would be so deceitful that I would love someone falsely? Tell me, what has your Shardasko training taught you concerning the structure of your transpersonal consciousness?"

"Fundamentally, that it is pyramidal. I am a triumvirate of conscious body, mind, and feelings with my *Holder* at the apex point of creation."

"Why is this structure viewed as pyramidal?"

"Kyron says it can be no other because a pyramid is the strongest structure in the third dimension."

"Would you call your pyramidal relationship an intimate four-way affair?"

"Yes—what's your point?"

"Don't you think it would be odd if your *Holder* refused to entertain a complete relationship with your body, feelings, or mind because it thought anything other than a two-way relationship perverted? Besides, if you care to talk about perversions, the greatest perversion in the third dimension is the limited mind and its psychotic attempts to imprison the elemental universe in a strict dual-relationship between itself and the body's physical senses. My soul has left its black and white dualities behind and now I'm involved in a colorful and interactive flow of consciousness. I can do this successfully because my soul knows itself and is continually eager to know itself better. My knowing I accomplish through engaging and connecting totally with others. In all relationships, I can hold my subjective perspective while I can freely abandon my reserve to know the other as myself."

"That's a great deal to consider." His mind wheels were spinning and I hoped they were engaging in new ways. "Since my life seems to depend on it, I will call Stellium. I'll do my best to explain the situation, although, I promise nothing."

"Ask Stellium to come and I will help you explain." Élan gave me nothing but a blank stare. "If you ask him to come, he will," I added.

"He definitely will come. Beyond that, I cannot predict what Stellium might say or do."

****

Élan's behavior remained that of a well-trained warrior facing the challenges of the unknown, his mind was cunning, his vigilance sharp, and his seamless reactions disarmingly smooth. Unfortunately, cunning, vigilance, and seamless reaction failed to protect him from his habitual patterns. When I offered to arrange sleeping accommodations for him near the school, he explained that he already had accommodations at the Star Inn, a hostelry in the village of Pointilla. He was unaware the Star Inn was where we experienced our one night of passion, in persistent reality. Searching for anything that might allow us to interact on a more grounded level, I suggested, "Would it be all right if I walked into Pointilla and we ate dinner together this evening?"

"Come and we will eat," he agreed.

"We have been so far removed from the persistent stream we might be creating unnatural difficulties in getting the two realities together."

Still noncommittal, he replied, "perhaps—" Then his mind darted off to a new topic while his eyes examined me from head to toe. "Your Trinity garb—what do you witches call your attire?"

"We call them rags." I flared out the ragged hem of my green skirt to show him the cut of the cloth.

"That's right—rags. Shardasko Warriors associate the color green with creativity and compassion."

"Trinity Witches wear green because it sits at the middle of the visible spectrum and therefore symbolizes balance."

"Will you please do me one favor?" he asked with a cunning expression of innocence in his eyes. Show me your balance is authentic." He took Kyron's *ackinayon* and held it in his hands. "Show me your creativity and the skill of your alchemy and heal Kyron's wand that you broke as a lure to bring me here."

The ramifications beyond the obvious of why I broke Kyron's wand, philosophers might debate for time immemorial. Now it was vital that we mend the wand so it might serve its true function. Élan held the *ackinayon* between us and I staggered my hands between his so each of us had a right hand grasping either end. Then together we concentrated on the healing necessary to mend the millenniums of strife that broke the wand of authority into two separate pieces. "Repeat after me, Ineffable Reality of The Eternal Waters, make fluid again this wand with your complete and balanced authority that now will serve the integrated soul."

I was experiencing an incredible energy rush from holding Kyron's wand and I suppressed an urge to explain that witches consider a wand a surrogate phallus. Élan gazed into my eyes with cool eyes and I knew how easy it would be to make physical love to him. He was powerful, intelligent, sensual, and a potent ambassador of his *Emayre*. Then he repeated my words with an emphasis upon his own addition. "Ineffable Reality of The Eternal Waters, make whole again this wand with your complete and balanced authority that through this new reality will now serve the integrated soul."

"So be it," I added. "You may open the case."

I felt a tad disappointed when he said, "No need, the wand is mended for my *Holder* tells me the alchemical transformation is complete." He demonstrated his complete faith in the voice of his higher authority by slinging the *ackinayon* by its strap, bandoleer style, across his chest and pushing it to one side without checking to see if the wand truly was mended. He nodded his appreciation and said, "Thank you, goddess. Now may we address the issue of Kyron's twenty-second journal that is my rightful legacy? When do you intend to return this book to me?"

"I will bring *The Universe* with me this evening." The twitch of his right eyebrow slightly jarred the serenity of his face. "All puns apply in this case," I added and his face went blank with uncertainty. "*The Universe*—it's the title of the twenty-second journal, is it not?"

"Kyron did not mention the title."

"Then you have not read it?"

"Kyron asked me to withhold reading any of the journals until he finished writing volume twenty-two."

"Why?"

"I don't know why, but felt it was ungracious to question his simple request."

"Does Kyron enjoy your unconditional trust?"

"Only my *Holder* enjoys my unconditional trust, but Kyron certainly has earned a level of trust with me that is unequaled by anyone I ever met in this reality."

"Did Kyron ever discuss pre-incarnate covenants with you?"

"No, but I'm familiar with the concept. Shardasko tradition honors the belief."

"Pre-incarnate covenants are more than concepts, they are fact. Such an agreement exists between Kyron and me. The pledge stated that if Kyron would educate you into your sacred manhood then I, through my soul mate Viobella, would fine-tune journal twenty-two for Kyron."

"So Kyron accepted me as a neophyte because of a pre-incarnate covenant? I thought he took pity upon me because I was a pathetic orphan."

"This pathetic-orphan business is an unresolved shadow in your personality and has nothing to do with Kyron. His reason for taking you on was undoubtedly an irresistible urge in his soul that pointed to his own completion through you. Beyond that, the idea I'm attempting to establish is fine-tuning. When I opened journal twenty-two, the pages were blank except for the statement, 'The Universe is the beginning and the end of the journey.' Viobella will need to do a lot more writing than fine-tuning."

"Is this different than what happened in the persistent stream?"

"Dramatically, *The Universe* never comes into my hands in persistent reality. Instead, Kyron writes the entire book himself."

"Something is amiss. Kyron is beyond charades and contrivances and I know he has been working on the last journal for many moons."

"I'm not implying Kyron did not write *The Universe*. I'm saying the words have disappeared from the pages for some unexplainable reason."

"Actually, Kyron mentioned that Taro communicated something along those lines. Taro said a greater configuration plans to write not only a new ending, but also plans to amend reality wherever its greater influence will take hold. That new ending must be the new contents of the twenty-second volume."

"That matches what my *Emayre* has outlined for me; but thus far, Viobella has written merely a new introduction."

"Have you read it?"

"Yes."

"What its gist?"

"It would be difficult to paraphrase because the writing is concise. What would you say to the idea of working personally with Viobella on the body of *The Universe,* to expand its theme?"

"'I've committed my life to carrying the Shardasko message to Humans, so I definitely want to be involved. What surprises me is you trust me enough to introduce me to your soul connections. A Shardasko Warrior would not do that unless the relationship was extremely intimate. I've never even met Kyron's *Holder.*" Kyron's *Holder* was a lot closer to Élan than he consciously was ready to admit. "I did meet Stellium's *Holder* because the sexual intimacy brought it forth."

"My *Emayre* is looking out through my eyes right now and promises to make a personal appearance when we conceive a body for Dulce." Élan blushed and I realized how self-conscious he still was. To make him feel more secure, I decided to take him into my confidence concerning my sexual limitations in this life. "I want you to know that I have endured my sexual frustrations too. I'm a virgin. I did this on purpose so no elemental accidents would upset this new reality. Sexual union will not happen between us, until you are ready."

He looked askance. "You're a virgin? That sounds as improbable as a vegetarian dulcerary. Rumors abound that Trinity and Hectarian orders mingle their sexual energies on a daily basis to gain insights."

"At the *Emayre* School, it's optional. Our focus is community service rather than metaphysical gymnastics."

He looked deeply into my eyes and was clever as any psychic Gathosian at reading the truth. "I see clearly that you are not lying." We parted a short time later and our parting was formal. We still had a long way to go. So far, we had not even physically touched each other.

# TWELVE

Freewill is not a privilege, but a test that evaluates our integrity. The *Emayre* endows us with awesome power, allowing us to intercede and change specific aspects within the persistent stream. This power manifests through us as a strong compulsion; however, we enjoy no special immunity. If we abuse the laws of creation, without exception, we fall from grace. Compulsions drive us, but it is our responsibility to manifest the highest possible expression of each compulsion. Personally, my unwavering desire is to soften the lives of everyone I meet. It's not that I harbor dark projections concerning death. I know the vast majority of souls go straight back to their soul groups at the completion of their lives. Within the folds of their *Emayres*, the bliss is so intense, millenniums slip by like sunny afternoons. My complete sympathy is for, what life calls, "survivors" for they abide the exhausting inertia of time and the muffled whispers from their *Emayres*.

Freewill is such a strange and elusive principle. I can use freewill to make choices or as an excuse to soften the impact of my journey. At this late stage in my career of lives, my freewill feels nearly nonexistent. One of my few options pertains to Taro and Cerebow. *It's up to you how far you want to go in helping Taro and Cerebow,* said my *Emayre. You may feed them enough tartan ratu until they are lost in utter bliss, and allow them to die when the meteor storm comes. Then Élan's soul group can decide if it wants to incarnate this unique expression of consciousness again or dissolve it as the anomaly it is, at this time.* Exercising my freewill by doing nothing felt like the easy way out to me.

My first impractical notion was to take Taro and Cerebow off-planet when I left, but I knew it would be impossible to transport them on a commercial spaceship. Even if they appeared tame and agreed to wear

184

muzzles and leashes, security agents would stop us at the first departure checkpoint, and declare me insane. Hiring a private spacecraft is expensive and difficult to secure in the short time remaining. More importantly, I could not risk my primary goal of saving Élan's life by introducing risky variables. That's why I decided the best plan was to hide Cerebow and Taro in the fourth dimension. Time was nonexistent there, but I could use the advantage of time in the third dimension, to make plans that would safeguard their future.

****

After Élan departed for the walk to Pointilla, I found Taro and Cerebow and gave them the new assignment of escorting Stellium to my door. "This is the last time I will ask you to do this type of chore," I promised. As soon as they ran off, I began to worry. Inside persistent reality, only a short margin of time remained until death came to claim Élan. *Not enough time remains to gain his trust,* said a familiar voice. Thus, I knew worry had cracked open a door and was allowing doubt to relay its fears.

I questioned my great prevaricator. *It's you again?*

*I'm unsure.* Doubt mirrored my uncertainty and I recognized its halting manner. Out here, as I sat on the fingertips of my *Emayre*, doubt was my frequent harpy.

Viobella calls doubt, "the cruelest assassin," for without doubt, almost anything is possible. Doubt is a free radical tributary stemming off from fear. Information on doubt commands many shelves in the Library of All Creation. Doubt, like all free radicals, came into being as a half-form, through the imaginings of immature soul groups. When the elemental universe attempts to manifest immature imaginings, an energy stutter occurs and the elemental universe, metaphorically, chokes and aborts these immature imaginings. Free radicals never manifest into physical form or evolve and carry the karmic legacy of their own miscarriage. The archetypal motivation behind free radicals is naiveté and voracity. Free radicals seek to know whatever they can about themselves, but in the case of doubt, doubt is never sure about what it needs to know.

****

On the way to my room, I encountered Brother Remette and he was irritated. A wave of pity came over me for his exhausting frustrations until he open his mouth and asked, "Who was that monkey-faced Human, I saw lurking around here a couple of hours ago?" I walked faster and so did Remette. "I saw you go to your room, but when I knocked on your door, you were gone. We needed your help gathering sarup nuts in the south woods. We need the oil for the temple lamps—reserves are low."

"If I was gone, then you must of seen wrong. Now, let's go about our appropriate duties and leave each other in peace."

His annoyance with me only increased, and his voice climbed to a higher octave. "If you can't cooperate, then expect nothing from me in return. I intend to tell Sister Sessabell of your continuing lack of humility to perform the necessary chores to keep this school afloat."

"Do as you wish, Brother Remette, your actions bring no blessings upon you."

His hands clenched into fists and when he spoke, spit came flying out of his mouth and I felt a drop hit my cheek. "And your virginity brings no blessings on you. You think you're so high and mighty; but to me, you stink of a sexual cavort with a meat-eating Human."

Remette was highly agitated. My best guess was his unconscious mind was putting plenty of pressure on him to resolve the issues I highlighted in his life, before I permanently disappeared. It was daylight and I dare not breach the confines of the herb garden to cast another spell. Instead, I used my eyes and, in the end, my eyes proved a more powerful metaphysical tool than herbs. *Look into my eyes*, demanded my *Emayre*.

Remette's "what?" was full of irritation, but his "—did you say?" trailed off and ended in a choked whisper. My *Emayre* snagged him with the rutilates of my eyes as a shiny lure snags a hungry fish. Remette stumbled forward and I caught him so he did not topple over and injure himself. He slumped sideways and managed to extend his hand in an effort to support his weight. He was awkwardly off-balance, but possessed no power to release himself from my eyes. "Aaaaah! Let me go," he gasped. My *Emayre* released him and he tumbled backward on the ground before scrambling to his feet and dashing away. The situation was reaching a critical stage. This time, Remette affected me too and my body was shaking as I returned to my room.

I went to the sink and splashed cold water on my face and Viobella said, *concentrate on Élan; Remette is not ready to change.*

*It's difficult.*

*Pay careful attention to my words, Iosobell. Remette is a fatal distraction, aligned with many errant shadows and several free radicals. He is not your true course. All your pity, he turns into self-pity. When you return from Pointilla, pack your belongings and be prepared to leave at a moment's notice. Chances are favorable that Stellium will be motivated to come more quickly than Élan did.*

\*\*\*\*

I took extra care in dressing for my evening with Élan. I owned one precious set of secular clothing, which I decided to wear. The garb was simple—a white peasant blouse, and an embroidered *soaple*-cloth skirt—typical of what any Sutcay Tay female might wear. I put on the clothes and looked at my reflection in the window. Now I was unsure of my physical appearance. Doubt was insidious. *Thanks to Kyron's influence, Élan is closer to balance than he's been in ten thousand phases, yet he still prefers the masculine façade. Perhaps it would be easier to give in to your impulses. Go ahead, you can do it. Outfit yourself in a masculine form. That will get his attention and respect.* Squeezing my eyes shut, I attempted to be objective before gazing at myself again. On the surface, I was a peasant girl with no finery or jewelry. Trinity Witches of this ancient time had few luxuries and none of the wonderful perfumes they would concoct in the future. I washed my face, brushed my teeth and combed my hair. My only cosmetic was a smile.

A short time later, I walked along the main street of Pointilla, weaving between the half-constructed booths. The booths were reminders that the phase of Air soon would climax with the Festival of Air. In three days, either Élan would be by my side or his *Emayre* would be standing before his soul group, rehashing the reasons Élan opted for an early exit from life. And in four days, as Sutcay Tay awoke to the phase of Fire, it would face an ecological disaster unprecedented even by the destruction of Ravenna. For millenniums, Gathosians would ponder the inexplicable reasons that meteorite storms always wreaked the most havoc during the final days of Air.

The Star Inn was an ancient structure near the north end of Pointilla. Many times, I passed the inn on my trips to market. The inn's weathered sign, hanging perpendicular to the door, featured the carved relief of a longhaired maiden. She was poised between a radiant star above and the unmistakable New Delphi Crystal below. I walked inside and saw another sign. This one said, "Star Inn, owned and operated by Natty and Lyle Nuith." Lyle Nuith was snuggled into an easy chair with his slippered feet propped up on an antique desk. His thick, white hair hung down his back and he appeared as unconstrained and commodious as his ancient inn. I cleared my throat to gain his attention, because he was engrossed in a book. He peered over his reading spectacles, then closed the cover, and placed it on the desk between us. The book was *The Dark Unspoken* by the Human, Gregory Haute. "Fascinating! All about time travel," said Lyle.

Persistent reality was exerting its stubborn bull influence because, not only was Élan entrenched in the Star Inn, he again was occupying room 21. The hotel possessed no communication system to its various rooms, so I walked up to the second floor and located room 21 with little effort. Élan was the perfect Shardasko Warrior and I heard no footsteps as he approached the door. He opened it before I could knock and said, "Good evening."

"I brought *The Universe* with me," I said with a smile. I took the journal from inside my shawl and handed it to him.

Instead of inviting me into his room, he said, "Just a moment, while I stash the book in a safe place." He did not even examine it. I stood awkwardly suspended in the open doorway, while he put *The Universe* away in his backpack.

We walked downstairs and decided to eat in the Star Inn's cafe. It was early evening and the café still empty of other patrons. Ten round tables sat scattered around the candlelit room. The tables looked like swirling disks, with their tie-dyed tablecloths. A gentle breeze blew through the open bank of windows and caused the candlelight to flicker and dance upon the plastered walls.

Élan and I chose one of the tables near the windows and sat comfortably. Between Élan's lingering distrust and my doubt, I could not restrain myself from asking, "This afternoon, you suggested that you were primarily heterosexual, yet you do not want children. Why is your distrust of the future stronger than your sexual urge to procreate?"

"It isn't—or should I say, it wasn't. I admit, I'm a slow starter in the sexual arena, but please remember, I lost my virginity only seven days ago."

"I don't mean to pressure you. After we parted, doubt came calling on me and suggested that you would find me more acceptable if I were a man."

A soft smile sailed across his face and he shook his head, which, I was about to learn, was an expression of disbelief. "If a woman as beautiful as you could doubt your attractiveness, there's no hope for me."

"That's not the reassurance I was hoping for."

He thought for a moment, his eyes staring through me. "I've thought about my abrupt heterosexual statement that I made this afternoon. As an adolescent, I would have told you, I was attracted only to females. Two phases into my Shardasko training, my *Holder* metamorphosed from a beautiful young woman, into an old man. Since Shardasko Warriors use their creative energy in sacred masturbation, offered up to their *Holder*, that old man scared the sexual instinct right out of me. At a time when Human men are experiencing their sexual peak, I was impotent. My sex urge did not return until I surrendered to the old man and absorbed the lesson my *Holder* was attempting to teach me. The lesson was appreciation for both male and female forms, in all their guises, and my ability to respond with compassion to them both. Now it's the virtue of the soul that attracts me, not the gender of the person. If the soul has virtue, I can respond sexually and that's what attracted me to Stellium. I still have preferences concerning attractiveness and you definitely are what I consider extremely attractive; however, I will not allow my preferences to seduce me into the superficial. On the other hand, I still regard children as a drunk might regard his morning hangovers. Children are the unfortunate result of creative ecstasy."

"You can't mean that?"

"Perhaps I don't mean it entirely. I adore my nephew Valent, but I'm glad I'm not responsible for guiding his future."

Élan's outlook on children annoyed me and I was on the verge of declaring him self-centered, which certainly would not have helped. The proprietress of the Star Inn came in the nick of time and set a bowl of warm water between us. The sparse woman walked with a limp and told us, "I'm Natty Nuith, Lyle's wife, welcome to our inn." When I looked at her with my psychic vision, I saw a torn ligament in the small of her back was pulling her off-balance and causing her to limp. I immediately wanted to help with a cure, but my *Emayre* forbade me to perform miracles of this sort. We chatted with Natty for a couple of minutes. "Would you like to select your vegetables from my garden?" she asked, like the good Gathosian cook she soon would prove herself to be.

Élan responded first. "We'd be honored if you'd do the selecting for us this evening. This lady and I could use the extra time to talk about our future together."

"My husband Lyle discovered a bounty of fresh numidian deliciousos in the woods this morning. Would you be interested in trying a few with your meal?"

Élan looked to me for my approval. "Sounds lovely," I agreed.

Élan waited until Natty walked away before saying, "you first," meaning I might rinse my hands first in the bowl of water. I did and he remarked, "Your hands are lovely."

Staring at my hands, I told him, "They're exactly like my mother's hands. She died when I was young, but I have a fleeting memory of her hands and they way they danced up and down, when playing her flute."

"Did she play Gathosian folk music?"

"She did. She wrote hundreds of chants. She liked to create *sagas** too. My father said she was clever and could make up lyrics on the spot for other's amusement." Again, I reached for the memory of my mother as music poured forth from her soul. One of her songs began playing in my head. I hummed a few bars and it made me remember the lyrics, which I sang softly to Élan. "'Lovely-ebonbirds-come-from-distant-lands, to-savor-the-dormant-seeds-of-*tartan-ratu*-from-my-hand. What-sorcery-does-your-spirit-breathe-that-brings-these-seeds-to-life—in-me? Song-so-distant, wings-poised-for-flight, guide-my-heart-through-this-dark-endless-night. Carry-me-to-my-lad's-open-arms-and-I-will-surrender-my-sweetest-charms—to-him, only-him. Song-so-distant-and-wings-poised-for-flight, carry-my-spirit-with-you-in-flight—to-him, only-him.'"

"Your voice is lovely," said Élan.

*Sagas* are dances that increase in intensity and rhythm as they build to a finish. Some have lyrics, but the lyrics are an undercurrent to the music itself. The music is always lyrical, textural, and sensual. Gathosians say, "*Sagas* smolder until they catch fire and burn themselves up."; language origin, Mescale.

"Do you like Gathosian folk music?"

"Love it! I adore its distinctive rhythms and the way it invites people to dance."

"Do you dance?"

His shy little laugh was charming. "A little. Can you tell me the story behind that particular song—about ebonbirds and *tartan ratu*?"

"It's a Gathosian legend involving a great Trinity Witch alchemist named Bellomead. On the planet Namor, grows a white orchid called the *tartan ratu*. Blooms can last up to five phases long. Since a flower is the symbol of the fragile sacrifice of each plant, *tartan ratu* is closely associated with patience and wisdom. Legend says that Bellomead was the first witch to notice that when the *tartan ratu* produced its flowers, flocks of ebonbirds came to feast upon the plant's sweet nectar. The more nectar the ebonbirds consumed, the more sweetly the birds sang and the more exuberant became their mating. Bellomead discovered that *tartan ratu* orchids contained a potent aphrodisiac. She tried eating the flowers, but was unaffected. When she investigated further, she realized that the ebonbirds used *tartan ratu* as an energetic catalyst. During breeding season, the crop of both male and female ebonbirds becomes softer. Their crops secrete a milk-like substance, on which the newly hatched nestlings feed. Ebonbirds produce the hormone prolactin, which is responsible for the production of this milk-like substance, and is similar to the hormone prolactin that controls the production of milk in mammals. Eventually, Bellomead found that the nectar of *tartan ratu* was an extremely potent aphrodisiac when mixed with her own breast milk. *Tartan ratu* nectar mixed with prolactin, is what we call, 'harvest cream,' and what Trinity and Hectarian orders use in their sacred rituals. In it's present form, it's addictive."

"How did you maintain your virginity under the influence of a powerful aphrodisiac?"

"I was strong willed until I saw you."

He blushed and bit his bottom lip before glancing away. When he looked at me again, he asked, "Where are your Trinity rags this evening?"

"It's better that I remain anonymous—don't you agree? A Gathosian woman having dinner with a Human is conspicuous enough, but a Trinity Witch having dinner with a Shardasko Warrior might be cause for much gossip in this small village."

"Shardasko Warriors also try to remain anonymous. We believe that after we are gone, nobody should realize we were ever there."

"I agree with that reasoning. Did you notice the Hectarian brother staring at us in the school courtyard this afternoon?"

"He was difficult to miss. I sensed that he was sexually interested in you. At the time, I wondered if he was your current intimate and regarded my presence as a challenge."

"Brother Remette is the school's assistant administer. He knows that I'm a virgin and he wants to initiate me. I keep a low profile to protect myself from his constant interference, but unfortunately, Remette is as persistent as the reality that motivates him."

"That nervous quiver in your voice tells me there's more to the Brother Remette story than you're admitting."

"In persistent reality, when you leave me, I return to the *Emayre* School and trap myself in a painful relationship with him."

"I'm so sorry, Iosobell."

"It was my mistake, not yours."

Élan was quick to answer. "This time around, I don't want to make any mistakes either," and he moved the bowl closer and scrubbed his hands clean. He stretched out his wet hands and stared at them for a moment before saying, "I used to think my hands were ugly—certainly too large. When I was a child, I hid my extra finger behind the others in a futile attempt to make my hands appear more Gathosian."

"Your extra finger is called a 'pinky' in English?"

He brightened. "The goddess speaks English?"

"I have memories of lives on Earth and speak many Human languages."

"Then perhaps you can help me because Human words have been spinning webs inside my head, all day long. In particular, I remember the word *moksha*. Do you know what it means?" I shook my head no. "It's a Sanskrit word that means liberation."

"What kind of liberation is *moksha*?"

"That's what I am struggling to remember. I think *moksha* represents the yearning for the goal and, perhaps the goal itself.'"

"Trinity Witches call this yeaning, 'self-possession,' meaning the *Emayre* has complete fusion with its lives."

"Do you think self-possession or *moksha* is possible? Can we become both the lover and the beloved? Can the dream ever become the dreamer?" Élan gazed off toward the bank of windows. "I'm remembering more than I did this afternoon about the persistent stream. My *Holder* said it was releasing the truth in doses, so I could consciously digest the information. Many shadows or old moods are attached to my remembering." He reached across the table and covered my hands with his and to my amazement, we were touching for the first time. "Throughout this life, dreams of a dark Gathosian woman have haunted me. That day in persistent reality, when I walked away from my life as a Shardasko Warrior, I thought I might die if I did not find this dark Gathosian woman. When I first saw you, at the Festival of Air, you were holding a parishfruit. As I stood gazing at you for the first time, I recalled a story Kyron told me as a neophyte. When he first saw his future wife, Belinda, she also was holding a red parishfruit in her hands. Were you Belinda, Iosobell?"

"Not exactly. Reincarnation is not a simple linear phenomenon."

"Tell me more."

"When Belinda died, the conscious pool of our mutual soul group experienced her life. My conscious patterns were present within that conscious pool and voluntarily resonated with the full pattern of her being; therefore, in essence, I know her life as I know my own." I waited for him to flinch, but he was as steady as a rock.

"Does Kyron know you carry Belinda's conscious memories?"

"On a spiritual level he does, but whether Kyron, the life, remembers, I cannot say."

"You are as beautiful as Kyron said you were."

"My beauty belongs to this body."

"I was addressing your soul." He looked at me intensely and his eyes drank me in. It was the first look of love he granted me and what fueled it was his memory of me from the persistent stream. Perhaps it was the first sign that persistent reality was yielding to our new agenda. He relaxed and I loved him even more because his passion flowed more strongly. "I intend no exaggeration when I say that you are the most beautiful woman I have ever had the pleasure to behold in any reality. However, your eyes are different from your eyes of persistence. They no longer pierce like most Gathosian eyes. Instead, they are invitingly translucent." He squeezed my hands affectionately. "Now, this evening, in this soft, yellow candlelight, your skin shines with its own darkness and it seems safe to accept my total fascination with you." His mood lightened even more. "Please, tell me more about your ordinary self. Where are your genetic roots?"

"I was born on the planet Oceania in a northern seaport village on Noer Island. Gathosians from Oceania generally have darker skin and I am typical of the women of Oceania. My mother named me Follie Lanai after the purple follie flowers that are abundant on Noer Island."

"Follie Lanai! What a sweet and delightful name. It sounds like a sunny disposition. May I call you Follie?" I smiled and nodded yes. "Tiny follie flowers bloom on the foothills between the Sutcay Valley and the Tyburnian Mountains, especially at the end of monsoon season. The day I gave into the physical urge to love Stellium, the hills were ablaze in a profusion of purple follie flowers. Were you there as a flower watching us fall in love?"

"I don't think so. Perhaps the follie flowers were an omen of what might come, if you learned how to love Stellium."

Élan broke eye contact with me to stare into the light of the votive candle between us. "As I promised, I spoke with him. He was surprised to hear from me so soon."

"But none the less delighted?"

"He said as much and promised to come immediately. I felt

uncomfortable discussing the details over the multidex."

"Did you tell him that I was sending Taro and Cerebow to guide him?"

"Oh! I'm sorry, I forgot to mention that detail because so much was on my mind. When he gets here, I want to talk to him first without you present. You are so radiant that it might be daunting for him. I want to make it perfectly clear that my commitment to him stands."

"Certainly, but Stellium is not as fragile as you might imagine."

"I pray you are right."

"No negative karma exists between Stellium and me. The truth is, you concern me more than Stellium."

"Me? You've owned my imagination since Kyron first mentioned you as Belinda."

"I'm concerned because persistent reality will continue its magnetic attraction for you until you clear the time of your death. As the critical time grows near, it's important that you trust my greater perspective. Once you clear the time of your death, your memory, of what you once regarded as reality, will change."

"If I do manage to survive, how do you see our future unfolding?"

"I believe the best plan is for the three of us to leave Sutcay Tay as soon as you speak to Stellium. We should be long gone from this place before the meteorite storm arrives."

"We will need to go to Gathos so I may retrieve the journals from the bank vault."

"Certainly, and then I want to go to New Delphi."

"Why New Delphi?"

"If we could conceive our child on New Delphi, we could channel greater refined energy into our creation through the Crystal."

"Can you—please give me a little time to feel comfortable with the notion that I am going to be a father? Obviously, I want to make love to you; but fatherhood seems a daunting responsibility."

"We have time for creation as long as you are solidly with me."

"If Stellium agrees, it will be easier for me to accept. One stipulation though—before we leave Sutcay Tay, I must see Kyron. I promised to place his mended wand in his hands and I must keep my promise."

"Not enough time remains for you to return to the Sutcay Valley. The meteorite storm will be here in three days. If you like, I will ask Taro to return Kyron's wand. He can make the round-trip in a few hours."

"I personally promised to return Kyron's wand. It's important to me to keep this last commitment to him."

"This is exactly what I mean about trusting my greater perspective. The condition of both realities is still highly unpredictable. The mere act of you returning to the Sutcay Valley might be enough to initiate your death. Your next few hours should remain calm and focused as possible. We will succeed only if we concentrate on the reality we wish to create."

Élan looked at me oddly and released my hands. "I'm not exactly sure what you mean, but I sense a dark spot in your aura. It's something you're blocking—not telling me—what is it, goddess?"

"If I tell you, you must promise not to react rashly."

He immediately turned into a stony Shardasko Warrior. "If I react rashly, I fail The First Adaptation principal. So tell me what you are shielding and I will know the truth, and we both will know if I fail to adapt."

"As you wish. The coming meteorite storm will cause great devastation to Sutcay Tay. The loss of life and property will surpass the loss on Ravenna thirteen phases ago."

"Kyron—"

"When the storm comes, Kyron will remain in the third dimension and hold open the door to the fourth dimension for neophytes unable to jump."

"I must go—forewarn him so he can prepare."

"He knows—and he also knows he will die as a result."

"You expect me to do nothing?"

"Your urge to go to him is the pull from the persistent stream. Kyron has known his fate for many moons. Why do you think he insisted you take his journals off-planet and place them in a secure vault on Gathos? We do not have the right to interfere in Kyron decision to die."

"If that were strictly true, then your machinations in my life I might classify as both impudent and judgmental."

"You are unprepared for death, while Kyron is at peace because he has fulfilled his core purpose. I'm offering you a chance to take an authentic evolutionary leap. Don't throw this chance away through foolish actions."

"If Kyron dies, he takes the best part of me with him."

"I'm sure Kyron, himself, would tell you that is untrue."

Natty returned with our dinners, interrupting the growing intensity between Élan and me. She chuckled. "Here you go, young folks. Fresh from my garden and hot from my grill." She fussed for a couple of minutes to make sure the table was set to her standard. "Will you be staying in Pointilla for the Festival of Air?" she asked.

"We're leaving in a couple of days," I said.

"Too bad, the village council is planning balloon rides. It should be fun; but it will not be as colorful as a Fire festival or as romantic as a Water festival. Lyle and I met at a Water festival, many phases ago." She chuckled again as she joined with her memories. "I came down a water slide and landed right into his arms. We've been swimming along together ever since."

"That's lovely," I said. "So your life is happy with Lyle?"

"Like most folks, we experience our little deluges; but I can't imagine my deluges with anyone except him."

"Then bless you and Lyle too."

"Thank you, sister."

Natty left, but Élan sat stubbornly staring at his plate of food. "I must go to Kyron," he still persisted.

"If you return to the Sutcay Valley, you will choose death again. Choose death, and it will be a selfish death without Shardasko valor. Choose death, and condemn Stellium to a life without your love and our son to a life without a father. Choose death, and leave Kyron with an unfulfilled dream of you taking Shardasko truths to Humanity and Humanity to a future of perverted Shardasko concepts through Aytinous. Choose death, and you will desert your potential and endorse your own willful ignorance—"

"Stop—" he demanded. He seemed frozen in his dilemma. "What do you mean—my willful ignorance?"

"Willful ignorance, it's the crime that continually breaks the back of the evolutionary camel. Willful ignorance is ignoring our personal opportunities for illumination through rationalizations and reducing every miracle to happenstance. Do you honestly believe that if you die in three days that your *Emayre* will stand before your soul group and proclaim you were an innocent victim? Believe me, Truth will be there as your personal perspective and this time you will be your own harshest critic. You will remember these moments with me, this miracle of opportunity, and you will remember your willful ignorance and become the martyr of your next life."

"But face to face, I know I could persuade Kyron to change his mind."

The compulsion Élan felt for Kyron was even stronger than I imagined. Was the real reason Élan left me that morning in persistent reality, his incredible need for Kyron? "Contact Kyron through meditation or even the multidex. If he agrees to change his mind, then I certainly will welcome his continued presence in the third dimension."

"I've tried that approach. All the way to Pointilla, I struggled to establish a psychic link with him through the prayer beads he gave me. Each time, I sensed him refocusing his mind as if trying to avoid me. As soon as I arrived here, I sent him hourly messages and he has not answered one."

"Kyron has made peace with his fate and released his love for you into his *Emayre*. You must do the same with your love for him."

"When I die and stand before my soul group, truth will ask me why I did not make every effort to save my precious master." Élan was persuasive as he stared at me with his blue-green eyes. "Help me, Follie. You possess incredible powers. Use a little of your power to help me convince Kyron. I know he will listen to the voice that was once his precious Belinda."

"It would be unfair of me to use Belinda's influence over Kyron to get him to change his mind. Don't you understand that temptation counterbalances my gifts and I am the freewill between? I can do only one thing. I will help you contact Kyron, so you can make your own plea."

He brightened considerably. "That's enough, if you help me contact Kyron, I will take it from there."

"My only condition is—let's honor the efforts of this kind woman and eat first."

****

After dinner, we went to Élan's room so I could help him contact Kyron. Standing inside room 21, my memories turned toward persistent reality. A slight nudge and my attention moved forward into a parallel slot of time. Again, I was the innocent girl who awoke to find a hastily scribbled note on the pillow next to mine. A slight flicker of light hit my eyes, and again I rushed toward the window, to glimpse any sign of Élan. As I peered up and down the deserted street, the light was as sharp as glass. His retreat had been soundless. The night before he told me, *A Shardasko Warrior takes what he needs and after he is gone nobody should know he has ever been there*; however, his getaway with me was not so clean. I was pregnant.

Memories kept coming—cruel waves like icy breakers on the northern shore of Noer Island. I trusted a handsome stranger and he left without even a goodbye kiss. Pulling back, my perspective widened. Now I could see that Élan's death was instantaneous and fiery, while mine was slow and bitter. I had metamorphosed into an aimless zombie—rarely present for our child, allowing him to falter in his personal life. I had betrayed myself. It was time for me to face the difficult questions. What personal shadows called to me from that gap, between what was and what could be?

"I apologize for my reverie," I told Élan. "Are you aware that this is the same room we occupied in the persistent stream?"

*Élan* flushed red with embarrassment, as if he committed a social faux pas by again checking into room 21. He quickly handed me the prayer beads, hoping to change the topic. It made no difference. Whatever topic we entertained, the twisting spiral would bring us back to our mutual passion, until we faced our truth. "This is my strongest talismanic link with Kyron," he explained. "If the power of these beads cannot make Kyron respond, then I do not know what can."

Holding the beads in my hands, I tuned into Kyron and told Élan, "Kyron is bathing, in preparation for his evening meditation. Let's wait until he sits down before his altar and then we can engage his full attention."

While waiting for precisely the right moment, I examined the prayer beads more closely. They were beautiful. Considering how important they were to Belinda, and then Kyron, they were a precious gift for Kyron to bestow on Élan. When I examined the two triangular inscription plates, on either end, I was startled because words were missing. "Are you aware words have been eradicated from one of these inscription plates?" I asked.

"I noticed the gap between the phrases, 'I am The Chalice of All Understanding,' and, 'the essence of Love therein.'"

"Words are missing that change the meaning."

He was alert with Shardasko attention. "Is this gap anything like the gap you described between the original intent and where we are at this moment?"

"Exactly."

"Do you know the missing words?"

"I do. The inscription should read, 'I am a Trinity Witch, a Chalice of Understanding. I am The Truth holding The Cup and the essence of Love therein. I drink of my *Emayre* and The Elements that fuse my soul with Life.'"

Élan's eyes glazed over with realization because he heard the truth and knew it. Both of us realized the props of physical reality were slightly askew. Now in this pregnant moment, the persistent stream was losing authority and sinking down into the thinness of nonexistence. "We are Trinity Witches and we are the truth holding the cup," he said.

"Together, we will create a better future. It begins here and now, with you and with me."

Élan's eyes filled with emotion. "When I was crossing the Great Verdant, a moment came when I felt exactly as I do now. The day was particularly difficult for me. Toward evening, I climbed to the top of a mountain and stood gazing out, over the valley I just traversed. My *Holder* told me, 'Physical reality is not a place, but a conjunction of conscious elements that dances intimately before moving on.'" Élan looked up and a tear trailed down his cheek. "Here, with you, I feel myself standing back from the accumulation of indifference with greater perspective."

"What does your greater perspective see?"

"—that my physical senses rarely question reality. Instead, they perpetuate their own blind myths."

We prepared a sacred space to perform our metaphysics and the ceremony was a potent combination of our instinctive efforts, not something we learned through Shardasko or Trinity training. We robbed the bed of its blanket and folded it into the shape of a triangle. Arranging the blanket on the floor, we made sure the vertex of the triangle pointed southeast, toward the Sutcay Valley. Élan took three quartz crystals from his backpack and placed them in another triangular pattern, near the vertex. Élan took the mended wand from its *ackinayon* and draped the prayer beads around the wand several times. Then we sat down on the blanket, not facing each other, but I rested my back against his chest. He wrapped his arms around me so his hands rested on either end of the wand with my hands between his. "Are you ready?" he whispered in my ear.

Was I ready? With Élan's arms wrapped around me, my energy surged up like a fountain of light. I realized then that Cerebow was correct about his smell. I could smell his sweetness, as clean as daybreak in the primeval forest. Within seconds, our combined energy was so powerful that the zaqurlite crystal began glowing with fiery intent. The wand vibrated until it turned itself and pointed southeast.

At that instant, Kyron gasped in shock for he lost control and found himself split into two pieces. His senseless body remained in his *tritum* in mock meditation, while his consciousness materialized a half-form that sat before us at the vertex of the triangle. He struggled for several seconds either to disengage or gain control of his new circumstance. He could do neither. When he realized the truth of his situation, he abruptly stopped struggling and nodded toward us like the adaptable master he will forever be.

Élan nudged me gently with his chin to greet Kyron into our future possibility as planned and I said, "Élan and I want you to reconsider your forthcoming egress from life and instead, consider coming to Earth with us, to help us establish Shardasko truths with Humanity."

Kyron answered with humble authority. "Thank you for your offer, but my *Holder* and I have alternate plans. I am honor-bound to remain on Sutcay Tay during the meteorite storm. I have promised to save the lives of neophytes who cannot yet jump dimensions. When my commitment is complete here, no reason exists for me to remain in this dimension."

"Untrue," challenged Élan. "You have an unfulfilled commitment to me."

Kyron appeared shocked. Despite his shock, his voice became soft, with an indulgent and playful edge, when speaking to Élan. "My prince," said Kyron. "I cannot believe you capable of such blasphemy. As truth is my witness, my finest efforts I've poured into your education." Kyron searched my eyes for support. "Iosobell, do not listen to his foolishness. I more than fulfilled our agreement with this divine neophyte. Please, you must fine-tune journal twenty-two, as agreed."

"Journal twenty-two will be completed," I promised.

Élan persisted, "This has nothing to do with your pre-incarnate agreement with Iosobell. You made a commitment to me when I first knelt at your feet and begged you to guide me to Shardasko mastery. Shardasko precepts are explicit concerning your responsibilities to me. You cannot walk away from me; only I can walk away from you; and I certainly do not release you when I still need your guidance."

"This is ridiculous," said Kyron. "Besides, the morning you left the Sutcay Tay campus, you reclaimed your personal authority."

"I resigned from the school, but our commitment goes deeper than the

Sutcay Tay School."

Kyron shrugged and casually said, "Okay, my fiery prince, you now are a master, a full fledge king of Fire. Are you satisfied?"

"It's not that easy. You cannot make me a master unless a committee of masters examines me and approves my commission to mastery. That committee must interview my peers and students and all must support my ascendancy. Finally, you cannot make me a master unless you place your wand of authority upon my head and declare my mastery with your sacred blessing. How are you going to do that, when you are in the Sutcay Valley and your wand rests here in our hands?"

"It's your Humanness," swore Kyron. "I have nurtured countless Gathosian warriors and not one was as obstinate as you. If all Humans are as stubborn as you are, your task on Earth will be difficult."

Élan abruptly lowered his voice. "My dear master, if you were ill and suffering, my love is strong enough that I would be the first to help you die. But you are healthy and could live another forty phases. Think what we could accomplish in forty phases with your wisdom and Iosobell's knowledge. Help me, even as she is helping me now. Help me become a full-fledged Shardasko master; then I promise, I will let you go."

Kyron weakened a little and I knew his love for Élan was great. Kyron confirmed it with, "My eternal love for you wants to say yes, but I can promise nothing without consulting my *Holder*."

I was impressed with Élan's unique approach and decided it was permissible for me to give Kyron an additional incentive to reconsider his decision to make a heroic exit from life. "Kyron, there's something I think you should know. When I opened the twenty-second journal, the pages were blank except for your words, 'The Universe is the beginning and the end of the journey.'"

Kyron was further shocked and I felt sorry for him and his new dilemma. "I swear! The journal was complete as I could make it. Those twenty-two journals are the prime focus of my life. Do you believe I would skimp on my duty to them?"

"Ask your *Holder* if you do not believe me. Perhaps you are being given another opportunity to remain in this dimension to help us rewrite *The Universe*."

Kyron went internal as if his *Holder* was demanding his attention. Then he said, "I concede that I have much to consider."

"Then I will let you go," said Élan. "One last thing, Iosobell believes not enough time exists for me to return to the Sutcay Valley before the meteorite storm. Whatever you decide, I want to place your mended wand in your hands, as I swore to do."

"As I told you before, the wand is of little importance to me."

"Please?" begged Élan. "I feel as if I've jeopardized my integrity in several ways. I need to keep this pledge to you."

Kyron leaned forward with outstretched arms. "You broke no pledges, my sweet prince. You finally are completely on course. Has Stellium arrived?" asked Kyron.

"I expect he will be here by tomorrow evening," said Élan.

"When he arrives, call me via the multidex. We can meet on Gathos, a few hours later, and you can give me the wand. Now, release me so I may meditate."

Élan and I moved the wand until the zaqurlite crystal again sat in a neutral position. As soon as we did, Kyron's consciousness escaped from the half-form and returned to his body in the Sutcay Valley. So much magnetic energy existed between Kyron and Élan, a glowing outline of Kyron's body remained in the room for ten minutes after he was gone. I've been in many places, both incarnate and disincarnate, and seen many marvelous things; but this special trick—referred to as, "the sentinel glow of love"—is an act of radical passion performed only between soul mates in moments of crisis because they can never fully let go of each other. The glowing outline of Kyron's body slowly dimmed to a lovely amber light. The light so mesmerized Élan that he felt compelled to get up and touch it reverently with his hand. "Perhaps it's not my place to mention this to you," I said, "but it's fairly obvious to me that Kyron is your soul mate."

"Are you sure?"

I explained to Élan about the sentinel glow of love. "Kyron probably did not tell you because he knew it would give you greater power over him, a power that is more like an obligation of mutual surrender. Even if Kyron decides to die, he cannot leave you. He might even believe that he can serve you better from the perspective of your *Emayre*, than here from his body."

"If we truly are soul mates, then Kyron and I share one *Holder*?"

"That's the way I understand it."

"I'm not surprised. Along the way, many clues suggested as much."

I glanced down at the prayer beads wrapped around the wand and noticed the gap between the phrases had vanished and I wasn't surprised either. I picked up the beads to enjoy a closer look. Examining the two end pieces, I could see that all the words appeared, as they were meant to be.

·

# THIRTEEN

**M**y emotions were still in turmoil when we said goodnight. Convincing myself that Élan had enough to consider, I deliberately suppressed the expressing of my emotions in his presence. All this suppression made me jittery as we said goodnight. I walked downstairs and rationalize my anxiety by telling myself that I was overtired. The strange agitation continued to build; and by the time I reached the outskirts of Pointilla, I was uncomfortable with a pressure coming directly from my unconscious mind.

As I reached the trail, leading into the woods, visions of the near future began appearing as staccato flashes between the trees. The farther I walked, the more prolonged and graphic in detail the visions became. My mind filled with morbid snapshots of what soon would befall Sutcay Tay and its people. I could not convince myself that these gruesome visions were unreal nor could I make the visions go away; for through experience, I knew what I foresaw soon be evident in both realities. Then the visions vanished and my personal reality felt so constrained that I seemed to be standing inside an eerie and expectant void.

Physically, I felt wobbly from the abrupt shuttling of my emotions, so I stopped and clutched a tree trunk. Scanning the darkness with my psychic vision, the scene felt singularly suspenseful, as if armies of ghosts hid behind the dark pillars of trees. As I stood there, clinging to my tree, my feelings catalyzed into something lethal that felt like a butcher preparing to carve me up. On the verge of screaming for help, my *Emayre* interrupted with, *accept it*. Its voice so startled me that my body jumped. Now I knew I had nowhere to go but deeper inside, to that pregnant wall at the back of my mind. When I did, all my unrequited emotions from the persistent stream broke through the wall with a flood of painful memories. *You must bridge the gap*, warned my *Emayre*. When it was finally over, silence reigned and I was free as never before. Despite my new sense of freedom, I found myself on the ground and still clinging to a tree trunk. My *Emayre* hovered over me everywhere, telling me in the future, in the present, and in all corners of my being that, *now your knowing has greater meaning, because you can feel the truth.*

Wisdom spoke through the eyes of my *Emayre* telling me, *No one can hurt us like those we love the most, for only those we love the most know how to enter those places within us that truly hurt.*

****

Exhausted from my ordeal along the trail, I was thankful not to encounter Remette upon reaching the school. Once in my room, sleep was the last thing on my mind. I busied myself, packing my personal possessions in my tapestry valise. My belongings were few and my valise sadly limp, even after I packed it with everything I owned. I took my personal toiletries, a foiled box of *tartan ratu*, my mother's flute, that fateful stack of unopened letters returned from my father, and my personal journal. I left my Trinity rags, for that part of my life soon would be over. Once packed, I secured the valise under the floorboard again to retrieve at the last moment before vacating the room.

After packing, I sat in recuperative meditation before my altar and waited for my *Emayre* to speak. Hours of silence followed. Where was its attention? Was it cohabiting with other spirits, as it often said it needed to do? The virtue of my *Emayre* was untainted, as pure as an unblemished flower, but it was candid when it said, *what incarnates consider promiscuity, I consider gaining greater perspective through energetic ecstasy.* Whatever it was doing, it ignored me. I felt alone, but not lonely. This type of silence happened often, especially after emotional clearings, and I knew this is why we incarnates invented the word, "faith."

Right before the emergence of *areé didamé*, I heard the distant wail of the alert sirens in Pointilla. I rushed to the window and watched a fire trail of bright orange meteorites plummeting toward the ground. *It's too early*, I argued with the Queen of Air, who was celebrating her forthcoming nuptials with the King of Fire. The first hail of meteorites struck farther down the mountain. The ground quivered like jelly and I heard several loud explosions. Fire and smoke followed and the screaming seemed to be coming from everywhere.

Lights went on all over the school and many of my Trinity sisters and Hectarian brothers ran out into the courtyard to peer toward the heavens. A few panicked and all questioned what might happen next. My connection to them felt intense, for I knew each person well and loved some as family. I heard each one of their souls humming like a perfect *vitaroon\**. Shame welled up in me because I could not face their incarnate façades with my knowledge that many soon would be dead. My compulsion to rescue them was intense and I wanted to rush outside and scream—get off this doomed world as fast as you can. The familiar voice of Sister Sessabell sounded strained with uncertainty when she suggested that it would be safer to remain inside in case more meteorites were about to fall. Sisters and brothers dashed back inside to various rooms, some alone and others doubling up with closer friends. Remette was not among them and I fully empathized with his cowardice. *I must go to Élan*, I begged, hoping my *Emayre* might answer. Then it was there—*back from your energetic orgies?*

Wait, it advised. These meteorites are only the harbinger to the great storm that will come in two days.

A great deal of frantic activity was happening on the main path to Pointilla. People scurried about in an effort to put out the numerous fires lower in the valley. Plumes of smoke rose in the distance and choked out the green light of *areé didamé,* while black clouds scorched the morning horizon and foreshadowed death. Sisters and brothers again emerged from rooms, to stare questioningly toward the sky. I considered feigning sickness, because I could not bear the notion of seeing the innocent faces of the children.

I peered out the window of my room and saw Remette telling the others, "I slept through the whole thing."

*We both are cowards*, I told myself, *you because you realize too little and me because I realize too much*. I watched as Remette walked toward the administration office and then the white-clad figure of a Shardasko Warrior caught my attention as he walked through the main gate. *I knew it was Stellium*. In response, I instantly sent a telepathic message to Taro and Cerebow to meet me at the Mother of the Forest.

Stellium stopped to speak to a few of my Hectarian brothers standing in the courtyard, apparently to question them concerning my whereabouts. A few seconds later, he was poised before my door. I opened it before he could knock. "You must be Iosobell," he said.

"Stellium?"

"I am forever at your disposal," he said like a typical Shardasko Warrior and we were off to a good start. Peering around him, I could see my Hectarian brothers staring in our direction. Stellium glanced over his shoulder to see what I was peering at and then quickly maneuvered me into the room before shutting the door.

"How did you get here so quickly?"

"My psychic sense advised me that time was of the essence. I took an

---

*A *vitaroon* is a single tone persisting through a piece of Gathosian folk music and is considered the thread on which the melody hangs, like a string on which beads are strung. The *vitaroon* represents the persistent core of perfection that supports each life; language origin, Mescale.

Airfloat to Sheebrun and then hired another airfloat—despite the high cost—to bring me to Pointilla. Apparently it wasn't fast enough because Élan is gone."

I thought I might faint. "Gone where?"

"His note says he went back to the Sutcay Valley to see Kyron." Just then, Remette began hammering on the door. "Who's that?" asked Stellium.

"The bane of persistent reality. It's better Brother Remette doesn't see you."

"No problem. I'll flash to the fourth dimension for five minutes. Is that enough time?"

"I hope so."

"Then back in five and hide my clothes." Stellium sprang into Primal Stance and like a sudden gyrating top, began to spin. In the process, his body slipped from his sandals and out through the neck of his *moodarry* that more or less landed at my feet. At the same time, his long hair came lose from its binding and flared out around him like a circular fan. There was a slight whirling vibration and then a dim flash of light as he vanished upward, inside his hair. The spectacle was so startling and beautiful that I ignored the incessant noise at my door, and watched in wide-eyed wonder.

Remette was screaming, "I know you have a strange man in your room. Open this door, before I break it down."

Snatching Stellium's *moodarry* and sandals, I stashed them under my bed pillow. Then I slipped my robe over my secular clothing to conceal my appearance. As soon as I opened the door, Remette pushed his way inside. Now breathlessness with anticipation, I managed to say, "Sure, come right in. Why wait for an invitation."

Remette continued to rave about "a strange man" as he searched my room. He inspected the bathroom and peered into my closest and when he leaned over and looked under the bed, I resisted a strong urge to kick him in the ass. As usual, he was expecting the obvious—something like a body—so he missed the detail that the strap of Stellium's sandal was hanging out from under my bed pillow. "This is the end," he swore. "Your hours here are numbered." Remette was finally right about something.

I managed to appear only casually annoyed, which made him even angrier. I went to the open door and smiled at my curious Hectarian brothers still across the courtyard. They would not betray me because they disliked Remette too. "Brother Remette is searching for a man," I called out to them. "Would any of you care to help him out?"

Suggestive mutual laughter arose and Brother Sontag yelled, "Yea! Brother Remette! You silly-ass-lily! This is no time to be looking for connections, we may have an elemental crisis on our hands."

"You're infected with meteorite hysteria," I said to Remette. "It happens to lots of people who have never lived on headwater planets before. Why don't you try to rest before classes?"

Remette was fuming. "You're evil. May your soul burn in Chaos." He stalked out through the door and left it standing open. I went over and slammed it shut because Stellium was bound to reappear from the fourth dimension in a few seconds time.

Then the light flashed and again there was a whirling vibration and sure enough, Stellium twirled into the third dimension. The only difference was, this time he appeared to be falling down from his hair. "Keep your voice down," I warned him. "Brother Remette enjoys playing the role of the interminable busybody in this life."

"Sorry," Stellium said. "Spectacular entrances and exits are considered bad form for a Shardasko Warrior."

"You handled it beautifully." Questions swamped my mind, but we needed to find a secure place to talk. "I'm afraid Brother Remette's anger has amassed enough energy to attract some desperate free radicals and we need to leave immediately."

"Is there a rear door?"

"In the bathroom, we can escape through a window."

He glanced down at his nude body. "My clothing, if you don't mind?"

"Under my bed pillow."

Stellium's unexpected arrival and quick disappearance afforded me only a teasing glimpse of his physical beauty and now my eyes took delight in seeing him quite fully in the flesh, for the first time. He crossed the room to my bed to retrieve his clothing and his genitals peeked out between the long tresses of his hair. He had a lingering semi-erection from the energy charge of jumping dimensions. When he turned away to slip his *moodarry* over his head, I could not help noticing the graceful curve of his waist and the smooth, golden skin of his backside. The way he moved forward with one of his hips, suggested his spine was supple and he probably was a natural dancer. He balanced on the edge of my bed to lace up his sandals and retied his long hair, showing me a profile as precise as a carved cameo. His soul group ideals of beauty stamped his physical appearance. His soul group prefers to incarnate through Gathosian forms that burn with a need to express their artistic creativity. They are easy to spot for the fertile light of their creativity burns vibrant blue, around their bodies. When Stellium faced me again and showed me his distinctive face, he came into sharper focus. He definitely reminded me of Dulce. Just like Dulce, Stellium's face was more beautiful than handsome, and both carried the greatest creative compulsions from their soul's group. The scraggly new growth of black beard on his upper lip and chin made him appear wild and that was the epitome of Dulce too. *No wonder Élan is attracted to Stellium.* I told Stellium, "Élan said you were handsome and I definitely agree."

Stellium's blue-black eyes twinkled with psychic clarity. "Élan is eloquent, sometimes his eloquence tends toward hyperbole." Stellium focused on me as he finished tying his sandals. "I must admit that Élan was right on the mark concerning you. He told me you were the most beautiful woman he has ever seen. Élan also said you were wiser than any Shardasko Warrior he ever met."

"Now that is hyperbole!"

"How old are you, little sprite?"

"I'm five Water phases (about twenty years) while my greater consciousness is as old as time itself."

Stellium stood up and took me by the chin, as a mother might hold the chin of a child. His blue-black eyes were uncanny crystal balls of perception. "I see glimpses of the real you through your eyes. On the surface you are a dark woodland nymph, a sexy little elf. Behind your eyes, I see calm black water. I definitely will paint the real you and perhaps this face as well."

****

Stellium was quite a different individual from Élan. From the start, Stellium had no compunctions regarding physical contact with me. After I retrieved my valise from under the floorboard, Stellium went out through the bathroom window first. All the way up the trail, he remained vigilant, as he scanned the entire area for possible danger. In the process, he managed to put his hand on my elbow and waist several times, as if preventing me from tripping over a rock or rough spot on the ground. His gestures of concern for my physical safety were attractive lures and I did not tell him I could walk this trail blindfolded. "Where are we going?" he eventually asked.

"We are headed into a dimension of new possibilities, where we can talk undisturbed."

As confident as can be, he assured me, "I could use a few new possibilities at the moment."

Taking him directly to Mother of the Forest, he again showed no hesitation about sitting next to me on my rock throne. As soon as we sat, he extracted some sheets of folded paper from the pocket of his *moodarry*. "Élan left this letter for me in his room at the Star Inn. I certainly hope you can explain what it means."

I unfold the sheet and saw that Élan's handwriting was small, his Mescale *rilets* (letters) perfect as those of a skilled calligrapher. My eyes could not focus on the handwriting because my hands were trembling. I returned the sheets to Stellium and asked him to read the letter aloud. As Élan's words came through Stellium's mouth, they took on a synergy of emotion that was difficult to abide.

"'Dearest Stellium, when you read this letter, I hope you do not believe

206

I've gone insane. I assure you, I am more conscious than I've been throughout my many twisted lives. These last few days have been pivotal for me. Changes are occurring that I cannot explain to you in this letter and must explain face to face. One thing is clear through this ongoing change— and I wish with all my heart that I could hold you in my arms, at this moment, and convince you of my sincerity—I love you.'"

Stellium stopped reading and began to weep. My immediate compulsion was to comfort him. I restrained my urge because I did not want to short-circuit the expression of his grief. After all, that's what I, as Iosobell, did within the persistent stream. Élan deserted me and I pretended to be okay until I discovered I was pregnant. Then terrified, I indulged in sexual relations with Remette to conceal the truth to the outside world. What a fool I was. How in creation did I think I could conceal that Dulce was half-Human when he was born? Now, as I sat next to Stellium, I felt his abandonment as my own.

Stellium sniffed and wiped his nose with the back of his hand before returning to the letter. "'Thank you for coming into my life and showing me the nonsense of abstinence and the glory of love. Lamentably, I'm still an awkward barbarian compared to you—'" Stellium looked up at me and a slight smile offset his tears. "I once told Élan that he was barbarian because he lived in a stark all-male environment for most of his life." He quietly studied the letter as a ruse to gain his composure before continuing to read. "'—because I lack your creativity, tenderness, and even your incredible Humanity that shines through your gentle, Gathosian heart.' Stellium looked up again. "That certainly is not true. Élan is the most tender and compassionate soul I know.'" He studied the letter again and a tear dropped off his cheek and splashed on the page. "'My desire is to spend a lifetime with you, so that perhaps, I could learn to emulate your unselfishness. Until then, I feel as if I possess only one thread of goodness in me that I must follow. That thread is my conscience telling me that I must act with integrity. I know that I asked you to meet me in Pointilla, but I did not realize then that Kyron's life was in peril. As you also know, I pledged to place his wand of authority in his hands in a mended state. Now I must return to the Sutcay Valley and fulfill this obligation before it's too late.'"

"That makes no sense," I interrupted. "Kyron promised to meet the three of us on Gathos, so Élan could return the wand."

"Wait until the postscript."

"I'm sorry, go ahead."

"'I ask you to extend your faith in me, dear Stellium, for a couple more days. As soon as you read this letter, go to the *Emayre* School and seek out the Trinity Witch Iosobell. I have scrutinized her with all the powers at my disposal and believe she is trustworthy. I'm sorry to be so cryptic concerning her and her part in this matter. Please extend your trust and everything will be clear to you in time. Listen carefully to all she says and she will lead you to safety. By the grace of my *Holder*, I will meet you both in the city of Wacar on the planet Gathos in two days time. Wait for me at the Lord of Eights Hotel, which is a short distance from the spaceport. All my love, Journey. P.S. Dear Iosobell, a couple of hours after you left the Star Inn, Lyle Nuith brought me a message and slipped it under my door. The message was from Kyron and he asked me to return to the Sutcay Valley instead of meeting us on Gathos as we discussed earlier. Obviously, I could not refuse. I plan to be quick and meet you in Wacar as promised. I'm aware of my responsibility to you and I hold this committment as sacred as my allegiance to Kyron and my love for Stellium. My first wish is that I could tell Stellium the details of my persistent missteps face to face, but as circumstances stand, it is impossible. I do not expect him to wait even another hour to hear the truth; therefore, feel free to tell him everything, even as you told me. If I can be proud of anything in this life, it is that I have been completely candid with Stellium concerning the sordid details of my life. Love to you both, Journey.'"

Later, when I read the letter over several times, I would feel the cruelty of the persistent stream and realize it still had enough authority, to dig its claws into my heart. I understood more fully that Élan did not hastily scrawl the letter—at least this part was different from the persistent stream. And this letter he addressed to Stellium, not to me. Its words were passionate, committed, and bled with the agony of dilemma. Élan possessed a deep abiding love for Stellium, but I still regarded the letter as another farewell note. Élan had left again and this time he left two people in the lurch.

****

"I don't believe Kyron would ask Élan to jeopardize his life by returning to the Sutcay Valley at this dangerous time," I said.

"As Élan suggested, you need to tell me everything."

Like Élan, Stellium was not prepared to share energetic ecstasy with me, so I could not give him my truth in an instant. Still he expressed fewer apprehensions than Élan, mostly because Élan had laid a foundation of trust in Stellium that helped me cut through his protective façades. It was difficult for him to believe that in the persistence stream, he never came to Sutcay Tay or met Élan. Stellium could not help crying when I told him Élan might die in just two-days time.

It took three hours to bring Stellium up to date and answer his questions. Afterward, he swore to be solidly with me and was prepared to do anything to make sure Élan lived. Then Stellium told me about an incident that made me think Kyron might be supporting the new agenda too. Stellium cryptically informed me, "The subject in this painting is still hiding in the shadows."

"What do you mean?"

"What I mean is after Élan contacted me and asked me to come here, Kyron arrived at the door of my *tritum*. He was eager to endorse the idea that I should leave for Pointilla immediately. I possess a couple of paintings that are precious to me. They were too bulky to pack and bring along and Kyron was so insistent that I leave immediately, he helped me pack my paintings and art supplies and promised to ship them to my mother on Earth for safekeeping." Stellium put a hand into his pocket and pulled out a lumpy sealed envelope. "And then there is this. Élan left this envelope behind for you."

Taking the rather weighty envelope, I read, "Follie," that Élan wrote in the middle. Inside, I found the jade prayer beads along with another letter. Stellium gave me a look of concern. "Those beads are Élan's talismanic connection to Kyron. I can't believe he would leave them behind."

I read the letter aloud. "Dear Follie, after we parted this evening, I sat in meditation with my *Holder*. It told me that it wanted me to view the critical events within the persistent stream, in detail. Then I saw a future that I hope never to repeat. I saw myself running away on that fateful morning and leaving you alone in room 21. This part truly was not new for me, for I have relieved broken segments of my egress, since you unveiled the truth, earlier today. This time, however, my perspective broadened, because part of me stayed behind to watch my escape. The first thing I noticed was I forgot my knife on the bedside table. This knife is a real physical object in my present life and my one tangible legacy from my father. My vision skipped forward and I saw Dulce on his ninth birthday—the morning you gave him this same knife and told him it once belonged to his father. Then, time went into a sprint and I was many phases into the future and living my next life. It's difficult to explain my future perspective in actual words, but somehow I'm simultaneously live inside both a male and female body. A scene jells and I find my two future selves face to face with Dulce. He gazes into the eyes of my masculine self, yet does not recognize me as his father or his loving soul mate that he married on the steps of the Library of All Creation. My knife is poised in his hands and then he abruptly conceals it inside his shirt. His intention is to do as much damage as possible with the knife before committing suicide. I know he is insane and insane partly because of my neglect. That's why I take the knife away from him—for safekeeping. Then I am killing something with the knife that is not manifest, yet has a direct effect on reality. The male part of me dies in this confrontation and the female part of me lives on to mourn my masculine self.

When I emerged from the vision, and was fully myself, I remembered the knife no longer was in my possession. I gave the knife to Kyron, the morning I left the Sutcay Valley. This cheered me—to realize that circumstances were at least a shade different, this time. You told me it's more difficult to change the stream of persistence than we believe, but I am committed to trying. Dulce will be born between us—this I now accept as my true destiny. As I write this letter, I want you to know that I accept and welcome this destiny with my whole heart and pray you will forgive my initial shock upon hearing the truth. I swear I will father our child in the most loving way I know how. As a symbol that I will keep my promise, I consciously give you my most precious possession, these prayer beads instead of a forgotten knife. These beads represent much more than my connection to Kyron or even my promise that I will return. These beads once were a symbol of your Trinity Witch authority. By returning them to you, I feel the gap between the persistent stream and new reality bridged with the love they represent. Through the grace of my *Holder*, you, Stellium, and I will read the inscriptions plates to Dulce. Together we will explain the whole truth, so he can remember the music that first spun out life from the conservatory of creation.' *Ejesay epay*, Journey."

"I understand even less than before," said Stellium. "What in creation is he talking about?"

"His *Holder* showed him his next life as a martyr if the persistent stream remains a dominant force."

"How does Élan come to find himself in two bodies in his next life?"

"If Élan dies in two days, he will be reborn almost immediately. When a soul is reborn under pressured circumstances, it carries a strong karmic burden. In his next life, he will be a woman named Mellé. As Mellé, she will eventually meet and marry Dulce. Mellé will continue her relentless obedience to the glittering illusions of the persistent stream and Dulce will continue to cheat his soul mates, and deny his *Emayre*. Eventually, an unscrupulous scientist will become involved in their lives and he will clone Mellé and put part of her consciousness into a male body, which she will call Michael. In the persistent stream, these three shattered souls—Mellé, Michael, and Dulce—finally find themselves at the foot of the New Delphi Crystal. There, they encounter a free-radical specter lured into this dimension by the Trinity hierarchy of New Delphi. This specter kills Michael and because of his abrupt death, he will remain a split-off from Mellé for six thousand phases."

"That's horrible. What happens to Dulce?"

"Dulce, who is the quintessence of creativity between Michael and Mellé, lives on in obscurity and pain. When he dies, his soul does not incarnate for eons. When the Dulce stream of consciousness finally resolves to be reborn, it immediately finds itself in the position of resolving its ancient dilemma with Mellé and Michael."

****

The only reason for lingering so long at Mother of the Forest was to wait for Taro and Cerebow to return. Six hours after Stellium and I arrived at that sacred spot, they still had not appeared. Stellium agreed to help me search and we spent an additional two hours combing the woods, while I frequently made my gnosis bat call, to alert them to my presence.

Stellium suggested we take a break and find food and water. This sounded like a sensible suggestion. I was weary from not sleeping the night before. We walked into Pointilla and the open-air markets were on the verge of closing, so we were able to buy pears, bread, cheese, and beer at bargain prices. We stopped in the lobby of the Star Inn and Natty was on duty at the desk. "My goodness!" she exclaimed to Stellium. "When you said that you wanted to locate your sister, I had no notion that you meant this lovely young lady."

"Élan is my betrothed," I told Natty, "Was there anything unusual concerning the message that came for him?"

"Lyle was at the front desk and mentioned the message for *Jai* (mister, or sir) Cœur was the last to come through before the meteorite storm struck. Ten minutes later, he came downstairs and told Lyle that he needed to leave. He paid for the room for two extra nights with a generous tip and said he wanted to leave his backpack in the room for you two to find."

"Did he seem agitated?" asked Stellium.

"Lyle said he seemed to be in a rush. Is anything wrong?"

"No," said Stellium, "only an unanswered mystery. Do you mind if I use your multidex to see if I can locate him?"

"Help yourself," said Natty. While Stellium sent a message to Kyron to inquire if he, indeed, asked Élan to return to the Sutcay Valley and if he had—why, Natty took me into the café. She loaned me a couple of plates, a knife, and two beer glasses. While we were there, she advised, "Your young man loves you and he will return. I saw the way you two were holding hands last evening. He's a fine man." Then she gave me a gentle and reassuring squeeze. When she did, she pulled healing energy through me and mended the torn ligament in her back. It wasn't anything either of us did consciously, but rather something her *Emayre* helped her to do. Naturally, I was delighted to act as the conduit for her healing. Neither Natty nor I acknowledged this miracle openly; but the incident taught me a valuable lesson. It was inappropriate for me to project healing on anyone. I merely needed to be receptive to others and allow them to take what they needed, through me.

Stellium and I walked upstairs to that fateful room 21, and I gave a cursory inspection to the few belongings Élan left behind. On the end of the bed, sat his backpack, exactly where I saw it the night before. He had left most of his possessions behind—his personal journal and quartz crystals, his lucky tortoise shell, extra clothing, and even his money.

Between Stellium and me, we determined that the only missing items were Kyron's *ackinayon* with the wand, the twenty-second journal, and the clothing Élan was wearing.

****

Now that Stellium was here, all my previous aversions to room 21 disappeared. The security I felt with him surpassed any lingering doubts about Élan. Stellium and I never met in the persistent stream and our freedom from that deadweight, afforded us an opportunity to dance to any tune we could imagine. Regardless of the specks of cynicism in his personality, I felt an enthusiastic sexual attraction for him. He was tenacious, compassionate, psychic, and completely spiritual. When I gazed into his rutilates, I witnessed his foundation in the Library of All Creation and realized how essential he was in bringing Élan up from the rut of the persistent stream.

I sat on one of the chairs and took off my sandals. Stellium sliced one of the pears and gave me half, along with a wedge of cheese and a piece of bread. I handed Stellium a glass for his beer and he said, "I prefer drinking mine from the bottle—thank you." While we ate, Stellium told me more about his present life. He still claimed that it was difficult to believe that in the persistent stream, he never met Élan. Stellium shook his head as he pondered a life he nearly missed. "The way you describe the persistent stream—it sounds more like the reality that trapped me, before I entered Shardasko training." He laughed with a breathy huff. "Who knows? Maybe I arrived in this new reality ahead of you both and I've been waiting for you for the past five phases."

"Can you tell me how you got here ahead of us?"

He fidgeted, bringing both of his feet up so he was sitting cross-legged on his chair and his plate was balanced on his lap. "I'd need to go all the way back to my feelings when I was growing up to explain my initial jump."

"I'm listening."

He thought for a moment and took a slug of beer from his bottle. "Most of this life, I felt grossly off my proper path—deeply flawed, as if my constant missteps set me aside from real happiness."

"Someone as beautiful and talented as you?"

"I felt neither beautiful nor talented, just odd and slightly out of sync. I certainly chose a difficult path when I agreed to be born as a Gathosian on Earth between the cold Pacific Ocean and the ugly strip malls of Southern California. As a child and adolescent, it wasn't as if I was a willful problem for my parents or society. If anything, I acquiesced too freely to the indignities that leave most people in a rage. My exterior control always remained smooth, so no one guessed I felt angry and cheated."

"What was going on inside you?"

"My feelings were spastic with violent mood swings and I was self-destructive as a teenager; although, I was notorious for making overly optimistic new starts. You know—I became the strong starter who finished last. As soon as I was old enough, I recklessly began falling in love with a string of controlling people, hoping they might rescue me from my bewilderment. Sometimes I would abruptly wake up and come to my senses and find myself trapped in the most humiliating situations and wondering how I could make my fastest escape."

"Were these lovers men or women?"

"I was attracted to both women and men, but my earliest relationships were with Human girls—all blondes. A blonde would walk into the room, and for me everyone else disappeared. To this day, I've never even kissed a Gathosian woman, but you make me want to try." He flexed his eyebrows in a suggestive way, which made me smile. "Anyway, my experiences with Humans all ended in dramatic failures. I lost my virginity to a honey-toned blonde, named Heidi, when I was fifteen. From the start, she said I was 'too intense.' She mocked me when I cried and for some reason, I couldn't make love without crying. She criticized my art, especially my erotic drawings of men and eventually, she created off-limit zones on her body—her breasts, her ass, and her armpits. Then came a short affair with the blonde Kate. Everything needed to be in perfect order before we could make love, which warred against my need for spontaneity. She insisted that we hang our clothes up in the closet before making love, and was adamant that the closet door needed to be shut. She said I was a lousy lover and it was my fault that she couldn't reach orgasm. She was right; I was a lousy lover. Then three dates into what I thought might be a promising relationship with a sun-streaked blonde named Lori, she said, 'Oh Gawd! I never realized your tongue was black. Is your thing black too?' When she said that, my black thing shriveled up with shame."

"A few Human women told me they were attracted to me because I was different. Since it seemed to my advantage that I was different, I eventually went to great lengths to exaggerate my differences. This drove many women away and me into absurd parodies of myself. Granted, my forced idiosyncrasies sabotaged my relationships with the Mexican beauty Flora, my fellow art student Heather, and even my fellow surfer, Nicole. If the relationship reached the stage of making love, they set their conditions and I set mine. Under these circumstances, I experienced increasing difficulties reaching even minor physical orgasms and I no longer cried when I made love. When the strawberry blonde, Amy, took me home to meet her folks, as an act of rebellion against her parents, she told me afterward, 'Let's just be friends.' 'Let's be friends' meant I agreed to be forever at her disposal, which gave her carte blanche access to me as a sounding board for her unrequited miseries."

"When I was nineteen, I experienced a brief affair with a man. His name was Charles and he was an artist from England, teaching a class in holographic kinetics. He was fifteen years my senior and knew how to give me the unmitigated intensity I desired. When we first made love, I was able to cry again. Charles really wasn't interested in a relationship either and I thought my heart was going to break when he said, 'It's time to dry your eyes and learn the rules of the game.' He said a few other cruel things too like—'Face it, you're a bloody queer, just like me.'

"Only in retrospect, can I understand that the polarized society of Earth dominated me and made me believe I had to decide that I was queer. I already considered myself odd, so why not queer. After Charles, I forgot about the relationship part and decided to be tough. I lost myself in sexual lust. My favorite expression was, 'no strings attached.' About two hundred men later, I got into a life-threatening situation, when I went with a complete stranger to a motel room and found three other men waiting. I had years of martial arts training, but was no match for four Human men. The last thing I remembered was one of them calling me, 'a goddamn queer,' and telling me, 'Go back to whatever Gathosian hellhole you crawled out of.' As soon as I was released from hospital, I decided to take their advice and a few weeks later, I was on my way home to the Island Worlds of Gathos."

"How did you get into Shardasko training?"

"My ship made a layover on Mars, which gave me a few days to see my dad. One evening, I went into a tavern and an old Shardasko Warrior was there. A circle of people were sitting around him and he was telling stories—absolute legends about Shardasko Warriors jumping dimensions and masters he once knew. That night, my *Holder* came to me in a lucid dream, only at the time, I did not realize it was my *Holder* or that I was experiencing a lucid dream. In the dream, I see a big wave coming and I'm terrified that I am going to drown. This relentless wave comes crashing over me and yet afterward, miraculously I am still alive."

"One month later, I found myself on the planet Numida, kneeling before the great Master Lumenet. To him, I confessed fully what I thought were my many sins. I told him I considered myself homosexual and did not know if I could endure being in a society of abstinent brothers. I desperately needed to find new direction in my life, so I told him about the dream and the voice. Lumenet told me, 'you awoke your *Holder*. It washed over you and left its imprint upon you. That imprint has brought you to me. Together, with your *Holder*, I will teach you what I know about the meaning behind reality. All the love and intensity that you have been wasting on the shadow forms of men and women now belongs to your *Holder*. If you want the intensity and love to grow, your complete loyalty is required. Masturbate only in a mood of complete trust and surrender and offer your complete creative essence to your *Holder* and your past encounters with mere mortals will pale by comparison.'"

At the time, I wasn't exactly astounded with Master Lumenet's interpretation of my dream nor was I impressed with the advice of an abstinent master on the proper way to masturbate. Only my desperation to find a new way made me accept the vow of abstinence. Master Lumenet made the situation easier by giving me a private room. One of the first things he did was help me unravel my past behavior. He said I had sought another person who could mirror me, so I could better understand myself, but when I looked outside myself, to better see myself, I ran into endless difficulties because of the distortions everyone projects." Stellium was quiet as he took another slug of beer. "It was my *Holder* that helped me find what I was looking for. When I found my complete self, it was a flawless mirror and directed me toward my higher purpose. Only then did I realize that I was not flawed; rather, I knew I was divine and blessed with unique gifts."

"Did your *Holder* tell you how beautiful you are?"

Stellium gazed at the floor and was slightly self-conscious. "We experienced our moments. When I finished my *quarrying* a day early, Master Lumenet—like all Shardasko masters—told me I was not living up to my potential. When I heard that news, I did not feel despondent, as many warriors do. I felt stronger. I knew I could do whatever I wanted with my life. I felt positive, healthy, and connected to my higher purpose. It did not take me long to decide to return to Earth and pursue my artistic career with greater zeal."

"What prompted you to come to Sutcay Tay instead?"

"Master Lumenet reminded me that the Sutcay Tay School needed someone to refresh the frescos on the Celestial Air Palace, but I think I came to Sutcay Tay to prove to myself that I could be complete no matter where I am geographically. Then the moment I laid eyes on Élan, I felt that old, familiar catch in my heart. For me, Élan felt like the ultimate test. I had to know if I could trust myself in a loving relationship and if I could honestly love him minus my projections. Élan was eager, but I made him wait." Stellium laughed again and his laugh was delightful and filled with compassion for his previous self. "It was the first time I ever made a potential lover wait for me."

"What did you learn by waiting?"

"I learned that Élan and I are different, but I could love him in spite of our differences. Élan was a virgin struggling to come to terms with his sexual need, while I was a reformed, sexual clown, struggling to balance between my past cynicism and Élan's obvious purity of heart, which I very much envied."

"You envied Élan?"

"Absolutely, I envied him. I envied his ability to keep himself pure and yet be open and wise."

"He must have convinced you of his purity of heart. It appears to me as if you trust him implicitly."

"Do you think I'm foolish to trust another person again, as much as I trust Élan?"

"If Élan were the same individual as he was in the persistent reality, perhaps; but you are in love with the Élan of unlimited potential."

"So why has even the unlimited-potential Élan deserted us?"

"Don't give up hope, Stellium, I want this new reality to succeed for you too. A great deal of genius is waiting to collaborate with you if your evolution continues. Many soul groups will offer you inspiration and I'm sure you will manifest an art that will be unique genius at its finest."

"I don't know what to say to such a magnanimous offer." He fell silent before confiding, "I think I might have come to this wonderful party merely to love you and Élan."

"*E tres zolee\**," I said.

"*E tres zolee*," Stellium offered in return. He hesitated, "Although I'm no longer certain I remember how to love a woman."

****

Stellium and I filled our empty beer bottles with drinking water from the inn before returning to the woods a second time to look for Taro and Cerebow. While we were searching, another meteorite storm hit. In daylight, the fireworks were not as obvious, making the situation even more dangerous. This time, the meteorites appeared smaller and more numerous and fell toward the southeast, nearer the population centers of Tacings. Both of us stopped in our tracks, as hundreds of meteorites caught the late-day sunlight of Insanio. It was certain these fireballs were now destroying lives. I held my breath, wondering if again this was the start of The Big One.

We continued to search for Taro and Cerebow, but to no avail. The day grew short and the woods took on the hushed and drowsy songs of early evening. The serene forest seemed a contrast to my worrisome mood. The temperature cooled slightly and the trees perfumed the air with a sweet balsamic scent. None of this soothed me, because the smell of burning wood in the distance, undercut the calm. For the third time, Stellium reminded me, "We better think about wrapping up our search until

*\*E tres zolee*, meaning, "I love you." On the scale of I-love-yous, *e tres zolee* is probably halfway to *ejesay epay*. *E tres zolee* has sexual connotations and comes close to meaning, "You fascinate me; and if this fascination holds between us, I am willing to pursue this relationship all the way to *ejesay epay*; language origin, Mescale.

tomorrow morning. It's going to get dark soon."

"Okay, but first let me talk to Mother of The Forest. I want to offer her my gratitude for all she has done to help me and ask her root eyes to watch throughout this night for Taro and Cerebow."

"You have the ability to communicate with trees?"

The tone of Stellium's voice suggested that he thought communication between Gathosians and trees was slightly odd. "It's a common Trinity Witch skill, taught to novitiates in their first few moons of training. Some witches are better at it than others.

"Okay, why not?" We walked a short distance to a nearby streamlet, rinsed out the beer bottles, and filled them with fresh water. Stellium was a curious and eager student and asked, "What next, sprite?"

"Hold the bottle against your chest and allow your love to flow into the water. Now repeat after me—Eternal Waters, Primordial Ocean of All Life, bring your love and blessings into this water and make it a sacrament that I might offer to Mother of the Forest." Stellium did as I instructed and repeated my words. Then together, we returned to Mother and stood beneath her sheltering limbs. "Listen," I told Stellium. "This tree is one with the element Wind. She knows how to lean into the evening breeze, in specific ways, that will allow her to speak to us."

"But there is no breeze. It is extremely calm this evening."

"The Mother will call out to Wind and it will come to serve her." Wind was still far away, but I could hear it approaching, hear it tickling the faraway treetops, as Mother beckoned with her need.

"What's that?" asked Stellium.

"It's the voice of Wind coming over Mount Tyburnian."

"What's it saying?"

"Wind says that it's coming to help Mother speak. Put your ear against her trunk and listen carefully." He hesitated. "Go ahead, she is a friendly tree, quite extroverted." He decided it was okay to play my game, so he put his ear against the trunk and I put my hand on his shoulder and tuned his energy, just a tad, to help him hear with better clarity. "Now you tell me—what is Mother saying?"

"I think I hear her calling out to someone she calls, 'black daughter.'"

"That's me. Mother calls me black daughter."

His eyes squinted to better concentrate on the new language he was hearing. "Wow!" he said after a moment. "I understood that clearly. Mother says she personally has not seen Cerebow or Taro. However, her sister trees, farther down the mountain, tell her that Cerebow and Taro encountered Élan along the trail and they went with him."

Mother spoke privately to me. *I hear—hear your concern; but do not fret,* she sang through Wind. *I—I have a direct connection to Divine Love for she is Queen of The Universe. She—she tells me Cerebow is deeply connected to your sensual body and that's is why she remained with Élan. Don't you know by now, Iosobell? Even the body seeks eternity within Source?*

Upon hearing that, I staggered for The Mother's one brief statement destroyed my structure of reality. "What's wrong?" asked Stellium.

I ignored Stellium, asking, "Is that right, Mother?"

*That's right, right, right, right,* she laughed through Wind. *My innocent child, nothing is outside the queendom of Source. We are One.*

"Tell me!" demanded Stellium. "What's she saying?"

I repeated Mother's words and Stellium said, "Okay, we are all one. What's new about that statement?"

A universe of difference exists between the statement, "We are one" and the experience, "We are One!" How could I explain the experience without rolling myself in a ball of ridiculous superlatives? In vain, I tried to explain. "I am a wave that's been swallowed by the ocean."

"Yeah, I still don't get it," he admitted.

"How about? I am now Mount Tyburnian and capable of swallowing all of Sutcay Tay in one gulp."

He shrugged. "Can you throw anymore metaphors my way to help me understand?"

The experience of, "We are one" is a series of experiential gates we pass through. Each time we do, our consciousness opens a wee bit more and we include more and more of reality into our hearts. The ultimate epiphany is that we always have been and forever will remain within Source. I struggled to explain this to Stellium, but the experience was impossible to explain to anyone. It proved to me that language reduces the sensations of transcendental experience. Perhaps the supreme irony was that consciousness was not a communicative gesture, but rather an experiential interface, our understanding surrendering to The Whole.

I told Mother of The Forest, "I might not see you again in this life; but before we go, we wanted to offer you our love and gratitude for allowing us to use your energy to create this outdoor temple."

*You—you are so welcome,* she sang. *Your—your tiny dilemma has brought excitement into our lives. I—I hope you do not mind, but I have shared your love story with all my sisters between here and the Sutcay Valley. Many, many trees even now repeat your name in Élan's ears, so he may not forget you.*

"Thank you, Mother. Élan and I are pleased to perform our small gestures of love for your amusement. Stellium and I have brought you a token of our gratitude, water that we have infused with our love. It's blessed by the Eternal Waters from which we all sprang."

*I—I will accept it,* she said. Taking turns, we ceremoniously poured the water from each of our bottles upon the roots of the tree. I got down on my hands and knees and tenderly kissed one of the Mother's eyes, the one that had always seemed profound to me.

****

It was early evening when we returned to Pointilla. From the numerous and lingering fires, smoke spiked the evening air. When we walked into the inn, Lyle Nuith handed us three messages. All three were from Kyron. The words on the first message leapt off the page. "Iosobell, I could say much about your inattention to your goals and in my defense. Instead, I will say only that I positively did not ask Élan to return to the Sutcay Valley and, as far as I know, he is not here now. If he shows up at my threshold, you can bet your precious patch across persistent reality that I will put him on the first flight for Sheebrun and then Gathos. La Teeair Forma, Shardasko Master, Sutcay Tay School."

After Stellium read the message, he waved it in the air as if it were too hot to hold. "I feel the heat!" he exclaimed.

I held up the second note, posted a half hour later and Kyron's tone had turned conciliatory. "After searching the campus, I found Élan meditating in the Eternal Waters Sanctuary. For the moment, he is safe. He told me that neither of you knew he planned to return here; therefore, I sincerely apologize for my previous outburst. La Teeair."

The third message said, "Dear Iosobell and Stellium, please do this new reality a favor and get off Sutcay Tay as soon as possible, so at least Élan and I do not have to worry about your safety. Élan asked me to tell you that he encountered Cerebow in the woods and she would not leave him. Of course, Taro would not leave Cerebow. Élan put them both in the fourth dimension and they will stay there until someone can retrieve them and escort them to safety. Frankly, I feel frustrated at this moment. Élan refuses to leave me and I certainly cannot put him in stasis in the fourth dimension. I have never signed my Shardasko moniker before, but I do so now. I, Kyron, swear upon my moniker that I will find a way to protect my most precious legacy. Kyron."

I could do nothing to impede Élan's freewill, but I wanted to jump over to the Sutcay Valley and giving him a piece of my agitated mind. Stellium thought this was the wrong approach and after consideration, I did too. "Kyron has more influence over Élan than anyone," said Stellium. "We should take Kyron's advice and get off Sutcay Tay as soon as possible. If we are off this planet, in a place of relative safety, we will act as a beacon for Élan and bring him safely to us."

*I completely agree*, said my *Emayre*.

I agreed to go and allow Kyron to handle the predicament of keeping Élan alive, but it was difficult. I had initiated the changes and now the situation suggested I had to release my control and trust others. "It's probably another test," Stellium reminded me.

****

We went upstairs to room 21 to retrieve Élan's belongings and the moment we opened the door, I spied a woman standing across the room. She was gazing out the window with her back turned toward us. She turned when she heard us enter and Stellium exclaimed, "Holy shit!" in English vernacular, when he saw the woman looked exactly like me. Even I was baffled. Had Élan's decision to return to the Sutcay Valley caused the persistent stream to loop back over the new reality? Was I now seeing myself in a parallel timeline? The woman wore a red dress I never owned. Then I realized that this dress was Belinda's wedding dress from the day she wed Kyron. The figure was a half-form and that meant it did not have access to a third dimensional body. This was an advantage for Stellium and me, because apparitions rarely possess the power incarnates believe if a safe distance of a few meters is maintained. Stellium demanded, "Who are you?"

"Good evening," she said. "I'm sorry my appearance startled you, but I've sustained this vision of myself for so long, it feels quite comfortable." She read my mind with ease and laughed over my apprehension and fear. Her laughter made my ears ring for her voice was the sound of the tinkling bell of illumination. "Please relax, you have nothing to fear from me. Allow me to introduce myself. I am Kyron and Élan's *Emayre*. I'm here to help my lives fulfill their chosen destinies. This evening I've come to open a path to understanding for you both." She extended her hands to me and expected me to grasp them.

"Your energy is strong and sufficiently dissimilar to mine," I said.

Her laugh again was a tinkling bell. "I've been dancing with your *Emayre*. Inside the dance, we synchronized our energy as we drew energetic meaning from are physical lives. That encounter gave me intimate knowledge of you. Now, do not delay. Gather your courage and find the strength to take my hands and gaze deeply into my eyes." When I did, it was uncanny, because I was looking into an infinity mirror of myself. Then she gave me the truth in an instant, in a moment of energetic union filled with unblemished love. "Now you may give it to Stellium," she said.

"I will," I told her.

"Good, now have faith in your *Emayres* at these dark hours, as we have faith in you," and she promptly disappeared, leaving not a speck or whiff of herself behind.

# FOURTEEN

"Okay Sprite, give it to me as Élan's *Holder* gave it to you," said Stellium. We embraced and it took a moment to synchronize our energies. Then eye into his eye, I led Stellium into an energetic dance created by the impressions Élan's *Emayre* left in me. The dance, not I, opened Stellium and reflected the message onto the screen of his conscious mind. On the tail of this great reflection, clung my hopes and desires, so he received a bigger package than even I received. His mouth dropped open in shock. "Me, Noveil Esay, father a child?"

"Then you're keen on the idea?"

"Keen? I feel all pink and fuzzy over the mere notion of being a father. I can see her already. She is exquisite." Neither of us comprehended the larger fate we set in motion, when Stellium agreed to help me create a body for Kyron's next incarnation.

When Élan's *Emayre* took my hands, I was overwhelmed with new information. The *Emayre* had ebbed away, yet as one can see the pattern of waves imprinted in the sand, I could look back into my memory, and comb the imprint for clues.

Despite our initial confusion, we understood this *Emayre* had asked Élan to return to the Sutcay Tay Valley on Kyron's behalf. Kyron wanted to spare Élan further pain; however, their *Emayre* realized that Kyron's death offered Élan an unprecedented opportunity. During the meteorite storm, a moment would occur when their *Emayre* would descend into the fourth dimension and fabricate a zone of safety. The three would meet within that safety zone and their interactions would affect the future in a profound way. As I examined the clues for further information, I sensed a greater danger awaiting Élan than the meteorite storm. The danger was something fateful, engulfing, and perhaps too enormous for one soul to sustain.

****

Stellium and I caught the last airfloat for Tacings. The airfloat was a local and made a dozen stops on route. The smokey air created a black underbelly to the clouds and each time we landed, I felt pressure on my chest from the air pollution. When the airfloat landed at the Tacings spaceport, it was half past *shahaut*. For over two hours, we waited with a few other subdued and drowsy travelers for the night flight to Wacar. We stared aimlessly at a screen that ran perpetual news coverage from Gathos. A simu-image of a male reporter dominated the screen that called itself Max Construe. In this time, simu-imagining was in its infancy, so Max appeared synthetically good-looking. The hair gleamed but never moved and the occasional blinking eyes were two lifeless, black holes. The voice was a better simulation—a reassuring, deep baritone that maintained an even modulation throughout the most grisly news reports. Six thousand phases in the future, later editions of Max Construe still existed. In the future, it appeared impressively physical—programmers would solve the vacant eye glitch—but the black, shiny hair would remain Max Construe's trademark.

Max reported that the Afen comet would conjunct Insanio within the next twelve hours. A backdrop screen showed yellow arrows fluttering and arching, which illustrated the assumed trajectory of Afen. This killer comet appeared harmless and even pretty as a simulation—similar to a bright burst of fireworks against a nighttime sky. "This is Max Construe reporting, keeping you updated with continuous live coverage on the approach of the Afen Comet. Meteorscopes on orbiting satellites are giving us minute-by-minute updates. Again, for you folks just tuning in, the Galaxy Council has issued a meteorite watch for the planets, Hubbard Station, Kujairani, Lalaseair, and Sutcay Tay. Citizens of these four headwater planets should stay close to shelter in case the situation takes a turn for the worst."

Tacings was one of the larger cities on Sutcay Tay, with a population of slightly over three million. The second meteorite storm, earlier that afternoon, had killed dozens of people in the outlying areas of Tacings. Max did not mention—at least while we watched—this disturbing news. Out in the hinterlands, in places like the Sutcay Valley and remote hamlets such as Sheebrun and Pointilla, people were carelessly blasé concerning meteorites and ignored the alerts. To these people, meteorite storms were part of their daily lives.

On the verge of falling asleep, Stellium brushed my cheek with the back of his hand. "Wake up, sprite, time to board our flight." It wasn't until after liftoff that he asked, "How bad is it really going to get down there?" We gazed at each other intently and he insisted, "Tell me the truth."

"I don't know the truth; I only know what I remember from persistent reality." What could I tell Stellium without fueling more painful memories?

"We have a chance to change our lives through the modification of our thoughts and actions, but we cannot change the laws of the elemental universe."

"Then the fate of Sutcay Tay is sealed?"

"As far as I can see, the tension between Insanio and Afen is identical."

"Then all our costly satellites, with their sophisticated and sensitive instrumentation, all those millions of triserabits of information compiled on the Afen Comet by cosmic meteorologists—none of this gives us any clues about this impending catastrophe?"

"The problem is not as obvious as you may think. In this time, scientists are unable to calculate the variables involved with the structural fissures inside Afen or the way Insanio and Gearthot will act upon those fissures."

"How soon will scientists know a portion of the comet will break free?"

"Sometime in the next three hours. By then, the people of Sutcay Tay will have only six hours to prepare."

"Tell me again that Élan will live through this catastrophe."

I felt myself sinking into clichés. "We cannot lose faith." Experience told me that when we lose faith in difficult times, we attracted the free radicals of the fourth dimension.

Stellium remind me, "Faith is what we hang onto when situations feel beyond our control and we have no hope of understanding."

"If I led you to believe that I controlled our fate, I'm sorry. Thus far, I've merely provided a few narrow escape hatches through which we may evolve."

Stellium shook his head in frustration. "I sure feel the squeeze. Something new and inevitable is troubling me. It feels as big and unavoidable as death."

"What we might be feeling is the passionate urgency every *Emayre* exerts on its lives."

The rutilates in Stellium's eyes brightened and flashed. "Your words just caused a vision to catalyze in my mind. Watch, I'll sketch it for you and perhaps you'll see what words struggle to explain. I usually don't title my paintings, but I'll make an exception this time and call it, *Passionate Urgency*."

Stellium gazed at the empty space before his eyes and his right hand began to move, as if poised with a drawing pencil in hand. He drew a rectangle in the air in front of us and said, "See here, in the lower third of the canvas, Élan's back is turned toward us. He crouches in fear and is slightly off-balance. The earthy pigments of claret wine and timber-brown stain his white *moodarry* as he hovers in a moment of divine suspension. The hem of his garment sweeps below the lower frame and to the right his body is lost in the darker shadows. His stance gives the impression of movement, as if he is standing in a powerful wind, but in reality, he is absolute stillness. Mid-canvas and to the left, his *Holder* dominates the space. She looks exactly like you and is dressed in pure tones of porcelain white and primavera green. Her appearance is arresting because, at first, her position seems so peculiar. She hovers above Élan, yet kneels before him in complete humility. See the bodice of her flowing gown? The collar is open and exposing her flaming heart. Look at her sweet dewy mouth. The word 'please' is poised upon her wine-stained lips."

"Then your painting is an illustration of the many decisive moments we face in life?"

"Exactly, those moments when we must decide if we are going to be responsive to the passionate urgency that supports our life or if we are going to ignore the divine please."

The airfloat banked and Sutcay Tay loomed into perfect view through the portal next to my seat. Stellium stared out the window, toward the tranquil image of this innocent world. We did not speak for several minutes because this was our last opportunity to see Sutcay Tay, as she would never be again. "What kind of day will Sutcay Tay awake to tomorrow morning?" Stellium asked. It was a rhetorical question, but it caused my mind to jiggle with anxiety. Persistent reality was so close that I felt its breath on the nape of my neck. I watched as persistent reality sketched its own canvas of the gray and ashen survivors, leaving for brighter worlds. I saw the jumble of cacophonous colors, The New Breed—a few would be saints with missions to heal the wounds of this shattered world, while others would be selfish and brassy charlatans. Graphic tricksters would prey upon the afflicted and, like vaspray, have no pity upon the ancestral bones of Sutcay Tay. Purple rage would distort perception into illusion. Superstition filled with meaningless ritual and vivid extravagance would replace simple and direct worship. Charlatans, so realistic and alluring, would accuse spiritual leaders of collusion with elemental forces—especially the order of Trinity Witches. Even the simple word "witch," which now meant "female visionary and healer," would be smeared with contempt and loathing. One day, the canvas of Sutcay Tay would be black and white and splattered with the blood-red stains of the women who died as futile martyrs.

"This time, Sutcay Tay will live through her trials," I promised Stellium.

He swallowed a lump in his throat. "This time?"

"Afen will return in approximately one hundred phases and Sutcay Tay will not survive." A tear spilt over the rim of his eye and I questioned if I was being too blunt. How could Stellium possibly understand the grim reality I lived through on post-apocalyptic Sutcay Tay, when even my words hurt him so much? Words were fleeting icons, not the actual grind. Vainly, I attempted to soften the future for him. "A bright side exists to this inescapable tragedy."

Stellium's cynicism woke up and he let go a shuttering laugh. "What? Everyone dies happy and fulfilled and they have a hearty chortle over the angst of the living?"

"When the end comes for Sutcay Tay, astronomers will know well in advance. Brave and beautiful souls, not yet dreamt possible, will risk their lives to save many of the people of Sutcay Tay."

He turned toward me and peered so deeply into my eyes that he provoked my *Emayre*. "How can you bear it—to know?" His question came out, almost as a demand, that I change what for him was still the future.

"Now you know too and your shared knowing is a great comfort to me."

"I'm sorry, I don't mean to pressure you. I want to help you. Please, share all your doubts and concerns with me."

"Doubt shows me pictures of us staggering under the awkwardness of the past and projecting the past on the future. Doubt reminds me that the newly enlightened lie like broken kindling along the trails. Doubt suggests that souls better prepared than Élan have ended up as ashes, destroyed by their supposed bits of power, fame, and wisdom. Don't you understand, Stellium? Élan has changed something critical by returning to the Sutcay Valley, something that transcends even this new reality. For some unknown reason, Élan's *Emayre* is prepared to risk a great deal more through him than was agreed upon in our pre-incarnate agreement."

Stellium thought for a moment and the rutilates of his eyes flared with golden light. "Did you know Kyron had a penchant for teasing Élan by calling him the prince of Fire?"

"Yes, I heard Kyron use that soft mocking tone when we conjured him last evening. It sounded as if he was playing games with Élan. What's the connection?"

"The connection is Élan once suggested to me that the prince of Fire reference was the equivalent of a master's conundrum. Élan interpreted it as a warning that he needed to burn away his sexual desires in order to reach mastery. Now I'm wondering if the prince of Fire reference might mean more."

"Like what?"

Stellium snapped his fingers. "Like a symbol for a match, a fire starter. A match is a catalyst that lights quickly and burns itself away in a few seconds time. Kyron might have been warning Élan that his life was to serve as a catalyst and that he would not live to enjoy the warmth of the greater fire he ignited?"

That was entirely possible, especially with The Divine Dulce waiting in the wings for life. Stellium put his arm around me then and said, "You're exhausted, little sprite. I have a comfortable shoulder, if you're interested. Why don't you rest your psychic eyes and I will watch the canvas for changes?"

****

Even on Gathos, Afen was affecting the weather. Wacar was cold for late summer and torrential rain was falling. Stellium and I were unprepared for cold, wet weather. We stopped at a shop near the Tacings spaceport and purchased a few additional items of clothing, but our new clothing still was inadequate for the cold. I borrowed Élan's raincoat and wore it to stay dry, while Stellium wore Élan's extra shirt in a vain effort to do the same.

The Lord of Eights Hotel was within walking distance of the spaceport. The short walk seemed like a veritable trek in the wind and rain. We were grateful when we spotted the hotel placard swinging wildly in the breeze. Our room, by Gathosian hotel standards was quite basic; but for us, the room seemed cozy and luxurious after our monastic lifestyles. We had a retro-gravity unit for sleeping and a heat closet, which is similar to a sauna, and helpful in reducing spacelag, a bath, and separate toilet. We also had a tempmaster for food, a multidex; breakfast service, a basket of fresh fruit, and even four aromatherapy candles consecrated to elemental spirits.

We were startled when the loquacious desk clerk, with his pencil-thin mustache at full alert, informed us, "Your bill was paid in advance by madam's brother. *Jai* Cœur multidexed the hotel earlier today and told us that you were on your honeymoon and paid for your room for the next three nights." The clerk assured us room 202 had an especially charming view that overlooked the rear garden and, "Weather permitting, breakfast will be served in the garden, tomorrow morning. So sorry it's raining," he apologized as if the weather was his fault. His mustache twitched and he raised one finger in the air. "My dear mother used to say 'rain on a honeymoon means good luck and many children.'" Then he abruptly seemed embarrassed and said, "I'm sorry, I guess I'm getting ahead of myself."

As soon as we reached our room, we sent a message to Élan, to let him know we arrived. Forty minutes later, he called us directly. Overpowering emotions welled up between Stellium and Élan. Stellium felt awkward because Élan no longer seemed shy, but passionately open and frank. I could not decide. Either Élan was trying too hard to breach the gap between what he was and what he wanted to become or he was metamorphosing so quickly, we could not adjust to the rapid changes. Moments of intense silence punctuated our conversation, as we all visually feasted upon the iconic projections of each other through the multidex. Élan seemed to dissolve into a pool of sentiment when he confessed, "My selfish heart wants only to be with you."

"Thank you for securing the hotel room for us," I said.

"Kyron and I stayed in room 202 several times when we traveled to Wacar," said Élan. "He always said room 202 possessed positive energy. About Cerebow and Taro—"

"We are on the same wavelength concerning Cerebow and Taro," I said. "I planned to put them in the fourth dimension myself until we can figure out how to get them to safety. Your *Holder* appeared before us in your room at the Star Inn and explained that it sent you the message on behalf of Kyron."

Élan brushed back his pale hair along his temple in frustration. "I begged my *Holder* to explain the situation to you both. I swear—I did not know how to tell you myself, or even if you would believe me." Another pregnant silence followed as Élan glanced down to avoid Stellium's eyes that seemed to be boring holes through the multidex screen. Then Élan abruptly looked up and his eyes—so blue-green and completely poignant—fractured my willing heart. "Please forgive the confusion I've caused you both. I had no conscious idea my *Holder* sent me the message until I was back here in the Sutcay Valley."

"We understand completely," I assured him. "No apologies are required or needed."

"Stellium, say something to me," Élan finally begged.

Stellium put a hand to his neck to help him swallow the tension accumulating in his throat. "What should I say?" his voice trailed off.

"Please say you forgive me for leaving Pointilla before you arrived."

"I say only that I love you, with each breath I take."

Élan put his hand forward as if trying to touch us. "Listen carefully to me. Kyron, above all, is being explicit with me and I realize the peril I face. Please, I beg you, Stellium. If I die in the next few hours, do not waste your life or your precious love on the memory of a dead man. Please, do not even wait for me to make love to that beautiful woman standing by your side. Always and forever, you are my bridge of light. Please understand. Through you, I can love her too."

The energy within Stellium staggered. "Don't say, 'if I die.'"

Élan was relentless and the daylight was too much for Stellium, the night-blooming orchid, to endure. "If I die," Élan repeated more forcefully, "I carry no regrets, save one, into my next life. My foolish evasions continue to shame me. Through you, I know only an idiot would waste his life drooling down his leg when so much love waits for expression."

"You will live," I assured Élan. "You can and will meet these challenges, whatever they may be. I believe your *Emayre* is shifting some of the responsibility, which Dulce originally was destined to carry, upon you. Your *Emayre* believes in you and this belief streams out into many soul groups that now pray for your success."

An ironic smirk clouded Élan's face. "I never thought of that before, the transcendent praying for the living. What a humbling thought." He seemed to look straight at us then. "I must go because many brothers need to use this multidex to contact their loved ones. *Ejesay epay*," he mouthed as if the words were too precious to speak aloud. "I will see you soon." Stellium and I held Élan's last words in sacred trust. Élan's, "I will see you soon," became our prayer, an unwavering mantra that soon he would join us and our love would know its full expression with him.

****

Stellium was subdued afterward. He seemed testy when I questioned him about his new mood, but insisted, "I'm okay, go take your bath and put on dry clothing before you get ill."

"Okay, I'll do that," and I leaned over and kissed the top of his head.

Physically, I was exhausted. If possible, I wanted to sleep for a few hours before the conjunction occurred. Grabbing a handful of blue skyfruit from the fruit basket, I went to take a relaxing bath. A few minutes later, Stellium peeked around the bathroom door and said, "I'm going out for a few minutes to buy a couple of things we may need." When I emerged an hour later, he had not returned. My concern turned to worry at the two-hour mark. Élan had called Stellium "tender." Stellium's tenderness was vulnerable and sensitive as a night-blooming orchid. Stellium's evolution was reaching a point where he needed to question what he knew and where he wanted to go. This was good, but the challenge was risky for someone as sensitive as Stellium. *Help me*, I prayed. *Help me be with Stellium in the way that will help him grow into the perfection of his Emayre.*

I went to the window and peered out into the garden. The strong wind pelted the rain against the windowpanes and distorted my view. The soft, flick-flick-flicking of raindrops sounded like coded messages for those with the proper interface to understand. I listened carefully, but the elemental sounds of Gathos were a foreign language to me, especially when I was ensconced in a hotel room with a layer of glass separating me from the natural world. At the moment, I missed Cerebow's confidence, her humor, and especially her spirited challenges. She enjoyed a healthy and nonchalant connection to the elemental universe. My block was my limited mind, which preferred to reduce the elemental universe to an inert object. Down in the garden, a damaged, tree limb dangled like an awkward, fractured arm. Every time a gust of wind tore at the limb, it flailed and waved as if in acute agony. Limited mind quickly assured me that this meant nothing and I was anthropomorphizing the broken limb. This was the easiest explanation to believe, a quick and efficient rationalization, which allowed me to relegate suffering to the dead zone of the fourth dimension. Limited mind rationalized the pain of others, while mind's big sister, feelings, sent forth tendrils of empathy and sensed the agony between tree and limb.

When Stellium returned, I was relieved. He wore a new raincoat and carried a box in one hand and a bag in the other. "You were gone a long time," I said.

"I'm sorry, I decided to go shopping for a few essentials I thought we might need and got distracted by the frou-frous along the way. I bought a new raincoat. What do you think?"

"Midnight blue is definitely your color." Then he handed me the box with a gallant nod of the head. When I opened the box, I was delighted to find a lovely, white nightgown and a pink, snuggly-warm sweater. I went in the bathroom and put on the nightgown with the sweater on top. When I returned to show Stellium how the new clothing looked, I found him slouched in one of our two chairs, with his legs sprawled out in front of him. He was sitting in front of the multidex and he and Max Construe looked like two zombies vacantly staring through each other.

Stellium abruptly glanced up and smiled rather dryly. "Max is on replay," he informed me. His response to my nightgown and sweater were not what I expected.

"Wrong size?"

He laughed nervously. "No, the fit is—perfect," and he made a gesture toward his own chest. "I guess when I pictured you wearing the nightgown, it wasn't with the sweater on top."

I flirted with him a wee bit by asking, "Which one would you like me to take off?"

He sat up straighter. His hands waved around as if trying to stir up the right response. He laughed again, although sadness and worry seemed to shadow his every expression. "The room feels chilly," he replied and I knew I needed to go slowly with him. He continued to smile and finally his smile deepened. "That pink sweater makes you look like a pet bunny my friend Yancy had when we were kids—soft, warm, and cuddly." He looked away and seemed on the verge of tears.

At that moment, I wanted to rescue us both. "We don't need to rush things between us, Stellium. Remember, we are free to create whatever future we want."

"You are so beautiful, you almost seem impossible to me. In truth, you are so beautiful that every other woman is plain by comparison. I keep asking myself, dare I touch you without you evaporating like an illusion?" He reached down, picked up the bag next to his chair, and handed the bag to me. I peeked inside and found shampoo, razor blades, and a package of his and her contraceptive patches. "The razor blades are for me," he explained and he patted his cheek. "I thought we might share the patches, if you feel in the mood." I pulled out the box of Magic Moment patches and read the back of the box. "What does it say?" he asked after a moment.

"It says, 'Follow instructions precisely to prevent pregnancy,' and, 'Make sure your hands are clean and dry before handling patches.'"

Stellium relaxed and showed me the palms of his hands. It was a Gathosian gesture of surrender and honesty. "I think I can handle that much—what else?"

"'Do not confuse the gold envelope containing male patches and the silver envelope containing female patches and do not mix patches between envelopes and do not attempt to reuse patches.' They're even elementally correct. The his-patch is shaped like a golden sunburst and the her-patch is shaped like a silver, crescent moon."

"Sounds either erotic or ridiculous, I can't decide."

"The erotic and the ridiculous are frequent bedmates."

He laughed and admitted, "This is kinda sexy. Read me some more about Magic Moment patches."

"It says to 'achieve maximum contraceptive effectiveness,' we are supposed to apply an appropriate patch approximately one centimeter below our navels on clean, dry skin, one hour before expected intercourse."

"Show me where they go?" he asked right away.

I took his hand and placed it on my lower belly. "Right here, it says."

He looked up into my eyes and his eyes were eager. "What makes it work? Please tell me it's sprightly magic."

I checked the box again. "Sorry, no sprightly magic involved, it is 5 micrograms of protogestant for females and .05 milligrams of prototestudo for men."

"Side effects?"

Maybe I should have made up something silly, such as the patches caused insatiable lust, but I was a disciple of Mother Truth and read the side effects to Stellium. "'Warnings: prototestudo may exacerbate lipid disorders, high blood pressure, and impotency in men;' and 'protogestant may cause fluid retention and emotional anxiety in women. Overdoses may cause nausea, vomiting, and ataxia.'"

Stellium came down fast with that news. "If the drug doesn't prevent pregnancy, the side effects will?"

I struggled to recapture the mood of sensual playfulness. "There's more—want to hear the rest?"

"Okay, I guess I've faced a lot harder stuff than a few drug side effects."

"If you're worried, the package says we can, 'address inquires to Atlas Pharmaceuticals via multidex at Atlas Universal.' Listen to this crazy bit. 'Check out our live group forums on sexual dysfunction and allow our on-staff intimate-relation specialists teach you the techniques for improving your sex life. Mention your recent purchase of Magic Moment contraceptives and receive a free video on masturbation and advanced oral-sex techniques, along with our new catalogue filled with adult products designed to help you spice up your sex life.'"

Stellium groaned and sat back in his chair. "I was surfing on the kinky notion of sex patches, but you lost me on sex clinics. Sounds about as exciting as learning to dance from footprints they paste on the floor and as original as a paint-by-number da Vinci." He twisted his head as if trying to relieve a stiff neck. "It's that damn one-size-fits-all approach again. That free video will start with a dried-up clinician, in a white lab coat, giving us a frank pep talk about self-masturbation. Then he'll move on to the topic of masturbating your partner; then, without a doubt, mutual masturbation; and finally the ideal couple will dosàdo home to orgasm." Stellium made a silly expression and rolled his eyes. "Let's all fast-forward and get to the live couple doing it at the end." Suddenly Stellium started talking about art; and while I wondered how he planned to connect the dots between sex and art, he unleashed a storehouse of criticism for an artist he once knew on Earth, named Denny Pratt.

"Denny Pratt was a master of technique," said Stellium. His hands quickly gesticulated through the air making fancy curlicues as if he were painting another impromptu picture on an imaginary canvas. "See! All done. It's my latest masterpiece. Did you notice how this masterpiece looks like my last masterpiece and the one before that? Denny was one of the most predictable and stilted artists, I ever encountered. His true creativity never got a chance to surface because his technique always managed to seduce him and get in his way. He was the worst kind of idolater. A vulgar gymnast! A perfect Don Juan and an obvious victim of his own bad taste."

"Is Denny Pratt one of your ex-lovers?"

Stellium let go an irritated huff of air. "Our affair lasted two weeks."

"Give me a clue. What are we talking about, Stellium?"

"Don't you understand?"

"I have a feeling you're going to explain it to me."

"We're talking about the art of living and tuning into the motivating spirit of creation. Lovers, like true artists, must leap beyond technique and express themselves from the whole of their being. Dancing, music, art, and loving, are chances for true self-expression, the release of tension between beauty and pain, the agony of desire and the ecstasy of creation. These unique expressions of the soul are beyond clinical methodology."

"I agree, but perhaps sex clinics are attempting to give lovers an opportunity to address those ancient difficulties that always emerge when we try to match the wants and needs of another person."

"That's an ideal. The reality is sex clinics are trying to make money by reducing sacred and intimate expression to the level of physical technique. Tell me, what do you believe are the real causes of impotency?"

"I think shame alienates us from our *Emayre*, which causes us to become paralyzed within the ruts of our limited mind. This leaves the body to stew in the rage of impotence."

Stellium was bobbing his head in agreement and added, "Impotency is the exclusive bane of higher consciousness."

"Or perhaps, mediocre consciousness."

He laughed, but it was fleeting. "We've lost so much more than we've gained. I ask you—does a mother bird take her fledglings to flying clinics or does she push them out of the nest and allow their souls to take flight? My mom told me that when I was born, the hospital gave her stacks of pamphlets before she left for home that discussed sleeping and feeding schedules. These pamphlets were nothing more than advertisements for products like powdered infant formula and pulverized baby food. Is it any wonder children grow up to be impotent nihilists and are alienated from the inspiration of their own creativity, when all they eat is dead food? Anyway, mom, being an neophyte at motherhood and alone on an alien world, felt obliged to follow the clinical claptrap promoted by these so-called experts and the one-size-fits-all approach these pamphlets endorsed. She believed that if she held me too much that she might spoil me, as if I was a ripe banana."

"Where was your father?"

"He was on Mars most of the time."

"Mom told me I cried constantly and when she called the pediatrician for guidance, he'd spill out some new bit of twaddle like, "Try feeding him every three hours instead of every four." Finally, he told her, 'Mrs. Epay, you need to learn to ignore his fussing and crying because that's just what babies do.'"

"Sounds to me as if the three free radicals of shame, fear, and rage controlled that situation."

"In what way?"

"The experts, with their pamphlets, were the fear of the limited mind with its handy yet incomplete answer; your mother was the shame, believing she lacked the innate motherly wisdom to care for her child; and you were the rage with your crying."

He thought about it for a moment before saying, "Fear, shame, and rage, I think you've on to something with that theory."

"Did your mother explain to the pediatrician that Gathosian infants rarely if ever cry?"

"I don't know. What happened was Mom multidexed Grandmom on Numida and Grandmom said, "Lavish—my mom's name is Lavish— Gathosian men and women have been delivering and caring for their children for eons without the advice of Human pediatricians. Do what you feel is right for you and your son." Stellium stopped dead in his conversational tracks. When he spoke the next time, his voice was soft with reverence. "Grandmom came and lived with us for a while. I remember her holding me. She was the kind of person that brought her calm with her, wherever she went. In a way, I think her holding me saved me from complete cynicism."

"Your cynicism still seems rather bold."

Stellium rolled his eyes. "Sorry, when I get started, all saints seem insincere and even the Sistine Chapel looks like vulgar art."

"What's really bothering you, Stellium?"

He shrugged, "I'm not quite sure, but I really seemed bugged—don't I?" He laughed a little and let out a deep sigh. He closed his eyes and leaned his head on the chair back. "Maybe it's the strangulation I feel when others presume to limit and categorize, what for me is sacred expression."

"No one is doing that here."

"I know—"

"Stellium I need to tell you something important before we take one more step into the future. You are under no obligation to make love to me, simply because Élan suggested that you should."

Stellium grew quiet and his expression turned sober. "That's a huge part of my dilemma. I really wish Élan had not said that. Granted, he is under tremendous stress, but his statement made me feel—" Stellium shuddered and shook his head. "No matter how eloquently he put it, I cannot—in fact, I refuse—to play the role of his surrogate with you." Stellium put his head back and stared up at the ceiling again. "Bingo!" he exclaimed. "Now I understand what is going on in my head," and he clammed shut. After about thirty seconds of complete silence between us, he said, "Here's the deal, sprite. I, Noveil Epay, with all my ugly cynicism, must matter as much to you as Élan does." He raised his head and stared at me while the rutilates of his eyes seemed to do gymnastic tricks. "Maybe I'm expecting too much. After all, you've returned to the past to get straight with Élan, not me."

"My purpose always is to enliven love consciousness with everyone in the most appropriate ways I can find. Yes, I want to get straight with Élan, but you are the sacred variable that's already tipped the scale toward my success. We have no negative karma between us, Stellium. Do you realize what that means? We possess infinite freewill to express our love for each other in any way we decide is appropriate."

"You're wrong; negative karma does stand between us. It's not yours; it's mine. I'm the one that's been slowly closing the door on my capacity to love a woman for the past few phases. Right now, I'm asking myself—in a sexual encounter with you, can I jump beyond my definitions of the feminine, to actually make love to you?"

"The first moment I saw you, I was sexually attracted to you. In our last few hours together, you have seduced me with your sincerity, your humor, and obvious passion. The moment you take me in your arms, I'm eager to express my desire for you."

"And what exactly does desire mean to you?"

"My desire is to realize your perfection and join with that perfection in perfect bliss. How about you? Do you want to connect with my perfection in the full glory of your personal freewill?"

"It seems like a fairly large challenge. I'll need to meditate for a while and see if I can bring all we've said into perspective." He got up, collected his belongings, and went into the bathroom. The room was warm now, so I took off my sweater and put it in my tapestry valise. Then I decided to paste a silver crescent moon below my navel—just in case. I checked the multidex for news and the universe was steadily grinding away toward the inevitable conjunction. While waiting for Stellium, I fell asleep in a half-upright position in front of the multidex screen. When he emerged from the bathroom, he awoke me and said. "Why don't you climb into the regrav unit, where you can sleep in comfort?"

I gazed at him sideways through my sleepy haze. He was standing there with a towel draped around his waist. His scruffy beard was gone and he had trimmed the hair on his upper lip into a thin, naughty mustache. His long hair was damp and hanging loose around his shoulders and chest. It sure felt like a Magic Moment to me. "You look handsome standing there all damp and seductive," I said.

He leaned over and kissed me. It was our first kiss and I quivered in the absolute joy of his warm lips. "Warm the regrav unit up," he said. "I need to sit here and dry off, so my patch will stick to my skin."

****

The regrav unit is an equal opportunity environment for making love because no on-top position exists. The usual thrusting by the male and the bump-and-grind of the female, pushes lovers farther apart and those that make love only with their physical bodies, can find the experience frustrating and unsatisfying. However, in the 360° ambience of reduced gravity, lovers have a unique opportunity to enjoy the subtleties of mutual surrender and the magnetic attraction between the major energy centers of their bodies. The magnetism, which most of us acknowledge only as a special attraction for a lover, when fueled with our full attention in reduced gravity, has the ability to fuse lovers into one ovum of energetic light. Safely held within this ovum, compatible energies surrender to each other, in a dance of complete abandon.

Inside the regrav unit, I took one of the pocket blankets from the floor and climbed inside. Then I adjusted the temperature, humidity, lights, and finally the gravity. Slowly, I floated upward and fell asleep. Later, I heard the soft "swoop-swoop" of the regrav door as it opened and closed. Peering down into the darkness, I saw a dark outline floating up toward me. "May I come inside your blanket with you?" Stellium whispered. Love has a way of hushing us as it draws near, so we honored love with our perfect silence. Lifting the top edge of the blanket, his naked body slid between the layers.

Gathosians generally have little bodily hair, except for the exuberant hair on their heads and the pubic area and, of course, on the Gathosian male his facial hair. In preparation for the wedding night, it is the custom for both sexes to remove their pubic hair, except for a tuft at the top of the pubic bone, which they embellish with fancy ribbons. This wedding braid has many names and, as expected, they are stereotypically funny and sexually suggestive. Stellium placed my hand on his wedding braid and I apologized for not preparing myself for him with equal care. I used this braid to pull him even closer. We instantly clicked together, making me think, *we fit perfectly.* He smelled good enough to eat—fresh and clean—like citrus and spicy ginger. His hands were delicate and gentle and now that he was committed, he was not shy. He boldly lifted the skirt of my nightgown so he could feel my lower belly. He wanted to make sure my patch was in place. Then he took my hand and placed it on his patch to assure me that he was equally safe.

The space suddenly felt hot and we quickly discarded the blanket. It floated to one side and a moment later, he helped me remove my nightgown. Sexually, he was ready. I was not surprised because he was a visual artist with a creative imagination. He gallantly ignored his erection that began spinning binding webs against my inner thigh. We got involved in a long and languorous kiss and his mouth tasted as good as he smelled. His tongue was velvety smooth and wet as a newly dipped paintbrush. Our kissing led to unbridled exploration and his trailing kisses kept ending up closer and closer to my heart. He was an experienced lover and had no problems finding my most sensitive places.

Emotionally, spiritually, and mystically, his active and receptive polarities began dancing with mine. He was utterly romantic and possessed a unique ability to be both dynamic and sweetly vulnerable. It was a marvelous freeing adventure, to play unfettered by the limitations of dominance and pressing gravity. My physical virginity concerned him and when he could no longer ignore his erection, I helped him find his way inside me. We both were slick with yearning, so I experienced little introductory pain, just the pleasure of his growing eagerness. Only contraceptives prevented me from getting pregnant, because I was ovulating and this was the time in persistent reality when I became pregnant with Dulce.

Within minutes, our sex centers were burning with desire. He finally spoke saying, "I'm feeling dizzy; hold me so I don't fall." My solar plexus clamped onto his, which gave him the security to surrender farther into the experience.

Our heart energies began seducing us and he groaned softly and took a deep breath. Our dancing energies vibrated, looped, twitched, and teased us with such delightful shenanigans that orgasm would have been easy. Floating motionless, we clung to each other as our hearts filled with so much love, that it was difficult to believe our journey inside each other was just beginning. Our desire was to create a synergy of love, so our *Emayres* would join our play. It did not take long, for lovemaking is an irresistible magnet for the *Emayre*. When those greater energies came, they swooped down upon us like two golden wheels of spinning fire. Then we were traveling in a direction that seemed to be upward, through a narrow tunnel of undulating darkness. The unrequited murmuring of the ages protruded, and tickled us from along those tunnel walls. Each expression was like a tongue babbling and gurgling, trying to find a conscious voice through us. It felt confining in that long narrow articulation and, thankfully, we were there for only a moment before our *Emayres* spit us forth and into the vast primordial wetlands.

New creation greeted us with the silence of a perpetual rosy dawn. Our divine nursery was so warm to the touch—so pregnant with its nurturing embrace—we were filled with the most vibrant of possibilities. Bathed in the milk of blue-white water, we emerged from the primordial soup as our true selves. "Look up!" said Stellium in complete wonder. "A star hangs above our heads." In this new space, freewill truly was ours and because we owned our freewill, seductions approached from every side. The universe has many self-protective mechanisms built into its system and many lovers gently return to the heart energy at this point, believing their journey complete. The seductions were most intense between Stellium and me for, again, we could have ended it by worshiping the perfection within each other. There was mutual worship aplenty, but mutual worship is merely the first glimpse of the greater experience, for greater experience boldly invites perfection to bond with the lovers and worship them.

It took indescribable courage to go on, to open our love to the infinite, to lay naked, vulnerable, and believe we were worthy to receive. We lingered, allowing the curious energies, like hands, to move through us, touching our secret urges that surprised even us. Now, like roe-rich fish, we swam toward home and our mutual gaze fixed upward, toward the black universe above. Then auroras of rainbow light dawned on all sides of the horizon—expanding, rising, and squeezing the black universe upward and into a dark quivering ring. The dark ring began to oscillate, faster and faster, until I heard one sharp "ping!" With our energy peeking out toward the Creative Edge, we could have lingered forever in peace as unexpressed satellites. But Stellium was an exuberant child and his loving heart reached toward the black universe. Death came at that instant and since our energy was one, like a font of light, my love joined his and together we leapt up and kissed the Creative Edge seven times with complete abandon.

Afterward, we felt spread out like froth upon water. Tasting deeply of ourselves, we could not help sampling the hopes and dreams of those who joined our dance of love. Stellium's *Emayre* dipped itself into the darkness and when it emerged, it was dressed in a fragile web of light. Its every gesture became a dance and its every expression oozed with passionate love. Rarely does a soul have the privilege to witness the interplay between another *Emayre* and its own life, but I certainly witnessed this. *Always and forever, without end, is my absolute passion for you*, it told Stellium. *I will take you everywhere within me*, it swooned and then it sank down into the darkness, leaving its web upon the surface, like a net of golden light.

\*\*\*\*

Later, Stellium experienced a case of the giggles. He kissed my breasts, calling them "rose buds" and made me giggle too. "I'm too excited to sleep," he whispered. After a moment, he confessed, "I feel so light, almost as if I've lost my mind." I started giggling too, which led to more kissing. His passion turned serious and told me, "You showed me a place beyond doubt and now I know how to get there. It's through you, sprite. It's through you."

"It's not really through me; it's through love."

"You're right; it's through love; but you are so open to it, like no one I ever met before. When I was inside you, vivid visions came and then I was beyond visions. The experience was so—so utterly fulfilling that I don't know if I have the ability to put it into words."

"Maybe you were not meant to put it into words."

His body relaxed into me even more. "What I really want to do is paint the experience, but I don't know if I could do it justice."

"Painting is exactly what you must do. Your art could serve as a great comfort to living souls—touch them on a deeper level than their conscious minds. Your creative effort could bring divine love into this dimension and make it graphic for those not yet able to see."

"An honest artist always uses the tools at hand," he said and his tongue trailed down between my breasts and dipped into my vessel that brimmed with our commingled love. With his tongue, he drew an eye around my navel. "It's the finest eye I've ever drawn," he declared and with that, we begin to make love a second time.

\*\*\*\*

Stellium eventually fell into a beautiful slumber, but my mind lingered on Élan. I knew he was not sleeping—that much I knew for sure. I saw him praying. Maybe not the sitting-in-the-temple-kind-of praying, but prayers were on his lips. Then I drifted into a dream. I saw nothing but Élan's eyes floating in the darkness, those sweet, blue-green orbs of Human perfection. *Do you really think this state of moksha possible?* he asked me again. *Can we become both the lover and the beloved and see with the eyes of our Holder?*

*The scene abruptly changed. In a solemn cortege, moodarry-clad warriors are filing into the interior of the Eternal Waters Sanctuary. They are bringing their sacred belongings here for safekeeping. I'm among them as the press of the crowd pushes me forward. I call his name. "Élan?" My voice, once spoken, takes physical shape and possesses independent volition. It darts and swoops through the Eternal Waters Sanctuary in search of him. Then I see him. Élan is hovering above the surface of the center pool in a mood of passionate urgency. One by one, each warrior comes forward and offers him their sacred treasures. The booty is enormous, for thirty thousand phases of Shardasko wealth lay at his feet. Even in the dream, I question, "What does this mean?" Then everyone withers into the shadows except Élan. He extends a hand toward me as if he knew I was there all along. I respond by sending forth my love as a floating bubble that lands upon his outstretched hand. "We haven't even kissed," he says and with that the bubble bursts. He looks into the palm of his empty hand and asks, "Will I ever see you again?"*

*It will be a long time before you see her, says a new voice between us.*

"Élan?" I heard myself calling.

"It's okay," Stellium was saying. "Tell me the dream."

****

The conjunction between Insanio and Afen occurred in early afternoon, exactly on schedule. A half-hour later, astronomers announced to the citizens of the Island Worlds of Gathos that a portion of the Afen Comet broke free from the main mass and was heading toward Sutcay Tay. Max Construe never blinked an eye when it announced that the worst-case scenario meant Sutcay Tay might lose orbit. Twenty minutes into the crisis, two real people replaced Max and grimly announced that if Sutcay Tay lost orbit, it would destroy the moon Eno and the populous planets of Kujairani and Lalaseair too. A great deal of panic followed. Space and atmospheric disturbance in the area caused massive energy blackouts and communication was impossible to or among the headwater planets. Energy blackouts were as common during meteor storms as the alert sirens, so both were ignored. The only individuals on any of the headwater planets who knew of the fractured condition of Afen were those who were psychically aware.

The ill-equipped Gathosian Space Corps, which is a third-rate, space power at its finest, decided to shoot missiles at the breakaway meteor mass. This was a waste of precious time and created more ash that eventually fell into the atmosphere of Sutcay Tay. Roughly, a window of five hours still existed to do something constructive. The Gathosian Space Corp could have landed on Sutcay Tay and helped spread the word that a meteor storm of apocalyptic proportions was approaching or even rescued as many people as possible. Nothing of this sort happened. The free radical fear and its reciprocal shame kept those who were sure to survive from landing and facing those who were about to die. Individuals, who possessed the authority and did nothing, would hotly debate and try to defend themselves

238

for many phases to come. I felt pity for the suffering of the dying, but also felt pity for the upper echelons of the Gathosian Space Corp. For it was these souls and their soul groups that would carry the karmic shame of indifference for lifetimes to come.

When the meteor storm finally ended, no one understood why the breakaway meteor mass veered toward polar north and merely clipped the upper atmosphere of Sutcay Tay. Scientists would point to their simulations and explain that the gravitational pull from the sun Gearthot acted as a counterforce. One ridiculous theory suggested that because the rotation of Sutcay Tay was robust, the rotation acted as a grinding wheel against the meteor and diverted the meteor toward open space. That this theory was an unheard-of-phenomenon in the history of meteor activity, made no difference. Scientists quickly adjusted their theories to fit the circumstance rather than admit that they did not understand the elemental universe. It was sadly ironic. Because the media originally announced that the destruction of Kujairani, Lalaseair, and the moon Eno might also occur, many people now rationalized that the devastation on Sutcay Tay as an equitable tradeoff by saying, "It could have been worse."

# FIFTEEN

Hundreds of thousands of metric tons of ash and small meteorites reached the planet surface of Sutcay Tay. In the span of five minutes, five million people died and thirty million more died, within the next four hours. In total, over seventy-five million people died from injuries and the resultant, environmentally born diseases. The southern part of the Western Hemisphere, in places like the Sutcay Valley, sustained the worst damage. For ten moons, sunrises and sunsets stained the sky crimson red and the green light of *areé didamé* did not return until the phase of Fire was long gone. The normally tropical environment in the Sutcay Tay valleys became one sweltering jungle of misery, killing to extinction many unique lifeforms, indigenous only to the Southern Hemisphere. Of the millions seriously injured, only the wealthy, the favorably connected, and the fortunate found their way to hospitals on Kujairani, Lalaseair, and Gathos.

In the mountainous regions, to the northwest, rain began falling two days after the storm and continued as a torrential downpour for the next five days. Debris and rotting corpses washed into streams and rivers polluting the groundwater. Cloud cover remained dense and the air so polluted, the old and weak began dying from respiratory infections. Children suffered permanent lung damage and strong men gagged on the blood from their own raw throats. Flies dined heartily on the abundance of new death and tiny raybitian mosquitoes multiplied rapidly and infected the living with ring fever, leaving thousands wandering the countryside in amnesic states. Since most Gathosians cultivated their food in private gardens, those with no stored provisions, began to starve. Flocks of emboldened vaspray descended upon towns and villages in feeding frenzies previously unknown on Gathosian worlds and infected thousands with their their deadly fungus. In the fourth dimension, vaspray also were active, for they were feeding on shocked souls who drifted aimlessly along the timeline. Despite the death, disease, suffering, and the pollution of Sutcay Tay's air, water, and soil, this small planet would survive for another hundred phases.

For those anxiously waiting for any scrap of good news, it was impossible to get personal messages through to anyone on the surface. Stellium sent a message to Sycottie Shardasko, requesting help from their psychic masters. An Emblematic Warrior, who signed his name, "Brother Guruda," was kind enough to send us this message:

Brother Noveil, masters at Sycottie Shardasko are in psychic contact with the situation on Sutcay Tay. We regard this once lovely headwater planet as a brother who entered the Great Verdant Abyss and now is lost. As you requested, I've asked our masters if they could locate the whereabouts of Master Kyron and his Emblematic Warrior Élan. It aggrieves me to inform you that our masters believe Master Kyron lost his physical life in the meteorite storm. They have no information on the Emblematic Warrior Élan. I also did a quick physical record trace and found Élan, a.k.a. Journey Cœur, resigned from the Sutcay Tay School on Aeon, day 1, phase of Air, 8432. He has a sister named Sophia. Her multidex address is Sophia at Gathosian Arts-Universal, Chevy Chase, Earth. Hope this helps.

Brother Garuda's pronouncement felt official. It made no difference that we knew in advance of Kyron's death, it still was shocking to hear. Stellium sent a second message to Brother Guruda, telling him that Élan had returned to the Sutcay Tay campus before the meteorite storm and to, please, recheck with the masters. This time, it took three long days for Brother Guruda to confirm that Élan was alive and at the Sutcay Tay School. Again, it felt official and Stellium and I celebrated by jumping up and down and bestowing lavish hugs and kisses on each other. That's when Stellium realized his mother probably believed he was still on Sutcay Tay. He immediately multidexed her to tell her that he was safe. I retired to the heat closet, so he could talk in private and afterward, he cracked open the door and peered at me through the dim light. "You can come out. The coast is clear," he said in English.

"I'm going to stay in her for awhile longer."

"Mind if I join you?"

"I'd love you to join me." He stripped naked and joined me inside. Reclining on the opposite, lounge chair, he twisted his neck as he stretched his arms over his head. Every time he went through his neck twisting gestures, it freed the energy in this area of his body and shortly afterward, he would turn loquacious. "You should have come out and said hi," he said. "She's going to love you—guaranteed."

"Was your mother worried?"

"Yeah, she used the word frantic a bunch of times. She's going to multidex Élan's sister and let her know that he's okay. She wanted to know why I was on Gathos when I told her that I was coming home six moons ago. Guess what I told her? I said that I was in love with a beautiful sprite and we were waiting for Élan so we could start our honeymoon."

"You dropped that news, so casually?"

"Mom's cool, especially concerning my love life."

"Why do you call her cool?"

"Not cool as in indifferent. Earth's cool means a person has savoir-faire. You know, they've seen everything and now nothing shocks them. My past behavior put her through lots of turmoil, especially when I ended up in the hospital, so not much can shock her, concerning me."

"I guess I'm not as cool as your mother. I've seen quite a lot and many things still shock me. For instance, what's going on Sutcay Tay right now shocks me, and I've seen it twice."

"You are cool," Stellium insisted. "Cool people possess a nonjudgmental compassion toward the idiosyncrasies of other people because they realize they got so many idiosyncrasies themselves."

"You think I'm idiosyncratic?"

He twisted his neck some more. "Sure."

"That's odd; I experience myself as quite ordinary."

"Well that's another facet concerning cool you don't understand. You cannot declare yourself cool, for that's uncool or conceited. Only other people decide if a particular person is cool. Authentic cool people merely go nonchalantly about their experiencing; but as they do, they radiate personal confidence, so no matter what they do or say, they exhibit pizzazz and style."

"So cool is the ability to be comfortable in one's body and other people notice this comfort and declare that person cool?"

"Hooray, sprite! Now you got it." He abruptly started laughing.

"Now what's so funny?"

He sat up and laughed even harder. "I just remembered that once I introduced Mom to Denny Pratt. At the time, I thought Denny was ultra-cool; but Mom said, 'Noveil, you've hit rock bottom.'"

"And how did Denny's idiosyncrasies mesh with yours?"

"Never mind that." Stellium pointed to his left cheek. "Anyway, at the time, Denny shaved his head bald. He sported a heart tattoo right here that said, 'kiss me.'"

"You're joking?"

Stellium smiled wily. "Just a little. Denny did shave his head and he did have a heart tattoo, only it wasn't on his face and didn't exactly say kiss me."

****

Five days after the meteor storm, we still heard nothing from Élan. Stellium and I were short of cash and debated whether we should check into a cheaper hotel. A growing compulsion was urging me to project my consciousness to Sutcay Tay and make sure Élan really was safe, Stellium finally called his mother, explained our financial dilemma, and she sent us two thousand Gathosian banknotes with her complete love. I wanted to meet this generous woman and told Stellium, "Your mother certainly is cool."

A message finally arrived from Élan. It was not a direct communication, but a relay multidex message sent via Sycottie Shardasko, from the Lucretion rescue ship, *The Delphi Queen*. The message said, "Will land at Loxaloo Spaceport around half-day today. Please meet me. Journey." We did not question why he was not coming to Wacar and presumed he had no choice, but to fly to Loxaloo, if he was aboard a rescue ship.

In Loxaloo, Departures and Landings directed us to Hangar Eleven. Passengers were already exiting the flight when we arrived. "We're late," said Stellium. "I hope we haven't missed him." Little chance existed that this might happen. Disembarkation was cranking along at the lethargic pace of slow motion. The handsome Gathosian people, who usually walk with such assurance and grace, now plodded. Passengers pushed forward in a halting and unsure gait, while many huddled together, as if still protecting each other from bodily harm. As we brushed shoulders, their collective smell oozed with pungency and suggested its own story, a story of days and nights of smoke-filled panic, old sweat and fear, then rotted food and foul water, and finally empty guts and diarrhea. The severely injured rode in autochairs and two vacant-eyed children lay upon gurneys with intubation tubes dangling from the corners of their mouths. No one spoke, but the sporadic disquiet of phlegmatic coughing—like static—occasionally interrupted the silence. The faraway sounds—the fluting tones of spaceships beyond the terminal and the indifferent swishing of vehicles, outside on the street, were louder as they skirted past the incoming depression.

"There's Élan!" Stellium gasped. I saw an effulgent light squeeze through the doorway from the space hangar. The light was lucid with colors of a rainbow after a rain and its sudden appearance changed the entire complexion of the huge public space. No speck of miasma marred Élan's beauty. He was carrying the twenty-second volume, *The Universe*, under his arm and wearing the *ackinayon,* bandoleer style, across his back and the now infamous knife, in a scabbard at his waist. He was dressed in a once white *moodarry* that now seemed held together with stains rather than fibers. His unshaven face and wild hair were dirty with soot and he was barefoot. A crowd of fellow passengers surrounded him, pressed in upon him, and

243

moved with him as if magnetized by his presence. Several people closest to him found excuses to touch him. Hands brushed his sleeves and a woman carrying a child stopped and embraced him intimately. Other hands came up and patted him on the shoulders. Two rescue workers emerged through the doorway. They were carrying an empty gurney and stopped briefly to tell him, "thanks."

A few seconds later, Aytinous appeared through the same doorway. His clothing was stained and splatter with blood, but his right arm hung in an immaculate white sling that rescue workers probably had bestowed upon him. His aura was bright, but I could see the specks of miasma in him. He came up behind Élan and took his arm.

"Élan! Over here," shouted Stellium and Élan turned his head in our direction attempting to find us through Stellium's voice.

"Prepare yourself," I told Stellium. "This is going to be difficult." Stellium shot me one quick glance. No time remained to prepare him for the shock about to unfold.

Seconds later, Élan was there, in our arms, embracing us and telling us, "I made it!" while his eyes looked through us. Stellium shot another look in my direction, this one questioning. "I'm okay," Élan continued to assure us. "I just can't see." Stellium already was crying and Élan was trying to comfort him by saying, "I'm lucky to be alive."

Élan introduced me to Aytinous, and I inquired about his arm. "Rescue workers tell me its a minor fracture," he assured me. "Élan, and I, and several of our brothers are going to go to Sycottie Shardasko for medical treatment."

"Sycottie cannot help me," said Élan a wee bit too quickly.

"We've been through this a dozen times," said Aytinous and the edge in his voice sounded strained, as if perhaps he argued with Élan over whether to make this trip to Loxaloo.

Several more people approached Élan and interrupted our reunion with, "thank you," and, "I'll never forget your kindness."

"What happened to you? Why are you blind?" demanded Stellium.

Élan's eyes were brilliant, but they missed contact with Stellium and maybe even his point. "I don't know why I'm blind," he said. "Why do Gathosians have black tongues?"

Stellium shot me a third look, this one confused. "Okay Élan, you tell me—why do Gathosians have black tongues?"

"I don't know, but they do. Gathosians have black tongues and Humans have pink tongues and it seems that Shardasko Warriors who face *manatees* must loose their physical vision."

The puzzlement showing on Stellium's face seemed bottomless. "What are *manatees*?"

"*Manatees* are not a what, *manatees* are a who," and he kissed Stellium on the cheek saying, "I'll explain later."

Aytinous informed us, "Élan was lost for three days."

"Not lost, merely detained in the fourth dimension," said Élan.

"That's what he continues to claim, but when a group of neophytes found him, they said he was incoherent and blind and now he hasn't slept in six days."

"Never was I incoherent. They merely did not understand me."

Aytinous raised his eyebrows and a slight smirk settled in around his mouth that seemed to suggest he believed Élan was deranged. It was condescending for Aytinous to make facial expressions of that sort, when Élan could not see. A large transport vehicle arrived from Sycottie Shardasko and we went aboard and found seats. It felt a tad peculiar since I was the only female among them. Aytinous sat alone in a seat directly behind us and stared out the window. Meanwhile, the exhausted Élan, managed to remain upbeat, despite the horrors he just experienced. Several times his eyelids fluttered and his head nodded forward. Once, the vehicle hit a rut in the roadway and he came to full alert. Then he leaned against Stellium and told him, "I missed you so much."

At Sycottie Hospital, attendants immediately whisked Élan, Aytinous, and the others off to examination rooms, while Stellium and I went into a chapel down the hall to ponder the latest turn of events. This chapel honored the element Air and was a typical Air facility. It had a few old books and discs, a couple of chairs, and not much else.

Physical vision is important, but Stellium is an artist and vision is so critical to him that blindness seemed like a curse worse than death. He sniffed back tears. "Now we know the meaning of your dream. It was prophetic. The dream was telling you that Élan would be blind and unable to see you for a very long time." Stellium's mood went into a complete nosedive. He sat down on one of the chairs and buried his head in his hands. "Why does the universe treat us like such fools? I thought this was a new beginning for the three of us."

"It is a new beginning, but we always knew problems would arise."

"You call Élan's blindness a problem? Help him, sprite. I know you can do it."

"Don't ask me to intercede. Élan will create his own healing when he decides it's appropriate."

Stellium looked up and gestured with a finger in frustration. "What higher purpose could the loss of his sight serve?"

"We knew Élan would face dangers in the fourth dimension. Besides, something more critical is at stake than Élan's blindness."

Stellium dropped his head into his hands again. "His auric glow?"

"He's almost too bright."

Tears spilled from Stellium's eyes. "I've never seen anything like it before, not even around the most advanced Shardasko masters. It's frightening. I keep thinking about him being a match—" Neither of us could finish the thought aloud—*that lights instantly, burns brightly and then quickly burns away.*

"I believe we're seeing the first glimmer of Élan's *latturtimelda*, the fulfillment of his original intent."

"Well that's good—isn't it?" I put on a deliberate hopeful face. What good would it do to tell Stellium that doubt was now reminding me of the thousand roadblocks on the first leg of the journey called *latturtimelda?*

\*\*\*\*

As soon as the hospital staff allowed us to see Élan, he told us, "I need to get out of this place." After a short and heated debate with Stellium, Élan agreed to stay and submit to an ophthalmological exam. Stellium again asked Élan what caused his blindness, but he offered no explanation beyond his first cryptic statement, "Shardasko Warriors who face *manatees* must loose their physical sight." I knew about *manatees,* but Stellium did not. *Manatees* were fourth dimensional creatures that possessed the ability to show us our own future selves.

While the ophthalmologist examined Élan, Aytinous invited Stellium to eat lunch in the hospital café. Stellium insisted that my lack of a personal invitation was an innocent oversight on Aytinous' part. "Besides, no way am I having lunch with Aytinous without you present," said Stellium. "I need your help in getting his angle on what happened to Élan." When I sat down with them at the luncheon table, it was clear Aytinous did not want me there. Stellium and I loved Élan. It was so obvious, love oozed out of our every expression of concern. Aytinous ignored the obvious and pretended Stellium was Élan's *tritum* mate and friend. I was a bigger challenge, so Aytinous ignored me as a fleeting *tra kirlium\** in Élan's life.

Over tea and *grash*, Aytinous told us, "Masters knew several days before the storm that Sutcay Tay would be devastated. Emblematic Warriors visited all the villages in the valley and warned that the conjunction between Afen and Insanio would result in environmental catastrophe. Those that ignored our warnings, paid for their indifference with their lives. Even on campus, masters were explicit with neophytes and used the impending situation to initiate a First Cut. All twenty-two masters presided over an open forum and told us that vaspray would be a wing-to-wing obstacle along the timeline."

"How many neophytes left when they heard that news?" asked Stellium.

Aytinous stirred his steaming *grash* with his *juet* to cool it. Spiritual pride

*\*tra kirlium:* "One's involvement in a situation is politely not mentioned because it's obvious and might be embarrassing."; language origin, Mescale.

peeked out from beneath another slight smirk and the miasma just below his heart took on a healthy glow. "Regrettably, a full two-thirds abandoned their training merely over the notion of vaspray. Masters held meetings among themselves and decided who would act as the prime stanchions in the Interlude Shading. When the critical time came, we each knew what we were supposed to do. I, along with several other Emblematic Warriors, held the safety zone around the neophytes, just inside the fourth."

"Élan was the only warrior not assigned a specific task, because he missed the prep exercises. I don't know how his position was decided. When the storm began, he stayed with Master Kyron in the third dimension and helped him hold open the door. We were nine minutes inside the fourth when I noticed Master Kyron and Élan slipping through a door. Master Kyron glanced in my direction and smiled and then he kissed the tips of his fingers and waved to me. Humor marked his face, as it often does. Then a vaspray flew up against the force of our safety zone and smacked it so violently, the impact fractured my arm. I, along with several other Emblematic Warriors, had to renew our efforts to hold our safety zone. When I looked back to where I first saw Master Kyron and Élan hiding, they were gone. At first, this did not concern me, because I assumed they moved to a more advantageous position. However, that was the last time I ever saw Master Kyron alive and I did not see Élan until three days later."

"Iosobell and I are concerned about Élan's physical and emotional condition," said Stellium. "Can you tell us anything that might help us understand what happened to him in the fourth dimension?"

"As I said before, I did not see him for three days. Master Kyron told me three moons ago that Élan was his soul mate. I've made my peace with the fact that they are eternally connected."

"Kyron confided that confidential information to you?" I asked.

Aytinous finally focused on me, but not for long. "If I said Master Kyron did, then he did. Master Kyron told me that he was sharing that information with me to demonstrate a fundamental truth—"

Stellium glanced my way and his eyebrows arched slightly before he asked, "Did you see Élan emerge from the fourth dimension?"

"No, but several neophytes noticed him and an Emblematic Warrior named Brother Dalini arrived seconds later. Dalini claimed that Élan's aura was so luminous that even the neophytes could see it. Since then, his aura has toned down considerably. Dalini sent a couple of neophytes to fetch me. They came yelling, 'come quick! We've found Brother Élan and he looks as if he is on fire.' I rushed to where they found him and he was rather bright, to say the least. His body was crouched on the ground in a rigid position, which is atypical for any warrior emerging from the fourth. The expression on his face made him look like a wild man. He wore a silver chain around his neck with a key dangling from it and he was clutching a white feather in his right hand. The key and feather made me realize that he had not just arrived from the fourth dimension, as the neophytes insisted. Most probably he was in shock from Master Kyron's death and had wandered lost and blind around the countryside for hours, or even days, before the neophytes discovered him."

Stellium put his hand on my thigh under the table and I sent him a private telepathic message. *Do you realize Élan was able to penetrate the fourth dimension with third-dimensional objects?*

"How was he crouching?" asked Stellium.

"His legs were tucked in toward his gut and his fists clenched to his chest," said Aytinous. When I commented that Aytinous was describing the fetal position, he jumped on my fetal-position statement with, "That's a projection, in fact, a feminine projection. All we know for sure is Élan was crouching."

Stellium quickly stepped in with a new question. "Did he say anything revealing?"

"Not at first, he was completely dazed. When he did begin to speak, it was gibberish."

"Not even the masters understood what he was saying?" I asked.

"No masters were present. Admittedly, whatever Élan was trying to communicate sounded urgent, as if he was asking us for help. I sat down on the ground in front of him and stared into his eyes, trying to make psychic contact. I repeated his moniker several times and this seemed to bring him slightly out of his stupor. I think he spoke some English words; at least the words sounded like English to me and then he said, 'Aytinous, I'm so happy to see you.' Naturally, he couldn't see me, but I suppose he did not mean it literally. His behavior remained peculiar from then on."

"In what way?" Stellium asked.

"The Eternal Waters Sanctuary was the only temple left standing after the meteor storm and we set up an infirmary inside, to treat the wounded arriving from all over the valley. I took Élan to the temple, so a master could evaluate him. A few hours later, I returned and found him wandering among the patients, praying with some—"

"That doesn't sound peculiar," I said.

Aytinous' voice turned harsh. "What's peculiar was several people claimed that Élan had healed them. I persuaded him to rest because I was sure he would burn out, but talking to him proved useless. He would not listen and the masters refused to intervene. Yesterday morning, he told me that he remembered he was supposed to meet you on Gathos and I jumped at the opportunity to get him to Sycottie Hospital for treatment. All the way here, his behavior remained the same. As soon as we lifted off from Sutcay Tay, he was up and moving around the ship, interacting with anyone that crossed his path. This time I saw it with my own eyes. He was indiscriminately healing the sick and wounded."

"Why do you disapprove of Élan's charitable compassion?" asked Stellium.

Aytinous had a ready answer and he filtered it through Kyron. "As Master Kyron might say, our lives present challenges so we may learn from those challenges. A mere mortal able to perform a few, cheap miracles should not whisk challenges away prematurely. If you are his friend, please try to talk some sense into him. If he has authentic new powers, then he should use those powers to develop his consciousness toward Shardasko mastery."

"Do you recognize Élan as a master?" I asked.

Aytinous nodded his head slightly toward me, for now he felt on solid ground. "Élan is not a master. Mastery is a Shardasko title accorded a man because he has earned the respect of his peers through dedication and hard work. Whatever supernatural rubbish Élan now chooses to wield, is transient. Whatever he is, he assuredly is not a Shardasko master."

It was time for my soul mate Viobella to have her say and I allowed her to use my mouth to deliver her edict on mastery. "For your information, dedication and hard work does lead to mastery; mastery leads to dedication and hard work. Mastery has nothing to do with external kudos, except the external world occasionally recognizes a master and respects him or her as such. True mastery is the alignment of our many selves throughout multiple dimensions, with the original intent of our *Emayre*. We honestly do not know what Élan's original intent encompasses. Élan may be the greatest healer this universe has ever experienced. Finally, what you choose to condemn as supernatural nonsense and indiscriminate healing is, in truth, the sacred gesture of compassion coming through a life blessed with complete mastery."

"And you certainly are a Trinity Witch to speak as you do," said Aytinous, and the way he said, 'witch," hinted at the disrespect that soon would befall that word.

A great deal of tension brewed between Aytinous and me. He seemed so distant, stern, and sure, like a solitary, stone icon sitting on a mountaintop. Only later, in meditation, did I see the gap between us. Stellium and I were swimming along in the virgin stream of this new reality while Aytinous lingered in the persistence of his familiar space. I wondered why a man so blessed with beauty, intelligence, and access to cosmic consciousness would prefer to remain a mere speck of his real self when he had come so far. Parallels existed between Aytinous and Remette, only Aytinous was far more complex and advanced and therefore, capable of a bigger fall. Perhaps that was the real problem. Maybe he was afraid to make the final jump across the gap—the real abyss—because any move was a threat to what he thought he knew. On the other side of himself, he would be in unexplored territory, a neophyte yet again. I wondered what he would think if I told him about the leaps of faith Élan's *Emayre* was taking to reach its higher goals. Unfortunately, the knowledge Aytinous mastered, as a Shardasko Warrior, had become his prison. His mind lacked true understanding (flexible receptivity) and his journey lacked the juice of surprise. If Kyron's death and the near destruction of Sutcay Tay had not broken open Aytinous' heart to his own compassion—what could? In the world of persistence, his influence in the future was powerful. His future power— now diffused by the introduction of this new reality—floundered without a goal. As I sat at the table, my *Emayre* suggested, *offer him your hand. Try to make peace.*

"Please take my hand," I offered in friendship, and then I explained, "It's not really my hand, but the hand of my *Emayre*."

"I am a Shardasko Warrior," he lectured me. "It is inappropriate for me to touch members of the opposite sex."

"No such Shardasko precept exists," piped up Stellium.

Aytinous insisted, "It is my personal Shardasko precept."

"Have it your own way," I said and I retracted my hand. "Trinity Witches say, 'Even if the hand of a *Emayre* is not immediately taken, the offer once extended remains viable until the bridge is crossed.' Therefore, my hand awaits your acceptance. I predict that in the future, you will accept my hand and remember this moment. In truth, my prediction has already come true and we are the best of friends. Now, I merely thought you might enjoy becoming friends sooner, rather than later."

"Do not flatter yourself," said Aytinous. "I predict that in the future, every soul involved in Trinity and Hectarian debauchery will be lost in Chaos."

"Please?" said Stellium. "We're supposed to be enlightened individuals. Isn't the future of the third dimension large enough to accommodate all paths to enlightenment without anyone falling into Chaos?"

Aytinous pushed back from the table, "I apologize for my abruptness. I'm exhausted and not slept in several days myself. Nonetheless, let me make this perfectly clear. Trinity Witch enlightenment is not Shardasko enlightenment. My hope is that Élan soon will realize that intemperance is several steps backward into hedonism."

I was about to say, *many paths lead to enlightenment, but there is only one enlightenment,* but Stellium again had his hand on my thigh. Afterward, he said, "Sorry, I just wanted to get out of there in one piece. Aytinous reminds me of my biological father in too many ways. Both are cold as stalactites."

"Does your cold have anything to do with cool?"

"No way! The cold around Aytinous is subzero. I tell you one thing, sprite, if Aytinous becomes a master, no neophyte will stay under his tutelage for long. I predict that he is going to be one lonely stalactite with no stalagmites to drip his bits of wisdom upon."

"Aytinous will break free and then he will be a fantastic master. Right now, he is so thoroughly connected to his Witness, he can't make the next move into empathy."

"You mean he's got his head so far up his own gorgeous ass, he can't come down?"

I laughed. "That's another way of putting it. Actually, there's no up or down; there's only complete subjective empathy in each moment and that's the point Aytinous is missing."

****

The ophthalmologist diagnosed Élan blindness as damage to his optic nerve. The damage was repairable through tissue regeneration surgery. The surgery needed to be scheduled and hospitalization and recovery would last at least a moon. Élan was in a rush and opted not to wait. "I will get surgery later," he said, "when I have time." He checked himself out of Sycottie Hospital and that was the end of any discussion concerning eye surgery, at least for the time being.

The last thing Élan did before leaving hospital was to give Kyron's wand of authority to Aytinous. This he did against my advice. Kyron's wand was a powerful talismanic tool and even more so, now that Élan and I mended it. To Aytinous, he said most seriously, "I know Master Kyron would want you to have his wand. You will be a master soon and will need this tool to carry on his work." Élan smiled innocently and focused on the infinite beyond Aytinous' face. Élan felt the *ackinayon* along its shaft until he found a smooth spot near one end. "Look," he said. "You can carve your moniker and its meaning, 'perfection will reign,' right here."

To Élan's face, Aytinous was more generous and made no mention that he believed Élan was on the verge of falling from grace. Instead, Aytinous assured Élan, "You are well on your way to mastery too, my brother."

"I'm still just a bundle of possibility," said Élan. "You were right when you told me I did not understand my genetic and karmic foundation. You also were right when you said I had built a *tritum* on a foundation that was meant to support a temple."

"Then you're going to Earth to build that temple on your Shardasko foundation?" asked Aytinous.

"Eventually, but first I am going on my honeymoon with Stellium and Iosobell."

Aytinous ignored Élan's reference to a honeymoon. "May your *Holder* be your true foundation," offered Aytinous and he touched his forehead and wished Élan a warm brotherly, "*afen.*"

****

Stellium, Élan, and I departed Loxaloo and returned to Wacar so Élan could retrieve the twenty-one journals from the bank vault. He fell asleep in the airfloat, but the fact that his disposition remained so light and cheery, seemed incredible. His Shardasko skills remained so acute that it was difficult to tell that he was blind. He neither groped nor needed to feel his way along, as the blind often must do. His assured stride made him appear as if he really could see where he was going. At times, he did hesitate, as if taking stock of new situations, but once he knew where he was going, he still moved with style and grace. I told him he was cool and Stellium had to explain what cool meant.

When we arrived at the bank in Wacar, Élan told Stellium, "I'll need to use your key for the safety deposit box. When I entered the fourth dimension, I forgot to remove mine," and he pulled a silver chain from under his shirt and showed us the key in question. "I do seem to be collecting a few charms," he admitted. "Somehow this particular key is important to me now, but I don't remember why. Maybe Kyron or my *Holder* told me I should never take if off from here on out." His decision to keep the key was more than sentimentalism. The key undoubtedly retained transcendental energy. "A *manatee* even touched it," Élan confided.

"Are you ready to tell us what, or rather, who *manatees* are?" asked Stellium.

"Tell Stellium about *manatees*," Élan suggested to me."

"You tell him," I said. "*Manatees* gave you your subjective phenomenon, not mine."

"Then you will have to wait," said Élan. "Physically, I'm exhausted and when I tell you, I want to tell you the whole story with a clear head. For now, suffice it to say, *manatees* are the guardians of the future."

Élan managed to hang on for two more hours. We booked passage on a Gathosian luxury cruise ship called the *Fecundity Star* and left Gathos that evening for New Delphi. It would take two hundred space hours to reach Delphi or about ten Gathosian days. Élan claimed he was finished living the austere life as a Shardasko brother and our accommodations on the *Fecundity Star* were wonderful. "No skimping," he insisted. "It's our honeymoon."

Honeymoon or not, the first day out of port, Élan slept. Stellium and I spent time in the rear of the ship in the Astral Observatory where Stellium created a series of beautiful drawings of the Crab Nebula from that view. In a few, he sketched pictures of me in the foreground and drew several sketches for the painting he would call, *Passionate Urgency*. I spent time writing in my journal. Every few hours we returned to our suite and one of us would slip into the regrav unit to make sure Élan was sleeping peacefully.

In total, he slept for eighteen space hours, which is equal to about twenty-three Gathosian hours.

It was early afternoon, on the second space-cycle out of port, when Stellium and I returned to out suite and found Élan soaking in the tub. "Stellium, come in here," Élan yelled. In spite of his blindness, he managed to find the necessary amenities such as shampoo, toothbrush, and razor.

Stellium peeked around the edge of the door and explained, "He's shaved, but wanted to make sure he did not skip any spots. He still has his vanity. I guess that's a good sign that's he going to stay in this dimension a while longer."

"Did he—skip any spots?"

Stellium rubbed his chin and shook his head in awe. "Smooth as silk!"

Élan emerged from the bathroom dressed in, what I would come to learn was his favorite accommodation to clothing, a bath towel. This was as nude as I had seen him since we met. He extended his arms and bowed in my general direction and claimed, "I can feel you staring at me." Then the shy Shardasko Warrior found the audacity to lift the corner of his towel and flash me.

Stellium began snickering. "You've—mesmerized her. She can't take her eyes off your towel."

I returned the gesture with the challenged, "Élan, can you take me on a journey where I've not yet been?"

"I would like to try, but my towel will have to come off and we will need to get a whole lot closer."

If I was a sprite then Stellium certainly was an imp and he urged us on with, "May I watch?"

"Only if you participate," said Élan. "Now if you truly love me, Stellium, come here so I don't have to grope around this unfamiliar room." Stellium walked over to Élan, fully expecting him to initiate a sexual advance. Instead, Élan took Stellium's arm and shook it gently saying, "Consciousness is not separate from the elemental universe and no man begins a journey to higher awareness unless his survival is secure."

Stellium shrugged and glanced my way. "Okay, I'll play neophyte. Isn't our survival secure, Master Élan?"

"Yes, but survival is only the first course. What is course two, lad?"

"Ah—food?" suggested Stellium.

"You're a genius, my wonderful ginger-scented, star pupil. Let's start with a double order of *grash*, stir-fried vegetables, and two bottles of *lume* wine." Stellium ordered food from the ship's kitchen and a waiter brought the food to our room on an autocart. The food was delicious and Élan ate his portion in a flash before finishing off the remainder of mine. I had no doubt that his good appetite would hold for the courses ahead.

*Lume* wine is a celebratory drink made from the flowers of the parishfruit tree. Its taste is slightly puckering, highly fragrant, explosive, dry and full-bodied. When Gathosians drink *lume*, no one wants to miss an opportunity to infuse the spirit of the wine with good wishes and extend those good wishes to loved ones near and far. This is what we did in toast after toast. In truth, the three of us got slightly drunk while Élan told us about what happened, since he left us in Pointilla seven days earlier.

****

"I had no choice but to go," said Élan. "My compulsion to return to Kyron was the strongest compulsion I've ever experienced. Halfway back, I met Cerebow and Taro in the woods. Cerebow would not leave me and Taro would not leave Cerebow. When I put them in the fourth dimension, the personal barriers shattered between them and me and I knew Cerebow mirrored the unruly naiveté of my unrefined senses, while Taro was that precious and active genius that promises—Élan, you can be more." Tears filled Élan's poor, blind eyes and he proposed a toast. "To Cerebow and Taro, for the time-being, two more shadows in the fourth dimension. May their *Holder* keep them safe until we again are one."

"To Cerebow and Taro," Stellium and I offered, and we all drank a toast.

"When I reached the Sutcay Tay campus, I went to the Eternal Waters Sanctuary to calm my interior agitation. There, the voice of my *Holder* became stronger and I knew I had returned for a momentous reason. Still I lingered, afraid to face Kyron and his continuing denial of me. Then Kyron found me—said he was searching for hours because he received a message from you, alerting him to my return." Élan's eyes turned misty. "At first, Kyron wasn't exactly happy to see me. He was angry and even cursed— called me a 'damn reckless fool.' I cried because his anger hurt like thorns in my flesh. 'I gave you everything,' he wailed, 'and you repay me by coming here and risking your life.' I managed to stay calm and I asked, 'If you've given me everything, why do I still feel incomplete?' He kept up the barrage of false anger and refused to answer this simple question. I needed him to acknowledge my incompletion, so he could acknowledge his incompletion as well. Through my training, he taught me how to cut through my illogical conclusions when they impeded my evolution, and now I used his own method on him. Finally, I said, 'You're my soul mate, Kyron, and I am incomplete without you.' Tears rolled down his cheeks, but the denial was over between us. When he accepted it, he accepted it completely and he expected me to do the same. He stopped crying long enough to warn me, 'Your destruction awaits, my prince,' and he spun around like a dancing warrior and left me alone."

"I was eager and terrified all at the same time, but now I knew my fate was sealed. I did not follow him. Instead, I waited and gave him time to prepare. When I finally arrived at his *tritum*, it was the first time in my life I did not knock. I entered and found him sitting in meditation. We talked for a few minutes, but I can't remember exactly what we said." Élan laughed, but it sounded more like a gasp for breath. "I do remember that he asked if I was prepared and I told him that as his prince of fire, I was prepared to burn down his entire *tritum* to glimpse the truth. 'Then open your eyes,' he said, "and when I did, he jumped into my mind."

Élan swallowed a lump in his throat and tears rolled down his cheeks. "Kyron proved that he knew me better than I knew myself. He showed me rooms within myself that I did not know existed. He was ruthless, and burned every false mansion, within me, to the ground. He took me to where I knew reason was an inadequate excuse, a repression of my true self. Funny me! I was the one that tried to contain it, thinking, if I can contain this, I can return to this reality and translate it into something that makes sense. Kyron kept urging me not to contain it. He said, 'Give your fire all the fuel it needs.' When I did, the whole thing became light—nothing but light! Kyron was light and I was light, yet light came toward us until we were light dancing upon light. I didn't know where we were or when we were, nor did I care. I was free and alive in a cosmic playground. Kyron and I took turns throwing each other out like gobs of living stardust. Then, nothing remained—no home but the experience of rapture in timeless awareness. Then everywhere was My Key, unlocking my destiny, my joy; and I knew vastly more than I ever thought possible."

"Kyron might tell you differently, but to me it seemed my viewpoint had always been askew until that moment. Once I pictured myself as a beginning, moving through incarnation after incarnation, progressing along an imaginary line of time. That was the first lie I swallowed without examination. I was, and always will be, my *Holder*, imagining projections of myself upon the layers of endless densities. From my new perspective, I could see Journey Cœur and La Teeair Forma were two projections on the screen of the third dimension. These two projections were living in a neighborhood halfway between nowhere and home. I also knew that for any projection, the way home was through the perspective of the *Holder*. My eye focusing through its eye is my only path. That accomplished, I can take endless journeys and never lose touch."

"When it was over, we were back in Kyron's *tritum*. Either, we never left or just returned. I only know that was the reality of the moment. I found Kyron still sitting in meditation, but slumped forward. Our *Holder* appeared then and I questioned why it was missing and it spread forth its arms, meaning it was everywhere. 'Kyron's life is nearly exhausted," said our *Holder*. "Carry him into the fourth dimension for me.' I picked up Kyron and his body was as light as a feather. The three of us jumped, but this time we did not stop at the timeline. We went deeper, all the way to the end of the time threads where my *Holder* said, 'Here lies the real abyss; this abyss is the effulgence of creativity rolling out from Source.'"

"Did you have vision?" asked Stellium.

"Not at first, only a sense of expanse, perhaps inside my head. Then out of sheer nothingness, a physical place mushroomed into a reality, which mimicked third dimensional space. The place seemed oddly concrete from anything I ever experienced before, in the fourth dimension. My *Holder* told me that I was here to witness, The Great Exchange. The scene was unfamiliar, but I've seen holographs of Mars and this terrain appeared similar. I was on top of a desert mesa and the rocky countryside was stark and russet brown in color. Below and to my left was an open expanse of valleys and to my right a canyon of perilous depths. A group of elderly men and women appeared in the closest valley. Their skin was wrinkled and was the same russet shade as the rocks. They were communicating telepathically and I understood their thoughts. They called themselves lovers and their function was to fly from the cliffs of higher dimensions, to these valleys in the fourth. Their energy was mercurial—that is magnetic, intelligent, sensitive, and responsive with compassion."

"A moment later, Dulce emerged from among them as a beautiful young man. His skin was pale and creamy as a newborn babe and his eyes burned liked two golden coins. His appearance was breathtaking, an incredible contrast to the aged figures surrounding him. He stared up at me and I felt his passion as my own. I wanted to go down into the valley, to embrace him, but I couldn't move." Élan grew quiet and sipped his *lume*. "I heard music then, Dulce's music, and I understood its meaning."

Stellium sounded excited when he asked, "What is the meaning of Dulce's music?"

"The music holds a suggestion, or request, that transcends words. The music is a glimpse of Love's dream, a dream to manifest greater expressions of itself in every dimension. Love's request is that we become as exuberant children, manifesting greater and greater expressions of love.' Élan fell quiet and was lost in thought. "Hearing the music changed me; it made me a lover too."

I purposed the next toast. "To The Divine Dulce." The three of us drank.

Élan said, "My *Holder* told me that I could go no farther with my physical body, but I might watch The Great Exchange from the viewpoint of the mesa above. My *Holder* took Kyron from my arms and I kissed him and he stirred slightly as if I disturbed his sleep. Élan smiled and lifted his glass of *lume*. "To the precious life that once was Kyron. I'll see you later, my master thief."

The three of us drank to Kyron and Élan broke down and sobbed uncontrollably for several minutes. When he picked up his story the next time, he told us, "From the mesa above, I watched our *Holder* and Kyron enter the deep canyon on the right. I could no longer hear their communications through telepathy, but seemed to have a sense of what was happening. I knew that Dulce had volunteered to die for the entire group and would do that by joining Kyron and our *Holder* in the canyon. I got the urge to stop what was about to occur. I loved them both exactly as they were, but was powerless to intercede. Then Dulce disappeared down the deep canyon too. A short time later, our *Holder* emerged from the canyon and began dancing with joyful abandonment. At the height of its wild dance, it threw one white feather into the air. The white feather caught the wind, and whirled around and around until it lifted and cleared the edge of the mesa and landed by my left side. I stared down at the feather, but did not touch it because I did not realize the feather was meant for me. I looked to my left and that's when I spied Aytinous. Just as he reached out a hand to take the feather, something stopped him. That's when I knew the feather was mine and I picked it up and clutch it to my breast."

"I still don't remember everything, but somehow the mesa and everything in it vanished and I found myself inside a lovely sanctuary. Outside, I heard vesper drums as Shardasko musicians play them in the temples at sunset. Only this time the sound of the drums fill me with dread and I was afraid to acknowledge their demands. The drums grew louder and I could not ignore their insistence. Bolstering my courage, I prepared to meet the full impact of the demanding future and declared, 'I am a Shardasko Warrior and I will not lose unless I lose completely.'"

"I walked out of the sanctuary and met a creature whose authority no soul dare question. I knew, or rather remembered, the creature was a *manatee*. This time the *manatee* appeared as a Human man. He appeared familiar to me and I was certain we met before. His body was slim and tall. His skin was pale, like mine, but he was handsome with long blonde hair, and he was dressed in a black, casual jacket that had a unique, round, silver buckle at the collar. The silver buckle was a clue and then I remembered. The last time I saw him, this silver buckle was not open, but tight against his throat."

"You see, when I died in persistent reality, I died so quickly, I did not realize my body was dead. I thought I managed to save myself—thought I had jumped to the fourth dimension and escaped. This same *manatee* appeared in the persistent stream and politely informed me, 'Your body is dead, Élan.' This time, he was just as polite and again told me that he was a *manatee* and that it was his job to keep track of my progress and his visit was routine, but seriously routine. I wasn't afraid anymore, but just the same, I began talking fast. It seemed self-serving to tell him what I did thus far, because it seemed piddling. Instead, I told him, I'm beginning a new project and need more time to complete my mission. I showed him the white feather I received from my *Holder*."

Then he asked, "Where's your key?" I did not answer him because I did not know which key he meant. I had so many keys in my life, the most important one being Kyron himself. Then he said, "I see! You're wearing it. May I examine it more closely?" I glanced down at my chest and spied the key dangling from its silver chain and was in shock that I had penetrated the fourth dimension with a third dimensional object. The *manatee* picked up the key and ran a thumb along the cut edge. "Twenty-two," he said. That's when he twisted the key slightly. The key caught the light and the light hit my unguarded eyes. An instant later, I found myself back in the third dimension and blind. No longer could I see as, so called, normal men see and I struggled for a reference point and a way to relate. Regardless of my lack of eyesight, I sensed the devastation and misery from the meteorite storm. My efforts to communicate telepathically, as I had in the fourth dimension, seemed futile. No one understood me. Then I began going through my repertoire of verbal languages until I found one that made sense to the crowd of curious neophytes surrounding me. When I got to Mescale, someone answered me and this caused me to remember that part of me still was Journey Cœur."

"Moving back into this small projection of myself, I recalled the details of this life, although it seemed as if I had to squint and shutdown the bigger parts of myself, to convince myself that this life was real. Doing that, I lost some of my psychic senses. A few hours later, the misery and pain of this reality tapped my heart. I knew then that all life's misery comes to the living because our perspective is so miniscule. I was fully back by then, but I retained a memory of my fourth dimensional journey and who I was."

"After a while, the Shardasko masters approached me. One by one they asked what happened to Kyron. I told them his body was dead, yet he lived as The Key to my heart. I volunteered the information that the original projection was perfect for I had just come from the creative body of my soul group and seen the projection was perfect. I told them the problems occurred when the projections hit the timeline in the elemental universe. Upon the authority of that one statement, they offered me mastery. I explained that Shardasko mastery no longer mattered to me because my eternal commitment was now clear and that was to alleviate pain and suffering through my own compassionate outpouring. Yesterday morning, I remembered that I promised to meet you in Wacar. When I remembered, I felt the first urge of personal need arise. I wanted to be with you, to talk with you. I needed two people in this little reality who could understand, as I do, and help me attend the suffering souls."

"Your commitment is mine," I told him. I lifted my glass in another toast. "To Élan Journey Cœur." Élan, Stellium, and I held hands and we swore our love for each other and our swearing we considered as

258

commitment vows. We toasted our marriage with brimming glasses of *lume*.

Élan got up from the table and went over to the acid free bag that held the now complete twenty-two-volume inheritance from Kyron. He took out the journal entitled *The Universe* and opened it. From between the cover and first page, he lifted a pure white feather. "Watch," he said. "He tossed the feather in the air and gently blew upon it. The feather twirled around and around, just as he said it performed in the depths of the fourth dimension. He extended his hand and the feather landed gently in his palm. "Take it," he instructed Stellium. Stellium took the feather and Élan said, "Blow upon it." Stellium blew on the feather; and again, Élan extended his hand and the feather floated into his palm. We performed this experiment several times and no matter who held the feather and blew upon it, the feather always returned to Élan.

# SIXTEEN

## PART III: THE DANCE

I am the dance of All Understanding
Chalice is the sweet eternal
For your song
Is the direct path
Through my heart

**W**hen love claimed our passion, the visually predisposed Stellium went to great lengths to get the rose-colored lights adjusted to the right level in the regrav unit. Élan responded by making a strong point that he wanted the lights turned off. He called it, "equity concerning my handicap."

"You, handicapped!' said Stellium. "If you were any more adept in the dark, you could qualify as a full-fledged shadow. Sprite, do you realize Élan prowess as a shadow dancer won him accolades from the masters, during First Cut."

"You're right," said Élan. "Forgive me, Stellium. I'm looking in the mirror and reading backward. Handicap definitely is the wrong word. I should have said that it's only fair that you assume the same advantage as me." Élan's point—just like the point of shadow dancing—was to make us aware of the seductive need for visual stimulation, which can overpower and short-circuit creative expression. Despite my evolved senses, I thoroughly enjoyed the ease of visual stimulation. When Cerebow frustrated my need for a visual boost, because she was unable to describe Élan's appearance, I was frustrated. Now, it felt easy and even voyeuristic as my eyes stole glimpses of Élan's physical nudity as he walked around the room.

****

Inside the regrav unit, the lights were out and gravity sat at zero. I felt confident that our three-way love affair would be honest and profound. The doubt that sometimes pursues me, I saw nowhere in sight. We formed an intimate circle within the regrav space and synchronized our separate breaths into one circular breath. Love responded and became an effulgent fountain, illuminating our sacred space within time. Élan placed his white feather in the palm of his hand. "Are you ready?" he asked. Stellium and I nodded and off we sailed on a voyage toward freedom and a perfect place to make love.

Every voyage needs a helmsman and every ship needs a masthead, so Élan volunteered to fulfill these two rolls for our journey ahead. A good helmsman uses active energy to steer the ship, while the masthead is receptive energy, clinging to the bowsprit and telling the crew what lies ahead. We had not sailed far, when a large obstacle appeared like a silver iceberg in the darkness. It was Stellium's cynicism and it was larger than I imagined. The moment I saw it, I felt sick. This cynicism appeared volcanic and I knew it was supporting an active free radical inside his aura. I chided myself and asked *how did I miss this*? In my eagerness to love him, I skipped over what could take down his life and torture his soul.

Élan seemed fearless and asked, "Stellium, do you trust me?"

Stellium was as docile as a lamb. He seemed unaware that the obstacle ahead was his projection; or perhaps, his denial prevented him from seeing it at all. Whichever, Stellium showed no fear and said, "I trust you both implicitly."

"Go slowly," I warned Élan. "I love Stellium just as he is."

"What's up?" asked Stellium suspiciously. Élan steered us closer to the coldness that hid in the darkness of Stellium's heart. We changed physical positions and I cradled him in my arms as if he were my child. I kissed him deeply and told him to relax. He began to cough and then he said, "I can't, my chest is beginning to hurt."

Élan explained the situation to Stellium in plain and direct terms. "My love commitment to you is unconditional. I will stay right here with you if you decide to go no farther; but our complete unfolding is frustrated as things stand. That's because you have a free radical, just under your heart."

Stellium laughed nervously. "No, honestly, I feel fine. I'm merely dizzy because I drank too much *lume*." When he mentioned that he was dizzy, I remembered that he also was dizzy on several lovemaking occasions with me. Eager to connect our heart energy, I had helped him jump over his denial, with nary a backward glance.

Élan said, "Allow me to tease it out of you and then you can glimpse it for yourself."

Stellium thought about it for a moment and challenged Élan with, "Okay, I'm game; tease away, sweetheart."

"Release him and allow yourself a margin of safety," said Élan and then he cupped his mouth to Stellium's left nipple. After a moment, Élan opened his mouth and exhaled sharply, spitting forth a spray of black and acid-green miasma. Stellium abruptly began screaming in terror, because this free radical did not disperse as an illusion, but like a lively fetus, clung to his chest. The amorphous blob writhed and twisted under the new light of our mutual scrutiny. It knew it was exposed and churned in on itself and quickly sought a new hiding place. It scuttled off Stellium's body and tried to hide behind his back. When this happened, The Thing tore at the umbilical and caused Stellium excruciating pain. We wanted to protect and love Stellium and give him strength to deal with this half-aborted curse; but in his fear and panic, he definitely wanted to escape. "You're safe," Élan said several times. "Calm down and attempt to give it a name."

Instead Stellium began thrashing and hyperventilating. Élan leaned over Stellium again and clamped his mouth to Stellium's mouth forcing him to slow his breathing. "Watch out!" I warned Élan. "That Thing can turn back on you."

"Let me—go," screamed Stellium in between deep, jerking sobs that sounded like spasms erupting in his chest. "You're hurting—me."

Élan spoke the truth in Stellium's ear. "Now who is looking in the mirror and reading backward? Say who is really hurting you."

Stellium quickly sank down into hopelessness and it was an important lesson for me about the virulence of free radicals in desperate situations. "Let me—sink into Chaos; no memory there."

"Never!" swore Élan and he pinned Stellium against one of the regrav walls so he could not escape. "If you're not in Paradise with me, its divine glory would be my Chaos. Now name this damn thing or I swear I will do it for you."

"You shouldn't do that," I reminded Élan.

Stellium turned desperate and his desperation made him violent. He managed to amass a maelstrom of rebellious energy and stuck Élan with a martial-arts blow across the top of his shoulder. The angry outburst caused Élan to fall sideways and crack his head on the wall of the regrav unit. Miraculously, he managed to hold onto Stellium's arm. A good chance existed that he would try to jump to the fourth dimension, which would be incredibility dangerous in his agitated state. "Name it," demanded Élan.

"Give me—a chance—to breathe," panted Stellium. After a few seconds hesitation, he choked out, "cynicism. My icy child is Cynicism," and he crumbled into a ball and wept. He was so raw, he convulsively jumped when I touched his shoulder and, for a moment, I was afraid he was going to strike me too. Making my voice soft, I communicated that I thought it might be possible to melt cynicism with the fire of our mutual passion. Stellium glanced up at me and his eyes were red with pain. "Only with you, sprite," he sobbed. "That bastard will never touch me again."

Élan glanced my way and warned, "Be careful that your own doubt does not get involved. It's my understanding, that in a crisis, free radicals help each other."

Cynicism showed no attraction for me and seemed unaware of my presence as I poured my energy into Stellium. Suddenly the icy crust of Cynicism broke open and out poured its fiery lies. Using Stellium's own mouth, Cynicism spoke saying, "Stellium is deeply flawed. I know he's flawed because I see the happiness and success of others and remind him that his flaws will forever keep him from the happiness others enjoy."

Élan and I realized the situation was worse than we anticipated. We were facing not only Cynicism, but also its free-radical cousin, Envy. Envy makes itself at home in the energy of souls whose creative gifts are frustrated in lifetime after lifetime. It accomplishes its dirty work by expropriating its victim's creative energy and using it against them. Envy, like all free radicals, can never manifest itself nor can it help a life manifest its unique gifts. If anything, Envy stymies creativity because it always seeks to mimic what it envies. Envy frustrates the ability of a life to focus on its original intent and isolates the life in moods of victimization and defeat.

How insidious our incarnate foibles are! Envy expropriated Stellium's once, wonderful realization of perfection, used the terminology of the higher mind, and set up housekeeping under his heart. Like all souls actively involved in their evolution, Stellium enjoyed great vistas of transcendence and extended periods of higher consciousness. Unfortunately, higher consciousness and vistas of transcendence were inadequate protections from free radicals. Obviously we were still on the subject of vision. Cloistered beneath Stellium's heart, the eyes of envy reflected its superficial and detached glimpses, telling him that its visions were real. How to free Stellium of this fetal leech was not easy. The scissors of logic could not be plunged into his chest to cut Envy away, nor could we transform this free radical with kind words and sincere praise. Élan and I knew only one way to free Stellium. We needed to take him on a journey to the stainless realm of his *Emayre*, so he could fuse with the strength of his true perspective.

Stellium wept and clutched his chest in agony. "This humiliation hurts more than the pain," he sobbed through his clogged throat. He now felt shame for the umbilical twisted around one of his legs and hung near his foot, like a millstone.

"Hurry," I said. "The free radical Shame is closing in too."

"Let's jump," said Élan.

Stellium fretted. "We'll get lost—jumping from a spaceship."

"Don't worry," said Élan. "This particular feather will allow us to jump not only time but also space," and he tickled Stellium under the chin with the white feather. From the regrav unit, we jumped to the fourth dimension where Élan again had perfect vision. We were vigilant and sheltered Stellium between us as we scanned the timeline for other free radicals that might consider Stellium fair game in his weakened state. Élan tossed the white feather toward deep fourth and blew upon it. Here it was easier to see that the feather retained the holographic pattern of its complete self and a white hawk of incomparable beauty sprang forth. "Guide us, Kyron," was Élan's simple request.

Our combined energy created a radiant sphere of protection around us. Kyron led us into a super-highway of spectral light that connected two galaxies. From our perspective, we could observe the gentle radiance of the inferior galaxy, which was green in color, and the superior galaxy, which was expansive and blue. The green galaxy sat below the blue galaxy and took its sustenance from the first. We took a side-path, to the right, and when we arrived at the green galaxy, it glittered like a brilliant emerald lake. We found ourselves in an atmosphere, a place of milky waters and subdued greens. A red rose, the trademark of authority representing Élan's soul group, appeared in Kyron's beak, as it flew directly into the soft mist. We were flying through sandwiched bands of green diaphanous light. Passing through these densities, the light actively imbued us with love and harmony. "Choose any world," I told Élan. "It will be made ready for Stellium by his mere need." We chose the next world in sight and when we cleared the fog, we found ourselves standing in a peaceful meadow of green and gold. A sweet chorus of birds sang in the distance and the tranquil gurgle of water came from just over the ridge. Although Stellium was in pain, he managed to lift his head slightly and say, "so beautiful."

Directly above us rotated the massive blue galaxy. Its blueness gave new meaning to the word blue and its light permeated the vault of black space as brilliance permeates a diamond. It radiated love—was Love. Élan placed Stellium gently on the ground. "Now, look toward the seventh dimension and ask your *Emayre* to come and it will." I said to Stellium.

Blood dripped from the corner of Stellium's mouth and stained the pristine ground of this particular paradise. He managed to sit up straighter, but immediately fell sideways on his elbow and then prostrate on the ground. The umbilical between Stellium and the free radical was black with clotted blood as it feigned unconsciousness and hung limply along his leg. Élan tried to help Stellium sit up, but he insisted, "Don't—touch me." His eyes looked up toward the intense blue galaxy and begged, "My pain is too great for me to carry this free radical any longer; please help me."

One raindrop of light separated from the mass of blue and slowly began descending into the garden as a flood of conscious love. The raindrop plopped to the ground and eagerly mingled with Stellium's blood droplets.

From that comingling, his *Emayre* germinated and burgeoned forth like a fast growing sapling. Its appearance was the same as when I saw it in the Primordial Waters, only now it was clearly visible in the full light of day. Its androgynous form was Gathosian and it wore a short, white tunic with a colorful girdle at the waist. Its long raven hair was twisted around a crown of pure white orchids. Its face resembled Stellium's face, but its magnificent aura fanned out like green and blue wings of gossamer perfection. It knelt, tenderly, picked up the half-aborted Envy in its arms, and embraced it with complete tenderness and love. With this action, it proved its own perfection for only an *Emayre* has the breadth of compassion and fearless authority to embrace a free radical without dire consequences. Then it took the umbilical, like a lead, and told Stellium again, "Always and forever, without end, is my absolute passion for you. I will take you everywhere within me."

"Am I going to die?" asked Stellium.

"Yes," said his *Emayre*. "But my hope is you will have the courage to be reborn."

"Do I have time to say goodbye to my loved ones?" asked Stellium.

"Time is barely a consideration when you have forever," said his *Emayre*. "Now come, my precious self and we will dance together and make a case for your freedom, before the great consciousness of the seventh dimension." Stellium's *Emayre* looked toward Élan and praised him with, "I salute you Master Élan. The seventh dimension has wanted to recapture this free radical for eons. They thank you for returning it and for the opportunity to embrace fully the lessons accumulated within its consciousness. Please understand that this free radical attached to Stellium recognized him as family when he stood in the Jumping-Off Place, before his birth. It was his burden, but never his fault."

"I understand," said Élan. "I also understand that you could have freed Stellium at any time. Why did you force me to jeopardize his love for me by putting me in this compromising position?"

"Because you have a need to save Stellium and be his hero," said Stellium's *Emayre*.

"That's untrue," said Élan.

"Consider this," said Stellium's *Emayre*. "You came here at your convenience and forced Stellium to the edge of his evolution. So be it! What you initiated, I will complete."

Stellium was unable to stand so his *Emayre* picked him up as Élan did earlier. We each kissed Stellium and promised we would faithfully wait for him. "I'm not afraid," he assured us. He even tried to comfort Élan and said, "I forgive you, Élan. I know you were only trying to help me." Then Stellium's *Emayre* lifted him in a direction that appeared to us as upward. The higher they rose, the more they appeared as one body until they became one dot of light. When they entered the attraction field of the blue galaxy, they began orbiting it in a clockwise direction.

"Do you know how long Stellium will be gone?" asked Élan.

"I don't know because too many variables exist. I do know that beyond this meadow, at the edge of the woods, we'll find a portico where we can wait in perfect comfort. His *Emayre* will bring him to us when the process is complete."

"Then you know what the process entails?"

"I know a bit. As the third dimension is made of elemental substances, the seventh dimension is made of complementary striations of love and truth. The love inhales the soul and exhales it into truth; then truth inhales the soul and exhales it into love. The closer a soul gets to the center fount of the blue galaxy, the more concentrated the love and truth. His *Emayre* will take him as close as he can tolerate."

"That's it?"

"That's basically how it happens; but, naturally, Stellium will emerge with his subjective memory." I knew more, but this was not the time to discuss the mechanics of the blue galaxy. We were in a room of Paradise and I decided why wait for New Delphi. I now was intent on getting Élan interested in making love to me.

****

I pointed toward a set of graceful stairs built into the side of the hill. At the foot sat a magnificent pair of black marble, dulcerary panthers with gems for eyes. At the top, we found the portico where I expected it to be. Kyron was waiting, perched on the roof, as if he were a sentinel weathervane. The bird let go a couple of squawks and careened around the area, just for the pleasure of flight. The setting was lovely, although the scene now loaned itself to Stellium's soul group and favored what they considered paradisean refinement and pleasure. "Dramatic, and completely sensual," declared Élan, "exactly like Stellium and everything he creates in the third dimension."

The roof of the portico was a cupola made of translucent slabs of moonstone and supported by four classic, jade columns. The portico sheltered a round table covered with a snow-white cloth and set with silver candelabra that held glowing candles of various heights. Upon the table sat crystal bowls and golden trays laden with fruit, nuts, and many Gathosian delicacies. Exquisitely scented orchids flourished here and there and their chromatophore cells expanded and contracted, producing rainbows of dewy light. The furniture scattered about was amorphous and seemed to be made of endless mounds of filmy gauze. Élan laughed and told me, "I've never seen anything this lavish before—anywhere!"

"Welcome to the abundance of the green galaxy," spoke a voice. Élan and I turned and saw a beautiful Human female and a handsome Gathosian male standing at the top of the stairs. Their beautiful fragile bodies were nude except for the moonstone medallions dangling from silver chains around their necks. Orchids crowned their head and their hair glowed internally, like light passing through fiber-optic strands. The woman said, "My name is Helen and this is my consort Nuary. We're here to serve your needs. If this banquet does not match your desires or you require anything additional, merely allow the thought to rise fully in your mind and we will be happy to manifest your desires."

Élan glanced my way before telling them, "This bounty is more than I ever allowed myself to imagine. What more could I possibly need?"

Nuary said, "We are skilled entertainers and would be pleased to play for you while you wait for Stellium."

The proper response to this offer is, play on; but Élan asked, "What instruments do you play?"

This question confused them and Nuary explain. "Naturally, we play each other and we can play you too, if you so desire."

The pupils of Élan's eyes dilated and he gave me another sideways glance. I explained to Helen and Nuary, "We are concerned about Stellium."

"Oh, I'm so sorry," said Helen, who sounded friendly and concerned. "But you must realize that he will be fine. If you prefer, we could sit and talk."

"Thank you for this elaborate banquet," said Élan, "You both are very kind and I hope you do not think me rude, but I would love some private time with my new wife."

"Whatever you wish," agreed Nuary. "We'll watch for Stellium from a distance and bring him to you when he appears."

They walked away and I made myself comfortable on one of the mounds of gauze that billowed up around me like fluffy clouds. "You're expected to indulge," I explained. "It not just about us. Helen and Nuary are here to fulfill their need to serve."

Élan helped himself to a handful of grapes from one of the golden trays. "They must of thought I was really dumb—asking them what they played." He popped a few grapes in his mouth and then abruptly stopped chewing "Holy Fecundity! These grapes are absolutely delicious!"

"It's better to eat them carefully, one by one. They usually contain aphrodisiacs."

Élan's expression went slightly aghast and he stopped chewing. He dropped the grapes remaining in his hand as if they were too hot to hold. "How many times have you been here?"

"I've been here several times with my soul mates and *Emayre*."

"Do attendants usually arrive that offer to entertain with a sexual performance?"

"Depends on which soul group is hosting the party and which level you are on. On this level, your soul group likes to drape garlands of roses everywhere and they always serve exquisite rose wine. They never ask, merely assume that if you've come to the green galaxy, you're interested in all the pleasures it has to offer. Dozens of ripe courtesans usually arrive, a few mythological animals cavort suggestively in the distance for inspiration, and you are gently encouraged to join in the orgy of fun."

"You must be joking."

"I swear! Do you think all, so-called, higher dimensions consist of choirs of angels and old mystics spouting their bits of subjective wisdom?"

"Of course not. I thought higher dimensions consisted of conscious energy."

"They do, but the question is—what do you want to do with your conscious energy once you truly possess the freewill to use it? Do you want to sit in a cave or do you want to share your energy in a great energetic dance of love and fecundity? This paradise might seem generic or even trite, but it is vibrant creation nonetheless. And this dimension serves as a good entryway to other dimensions, although many souls do get stuck here, just as they get stuck in the third dimension."

"Does it sound dull and prosaic that I want to return to the third dimension and help souls trapped there by their denial?"

"You could never be prosaic in any dimension. To me you are as majestic as your white hawk."

"*Ejesay epay*, my little Follie flower." Just to make sure I understood, he added, "I am facing you in this moment, and this moment, and this moment and I know my fulfillment lies only within you."

"Are you sure all those grapes, you just ate, aren't doing your talking for you?"

He laughed and penetrated my eyes. I surrendered to his penetration and my eyes promised even more. "I swear, my love for you is real, but the grapes did loosen my tongue at bit."

*Now! Now! Now!* my *Emayre* sang. Élan managed to make it over to where I sat—it was quite a trip. He wedged himself between my legs and the moment we embraced, my body felt like a bottle of electrified juice. We kissed delicately, and in the process, I pulled him down on top of me. We kissed again and his heart was beating so wildly, I could feel its fluttering pulse against my chest. "I'm a little afraid," he admitted. "I'm afraid because I realize how important this union is between us. I want you to find me completely worthy this time."

"You were completely worthy even in the persistent stream. Now I find you utterly irresistible."

****

Now, as always, a divine genitor simmered beneath the prince of fire and with the energy of lust as kindling, he was an instant flame. Bodily elixirs oozed forth from our excited glands and perfumed our auras. We kissed again, allowing tongues to mingle our words. He tasted Human and his hair smelled of the sweet meadow grasses we walked through moments before. He held me, burying his face between my breasts and I trailed kisses along the scar that ran from his elbow to his wrist. I took a strange and wonderful delight in that scar, for it was the only blemish marring his physical perfection. My hands stroked the powerful curving muscles of his shoulders. He lifted himself upward until his body formed an arc to mine. His eyelids fluttered and his words were breathy. "I sense things so powerfully here," he sighed. His blue/green eyes turned into jewels and I knew he was ready. I balanced on all his emerging fantasies and cradled his power in any and every way he needed cradling. His body trembled like a leaf as he committed himself fully to his destiny.

At that instant, a greater need emerged between us. Energetically, a moment comes when the greater self reaches down into the depths of the original intent of the soul, and brings its most honest imagining up into conscious light. Once this happens, the body automatically becomes one with its mind and feelings—they marry. The limited mind is baffled and grows quiet. The moment of honesty feels as if you are standing on quicksand; the passion stands upon you and you feel it breaking through your layers of reserve. As I struggle to explain, the moment honestly lacks metaphor, yet is direct and sober as cold water hitting the face. First there is implosion, then explosion; the implosion exposes the self, while the explosion launches a spherical hunting spree, in an effort to fulfill its most honest need. *Stay in me forever*, I told him telepathically.

My honest need for such a union so startled him that he instantly stopped moving, yet the love continued to undulate and buoy us toward the shore of orgasm. We held onto each other's essence with our eyes. *Only if you stay forever within me*, he returned.

Our divine marriage was sealed. Our energy mingled like blood running through one artery. I allowed him into my warehouse of eternal abundance—sensation, perception, impulse, emotions, mind, soul, experience, my gifts were his in an instant. My soul mates arrived and whispered their secret names, as did my *Emayre*. No sooner had I spread myself out as a banquet for his consumption, than he transformed his body into a new relationship with matter. He became a particle stream of golden light that danced through me with complete abandon. He opened his mouth and his own radiance poured forth as celestial milk. He spread his hands and his palms offered me his complete experience through time. His ears gave me jewels of perfect sound that once interfaced with his *Emayre* in the seventh dimension. His eyes showed me vistas of his original intent, while his lips spoke words of eternal love. We clung to each other and bobbed in the ecstasy of experience. No reason existed to move because the Universe was dancing around us and as one, we tumbled like a bubble across the waves of ecstatic space.

Our energy joined so completely that eons passed in perfect union. We would need to jump back through space, to the time and lives that were Élan Journey Cœur and Iosobell Follie Lanai, to resume their cause and allow the counter-flow of compassion to drain forth from our love. *I cannot return unless we free at least one particle of ourselves into the infinite*, Élan swore. He wanted to launch a new universe—and with me!

*Tease out any part of me you find worthy for the venture and I will do the same with you.* What else could he take but a drop of my love for this purpose? He gently held my love upon his tongue as I did the same. Ever so tenderly, we breathed forth these bits of each other, which mingled in their own dance of love. We knew then that we were gods, gods of our own creation. Our bodies climaxed together as our own energy went nova—suddenly and dramatically brightening. A few minutes later, I could feel creation happening inside my physical womb.

****

We opened our eyes and found ourselves exactly where we began, with our lips pressed together. "Don't ask me to tell you that I love you," he said.

"Why not, for I know that you do?"

"At this moment, it seems too narcissistic." He patted his chest with the flat of his hand. "You have taken up residence within me." He pulled back, separating from me.

"Can you tell me that you love me from there?" I asked.

"It's the same. You are my thoughts, my own tongue telling you that I love you." He ate some more grapes and glanced around before saying, "It may be terribly mundane, but it would be nice to bathe or go swimming."

The words no more were out of his mouth than Helen returned to inform us, "Your bath awaits."

"You're kidding," said Élan.

"Over there," she said pointing to a sheltered spot.

Élan stood and looked where she pointed. "I didn't see that before."

"Certainly you didn't," said Helen. "You didn't see it because you just put it there with your wish. Would you care for anything else?"

"A couple of towels," I said.

Élan added, "And a nice, fat bar of soap would be must appreciated."

"All those items are already waiting by your bath," said Helen.

On our short walk to our bath, we discovered a delightful surprise. "Look—up on that knoll," said Élan. I looked and saw a male siberlene a short distance away; he was standing majestically on the crest of a gradual rise. The siberlene stared in our direction, as if questioning whether we could be trusted and then he casually glanced away. "It's the siberlene that gave its life for me the first day in the Great Verdant, the one I've been praying would find his way home. I wonder if I can approach him." Just then, the siberlene pawed the ground with its cloven hoof and snorted. Two female siberlene leapt over the rear edge of the knoll and joined the male. Then the three bounded toward the woods and disappeared. "I guess he wanted me to know that I could stop praying for him."

The bath water felt refreshing, like bathing inside a warm cloud. The bar of soap was lavender in color and smelled like orchids. Because Élan requested a, "nice fat bar of soap," it was as large as a brick. Carefully, I allowed the thought of a medium-sized sponge to arise in my mind and, *voile,* before I could reach for it, a sponge sat on the edge of the tub. Every time we tried to pick up the huge bar of soap, it would slip from our hands and plop to the bottom of the tub. "It's those irritating little snarls that bug me when I am dreaming up Paradise," said Élan. "I can't even imagine a proper bar of soap." Eventually, we placed the huge bar on the edge of the tub and he held the soap while I made lather with the sponge.

Something reminded me of Stellium then; perhaps it was a sense that he was missing a special moment with us that we could never recreate. "Could we be serious for a moment?" I asked. "We need to talk about Stellium."

"Barely am I equipped to contend with the biggest bar of soap in any dimension, let alone be serious."

"Please, just for a moment. How did you spot that speck of miasma in him? We made love at least twenty times, while waiting for you. Together we went as far as the Primordial Waters on several occasions. He laid himself open with great abandon, but I missed that speck."

"Twenty times? Did you take time to eat or sleep?"

"What about the miasma?"

"Stellium has always been candid about his cynicism."

"Yes, but I foolishly thought his cynicism was merely on the level of his personality. I did not realize cynicism was affecting his soul. How did you know it ran so deeply within him?"

"I didn't, not until the three got into the regrav unit together. When I saw the free radical under his heart, I wanted to help him, just as Kyron helped me. In retrospect, of course, the clues were always there. When Stellium first came to Sutcay Tay, he believed divine fusion with his *Holder* was an illusion. At that point, I hadn't experienced divine fusion either, so I could not convince him that he was in error."

"But you knew he was wrong?"

"Kyron always allowed me glimpses of that divine state. Stellium didn't believe divine fusion was real because the passion Master Lumenet offered

Stellium was insufficient to raise his energy. Lumenet even offered to help Stellium find another master who was a compatible match. I no longer have any doubt about the power of love. Love clears the way for divine knowledge, especially with someone as passionate as Stellium."

"So what you described as your last night together with Kyron allowed you to finally experience divine fusion with you *Emayre*?"

Élan cocked his head and stared at me sideways. "I guess you want the juicy details?"

"Actually, I do."

"Let me see—please let me see!" Élan disappeared into thought. "As I sat in the Eternal Waters Sanctuary, I realized my life served no one without divine fusion with my *Holder*. I also realized that away from Kyron, I could cling to my pretenses and even siphon off my passion in a myriad of ways, but face to face with The Key, the truth refused to go away. On a literal level, I was desperately and deeply in love with Kyron The Life—his genius and his radiant soul. As soon as I went to his *tritum*, I knelt before him and told him that if he had any fault, he should give it to me and I would adore it as a karmic link between us. I knew he was a stainless vessel, so stainless that our *Holder* danced within his eyes. I was the one with the miasma. Kyron was not a handsome man, but his transcendent beauty was breathtaking and that's what constantly drove me wild with yearning for him. I cannot bath here in Paradise with this gargantuan bar of soap and expect to come clean in this divine water, stained with a lie. The miracle was one of realization with Kyron, a realization that no barriers ever existed between us except the barriers I had built."

"How did Kyron help you break through your final door?"

"It always happens when someone you love and trust wields the sword of truth in your face. Kyron showed me what real Fire was all about. He made himself into a torch and branded my heart with the truth." Élan laughed to himself. "How did Kyron put it? Yes! Now I remember. Kyron said, 'Love is so utterly primal that it imprints itself on the original face of every living creature of this universe.'"

"Did Kyron mention his future incarnation through Stellium and me?"

"Not in words, but it certainly was part of his transmission once he got inside my head. Based on the belief that it would be easier for me to let go of Kyron, our *Holder* allowed me to see that you and Stellium will create a vehicle for Kyron's next life. Frankly, letting go of Kyron was still difficult. I hope you understand why I intervened with Stellium. No way would I ever, knowingly, expose our child to cynicism and envy.

****

We took pleasure in drying each other and returned to the portico to indulge in the array of waiting food delicacies. "I can't get over the taste of

these grapes," Élan exclaimed, and he popped two in his mouth at once."
He shrugged. "It's our honeymoon." He glanced up toward the blue galaxy.
"Stellium?" he called softly. "We're waiting."

"He won't forget. If anything, he is acutely aware that we are here."

"Can you tell me more about the process Stellium is going through right
now?"

"I can tell you from my perspective."

"That's acceptable."

"Can I give it to you as a direct transmission rather than words?"

"Sure!" he smiled. "I'm sorry I was such a stubborn ass when we first
met. From now on, I promise to be so easy that you're going to need to
throw me out of your bed." He smiled like a clever child. "Put your
transmission in this grape and I'll eat it," he suggested. He put another
grape in his mouth, kissed me, and in the process pushed the grape into my
mouth with his tongue. I rolled the grape around my mouth and offered it
to him between the tip of my tongue and upper lip. He was eager and
accepted the grape with great relish.

*A soul periodically goes through a process of conciliation within the attraction field of
the blue galaxy, but usually does not remember the experience. The trick always is to
maintain conscious memory, but whether one remembers or not, each person returns from
the experience with a new sense of peace. The journey must be made within the embrace of
the Emayre for the blue galaxy is inaccessible by a fragile soul on its own. A soul could
no more withstand this journey alone than a physical body could expect to breathe in
outer space, without a spacesuit. The Emayre acts as the metaphorical spacesuit and
embraces the soul in an aura of protection and, through the Emayre's own energy, it
ferries the soul on an orbital journey around the blue galaxy. The trip is not limited to
one orbit, but usually involves multiple circuits, each one taking the soul closer and closer
to the fount of Mother Truth and Father Love.*

"Of all the grapes I've eaten here, that one was the very best of all," said
Élan.

****

Nuary and Helen appeared at the top of the stairs and the fragile Helen
was carrying Stellium across her arms as if he were a lightweight infant.
Wherever Stellium's consciousness lay, it did not appear to be in his body.
Helen laid Stellium down on the gauze and recommended that we—"Give
him a chance to resynchronize."

Nuary leaned over Stellium thoughtfully and stroked his forehead.
"When he awakes, he will not remember Helen or me. Will you please tell
him that we are creating reservoirs of love for his consumption?"

"Are you from his soul group?" I asked.

Helen nodded her head in the affirmative. "Tell him Helen and Nuary
love him and always will and perhaps one day he will remember us."

"What's this triangular scar in the center of his chest?" asked Élan.

"That's the scar from Envy. It will go away," said Nuary.

"Is he unconscious or sleeping?" asked Élan.

"Neither," said Nuary. "He is resynchronizing."

"Is it best to allow him to resynchronize here or may we take him back to the third dimension?"

"It makes no difference," said Helen. "Do as you wish."

Élan looked to me for my opinion. "Let's take him back," I suggested.

Élan put two fingers in his mouth and blew, making a loud sharp whistle. Kyron appeared in a flash and Élan said, "Please return us to the exact third dimensional space we left."

Helen and Nuary stood together and held hands as they waved goodbye. "Come see us again," they called after us.

We flashed down the side-path and in a twinkling, were back in the fourth dimension. Just as we were jumping to the third dimension, I glanced over my shoulder and saw a *manatee* sitting on a not too distant time thread. It wore the face of my next incarnation, waiting for its turn to live. It waved to me and made soft cooing sounds like an infant nursing at a breast. It was there to check up on me exactly as the *manatee* had checked on Élan.

****

Stellium floated like a corpse in the middle of the regrav unit. No eye movement appeared beneath his closed eyelids and his breathing was shallow. "We should flush his eyes with saline to keep them moist," said Élan. I reminded him that blindness was his subjective phenomenon and he said, "Humor me, I'd rather be wrong than sorry." So we flushed Stellium's eyes with saline and kept a cool, damp cloth pressed against his forehead. His eyes stayed fixed, but we knew not where. Three hours later, we knew he needed a sensual stimulant to remind him that he had a body waiting in the third dimension. I floated down to the control panel, on the side of the regrav unit, and tapped the key a few times. By slow increments, I increased gravity to normal. Forty minutes later, Élan sat patiently holding Stellium's wrist. "His pulse is steady, but his mind is wandering. Damn my blindness. Come here and peer into his rutilates and tell me if you can see what's happening."

Crawling over the blankets, I leaned over Stellium and gently raised his eyelids. "His psychic awareness is alert because he's fixed elsewhere. On the distant side of the fourth, the deeper streams churn with powerful energy currents capable of ensnaring the personal mind. He might be projecting his fulfillment along these currents instead of living in this dimensional reality. I could return to the fourth and search for his consciousness along these deeper streams?"

"Please—don't go anywhere. Think. You must know a Trinity Witch concoction, an herb that we could use as a stronger stimulant than full gravity."

Making my way out of the regrav unit, I went to the bathroom where our collection of toiletries sat on a glass shelf. Among the tubes, atomizers, and bottles, I found an hourglass-shaped vial of perfume belonging to Stellium. Like all perfumes, this one possessed an enigmatic and intriguing name. "Origin," spiraled around the fancy silver bottle in gold script. I spritzed the ginger-scented cologne on my wrists, and returned to the regrav unit where I wafted the fragrance under his nose. It worked. His head jerked and then a guttural sound bubbled up from his throat.

Stellium's eyes fluttered and he squinted at us with innocent suspicion. Élan's blindness prevented him from seeing the subtler changes in Stellium's facial expressions, so I reported, "Right now he appears to be going through something similar to what you described when the neophytes first found you. He's probably searching for a reference point in this dimension." The unwitting expression on Stellium's face sunk inward and he inhaled sharply. I was certain he was asking—where am I? "Listen, he might give us clues to lives manifested by his soul group."

Stellium mumbled something unintelligible and then he was speaking Kulupan Prime, saying *"Pa,"* meaning the primal force that first created this universe, which was quickly followed by, *"Seti, Seti, apata tut?"* Seti was a pagan star-god worshiped in the ancient Lan Culture on the planet Old Ulsha Bramanth and Stellium was saying, "Seti, guide my way." His body vaulted as if struck from behind and he was telling somebody, *"Volonté je n'oubile janais cetle lumière de corail de coucher do soleil sur notre visage doux,"* or, "Never will I forget this coral sunset light upon your sweet face." Back on Old Ulsha Bramanth again, he was dedicating his life to the rainbow goddess, *"Rooti."* With his next breath, he spoke Ivory Coast Mescale on the planet Euterpe and was asking for water. *"La? La?"* Apparently, his soul enjoyed a special affinity with Earth and he began calling, *"Diy´ a Biáe?"* or "Where am I?" several times in Greek. He squinted and managed to tell us in Portuguese, *"A luz fere maus olhos,"* that the light was hurting his eyes. Leaning toward the control panel on the wall, I dimmed the light a few degrees to make it more comfortable for him. The softer light gave him confidence to open his eyes wider, and he peered at Élan carefully as if trying to fix him in place and time. Stellium's voice got abnormally deep when he said, *"Gringo, usted parece familiar."*

"He's approaching interface with the present," I said. "Grab him with a few vital statistics."

Élan's voice turned urgent as he reeled off, "You're Noveil Esay, born in San Diego, California, in the Earth year 2142. You're a Shardasko Warrior and your moniker is Stellium. *Seif shonay Mescale ze tutay* (Do you remember Mescale and how to speak it)?"

Stellium understood Élan, but continued speaking English. "No, I do not remember how to speak Mescale," he said.

"Welcome back," Élan said.

Stellium jerked again as if snagged by a wheel cog and then he thought for a moment and said in Mescale, "*Oh*, now I remember how to speak Mescale. I hope I didn't hurt you when I struck you in the regrav unit. I've been worried about that this whole time; and please, forgive me for calling you a bastard?"

Élan sighed with relief and smiled. "As long as you are okay, you can call me anything you want. Forgive us for disturbing you, but we were concerned that we might lose you to another place and time."

"The experience was over, but I was shadow dancing with my *Emayre*. We were having so much fun. I saw different places and my *Emayre* helped me draw a series of sketches inside my head to remind me of the experience."

"Isn't 'fun' rather an insipid word to describe what you've just been through and why are you using the term *Emayre* instead of *Holder*?"

"Did I? I didn't realize I said that, but I guess I did. Anyway, envy is gone. After it left, I had a big hole below my heart that needed mending." Stellium touched his chest where the scar was slowly fading away. "My *Emayre*—there I go again—filled it with its own perspective. Now I feel incredibly—I guess—light! That's right, I feel light and kinda silly and innocent except for the memory of seeing you two making love while I was dancing with my *Emayre*."

Stellium smiled and the expression on his face suggested something at a great distance still held his attention. The glow around his face was pearly and his skin looked refined as the skin of a newborn babe. Two hours later, as he finished eating a bowl of soup, he said, "I just remembered something else. My *Emayre* suggested that Élan should begin reading those twenty-two journals as soon as possible, because he will find his greater perspective within those pages."

Élan leaned over the table and fixed on Stellium. "I'm blind, Stellium."

"My *Emayre*'s suggestion was not meant to demean you in any way," said Stellium and he reached out and held Élan's hand. "Actually, it's simple. If you face right, you will recognize your divine guide as the active *Holder* and if you face left, you will recognize your divine guide as the receptive *Emayre*."

"An authentic conundrum, Master Stellium?"

"Not really, read the journals and you will know exactly what I mean."

A quizzical expression took root on Élan's face, suggesting that he was keenly aware of the bizarre irony of the new situation. Why did contact with the great beyond blind him and bestow greater perspective on Stellium?

The recognition of irony brings every soul to an incomprehensible paradox. This recognition is a symptom, similar to a sneeze on the verge of a cold. Irony signals we've reached an impenetrable wall; and as always, the impenetrable highlights our reactions, which can vary between total rage and complete acceptance. Élan's ironic sneeze did not mar his auric clarity, yet frustration fluttered around as if searching for a door to his soul.

Symptoms continued to emerge in Élan. Later the same day he was annoyed, but would not discuss what was troubling him; and then he turned exceptionally introverted. That evening, he could not find his toothbrush and this disproportionally irked him. Then he stumbled over the threshold of the regrav unit and bruised his shin and it seemed odd that he was so clumsy. He even swore when it happened, saying, "Damn my blindness." The following morning, I suggested we take advantage of a few of the onship activities. While getting ready to go, he could not find his socks and one of his shoes. It was minor, but symptomatic. We took a walk and explored. While Stellium engaged in casual conversations with several people, Élan retreated into silence.

"I have a headache," he explained. That afternoon, he suggested we go to a musical concert and we had to leave in the middle, because his headache took a turn for the worse. By early evening, his headache was better and he wanted to dine out, in one of the many restaurants onboard. While we were eating, Stellium talked more about his trip around the blue galaxy with his *Emayre* and mentioned that he was able to join with the Line of Creation*.

"That's a rare phenomenon," I said.

Stellium laughed delicately and sipped at a small crystal glass, brimming with *lume*. "I thought every soul that orbited the blue galaxy joined with The Line of Creation." Stellium was sincere and understated when he bubbled over with, "It felt wonderful! In one instant, the Line gave me enough juice to finally paint something worthwhile."

Élan was astounded. The rapt attention of a true Shardasko Warrior seized him and again, irony cast its shadow over his face. "Paint something worthwhile? Do you realize how blessed you are already? Say whatever you wish about Master Lumenet, but he got it right when he named you Stellium. You are an exceptional conjunction of stars."

****

Viobella once suggested, "You can learn more about kinship watching a common ant, than a high priestess." Stellium's blessing made me realize how many layers of artificial elitism still exist in the third dimension. We

*Line of Creation is where energy turns into matter. Its location is beyond the seven and eighth dimension.

entertain feelings of superiority to creatures we regard as less evolved beings. This snobbery promotes the belief that self-realization comes to those with the superior mind, through worthiness, or even preferential connections to The Infinite. As even Kyron The Great once discovered, he built his self-realization upon the denial of his own warriors. Stellium's present state of illumination, illustrates how conscious evolution actually works. When I first met Élan and then Stellium, my evolvement surpassed theirs. Élan could not have reached his present level of illumination, without my intervention. My involvement encouraged and supported his growth and when Stellium and I reconnected with Élan in Loxaloo, it was evident that he made a major jump. However, even in this new reality, the free-radical Envy weighed down Stellium's heart. Out of total love, Élan offered Stellium an opportunity to make his own jump. Stellium's ability to wed with the Line of Creation was an amazing feat, despite his understatement that, "It was fun." Stellium reached this new level of consciousness through the support of those who loved him and his own warrior instincts that helped him grab what he needed at the instant it appeared. The only question left was—would Stellium now help us?

Stellium set his wineglass on the table, extended a hand to each of us, and made a brief, but dramatic speech. His words, while important, were not as compelling as the depth of feeling he packed into those words. "I want to do three things with the rest of my life," he announced. "Naturally, I must paint; but more important than that, I want to be a complete husband to you both and a dedicated father to our children. In our family, I vow that the legacy of abandonment from our fathers will stop with me, for I am swallowing their negative karma. I vow to do this for all Journeys abandoned to boarding schools, all Follies disowned by their fathers; and for all Noviels that even now sit on beaches drawing question marks in the sand."

Rejoice my future children! Your fathers are committed warriors and pure of heart. This commitment by Stellium has sealed my aura from doubt in so many comforting ways, for I never thought I would witness a phenomenon as generous as Stellium's gift to all our fathers.

****

We were four space cycles out of New Delphi and our days and nights increasingly confused. This is a normal side effect of space travel. One can be asleep one moment and completely awake the next. I was in the regrav unit, barely conscious of my body, when I experienced a distinct sensation that something tickled my cheek. A few seconds later, I realized Élan was missing. "Where's Élan?" I asked Stellium and he mumbled something about the toilet. When Élan did not return in a few minutes, I went searching and eventually found him lying on the floor with one of Kyron's journals pressed against his chest.

Lost in the dark shadows of the quiet room, Élan's voice seemed to echo. "My eyes awoke me from sleep and told me they feel dead" he said. "How am supposed to read these journals?" Sitting down on the floor next to him, I offered to read the journals to him. There was a long silence and then he said, "Follie?"

"Yes, dear one?"

"You can cure my blindness—can't you?"

"I must tell you something important—"

Élan raised his voice. Because of the delicate reciprocity between us, I felt the sharp cut of his irritation. "Don't tell me anything important, just tell me if you can cure my blindness."

Raising my voice to keep pace with him, I said, "I'll tell you what I choose." I took a deep breath. "I'm allowed to be a conduit for healing, but am forbidden to cure people or I will fall from grace."

"I'm sorry; I should know better by now. Please forgive me for pressuring you."

Despite knowing the grave consequences of such an action, my compulsion to cure his blindness pressed against my heart. "Élan, from the first moment we stood face to face at the *Emayre* School, I've been a vulnerable interface to your needs. Now tell me, how I am supposed to give you what you don't know how to take?"

The long silence that followed was packed with deeper thought. "That's my real problem," he finally admitted. "I don't know how to take what I need like a real Shardasko Warrior. Forgive me for complaining, especially to someone as generous as you. You've already given me so much, but my blindness—is getting difficult. I feel as if I am a thin wall, squeezed between my promise to Kyron and my inability to see."

"Practical solutions do exist. For one, you could reconsider surgery."

"Not an option."

"Why?"

"Because I know I should not get surgery, just as you know you should not cure me." This time the silence lasted longer. "If—there was a just reason for my blindness, I swear I would accept it." As I sat there gazing into the perfection of his blue-green eyes, he raised his hand as if shading his eyes from glare. "I keep seeing the last thing I ever saw—that blinding flash." The next silent gap between us felt like two gears grinding against each other. His voice quivered with intensity when he said, "I'm a fool; still a damn neophyte." More silence, but I could hear the grinding of his mind, struggling to mesh with understanding. "At first, my blindness felt like a novelty. I was cavalier and thought I will endure this inconvenience for a short time and then a miracle will whisk it away. For the first few days, I even thought I was omnipotent and could simply make my blindness vanish with some energy manipulation. Now my eyes wake me, speaking as an innocent voice, asking why they cannot see. Then new fears surround me— it's a chill—and sometimes, I can't remember where I am or even who I am—Follie?"

"I'm right here, Élan."

"The only way I can read these journals is to jump to the fourth dimension with them."

"That sounds like a marvelous idea and you have the white feather as your guide."

"It can guide me, but can't protect me from free radicals? It's occurred to me that my blindness might be a free radical that I picked up in the fourth after my encounter with the *manatee*."

I leaned forward and kissed his eyelids. "Your blindness is not a free radical. Your soul is spotless."

"If I am so spotless, why do I feel so sorry for myself? My eyes are grieving, reminding me that I might never see the face of our child."

"Élan, what do you think happened when the *manatee* turned the key and it caught the light?"

He shrugged. "Frankly, I think I lost concentration and looked a lot longer at the light, than I remember. I think that accounts for my three-day absence."

"Aytinous told us your aura was completely effulgent when they discovered you. He said you possessed the ability to heal."

"Aytinous clearly disapproved. It wasn't anything I consciously did; I was overflowing with love and those who were suffering helped themselves to a bit of divine compassion through me."

"Give me a chance to heal you," said Stellium." I abruptly glanced up and there stood Stellium in the middle of the dark room. He aura was overflowing with pink empathy.

"That's the worst idea I've heard in at least a millennium," said another voice that walked out of the shadows.

We all were startled, but especially Élan. He sat up and his hands automatically moved into Primal Stance. "Who's there?" he called out.

Viobella appeared and threw out a ray of white light, which she walked into like a spotlight. The inspiration for the half-form was none other than Élan, and looked like his female twin. "It's Viobella," I said.

"This room is not your public thoroughfare," said Élan. "This is a private discussion with my mates and this time, you're not invited."

"Poor Élan!" she mocked. "—feeling sorry for himself all dressed up in his pitiful blindness. Sorry, but when you start using my soul mate's love for you, to put pressure on her to heal you, I feel personally involved."

"Don't worry," I said. "No one is falling from grace in this particular room."

"What good is grace if someone you love is in pain?" asked Stellium.

Viobella raised her voice and shouted, "All you silly martyrs—hold up! Now, here's the latest scoop on Élan's blindness, hot from my interface with his *Holder.*"

Stellium asked, "Is that why you look like Élan—from your interface?"

"It's mockery," insisted Élan, "and I am not amused."

"Never thought of it as mockery," said Viobella. "I regard it as total empathy. Oh well, whatever flavors your soup." She raised her hands over her head, thereby adjusting her form with her own powers of creation. Her body vibrated like silver water in a sonic bath, which caused her to mirror Élan even more closely. She did that by turning into a man and the voice went down an octave to accommodate the new form. Now two Élans were in the room, one sitting on the floor and the other one standing with his hands on his hips a couple of meters away. Stellium was on the verge of mentioning this dramatic transformation and Viobella brushed the back of his two fingers sideways across his lips, which is the Gathosian gesture to be quiet. "Listen to me," he said. "Your blindness will help you concentrate on what is truly important to your purpose."

"Skip the clichés," snapped Élan.

"And hold that flaming tongue of yours or I'll toss a dipperful of Primordial Water down your throat and you will be speechless as well as blind." Élan fell silent and Viobella put his hand to his heart and sang a few bars of, "Silence-is-golden!" in a falsetto contralto. "Now, hear this, my hot little fire starter. I was involved in this whole kerfuffle since the pre-incarnate agreement was set up in the Library of All Creation. I'm the one responsible for fine-tuning volume twenty-two. Granted, circumstances have changed and I will need to do more writing than fine-tuning. I surrender myself to the present challenge and suggest you do likewise. When the time is right, together, we will jump to the far side of the sixth dimension where sits the southern wing of the Library of All Creation. There, you will be able to see clearly and together we will read the journals and make any corrections to *The Universe* that we consider necessary."

Élan admitted, "It's obvious that my present mood makes me vulnerable to free radicals in the fourth."

"Then get over your present mood."

"I'm not worried about me, I'm worried about my unborn son. He is in a vulnerable position right now in the Jumping-Off Place. If I make any contact with free radicals, I will automatically expose him as well."

"Don't worry about free radicals," said Viobella. "I can and will protect you and Dulce."

Élan said nothing, so Viobella was forced to ask, "What do you say, tinderbox?"

"If you can protect Dulce, then I say a provisional yes, with one stipulation. We must be equal collaborators."

Viobella pointed his finger at Élan and gestured no. "You will work as my apprentice until I say otherwise."

"What makes you such a superior intellect to lead this project? It can't be your humility."

"Well, let me see, under the circumstances, my sense of humor remains pretty damn good."

"I'm more interested in your writing qualifications and your knowledge concerning all things Shardasko."

"All you Shardasko Warriors are so suspicious and stringent—must be all the abstinence that ties your nuts into knots. Okay, here's a peek at my credentials. Part of my soul configuration lived a life as correspondent and intimate of Haspian. I'm sure you never heard of Haspian; but she was the greatest philosopher who ever lived on Calypso, a planet not yet discovered by sentients of your ilk. Closer to your current genetic base, I knew myself as a cohort of the Greek philosopher Candidus and in third-century Rome, I was a scribe serving Plotinus."

"You're right; I never heard of any of them."

"Strike your match on this, Élan. You ever heard of Master Jelud? I possess full memory of writing the definitive texts on shadow dancing that you studied, as a voracious little neophyte. Besides that, I speak a myriad of languages that are unknown to you; my intelligence is too high to allow me to re-incarnate into your present third dimensional ignorance, and I know my way around The Library of All Creation. Therefore, when you dance with me, I lead."

Élan shrugged. "You certainly win; let's go."

"Not so fast! Your *Holder* believes we should wait."

"Why?"

"Because you need time to recuperate. Listen to me, Élan; you are going to be fine. Great souls attract great challenges. I'm here to help you solidify Kyron's vision and make you strong. Let me give you some advice. Give up your attachment and detachment to Kyron's legacy. In other words, do not anticipate this challenge. When the time arrives to work, we will work with total concentration and when the work is complete, we will stand back from our results." Viobella sat down on the floor next to Élan and embraced him. "I've lived lives and learned many lessons through trial and error. Your blindness is a difficult challenge—"

"I would prefer not to discuss my physical blindness," said Élan. "Besides, you don't really know how I feel."

"I do know how you feel because my *Emayre* forbids me to speak of circumstances I have not experienced. Once I was blind and my blindness raged openly. My blindness raged until my illusions burned away. I tell you from hard-earned experience, Élan. We are children of Fire and Mother Truth. We are born of Fire and our eternal allegiance is to Mother Truth that hides no darkness from our eyes. Light and dark are one continuum. No imagining is real, either in the light or in the dark, until we see it as Truth. Now, listen to me, tinderbox, and I will give you insight into your present dilemma. Around your aura flutters the two-faced free radical, impatience-reticence. Impatience faces the light and projects panic. Impatience fabricates beautiful illusions in honor of light and encourages you to do the same. Impatience preys upon your desire for union. Do not fear impatience; instead, look at its other face and you will see its hidden character, reticence. Reticence is obliging and willing to wear a thousand different faces for your distraction. This free radical is neither a curse nor a blessing; it is an active continuum of Source."

Élan dropped his head into his hands. "How do I negotiate my way to freedom?"

"You negotiate your way to freedom through internal integrity and you begin by loving your integrity as you love your *Holder*. Now open your energy toward me."

"Why?"

"Remember, I'm leading. Now open your energy because I want to give you something."

Élan faced Viobella and then he touched his one forefinger to the center of Élan's forehead. "Ah!" gasped Élan. "I see light!"

"It will last only for a few days—enjoy it. Remember, do not speculate upon the future or you will use up your vision in a flash. Be in each moment, for that is your honeymoon. That's the best I can do for now," said Viobella and he disappeared.

****

Élan's eyes cried with joy. His vision continued to improve and within a few minutes, it was twenty-twenty. "I really can see!" he continued to assure us. He darted around the room, examining us, and various objects. He raced to the mirror and stared at his face. "I still look like me," he laughed through his tears.

"What are you going to do with your remission?" asked Stellium, as he followed Élan from room to room.

Élan's mind began jumping all over the place in anticipation. "I want to take a peek at Kyron's journals and do you have any new sketches I might see?"

"A few—"

"I want to see every one, and I want to see the views from the Astral Observatory that you and Follie mentioned. He glanced my way and said, "And I definitely want to see you up close and naked. I wouldn't miss that for all the *grash* on Sutcay Tay. Finally, I want to be looking at you two instead of a *manatee* when I go blind again." For the next three days, Élan did not sleep and he indulged completely in everything that came his way. While Stellium and I slept, Élan began reading the twenty-two journals. He started with *The Universe* with its short introduction. "Amazing!" he said afterward, and he gave the journal to Stellium to read.

Stellium came back with his own, "amazing," and added, "You should apologize to Viobella as soon as she appears the next time."

After a few hours of sleep, Stellium could hardly wait to ask, "What did you find out from Kyron's journals?"

"I'm reading the one entitled, *The Marriage of Fecundity and Air*," said Élan. "I loved sitting here in the silence of space and reading. I could hear Kyron's voice through his words, just as if he were speaking to me. The book is about the process a neophyte goes through between the time he enters Shardasko training and First Cut."

"What does a neophyte go through?" I asked.

"The goal of a neophyte is to become conscious of the inner workings of the body/mind relationship and balance his strengths and weaknesses to make the journey ahead. Kyron talks about the disciplines of physical exercise, the education of the mind, and the psychological and physical changes that affect us at this stage. I was sitting here thinking how First Cut eliminates three-quarters of the neophytes that begin training. That's a tragic loss of potential—don't you think? I was asking myself if it's because of the difficulty of clearing the seductions of their body/mind or the master's inability to interface with the neophyte. Stellium has helped me understand that the success of any student hinges on empathy with, and trust in, his mentor. I would venture to say that Kyron would agree. Kyron always mentored his neophytes one at a time." Élan opened the journal in question and read Kyron's words aloud. "'A master must act as the proverbial carrot before the donkey, keeping the neophyte on course. The master's own body/mind connection must be so clear that he can run between these two points of reference with endless ease and show the neophyte it can be done. If the neophyte markedly blocks his body/mind relationship, the master must love the neophyte enough to swallow his karma.'" Élan stopped reading and looked up.

"As a neophyte, about three months into my training, I started experiencing serious psychological problems. Up to that time, I allowed myself a narrow margin of feelings and projected many of my illusional problems onto other people. I believed people ignored me because I was unimportant. I mumbled when I spoke and then I would accuse others of snubbing me when they did not understand what I was saying. Meditation caused the neurosis to drop from my mind and directly down into my body. I would find myself staring in the mirror, afraid that I was going to disappear. Kyron helped me uncover the source of my disturbance through a series of dialectics. I discovered that my father treated me as if I was of little consequence and this twisted around inside my mind and I believed invisibility was my proper state. I was naïve and did not understand that every father dumps his karma upon his son. Actually, it was my father who felt worthless and invisible and that's why he worked so hard to be a highly visible diplomat. During one of my early sessions with Kyron, he flabbergasted me by saying, 'Since my earliest days as a master, I've prayed that life would bless me with a child with your incredible potential. Now, only you possess the power to break this bond between us.' From that point forward, I thought of Kyron as my father. I did not understand the ramifications of his magnificent gift, but I certainly do now. He swallowed my father's karma—swallowed the karma of a man he never met—for me. I'm no longer afraid of the future. How can I be? I have powerful friends across dimensions and two steadfast lovers. Truly, I am blessed."

The last few hours of sight, Élan told us his vision flickered on and off. Every time it returned, his sight became more distorted. We secluded ourselves in the regrav unit and near the end, the three of us made love. Élan gazed at Stellium and me with an insatiable hunger telling us several times, "You are the most beautiful people in all creation to me." When the ship landed at New Delphi Space Station, Élan was again blind and experiencing another throbbing headache. This time, he accepted his blindness without a murmur of complaint.

# SEVENTEEN

Trinity Witches and Hectarian Mystics consider the New Delphi Crystal one of the cornerstones of this galaxy. To the prosaically interested, the Crystal reveals itself only as an effulgent outpouring of sub-atomic particles that our universe uses as a tool for regeneration. To the psychically adept, the New Delphi Crystal is a transmitter/receiver of unpatrolled scope that acts as a promontory between this dimension and all others.

In this age, the Trinity and Hectarian hierarchy live in a state of corrupt fear, where their major preoccupation has become protecting the New Delphi Crystal. According to the supreme high priestess of New Delphi, "Saboteurs are everywhere." Down through history, the wealth of nations has been wasted on this type of paranoia and the solution always seems to be the same—greater and greater restrictions on the general public. The Trinity and Hectarian orders have gained both wealth and power through the promotion of this fear. Their ongoing campaign, to convince the public that the Crystal is constantly under threat, has, so far, been unsuccessful with the public. People come to New Delphi in droves because the Crystal itself draws them near.

Once blocks are established, they build upon themselves until the very thing happens that is feared most. Allowing free access to the Crystal would prove this fear is nonsense and the illusional threat of sabotage would soon become a non-issue. Greater than these immediate benefits, I believe, free access would allow inhabitants of this dimension to fuse openly with their *Emayres*. This would allow incarnate beings in this dimension to play on equal terms in other dimensions. No longer would we sit here, in our third-dimensional ignorance, and wait for our lifetime sentence to end. For the first time ever, we would sit consciously at the table with other dimensions and use our gifts to help consciousness everywhere.

286

New Delphi constantly overflows with elemental devotees, pilgrims, and curious tourists—all eager to tap into the magic, they hope the Crystal will provide. When newcomers arrive on the island, the visual spectacle alone—consisting of vivid aurora lights and an atmosphere charged with negative ions, initiates dramatic responses in most. The physical sensations vary from ringing in the ears and giddiness, to tingling in the extremities of the body. The sensations usually are uplifting and enhance the connections among body/mind/feelings. Trinity Witches call this feeling *beltania*, meaning "greatest bliss." When someone arrives on New Delphi and reports, "I feel nothing," I can only shake my head in bafflement.

The Crystal's negative ions and aurora lights affect the energy of free radicals, just as the Crystal affects everything else. No one knows what happens to free radicals at New Delphi. Their fate might depend upon the will of the person giving the free radical safe harbor. If the person can release the free radical, it will sense the dominant attraction of the Crystal and use it as a conduit to go home to the soul group that created it. If the person continues to shelter the free radical—by denying its existence—then the free radical will not leave its comfortable refuge. The New Delphi Crystal is both attractive and repulsive and long exposure can twist a soul harboring a free radical, just as surely as a free radical can twist a soul.

Shortly after space explorers discovered New Delphi, the Trinity and Hectarian orders took control. That was over two hundred fifty phases ago and to this day, the public remains mostly ignorant about the many caverns surrounding the Crystal. In these caverns, light seeps through from the Crystal and makes these places into temples of cosmic inspiration. The Trinity and Hectarian orders have consecrated these caverns for their private and exclusive use. A Trinity high priestess has supreme authority in temple caverns and I have witnessed them ejecting even the most elevated Hectarian Mystic with a mere glance.

A high priestess wears three rings of authority. On her Anointing day, the supreme high priestess of New Delphi pierces three zaqurlite rings through the new priestess' body, one through her bottom lip, one though her left nipple, and finally one through the hood of her clitoris. When she works as an active temple oracle, she saturates these three zaqurlite rings with *tartan ratu* to raise her creative/sexual vibrations. These rings act as lures for the Crystal, which will produce the flash of inspiration that results in vision and sometimes, prophecy.

Ideally, every priestess has located her two soul mates that act as her consorts. These consorts can be living in male or female bodies, but their deep psyches should balance the polarities of active and receptive energy of the priestess. If her consorts are not her soul mates, they certainly should be trusted soul intimates. These soul mates or intimates act as telepathic confidants and as interpreters, relating her visions to the Hectarian scribes as she experiences them.

Beyond her soul mates or intimates, a high priestess maintains a family of sixty-four devotees called *privileges.* Half are supposed to be female and the other half are supposed to be male, but rarely is this balance achieved until the priestess is advanced. Her sixty-four *privileges* are supposed to represent the thirty-two essential perspectives of illumination; which consists of the twenty-two pathways to illumination; the eight crystals of this galaxy; the black hole at the center of this universe; and the ubiquitous Eternal Threshold. Adept Trinity Witches spend years refining their energy through the perspective of their *privileges* and become experts at identifying those individuals that can supply her with the perspective she needs.

By the time a witch reaches the status of high priestess, she is a master of energy in herself and able to understand and negotiate the energy of others with considerable ease. She will select a spectrum of individuals based on her personal vibratory needs and the ability of these individuals to meld with her energy. Individuals should be uninhabited, or free of internal blocks, and efficient and stable energy sources for her constant use. The ideal is to assemble an array of *privileges,* beginning with the lowest body vibrations, capable of keeping pace with her all the way up, through the thirty-two levels, to undistorted vision. This, of course, she does through intimate sexual contact with these individuals. She uses her energy to climb their supporting energy as one climbs a rope or ladder. On the lower energy levels, she will attract many young and eager dilettantes to serve her needs. These individuals may have limited understanding concerning what is truly happening and they tend to come and go. These lower energy *privileges* are the ones that carry tales to the outside world and then individuals, such as my father, end up accusing all Trinity Witches of being whores. It's always difficult for a high priestess to find individuals with sufficiently high vibrations to match and sustain hers. During a "visioning session," tension may be so taunt between a high priestess and a high-level energy *privilege* that eye contact will be enough to catapult her into vision.

All sexual alchemy preformed by Trinity Witches and Hectarian Mystics is supposed to be secret. Both orders take life vows forbidding them to tell how they jump dimensions. Revealing any secret, especially a sexual secret, is punishable, not by death, but by one's own brothers and sisters calling up free radicals where the traitor is tortured and haunted by demons. Within the persistent stream, I know the Trinity and Hectarian orders called up these demons and set them upon Dulce for revealing the truth.

****

Élan, Stellium, and I waited at the New Delphi Space Station for the first available flight to Logan's Point, which is the main harbor on the Iris Sea. Crowds of people congregated and wait for the windships to dock. Windships are the only means of transportation allowed to land on New

Delphi Island. A protective radius of three hundred-kilometers surrounds the island and restricts access of all powered vessels.

As we stood at Logan's Point and gazed toward the Crystal, the northern sky was a wonder of dancing aurora lights. The crowd contained the usual mix of Hectarians, Trinities, pilgrims, tourists, the desperate, and the skeptically curious. Mystics and witches fingered their prayer beads and repeated their secret mantras; introverts were silent in awe, and the extroverts exclaimed, "Look! Isn't the sky beautiful?" Deaf to parental admonitions, irrepressible children danced around with hyperactive glee. Women wept and dreamt of unborn children and gardens of fecund beauty and men embraced other men and spoke words of meaning they actually believed.

A fragile boy caught my attention and reminded me of Dulce. His two desperate parents were guiding his autochair toward the pier. A closer look revealed that the child was unconscious. Again, my compulsion arose to heal. We took our place in line behind them and I opened myself as a conduit to the child. As far as I could ascertain, I established no connection. This time I felt squeamish when Stellium began chatting with the child's parents. It did not take long to learn that Hanib and Doh Eret, and their son Pirect, were from Sutcay Tay. By then, Stellium had told them that he was born on Earth, Élan was born on Ravenna, and I was born on Oceania and that Stellium and Élan were Shardasko Warriors and I was a Trinity Witch. Doh looked eagerly toward me when he learned that I was a witch. "Do you believe you could get us an audience with a high priestess to help our sick boy?"

Exhaustion and worry had fractured several of the rutilates in his left eye and I told him, "I'm sorry, I possess no special connections here on New Delphi. I was a music teacher at the *Emayre* School, just outside Pointilla. What ails your son?"

"He caught ring fever in the days following the storm. This is our last hope. Doctors on Gathos insist his mind was destroyed." Ring fever meant death and the fact that the child was strapped in an autochair, meant his case was advanced. Stellium and I were discreetly guiding Élan between us, advising him when to step up and down. Doh said to Élan, "I guess you're hoping for a miracle too." Élan blushed with embarrassment for the last thing he wanted anyone to think was that he was needy. He assured Doh that he was not expecting a miracle at the Crystal and came only to meditate.

Stellium laughed and added, "However we would welcome a miracle if one came our way."

The six of us boarded the windship and began our journey north. While we waited for our cabin assignment, I walked to the bow of the ship and said a prayer for my father. He was on another ship, on another sea, on another world, yet Wind brought me tales of his present life. He was now sailing west, perpendicular to me. His first mate had just told him an old familiar joke—the one about a monkey with a wooden leg, a beautiful girl, and a barroom scene and a bet. My father laughed and said, "Aye. They're all the same—those damn wooden-legged monkeys." He turned right and faced into the wind, and the wind blew tendrils of his long, dark hair loose from his ponytail and made his eyes tear. I turned left and now, across worlds and space, we stood face to face, but he did not recognize me as the sky above his head or the sea that kept him afloat. Rarely did he think about me anymore, because thoughts of me produced a range of uncomfortable physical symptoms in his body from headache to seasickness. Thoughts of me made him rage against members of his crew that they dismissed as, "the captain's melancholy over his dead wife and lost child." A sudden urge grabbed me to take the unopened letters I sent my father and toss them into the wake of the windship. I refrained from doing so because it was against New Delphi law to throw anything into the Iris Sea.

Walking back toward starboard, I found Élan involved in his introverted blind-man's stare, while Stellium continued to chat with Hanib and Doh. Stellium had moved on to the topic of San Diego and its friendly people and then he suggested we all eat lunch together. Élan said, "I'm skipping lunch today; I'm getting another headache." That's when Doh admitted that they planned to spend the next three days on the windship in the public lounge and were going to rent a tent on New Delphi Island when they landed.

Since Hectarians discourage visitors from coming to New Delphi, sleeping accommodations on the island are few and expensive. Even the wealthiest pilgrims must contend with stark cottages with no heat, electricity, and no communication facilities. People that cannot afford a cottage, lease a tent in one of the camping reserves. The public lounge of the windship was crowded with other travelers who also could not afford the price of a cabin. All these individuals deserved our help, but the facts were clear. Circumstances brought us together with the Erets, not for a specific reason, but for mutual exploration of possibilities. I could not heal Pirect and perhaps healing him was the easy way out for me. The situation with the Erets felt like one of those freewill opportunities, just like my freewill opportunity with Cerebow. I could do nothing or get involved. As soon as we set our luggage down in our cabin, Élan said, "We cannot ask the Erets to sit for three days in that public lounge, especially with a dying child on their hands."

"You're right," I said. "Stellium, why don't you go down to the lounge and tell them we want to share our cabin space with them."

"Thank you," said Stellium as if we were doing him a favor.

The cabin had two single beds, complete with lumpy mattresses and two tiny pillows as flat and hard as two stale loaves of bread. Stellium later said, "I knew the child did not have long to live. He was hot and light as a feather when I laid him on the bed." That night, we gave the other single bed to Hanib and Doh who slept sideways so they could fit. Élan, Stellium, and I used an extra blanket to create a space on the floor where we sat facing each other in meditation. This was not really a sacrifice, except Élan's head still hurt. If the situation demanded, the three of us could rest in meditative silence for many hours in this manner. About two hours into our meditation, we realized Pirect was preparing to leave his body for good. He appeared in our etheric midst and told us, "Tell mommy and daddy that Soso came out to meet me. He was barking at my heels and as usual, wanted to play ball." Pirect, the body, died moments later.

Hanib, like so many Sutcay Tay women after the storm, was resolute in her suffering and beyond tears; but her husband sobbed uncontrollably as the ship's medic, a young medical student, told them, "I'm sorry, your child is gone." The medic, a willowy young woman with both intelligence and compassion pouring forth from her eye rutilates, wore a nametag that said "Giceum Das." The use of nametags was a practice some Gathosians had adapted from Humans. Most Gathosians regarded nametags as gross self-advertisement, a gimmick that allowed a stranger to address a person by name without actually knowing that person. Giceum stayed with us until four deckhands arrived to remove the body and take it to cold storage in the hold. Giceum explained to the Erets, "No provisions are available for cremation on the island." Two torturous days remained on the outward voyage and then Hanib and Doh would need to turn around and accompany the body of their son back to Logan's Point. Giceum turned to us in a private aside and said, "I'd like to make just one trip to New Delphi Island without someone dying on route."

"Death is a real inconvenience," said Élan, which caught her off-guard. She left our cabin scratching her head, perhaps to go somewhere and ponder the persistence of death even in the face of *beltania*, "greatest bliss."

Despite the doctor's warnings, the Erets now were stunned. They sat huddled together and stared off into space on the edge of the bed. Their reason for going to New Delphi, their very purpose for living, was gone. Slowly they began to talk in those short revelatory phases, which say nothing, but reveal so much. "Pirect was a miracle baby," said Hanib. Her words were my words, ghostly waves of motherly suffering from the persistent stream. I remembered bringing Dulce to New Delphi when he was Pirect's age. "Pirect was tiny when he was born, but spirited, and the most thoughtful child Air ever blessed with life." Hanib and Doh were members of an Air worshiping cult.

I lacked proper prenatal care and nutrition and the pollution in the Sutcay Tay air, made me ill during my pregnancy. Dulce was small when he was born. Then came Remette's mental cruelty. It was always either/or with Remette, his and not his. Dulce was barely three when Remette told him, "Look at your hands. You're a Human monkey and your mother is a monkey's whore." That's the night I ran away, begging for food and shelter along the way. The Crystal became my goddess and New Delphi was a paradise that might shelter me and nurture the genius within my darling child. My constant prayer of supplication was, "Nourish the hunger in his eyes, the gift in his mind, and inspire his Human hands to create." I did not know Dulce was destined to be the divine hope of the ages.

"Pirect wanted to be a dancer when he grew up," said Hanib.

Dulce was born eloquent and while most children were baby talking, he was creating tunes and clever lyric in his head. Watching Dulce grow and develop was a gift, because through him, I caught glimpses of his father. One day, Dulce picked up my mother's flute and out poured transcendent sound. Every time he touched a musical instrument, he was able to make music that stirred the soul. When other children were struggling to learn to read, Dulce was a keyboard virtuoso and the supreme high priestess of New Delphi asked me to allow him to play in the Witches' Temple on special occasions. He told me often, "I'm going to be a composer when I grow up."

"Do you believe we angered Air because we boasted that when Pirect danced, he was lighter than Air?" asked Doh.

"I'm sure Air was honored," said Stellium.

Doh assured us, "Every breath we took, we worshipped as a gift from Air. With my own hands, I helped build the Air Temple in our village. We dedicated our son's life to Air's greater glory."

Élan said, "We cannot control the elemental universe, but we can negotiate our way through catastrophes, with compassion for ourselves and others," but they were too raw to acknowledge this truth. All grieving parents are deaf and blind. They are incapable of excusing the elemental universe or themselves. They need cause and effect justice.

"I'm finished believing in anything," swore Doh. "Never will I believe in any element again," and he started building a wall around himself.

Hanib was superstitious. "Don't talk that way, Doh; you may bring even more trouble down upon us."

"What else could possibly happen?" he sobbed and his voice was full of indignant rage. "No, from this day forward, I believe in nothing."

"They repeated variations on their monologues over the next two days. It was difficult for us all in that small space. We had no place to escape, but up on deck, and no place to begin with the Erets, no niche through to their souls. Their grief was too fresh and Doh's anger too great. We allowed them the gift of talking as much as they needed and challenged them on nothing.

\*\*\*\*

Up on deck, it was raining. I stood by the port railing and watched the deckhands go about their chores. Sails were slack and a sailor paused before tossing a thick rope to a dockhand that stood on the edge of the pier. As a child, my father laughed because I told him this moment was the most exciting part of the voyage. Wayfarers were reaching their destinations, disembarking, and embracing old friends. In a short time, a crane would hoist boxes and huge crates and, sometimes, even caged animals came up from the hold. Once I saw an excited monkey rattling the bars of his cage, screeching at the indifference of the surrounding commotion. Where did he go? Another time, an exotic bird spurned the land and gazed wistfully out to sea. Where was she? Did she escape one morning when her *Emayre* sprang open the door?

In my hands, I held all the unopened letters returned by my father. *I am sending all my thoughts into the Primordial Waters. Through her, will you please understand and forgive?* Ignoring New Delphi law, I allowed the letters to slip from my hands and into the Iris Sea.

Afterward, I gazed at the early evening sky. The steady rain muted the scene while the sporadic creaking of the windship reminded me that the body of Pirect Eret was still down in the hold. Doh and Hanib came topside to say thank you again. Stellium was kinesthetic with empathy and hugged both of them several times. "You might not believe this, but we saw your son's spirit right before his body died," said Stellium. "He said, "Tell mommy and daddy that Soso came out to meet me. He was barking at my heels and as usual, wanted to play ball." Only Hanib was ready to acknowledge that she heard Stellium while Doh, without a word, turned his back and walked toward the stern of the ship. We never saw the Erets again nor did we possess an address through which we could reach them. I don't know if we helped them, confused them, or even if they would remember us. Certainly, when I took Dulce to New Delphi, many people helped me and I did not remember their faces or names. My *Emayre* reminded me, *not everyone needs to come all the way to New Delphi for revelation.*

\*\*\*\*

The view of New Delphi from the deck of the windship was lovely and could have passed as a scene from Paradise. *Deceptive*, said my *Emayre*. *Paradise is easy. New Delphi remains a question without an answer.*" The island appeared as an innocent circle of land surrounded by the Iris Sea. The gleaming New Delphi Crystal sat in the highest mountain in the island's center. The sky was capable of assuming any color creation could conceive. It was particularly fantastic when it turned diachronic blues and metallic gold and bronze. *Spectacular vision shields the truth.* This evening rain was washing the sky, turning it shades of translucent gray.

The silver light of the auroras ignored the rain and played across the sky. Gazing at the light, for what seemed like only an instant, a particle separated from the steam, and came straight for my eye. It called me a lover and lured me with an invitation, *come, and cast your doubts into me.* That one solitary particle took me into an oceanic interface, where light casts a hook into memory and fishes for absolutely anything that needs to bite. I was reminded of the impossibility of what I had committed to do. I had pledged my lives to sort out time with nothing but energy and my animated bones. Perhaps to escape from this impossible task, my mind wandered into its private museum called memory. *Just one more trap of time.* But without my memory, I cannot perform these tasks nor can I escape what I believe is true, especially with the light particle fishing in the pool of my eye. There, the hook released a cascade of New Delphi memories, that one tiny particle washing away the New Delphi of the unfolding now. In my cloistered memory, I held secret recollections—wee treasures—nuggets of glittering images of being here many times before. Other eyes, I once called my own, had looked out at this scene from the deck of a windship and thought they knew what they saw. *What is real? Then, now, or what is to come? If nothing is valid in the past or future and my present is distorted with illusions, why did I commit to this impossible task?*

*Memory is a drifting consensus filtered through the now.*

*Help me? I'm trapped in this loop called time.*

*Calm yourself!* said my *Emayre. Billions upon billions have failed to solve this riddle.*

Thankfully, Stellium came up and touched my shoulder, saying, "I've got a map and the key to our cottage." He flipped the plastic tag of the old style key over and said, "We're staying in cottage 22 on Auric Lane. We should probably get going. It will be dark soon and Élan is getting another headache."

# EIGHTEEN

No sooner did we disembark than Élan's headache took a turn for the worst. He stood on the dock and hung onto a lamppost with one hand while clutching his head with the other. "This time it's more than a headache," he said. "Vision is injecting light and color inside my head—fast-moving patterns weaving intricate designs high up in the stratosphere of my brain. I think I am going to be—" and then despite New Delphi law, we supported him as he sacrificed the contents of his stomach to the Iris Sea. After he vomited, his visions only intensified and he felt trapped because he possessed no physical vision to distract him from the turmoil going on inside his head. No transportation existed on the island; so with our help, he walked two kilometers, in the drizzling rain, to our rented cottage.

As soon as we got inside, we helped him strip off his wet clothing and he fell face down across the bed. He was shivering and his forehead felt feverishly hot to the touch. I covered him with all the extra blankets in the cottage while Stellium sat on the edge of the bed and tried to comfort him. Meanwhile, I began setting deadlines, thinking, *if he's no better, we'll leave on the first windship tomorrow morning. We have no real reason to be here anymore. I'm already pregnant.*

"Leaving doesn't set right with me," said Élan. He was reading my thoughts. "We need to stay until I figure out what's going on. It feels important."

As ever, Stellium was as accommodating as a downy pillow. "If you feel it's important, then we'll stay right here and help you figure out what's wrong. For now, open your energy to us and we'll soothe your psychic agitation with our calm."

Stellium and I stripped off our wet clothing and got into bed, compressing Élan between us. The three of us were completely empathic and it took no more than a few seconds to tune into the vision inside Élan's mind. Just as he suggested, vivid colors were ricocheting around inside his internal atmosphere—blue-green circles switching like interchanging lenses. The instant Stellium and I realized the phenomenon was the inner reflection of Élan's own blue-green eyes, the visions ceased. Then came a short pause, a mere half-breath, like the tension between overture and first curtain. A pinprick of crimson light appeared in the center of Élan's vision that burst into a fast whirling disk. He groaned in agony while burning sparks flew off the disk and stung our faces with the sharpness of beestings. As suddenly as the disk appeared, it disappeared, leaving a soft pink vapor drifting through the dark.

The spinning crimson disk was none other than the trademark of eighth dimensional consciousness. Now I knew we faced the great destroyer, the butcher and scourge, the sword of almighty truth. *New Delphi is difficult.* Nothing is ever personal concerning the great destroyer and that's why the ordeal is so devastating. The eighth dimension acts without mercy, will not compromise, and is an indisputable and relentless force. Its truth annihilates in one scintillating flash. It draws our blood and watches indifferently as we die. The pink vapor is the exclamation point the seventh dimension tags onto the force, as it zips through that realm, a promise of compassion if the truth hits its mark.

I immediately relayed this information to Élan and Stellium. *The test is courage.*

Stellium swept through our combined energies to make certain the three of us were clear of blocks. Élan's psychic center possessed a block directly behind his eyes. It was his blindness. *Try to relax into your pain*, Stellium communicated. Élan took a deep breath to ease his tension and at that instant, the block vanished and left an epic story that exploded into a multi-faceted vision. The three of us did not jump; we were catapulted. This catapult brought us to a precipice, where the perspective beyond was expansive knowledge, opportunity, and even responsibility to change the flow of third dimensional reality.

Eighth dimensional consciousness communicates with a speed, intensity, and precision incomprehensible to ordinary third-dimensional understanding. The message usually is short, a few seconds to a couple of minutes in length, and probably would drive the personal mind into schizophrenic fits of insanity if the experience lasted longer. The message and messenger are one. In other words, the experience is a direct broad-faced interface with eighth dimensional intelligence. It is similar to a thousand multidexes transmitting their messages and the receiver possessing the genius to simultaneously assemble them into meaning. The interface usually contains dozens of scenes with multiple perspectives and from different lives and times. No psychic experience comes without its cipher. The cipher itself seems to be a tenth-dimensional conundrum to our third-dimensional senses, in that the cipher is not observable, has no boundaries or form, is empty, and yet is a receptive tool of interpretation. For lack of a better word, we call it, "understanding." Understanding comes with the message/messenger and will not leave until the receiver assembles the scenes and perspectives into continuity and meaning. In our case, all scenes, lives, and perspectives came from the conscious soup of Élan and Stellium's soul groups. As Iosobell, I knew I was experiencing a puzzle inside Élan's head, yet I could witness these lives or, even be these lives, just as Stellium and Élan could witness or be these lives. The eighth dimension gave us multitudes of fluid perspectives to experience the reality of the message in anyway we chose.

The psychic visions inside Élan's mind whirled like bright confetti as a multitude of scenes snagged our attention and left their impressions. From the standpoint of this time, the puzzle pieces were events within the persistent stream that began on New Delphi Island, thirty phases into the future and ended eighty-seven phases later. One scene featured a cavern with a natural jade icon. Concentrating upon the icon, the periphery of the scene turned into a dense blue and crimson pattern, as complicated as intricate lace. A peridotic light emerged from the darkness and caressed a darker specter of evil. Again we saw the jade icon, but when we concentrate upon it, the icon vanished and our combined consciousness fell directly into a scene.

Click! We were inside an event but the other actors, did not realize we were present. We found ourselves standing inside a cottage similar to the one we were staying in at the moment. A Human woman opened a door and walked inside. She was blonde and pretty with a distracted expression plastered across her face. She let go a surprised gasp because she saw a snippet of green fabric disappear out through a rear window. What she saw was the hem on the skirt of a Trinity Witch.

Élan had so many emotional prongs into this scene, it jittered and we could not hold onto it. This is understandable. Élan had just seen Mellé, his feminine half in his next life. Stellium also held an intimate connection with the witch who slipped out through the window. Stellium communicated to us that he was sure that he knew her. Her Trinity Witch moniker was Beltania, "greatest bliss," and she was the stepdaughter of the supreme high priestess of New Delphi. Her stepmother sent Beltania to Mellé's room to steal a *keylic*. This was part of a plan hatched by the supreme high priestess to reestablish her control over the New Delphi Crystal. The plan was to use this *keylic* to bring Dulce to his knees because Mellé was Dulce's wife and soul mate.

The eighth dimension began showing us another scene and Élan twitched and moaned. Mellé walked out of the cottage and Michael stood there, waiting for her. "Where's your map?" he asked.

"I forgot it," said Mellé and then she told him about the snippet of green fabric disappearing out through the window of their cottage.

"It's the Trinity Witches," said Michael.

Élan began breathing harder, because he knew he was both Mellé and Michael in the future. *Somehow I knew!* Élan thought.

Because Michael was Mellé's clone, his hair was identical to hers. The supreme high priestess never realized Beltania stole Michael's hair instead of Mellé's hair. Beltania gave the hair to her stepmother and she draped it over the jade icon while she prepared herself for the *keylic* ritual. Blue and crimson were the colors of the intricate lace curtains that hung across the entryway to her personal temple. Someone yanked these curtains closed right before the high priestess began her energy manipulations. Regardless, no curtain in creation could hide the truth from the eighth dimension that now presented the evidence to us in a vision. We saw the supreme high priestess disdain all goodness and manifest a specter aimed to destroy Mellé. The specter was a powerful demon whose energy came from the protective aura of peridotic light the priestess created around it. Keying the demon for the hair *keylic*, the demon killed Michael, not Mellé as the supreme high priestess intended.

Élan was trembling with emotion when he told us, "When Michael asked Mellé, 'Where's your map?' it was the precisely the same tone as when the *manatee* asked me, "Where's your key? Now I remember! After the *manatee* touched my key, it said, 'Safety deposit box number 22, how synchronistic and beautiful! You will be staying in cottage number 22 on Auric Lane on New Delphi. Wear this key and it will act as a talismanic link between us. Now I will turn the key toward the light and a vision will enter your unconscious mind. When you arrive on New Delphi, a whirling disk of eighth dimensional consciousness will emerge through the Crystal and unlock the vision. Then you will have all the information required to complete your mission. I'm sorry, but to keep this information safe, until the time is right, you will need to be blind. We can't take the chance that you will see something in your travels that will trigger the vision before it's proper time.'"

The puzzle pieces continued to arrange themselves into greater meaning and the next scene sucked us inside. We were sitting with Mellé, Michael, and Dulce in a darkened room that was illuminated by the light of one small candle. "I was already involved with Bell," said Dulce. "She was more than enough for any lover. She would drop by and cast the tarot for some of the regulars between my sets—earn some pocket change that we would blow on vials of *tartan ratu*."

"When was the last time you saw her?" asked Mellé.

Dulce shrugged. "Alive? The same night I last saw you." Dulce turned sentimental. "She was a hellcat, just like me. It was all bravado—hurt little girl stuff. Her story was mine."

"Dulce, listen to me," said Mellé. "Bell is not dead; she is alive. I saw her."

Dulce stared into the distance. "She is dead. I know she is dead, because I helped cremate her body. The Trinity Order is using the denial she left behind to manipulate her soul. They blame me for their loss of power with the New Delphi Crystal. Now, because of our bonding, they believe you know the sacred music too."

"Tell us the truth," said Michael. "Once and for all, did you steal the sacred music from the New Delphi Crystal?"

Dulce huffed. "Steal it? How could I steal something from the New Delphi Crystal? The Crystal fed me the sacred music as if I was its *foie gras* goose."

"Then we need to face these witches and find out what they want."

"Impossible!" said Dulce. "Don't you understand? They want their power back. I cannot restore their power and I have no control over which way the power flows. However, I cannot leave New Delphi—ever. This place protects me. All they can do is send in their goblins on crow's backs to try to frighten me. Outside, true madness awaits."

\*\*\*\*

Four souls launched the next part of the vision. It would be presumptuous to judge these four souls, for we would forever miss the contact point of empathy. We invited them to speak plainly, as themselves. We experienced their stories simultaneously, yet understood each one as if she commanded our complete attention.

Viewed through the spectrum of time, Belleth, meaning, "sound of primordial receptivity," was the first witch to appear. We saw her ensconced in her cavern temple. The cavern was small and she was not a high-ranking priestess, but she was a priestess nonetheless. Like all caverns, under the New Delphi Crystal, spectral light filled the space. Belleth was a beautiful Gathosian woman, with black curly hair piled high on her head. She was dressed in a long flowing sea-green robe and wore a necklace of jade cabochons around her throat. She was sitting on a bench with one barefoot perched on it and her arm stretched out over her knee. She opened a jewel-capped jar of *tartan ratu* and dotted its dust on the zaqurlite ring that pierced her bottom lip. Then she stood and went to her altar to light four beeswax candles dedicated to the Elements. She lit each candle with her will and the act was a sacred gesture of personal sacrifice, a gift of her energy given to the Crystal. "Goddess Crystal," she prayed. "Lure him with your greater charms and take this irrational desire from me."

"What's your quandary?" asked her *Emayre*.

"I climbed the tricky energy of a half-Human last night," said Belleth. "—a rogue by the name of Dulcerary Cœur. He's a brilliant musician who's been playing keyboards in the temples during the spring festivals. He likes to flirt with the boys and girls alike and he flaunts his brilliance wherever he goes. His liberal use of rose-scented *ratu* smells like a breath of fresh air, after all the Hectarian musk and piety that shows up for *privilege* auditions. Despite the shame I feel afterward, his irreverence makes me laugh. Cœur speaks Mescale with a charming Oceania lilt and the mere sound of his logos gets me high." Belleth means Dulce's spiel or line, or the manner in which he speaks, fully reveals his inner meaning. "His aura is golden light and his rutilates golden splinters of psychic cunning, while his smile is wistful and sincere. The first moment I saw him, my energy peaked. He seemed to know what was going on inside me and he laughed delicately when he asked, 'What's the fuss all about, Belleth? Do you want to taste love or satisfy your lust with me?' What could I say but 'yes' to an invitation as bold as his? He's imaginative in the doing and he manipulates his energy like a magician. He begins by offering himself up as ninety-nine percent heart energy, powerful, somewhat erratic, but again sincere; but in actual sexual transmission, he's high-level psychic—real fire! I immediately offered to make him my soul intimate, but he shrugged off my offer saying, 'I'm going to Euterpe to seek my fame.'"

"Love him," said her *Emayre*. "Bring him to me so I might love him too."

The scene changed and we were standing with Belleth in the southern gardens, just beyond the Witches' Temple. The day was cool and she was hiding inside a long, green cape with the hood pulled up over her head. Not even a fingernail was visible beneath, which made the yellow-green color of the free radical hovering near her aura even more pronounced. "Now that the rogue is gone, I understand that he represented something important to me, but I don't understand what it was. I find myself coming here to the rose garden just to recapture his smell. Lately, my life is full of frustrations and my visions are dwindling down to few. Yesterday, the supreme high priestess told me my visions were all minor, parenthetical expressions, which she could do without, here on New Delphi. She is sending Belsod, Omodobel, and me to Euterpe to open a Trinity Witch hospital.'"

A scene opened on a hospital ward, somewhere on Euterpe. The three of us meshed so completely, those who were living this reality, saw us and interacted with us as if we were part of it too. A witch named Belsod handed me a bedpan. "Here, dispose of this," she ordered.

I looked around for Stellium and he was holding the hand of a dying woman who thought he was an angel, while Élan was changing the sheets on a bed at the other end of the ward. I disposed of the bedpan and went to find Belleth. I found her in an office where she was shuffling through stacks of papers that littered a desk. She was dressed in a simple white caftan similar to a *moodarry* with her hair pulled into a tight knot at the nape of her neck. Her only visible jewelry was a snake armlet of healing on her upper left arm and the zaqurlite ring in her bottom lip. The free radical still hovered around her. It had not penetrated her aura, but it must have sensed an opportunity was near, for it followed her wherever she went. "No time to dally," she lectured me. "If you want to hear this part of my lament, we will have to talk as I work."

Leaning out the doorway, I beckoned toward Élan and Stellium, "She's down here." Belleth flew out of the office and the free radical and I were hot on her trail. She began shouting orders to Omodobel and Belsod. Belleth took one critical glance at the bed Élan just made and scolded him with, "That looks like a piece of shit." She tore the sheets off the bed and proceeded to remake it herself. "Here on Euterpe, I enjoy only two *privileges*, both females," and she adeptly folded the corner of the sheet under the mattress and yanked it taunt. "Belsod is always gloomy, but she's skilled at concocting the drugs we need from the local herbs, while Omodobel is lazy and dull as a doorknob. Now hand me that bedding," she barked at Stellium.

Stellium handed her a blanket and asked, "Have you seen Dulce Cœur since you've been here on Euterpe?"

"The rogue? I ran into him at a charity benefit about a moon ago. He hasn't changed. He's still handsome, conceited, and his energy is always alert and maddeningly independent. Afterwards, he invited Omodobel, Belsod, and I to go back to his rooms, to sit on his lap."

"Did you go?" asked Élan, and he handed her the pillow.

She hesitated and her voice filled with hurt. "What can I say? His energy remains irresistible to me. Besides, the rogue starts his journey where most *privileges* get lost. His energy goes straight for the heart. The first thing you know his tongue is wrapped around yours and filling you with his eloquence. Despite his charms, he's conceited. This time he possessed the audacity to tell me, 'Every lover is my perfect match.' His eyes even glazed over with tears when he told Omodobel that she was beautiful. She was so smitten that she released her own energy down his throat. In retrospect, I'm beginning to realize the rogue means everything he says, when he says it, but he has a short memory indeed. He's not serious about supporting the visions of Trinity Witches. Dulce Cœur is only serious when the energy goes his way. He still likes to laugh and afterward he asked us if we were interested in connecting with the energy of an exotic alien, pointing out that he was his father's boy—'half-Gathosian and half-chicken.' Belsod is as humorless as I am nowadays and she told him, 'We're only interested in higher consciousness, not dogs, lizards, or cows.' Peels of laughter came streaming out of him when she said that and he assured us, 'The person I have in mind is a highly-evolved, Tyrowsian white rat.'"

The scene faded and we were standing in a void with Belleth. "We did not see each other for nine moons," she said. "No day passed, when I did not think of him. Every sweet smell and every taste of beauty reminded me of Dulcerary Cœur. I was sure no *privilege* could ever match him. He was the most exquisite lover who ever graced my energy with his own. When we met in the flesh the next time, he was on the prowl. He was too thin and his hair hung down around his waist. I thought, 'Holy Elements! His poor mother certainly tagged him when she named him Dulcerary. He's a wild black cat and all he wants to do is stalk, kill, and indulge. He offered me no explanation about his absence and yet he managed to look sincere when he said, 'I missed you and love you more than ever.' Another affair began between us that same night."

"He was playing keyboards at a waterfront dive called Club Obbligato and I would drop by for his last few sets. I would read tarot for the patrons—you know—tell them what they wanted to hear. I considered it educational. I learned that drunken men always give the most generous tips. Both of us were poor as street *scrubs*, yet we spent every banknote I received on *tartan ratu*. I still entertained illusions that the rogue was going to fall in love with me. But at the same time Dulce was dancing with my energy, he was indulging in a cheap sexual affair with one of his fans, a Tyrowsian dwarf named Jana Revba. Dulce called him, 'Jananita,' and in jest said, 'He's a shadow's shadow and that's why he's so white.' Whatever Revba was, he had plenty of money and he was spellbound with Dulce. Revba showered Dulce with expensive gifts and Dulce started dragging Revba along to pay for the *ratu*. Dulce even tried to bring Revba into our bed. He was terrified of me and protected his anemic little wand with his delicate white hands. Like a typical Tyrowsian, he did not believe in the past or future, let alone jumping dimensions. We went nowhere together. Afterwards, Dulce laughed about Revba and told me that ninety percent of their lovemaking consisted of them stroking each other's hair. I did not realize until later that all Tyrowsians are what you might call 'late bloomers' and that Revba was still an adolescent."

In an abrupt shift, we were back in the hospital with Belleth and she was sitting by the bed of an old man, pouring her energy into him to alleviate his pain. "I'll take over for you," offered Élan. "Why don't you rest for awhile?"

"Thank you," she said. "I've been here for several days without a break."

"Have you seen Dulce lately?" asked Stellium.

"You again?" and she yawned. "Why is it that every time I see you, you ask me if I have seen Dulce Cœur?"

"Well, have you?" insisted Stellium.

"For your information, the rogue married a rich-bitch Human named Mellé about six moons ago. He told me about his decision right before they flew off to New Delphi together. He swore to me, 'This will help break the irrational compulsion between us.' His eyes were all teary with personal hurt when he said, 'besides, you don't need me anymore. To you, I'm just a rogue with an unexplainable gift.' Now that our affair is over, I feel relieved and I want to make it perfectly clear that the rogue never fooled me with his phony sincerity. He always was and forever will be a rogue. By the way, his new fame doesn't impress me either. I've known him with his pants down around his ankles and his honesty stiff with need." Belleth's haughty expression turned into a laugh that could sour milk. "His new wife runs his life and she employs an entire staff of experts whose sole responsibility is to bolster the rogue's popularity. It's disgusting! Exactly what he deserves. It's for sure that no self-respecting Gathosian would flaunt divine gifts for wealth. Nowadays, the fawning media follows him everywhere, calling him The Divine Dulce, a genius, and the greatest composer of the Golden Age of Euterpe. One never sees him or his rich-bitch minus their jeweled finery, pretense, and entourage of hired help. They always are smiling and waving at the rogue's obsequious fans, as if they are on their way to somewhere important. I don't know much about Cœur's genius as a composer because everything he writes, sounds like music I once allowed him to hear through me. Either another foolish priestess is now humming in his ear or the rumors circulating around him are true. Still, no man has ever shown the psychic ability to consciously interface with the New Delphi Crystal and it seems highly unlikely that an undisciplined rowdy, such as Cœur, could do it in one afternoon on his wedding day."

Stellium, Élan, and I were standing in a darkened room. Belleth was lying in her bed on her left side. She was not quite dreaming, but rather drifting in that halfway state of hypnagogic transition that struggles to make sense of the repetitive nonsense of the day. "I miss you," she called out to her *Emayre. I can't hear you from here.*

*If you could get the rogue alone, without the distraction of other lovers, you might be able to decipher the configuration of his energy,* said the free radical that lingered near her aura. *If you could figure out his energy patterns, you could find someone like him, only more receptive to your needs. Then your visions would return and you could return to me.*

The following morning we watched Belleth as she contentiously half-explained to Belsod and Omodobel that she needed to go to the Ivory Coast for a few days to raise money for the clinic. Then the vision jumped and we saw her sailing with Dulce along the Ivory Coast. She stood back from this part of the vision and said, "He came to me one evening at hospital and said, 'I'm ready to stop playing games. You need me and I definitely need you.' I asked him, 'What about your rich-bitch wife?' and he said, 'To her, sacred music is just another way to make money.' We went down to the Ivory Coast together and he did give me the money for the clinic, but, naturally, that's not why I went."

"The morning we arrived, he said, 'I hope you brought your tarot cards?' We both shuffled the cards and poured our energy into them. Together we pulled out The Star. 'The Rose of Manifestation!' he exclaimed. He was happier than I ever saw him before. We spent the next several days, sailing along the Ivory Coast and bathing ourselves in the blessings of The Star and setting the nights on fire with our love. I still had access to all the higher realms through him. I no longer wanted to jump anywhere without him or be with anyone other than him; but I still could not figure out his energy. As a priestess, I learned that love of his sort is nothing more than sentimental illusion; but even now, as a witness to this fiasco that could be/is/was my life, I love Dulce Cœur with my complete being, yet loving him seems as foolish as jumping off a cliff and expecting to live."

The next scene opened on a garden party and we understood that the artists of Euterpe had organized the affair to raise money for the thousands of Tyrowsian refugees that survived the destruction of the planet Pybatium. Belleth was in attendance and again dressed in white. Around her head, she wore a silver band featuring a crescent moon with a moonstone cabochon in the center. She was exquisite. Dulce came up behind her and said, "Belleth! You're so beautiful this evening," and he offered her a flute of champagne. She turned to face him and the scene faded to dark viridian green.

"I stopped the vision because I didn't want you to see what the rogue had become," said Belleth.

"Let us see," I urged her. "We can help only if you allow us to see the whole truth."

"No! I refuse to look at him that way."

Stellium took Belleth's hand and urged her to let us see what she was holding back. "I can't," she still insisted. "Instead, I will describe what happened for that's the only way I can get through this difficult part." She swallowed hard and said, "I turned to face Dulce and his appearance shocked me. He was high on *ratu* and champagne and it was obvious he was cruising for an easy heart so he could dump his energy. It immediately turned into flippant banter between us, a way to hide our inexhaustible love for each other. The dark circles under his eyes and his fractured rutilates made him look dissipated and I asked him, 'What's the matter, rogue? Your pretenses keeping you awake at night?'"

He laughed. 'No pretenses with you, Belleth, just lots of honest lust.' He was growing fat and hiding his fat gut with expensive hand-tailored silks.

His long hair was gone—it looked butchered. He had a characteristic habit of delicately brushing back the hair that fell over his forehead with his fingertips. The first time we made love, that one simple gesture of his caused one of the most ecstatic orgasms I ever experienced. Now he pretended to brush back his hair only this time his hair was gone. He continued to laugh—he still could laugh like a demon.

"What happened to your hair?' I asked.

"I surrendered my energy to a sadistic hairdresser who was in love with his scissors," he laughed.

I struggled to laugh too. 'Too bad, rogue, your hair was your best feature, above your waist.' Then he suggested that we slip away from the party. How did he put it? Yes, now I remember. He said, 'Let's ditch this boring dig and take to the heart.' I loved him so much, I would have gone merely to help him recapture his beauty and grace, but just then, his empty-headed, gourd of a wife, found us and said she was searching for him all over the party. 'Dulcerosa,' she twittered. He kissed her in front of me and introduced me as his cousin. That night he came knocking on my door and in our mutual desperation, an accident happened between us. A few weeks later, when I told him about it, he was not pleased. He was cold and indifferent when he said 'get rid of it.' I wanted to tell him I loved the life growing inside me, but, as usual, I matched him iceberg for iceberg and said, 'If it's a boy, I guess I will give it to the Hectarians to rear.' He smirked and said, 'It was good enough for me,' and he began to walk away. He turned back just once and told me, 'I've always loved you, Belleth, but right now, I hate you. Do you know why? Because all you've ever cared about is bringing me down.' I answered him right back with, 'And all you ever care about is getting high.' Now, sometimes in my prayers, I swear, 'I will bring you down, my lovely half-breed rogue and when I bring you down, you'll be down for many lifetimes.' I think I can do it too. I possess the most powerful *keylic* in the world, his genetic seed in my womb."

Belleth flared into sharper view and this time she was holding her infant daughter in her arms. The zaqurlite ring was missing from her bottom lip, leaving a gaping hole. The free radical had penetrated her aura and was shadowing her every move. She believed it was her *Emayre* and said, "Sorry, my *Emayre* was speaking to me and we needed to cry for a while." We waited until she said, "The child was female and I named her Duebel, which means 'sweet sound of receptivity.' Duebel was an embarrassment to the Trinity order and I took full censure for my crime of loving the rogue. The supreme high priestess testified against me before the Hectarian Council. They stripped me of my priestess rank and tore my zaqurlite rings from my body. Now those points of sensual interface are scared and incapable of capturing vision. The council blamed me—said I gave Dulcerary Cœur sacred vision that he was profaning for popular consumption and profit.

They separated me from my child as soon as she was born and sent me back to Euterpe while Duebel went into Trinity communal care. My crime was not that I bore a child, for most priestesses have children. I received censure because it was obvious that Duebel was the child of Dulcerary Cœur, the man who served no high priestess and who flaunted his direct connection to the New Delphi Crystal. My child was the daughter of the man who wrote and published the scandalous Panansha Symphony. Dulcerary Lanai Cœur broke all the rules and possessed the audacity to expose the transcendent message of higher dimensions to anyone with the ears to hear. He wrote the music and revealed the message through the Panansha chorus, 'Be birtha nei Michi. Cany suite waverred, a douterrye et douterrye et aunt dayee foe-emayre*.'"

Belleth began sobbing uncontrollably. "I made so many mistakes and possessed no courage to leave the only life I knew. I wanted Dulce to rescue us, but he never came—not even to see his daughter. For a long time, I thought it was because he loved only Mellé, but he didn't even love her. He loved nobody. He wasn't even a rogue. He was a cursed paradox, incapable of love, yet capable of taking me into the heart of divine love."

"What happened to your child?" I asked.

"Many terrible things. I was on Euterpe and received a message from the supreme high priestess, telling me that her soul mate, Bastion, a Hectarian surgeon, had amputated Duebel's extra toes and fingers. The high priestess said the modification would help Duebel fit in with other Gathosian children. I was horrified. When they allowed me to return to New Delphi for a sabbatical, the high priestess said, 'Unfortunately, she still looks exactly like her father and she acts like him too.' It was true. Duebel even found ways to make music with her poor little mutilated hands." Belleth pressed the body of Duebel to her heart before saying, "My lament has run it's course. I await your decision, as does my daughter, my granddaughter, and my great-granddaughter. May my *Emayre* have mercy upon all our souls," and Belleth disappeared.

Élan, Stellium, and I experienced Duebel's life in an empathic proximity that felt like terror itself. Her daughter's story already had run dry, because it was much shorter than her mother's. I merely write Duebel's part now, to allow the tale to unfold in a linear fashion, which fits third-dimensional strictures of perception.

Duebel was/is/would be fragile, confused, and full of birthing pain. "Help me?" she whimpered and it seemed the sound of perpetual crying had followed her from the beginning of time. She metamorphosed into a toddler before our eyes and her arms flailed in a tantrum until she became

*"I am your dancer of All Understanding. Chalice is the sweet eternal. For your song, is the direct path, through my Heart."; language origin Mescale.

an adolescent child. She screamed, "Pain, so much pain. I want my mother."

"Tell us what's wrong?" asked Stellium who was able to open a short dialogue with her.

"Everyone tells me I should accept responsibility for my actions."

"What did you do?"

"Nothing! I'm innocent, but nobody believes me. My belly got big after the high priestess shared energy with me. It was her fault, not mine."

"How could another woman make you pregnant?"

"The supreme high priestess put something inside me that hurt."

"How old are you, Duebel?"

"I don't know," and she started screaming until she attracted the attention of the free radical legacy from her mother. In one horrible gulp, the free radical devoured the child and used her energy to transform itself into a specter of rage. Now the peridotic light glowed brighter and moved with an independence of spirit for it had swallowed an entire soul in one gulp.

The three of us began frantically searching for Duebel through the multitude of visions. "She's gone," said Élan several times, "but her daughter is putting enormous pressure on me to speak." We took extra time within this vision because the other visions still were unwinding and telling us their perspectives. We were able to replay Duebel's brief message several times and as we did, we searched for more clues, but she repeated the same information and at the end, her daughter again was putting pressure on Élan to speak. Our understanding concluded that somebody had amputated Duebel's life, just as Bell's soul mate, Bastion, amputated Duebel's fingers and toes.

The child born to the child Duebel exploded like a volcano before us. As a soul, this child-born-of-child was so frozen with fear, so disconnected from her life, she chose to speak as a soul witness and view her life, along with us, from the safety of the third person. She created a window and we stood behind the window with her and viewed the reality of her life in the persistent stream. "The specter of rage was waiting for me in the Jumping-Off Place," she said. "Even before I was born, the specter had perverted me with its illusions and when I was born, the physical pain wiped away any memory of the real."

The four of us watched as a nameless child scampered along Jade Boulevard. She was barefoot and dressed in a smock of faded blue. She held up a tattered piece of cardboard that read, "*Samay* (Hungry)." Her movements were quick and she managed to slip through the crowd and pick the pockets of tourists while she held their attention with her sad, pathetic eyes. A fruit and vegetable vender threw her a few sarup nuts and she snatched them and raced into a nearby alley where she sat on her haunches and nibbled at the nuts like a hungry *tujet*.

"I was hard and clever," said the soul witness. "I needed to be to survive. As a young child, I knew my way around New Delphi, especially the underground caverns. Life itself taught me how to survive, including how to trade sexual favors for food. I sold my virginity for a bowl of *grash*. I had no name, but my tormentors called me Shibel (meaning, "female receptive," and the Mescale equivalent of whore). I didn't take the insult personally, for I was streetwise and knew thousands of Shibels existed on New Delphi and billions of other Shibels on other worlds too. To amuse myself, I created musical instruments from discarded trash. One day, my *Emayre* assumed the form of a tourist and when I approached her to beg for coinage, she gave me a toy flute instead. I mastered the fingering within minutes and by the end of the day, I could play simple tunes. Soon tourists began throwing coins at my feet; and suddenly, I was able to buy food instead of begging or stealing. A few days later, I spied a silver flute in the window of a music shop called *Douterrye Emayre* (Song of My Heart) and I vowed that someday that silver flute would be mine. From that day forward, every coin I spent on *grash*, I saved two to buy that flute."

"Dulcerary Cœur owned the *Douterrye Emayre*. One day he was standing near the open doorway chatting with his shopkeeper when I pressed my face against the front window to stare at the flute." The soul witness now pressed her own face against the window glass to show us exactly what she meant. "His shopkeeper said, "That street *scrub* comes her everyday and stares at that limited-edition Resart flute.""

Dulce glanced around the corner and asked, "Do you like music, wee one?" I opened my mouth to show him that I had no tongue. That's when he realized that someone had pruned my tongue to a stump. I never was shy concerning my lack of a tongue and I often displayed my gaping mouth to tourists and pilgrims. It was an advantage, which brought extra coins my way. I showed Dulce my few dirty banknotes and coins and pointed toward the flute. I meant to explain that I was saving to buy the flute. Dulce took the money from my hands, counted it, and said, "That flute is on sale today and you just happen to have the exact amount to cover its price." He invited me into the shop, as his shopkeeper watched in wide-eyed shock. Dulce plucked the Resart flute from the window, put it to his lips, and played a few bars of zippy music before presenting it to me with a grand flourish. I took the flute, put it to my lips, and played my favorite ditty. "You're an artiste," Dulce praised. "The flute is yours, little one. Go into your own heart with it and there you'll hear music like no other." He made out a bill of sale and wrote on it, "paid in full." Then he scribbled on the bottom of the receipt with his flamboyant Mescale script, "If anyone dares take this flute from this child or even accuses her of stealing it, I swear on my sweet mother's soul, I will find you and you will answer to me." I could not read; but Dulce told me what the bill of sale said and that I was free to show it to anyone."

For the first time, the soul witness felt confident enough to merge with its life. The window opened and we saw without the protective glass for the first time. Now we could see more clearly that Shibel was unattractive. Her misshapen head bore the evidence of passing through the narrow birth canal of her adolescent mother who died in childbirth. The frayed and dissipated rutilates of her Gathosian eyes were dull. The karma of her grandmother, mother, and the free-radical specter clung to her soul and cast a yellow-green pall over her countenance. The specter fed off her, adding to her hunger, and communicated its response of fear and rage that overshadowed the great psychic legacy of her ancestral mothers.

"Music became my goddess, the glue that held my life and soul together," said Shibel. "The flute's satin-lined box became my nighttime pillow and the flute my true lover, for it was not afraid to caress the stump of my tongue. I showed the bill of sale to old one-eyed Kejan, the vegetable vendor. He had attended school for a few phases under the Hectarians and knew how to read. He got a frame, with a real piece of glass, and put the bill of sale on display right in front of the red parishfruit. Coinage came my way as never before and old Kejan said I brought extra business his way when I played in front of his stand. No one ever tried to take the flute away from me. The street *scrubs* respected Dulcerary Cœur. The media called him, "The Divine Dulce," but we *scrubs* called him, "The Divine Rogue.' He never was a snob and the older street *scrubs* said that they remembered when Dulcerary Cœur was a street *scrub* himself. That meant he was tough and lived by his own rules and any threat he made, people took seriously."

"Did you ever see Dulce Cœur again," Stellium asked.

"I saw him around, but we never spoke and I don't think he remembered me. He became more reclusive as he aged and old Kejan said that Dulce Cœur needed his privacy to honor his Gathosian roots because his early life was so Human and public. Rumors circulated that he became a Hectarian Mystic, but I never believed that he would stoop that low."

"What happened to you?"

"I remained a street *scrub* until an old priestess named Kabelista heard me playing my flute outside her temple and offered me a place in her household as an entertainer. By then, I was paying my own way and even had a permanent place to sleep at night. I decided to accept her offer so I could see how rich folk live. Living in her family allowed me to learn social etiquette from her *privileges*. I was middle-aged when she died and I took her moniker, Kabelista, to honor her memory. By then, my musical talent had gained me audience to the sessions held by the supreme high priestess." Then Shibel, who now is Kabelista, informed us, "I will need to step back into the soul witness, for my life gets difficult again." Again she created a window. "I will try to leave the glass open this time, so you can see more clearly," she said.

"If it gets too difficult, we can close it," I said. Then the four of us looked though the open window and saw Kabelista and the supreme high priestess of New Delphi standing together in a cavern. Despite Kabelista's past as a street *scrub*, she now was dressed in jeweled finery.

The soul witness told us, "The high priestess has just cremated the body of her soul mate, Belshzar. She requested that I play the flute solo from Cœur's Panansha Symphony for the occasion. I was surprised that any Trinity Witch, let alone the supreme high priestess, would request anything composed by Dulcerary Cœur."

The supreme high priestess emerged into the scene. She was over two hundred phases old, but still a powerful figure, for she enjoyed the gifts of sixty-four *privileges* that kept her supplied with energy. Her aura was the same shade of peridotic green as the specter we saw in earlier visions, but as her mood changed, different colors fused to the green, before fading away. Despite her age, her hair was still black and arranged into frozen waves that dramatically swept up and back from her face. A perfumed paste spiked with *tartan ratu* rimmed her eyes and two green tattoo lines scrolled gracefully from the outside corners of her mouth and along her jowl to her chin. Her dress was an exquisite green floor-coat and underneath, she wore a translucent green slip that split up the center to her waist. Emeralds studded the zaqurlite ring through her bottom lip and every finger displayed a different ring. A large platinum medallion set with a cabochon opal and surrounded by baguettes of fire opal, hung between her breasts. This medallion was the sacred symbol of Trinity Witch authority handed down through thirty thousand phases of Trinity Witch history, to each supreme high priestess.

"I knelt before her authority," said Kabelista, "not yet realizing its defamation of the divine."

"Your rendition of Cœur's music was moving," said the supreme high priestess. "What's his secret? How do you think Cœur created his own interface with the Crystal? Oh, I know, you cannot speak. You don't realize how lucky you are that you can't speak. Our own voice drowns out the sound of the divine. I should know, I haven't heard anything worthwhile in years." She looked at Kabelista more carefully and after a moment said, "Believe it or not, I've had my eye on you for a long time. Let me show you my pleasure." The supreme high priestess pulled the bodice of her green slip to one side and showed Kabelista her left breast with its pierced nipple. She cupped her sagging breast in one hand. It was a symbol of honesty, like displaying the palms of the hands, only with more intimate connotations. "I've decided to take pity on you and give you an opportunity to become more than a temple musician. Your features are ugly, but I personally care nothing for beauty. All I care about is the quality and quantity of a person's energy and that's why I'm offering you a position as one of my *privileges*." Kabelista was stunned, insulted, and flattered all at the same time. "I'm serious. To prove I'm serious, I will allow you to serve me as a level twenty-seven *privilege*. That's where your energy interfaces with mine," and she patted her own ass to show Kabelista where she thought her energy belonged. If you allow me to climb your energy, to know and explore it completely, I promise to raise you up. Belshzar was my favorite soul intimate. Her ashes are still smoldering—too hot to fill an urn. Replacing her in my energy ladder, this early would be disrespectful to her memory; but in time, I will need another female to furnish Brother Bastion with visions. If it works out, I will consider you for her position. For now, I want you to write some music—something similar to what Cœur might write. Naturally, you will need to remain anonymous, but if you serve me, no telling how far you might go. There's even an excellent chance that you will outlive me. Play your cards right, Kabelista, and in time you might sit on the throne as high priestess." Kabelista leaned forward and took the ringed nipple, permeated with *tartan ratu*, in her mouth. Her fate was sealed.

The soul witness told us, "For several moons, I awoke from my nightmares that never went away and would experience my past as if it were my present. I thought of the irony of my life—an orphan girl with the public name Shibel sitting on the throne in the Witches' Temple as supreme high priestess. As a *privilege* to the high priestess, I could see the supreme high priestess was not as virtuous as she presented herself to the public, but saw no way out of my dilemma. I realized only in retrospect that I possessed more freedom when I was a street *scrub* than when I was a *privilege*."

Kabelista fell silent and Stellium said, "You must tell us the rest."

"It gets even harder," said the soul witness. "I think I will need the glass closed to finish my lament." Two pieces of glass swung shut and met in the middle of the window. This time, the soul witness turned her back to the window and looked into the void. "The high priestess could never penetrate the mystery of transcendent sound nor could she jump dimensions or see anything other than her selfish illusions. She blamed me—told me I was uncooperative and flaunted music in her face as a taunt. She was convinced that I held a secret I was unwilling to share."

"Did she know that you were Dulcerary Cœur granddaughter?" asked Élan.

"Of course she knew! I was the one who did not know my identity. One more thing I must say, before the void takes me back into sleep. The supreme high priestess thought she would have a better chance to understand this supposed secret if I bore her a child that she could raise as her own. The way she told me about her decision made the situation seem as if she was giving me something rather than using me. She always possessed the ability to twist reality around and convince me she was right. 'Bastion will do you the honor,' she informed me. 'Let's keep it simple. No need for you to show your ugly face at my next energy session. Let me know when you are fertile and Bastion will make a quiet visit to your bed.'"

"Did you bear a child?" asked Stellium.

"I don't remember. Everything is black for me and the void is straight ahead."

We knew Kabelista gave birth to a daughter because we were concurrently experiencing her daughter's vision on another track. Beltania was her daughter and she was the witch we saw in the earliest sequence, the one that stole the hair *keylic* from Mellé's room. Beltania launched her vision by emerging from the darkness and standing by the stoic soul witness that we knew as Shibel/Kabelista. "You may go to sleep now, Mother," she said tenderly. "I will tell them the rest of the tale."

Beltania showed us an androgynous face of youth that never changed throughout the vision. She was pert, eager, strong, and spoke with confidence. She noticed Stellium immediately and she came up to him and kissed him as an intimate lover. He was so startled that he neither responded nor resisted. "You don't know who I am—do you?" she asked.

"I have a psychic inkling," he admitted. "Tell me straightaway so I have no doubt."

"I am part of you and you are part of me," said Beltania.

Stellium sighed. "That's what I thought."

"Now, the three of you lean closer and listen carefully because I do not want you to miss one word of what I need to say. Have you seen the specter of rage yet?"

"We've glimpsed it," we acknowledged.

"It's growing bigger and will be my legacy when I am born into the persistent stream. I remind you that the specter's desperation gives it a blinding will to destroy each life that feeds it. In spite of the prospect of this karmic specter hanging over my next life, I will not succumb even if you refuse to help."

"We are committed to help wherever we can," I assured her.

"Good, now please allow me to tell you about myself and the way it will be if the persistent stream has its way. I will hold the distinction of being the youngest woman ever to become a high priestess. On my Anointing Day, I will be scarcely a woman past menarche. When I sit in the Witches' Temple, among my peers, I will sit among women many multiples of my age. My appointment will cause gossip and outright indignation that the supreme high priestess of New Delphi has made her daughter a high priestess."

"Despite my elevated status, I enjoy no *privileges* and therefore I have no visions. Mother will tell me, 'You're too young for *privileges*,' and everyone will agree with her because she is the highest authority on such matters. I will not meet Dulcerary Cœur until I am middle-aged, but I certainly will know who he is. When I am still a child, he will be an old man, a notorious legend here on New Delphi. He will have the audacity to maintain rooms near the northwest end of New Delphi Village and sometimes he will drink beer at the Hermit Inn. My Trinity sisters and Hectarian brothers will say he is crazy. Mother will hate him and call him 'maggot spawn' and 'Chaos trash' and 'a common street *scrub* that stole sacred music.'"

Beltania declared. "I've decided to live this next part for you, if you will live the next part as me." She beckoned us forward. "Come into me, through my eyes, then turn around and see reality as I do." In an instant, the three of us were living a fast-paced life as Beltania and the experience was immediate and vivid. We jumped scenes with no notice or excuses and no opportunity to reflect.

"I am an adolescent girl and my mother is in one of her dark moods. She tells me, 'Go to cottage 22 on Auric Lane and get me a *keylic*. Be quick about it and make sure you're not caught.' Then she turns sweet and allows me to kiss the ring in her nipple. I'm nervous because I'm sure Mellé sees me as I slip out though the window of her cottage, but I avoid Mother's eyes when I return. I lie and tell her, 'I got away clean.' She sends me away, saying, 'Go straight to your temple and pray for goodness and compassion to descend into all hearts. I will come for you in a few hours and we will eat the evening meal together.' I was curious to see what she was going to do with the hair *keylic;* so instead, I take an underground route under the Crystal and find my way back to her temple. There, I can peek through the cleft in the rock that sits to the right of the jade icon and see what she is doing."

"Her *privileges* arrive quickly, as if she has called an emergency meeting to discuss budgetary concerns. I know immediately that whatever is about to happen has something to do with sexual alchemy, for all sixty-four of her *privileges* quickly disrobe. Her soul mate, Bastion, yanks the blue and crimson curtain over the entryway, as soon as they all get inside. The men are fondling themselves to keep up their energy and I notice they all are blasé, as if they've performed this sacrament a million times and it no longer means anything to them. I see no ritual costumes, hear no prayers offered to the Crystal, no musicians or music, no incense or candles, no building eroticism offered up to the divine. Mother strips off her jeweled coat and slip and tosses them on the floor. Then she impales her bare wrinkled ass on the jade icon that she once told me was so charged with sacred Delphic energy that I should never touch it. Bastion has the hair *keylic* draped over the tip of his erect wand. He dusts the hair and his wand with *tartan ratu* and chants, "All free radicals, all shadows seeking electrons, gather unto my wand and become a specter of free radical cascade. I declare war."

In an instant, it seems as if all oxygen disappears from the space and I cannot breath. I gasp and notice a rotten stink filling the air. Bastion stuffs his wand into my mother's mouth and reaches orgasm. Then, each primed *privilege* comes forward to offer her their energy in exactly the same way. After a reverential bow, her thirty-two male *privileges* begin spewing their energy into her mouth, while her thirty-two women *privileges* hover around and keep the men's energy spiked with their tongues. This is all wrong. The energy is backward. Bastion is supposed to be the final *privilege* to offer his energy because his energy is the highest, but for some reason, they all are doing it backward and in her mouth. As soon as her twenty-seventh male *privilege* withdraws from her—he's a big man with a thick hair-trigger wand—she groans and begins to gag and vomit. Now I realize mother is not going up, but she is using their energy to go down into Chaos. She begins giving birth—giving birth to a demon through her mouth. Its appearance is hideous and repugnant. It looks like a large amorphous head when it emerges and it has row upon row of gnashing teeth. Its umbilical cord is hanging out between mother's lips and she is turning blue and choking on it. When it is fully born, it turns back on its own umbilical and bites it off with its own sharp teeth. The demon lifts and flutters like a huge bat around the cavern, presumably looking for a way to escape. It must realize that the blue and crimson curtains offer the easiest escape and the specter heads for that draped space. As it passes through the fabric, the curtains burst into flames. Mayhem follows as a few of her *privileges* rush to put out the fire and others search for something to hide the entrance and their shame. Nobody but Bastion seems to notice that Mother is choking to death. I'm so terrified that I use the confusion to make my escape. I run away and hide until the following day."

Beltania fell forward and she was so rigid with terror that we could not escape from her. We were on the verge of repeating the entire vision and being trapped inside its loop. "We believe you," I said. "We experienced what happened for ourselves," and with that she released us.

"Are you all right?" asked Stellium and he touched each of us to make sure we were.

"I'm all right," said Beltania, "but I still retain the feeling that I am suffocating."

"You are vey courageous," Élan assured her.

"I don't know about courageous, but I swear fear will never conquer me," and she sniffed back tears. She took a deep breath and said, "I could use a friendly hug," and each of us hugged her in turn. She glanced around and seemed to notice we were standing in a void. "Let's create an atmosphere a bit more friendly. Some pink walls and a table and chairs would be nice. And a cup of hot tea would hit the spot right now too." All those things appeared for us out of the power of the eighth dimension that was the wellspring of this entire experience.

We sat down at a round table with Beltania and she poured each one of us a cup of tea. After she sipped for a while, she told us, "Mother was dead, the specter killed her. Afterward, Bastion put on her robes and permanently took her place. I saw photos of him when he was young and he was a pretty man. Now that he was ancient, it was easier for him to pass as a female, for age robs both male and female bodies of their distinctive figures and sexual grace. Bastion lived another twenty phases. Nobody but his *privileges*, and I, knew that the supreme high priestess was a man. He actually was kinder than my stepmother and allowed me to have three *privileges*. I was nine Fecundity phases (thirty-six years) when he died and knew many secrets about New Delphi and the Trinity and Hectarian orders. Because I knew so much, I was a strong contender for the throne of supreme high priestess. On Bastion's deathbed, he assured me that I was his first choice. I thought, 'If I become supreme high priestess, I might possess the power to change things,' but decided the position meant nothing if I lacked authority. As soon as Bastion died, I told my three *privileges*, "It's now or never." They were loyal to me and cooperated. Bastion's keys were in my possession and I went to his quarters and helped myself to all his *tartan ratu*. That night, I jumped to the fourth dimension, while his *privileges* were cremating his dead body. When I jumped, I fell into my own gap. I don't know how I roused my courage to go back through that frightening door a second time, but I did. I would rest for a few hours and go straight back to the fourth dimension. On my third trip, my *Emayre* was waiting for me. It told me that it would help me cut through my illusion, pain, rage, cowardice, and so much more, but that it was going to take a great deal of effort and personal honesty. My *Emayre* showed me that the aggregate specter of rage that killed my mother also killed a Human man named Michael. Then my *Emayre* introduced me to a soul called Shibel who told me that she was my real mother. Between Shibel and my *Emayre*, I learned the truth. In the end, it was difficult to decide who was more corrupt—the supreme high priestess or her soul mate, Bastion. It was impossible to separate these two for they hatched and executed their plots together. They did many terrible things during their long lives. In my family alone, Bastion cut off the fingers and toes of my grandmother and then raped her when she was barely a woman. When Duebel began to hemorrhage during childbirth, Bastion told her it was proper punishment for her crimes and allowed her to bleed to death. He took the infant, cut out her tongue, and gave her away to be raised by a street vendor. Still, the web of negative karma was so powerful between them that Shibel spiraled back into his life as Kabelista. Now he impregnated his own daughter. When she gave birth to me, his penchant for mutilation, rape, and incest finally turned to pure murder and he killed her and took me to his soul mate, the supreme high priestess, to be suckled."

Beltania drained the last dregs of tea from her cup. "And all this because Dulcerary Cœur wrote the Panansha Symphony and proved that anyone could access higher dimensions without a high priestess. The supreme high priestess knew Dulcerary Cœur possessed an authentic doorway, but she thought he had a secret, a trick, or magical words. She never understood what Dulce was saying all along. No magic words are needed, there is only the direct experience of, 'I am your dancer of All Understanding. Chalice is the sweet eternal, for I am your song and your song is the direct path through my Heart.' Those words meant that all consciousness was the one movement within the willing receptacle of divine creation. The receptacle is forever harmonious with love. It is the song heard only through the heart—is there any tea left?" she asked.

Beltania had mesmerized Stellium. He shook his head slightly before picking up the teapot and jiggling it. "It seems to be full again," he said and he poured her another cup.

She sipped the tea and said, "It's still hot too. It's just enough to help me finish my lament. Are the visions of Belleth, Duebel, and my mother still running through your heads?"

"They finished with us a few minutes ago," said Élan. "Your vision is the longest."

"Good, that means I now enjoy your full attention. As I was about to say right before my teacup ran dry, I knew everything, but my knowing did not set me free, as the philosophers claim. As honesty descended into my heart, I could not pretend that I was a complete victim. True, my feminine genetic line suffered, but Bastion's blood coursed through my veins too. My *Emayre* told me that I needed to take as much responsibility, for the mess, as I could. If I took responsibility—then I might have the authority to change the outcome. My *Emayre* said I could not dwell on faultfinding or blaming my stepmother or Bastion for their choices or actions. It was difficult, for the atrocities they committed were heinous to say the least. Finally, my *Emayre* gave me a jewel. It said, 'Dulcerary Cœur is your great-grandfather.' That news came as a real surprise. The following morning I left New Delphi on the first windship without even saying goodbye to my three *privileges*. Aboard the windship, I felt free for the first time in my life and I vowed never to return to New Delphi. Dulcerary Cœur was living on the planet Euterpe and I went there expressly to find him. When we met, I told him I was his great-granddaughter and he invited me in for tea. It took me several more visits to confess my part in the tangled scheme that killed his soul mate, Michael. When I told him, he said, 'that was a long time ago. We've all made many mistakes, especially me.' Eventually, he took me into his spiritual confidence. He made me a believer in the direct path and that the only way to break the tyranny of the Hectarian and Trinity order was to open the experience of New Delphi to everyone. He showed me how to jump to many different dimensions and when I was proficient, I jumped to the eighth dimension and found the help I needed. Let me add that, with your help, I believe we can correct these perversions through your new reality. It takes only one soul, no matter what time they are living in, to say 'change begins with me.' You freed yourselves of your karma and now I ask you to help free my mothers and me from the persistent stream. I will not wait for your answer, for I know you need time to consider what I ask."

Beltania leaned across the table and kissed Stellium on the mouth before disappearing. After she was gone, her outline, the sentinel glow of love, lasted several minutes. Stellium told us that for days afterward, every time he closed his eyes, he saw it.

# NINETEEN

Élan's headache vanished and his vision slowly returned. He was weak and exhausted from his ordeal, so we suggested that he rest. Instead, he said, "Not yet, I'm remembering even more about what happened after the *manatee* touched my key. Please allow me to verbalize what I remember, so the details are straight in my mind." He rolled over on his back and stared straight up at the ceiling. "After the *manatee* touched my key, I returned to the sanctuary and found Dulce and Kyron there. Together, we experienced the easiest and most intimate telepathy, I've ever known. The door to my unconscious was wide open, because I understood more about my origins and connections than the third dimension usually allows. Kyron was now a female and she was beautiful, with blonde flowing hair and her eyes were the color of blue-green crystals. She said, "We are showing you our omega selves to remind you of your omega self. They asked me to gaze into a mirror and when I did, I again realized this face, the face of Élan Journey Cœur, was a mask."

"Do you recall the specific purpose for this rendezvous?" asked Stellium.

Élan nodded his head. "I'm getting to that part. Dulce and Kyron said they wanted to help me dissolve my naïve assumptions concerning the nature of karma. Through them, I recognized that karma was more than our legacy from the past. In fact, Kyron explained karma as a byproduct of energetic action. She said, 'Karma's disposition is centripetal and its psychic appearance is as moving sheen and shadow."

"That's quite a complex and exact memory," I said.

Élan let go an intriguing, "I'll say! Somehow, Kyron's words branded my memory, just as Dulce's words branded my memory when he spoke to me from the valley. Yes! In no uncertain terms, Kyron said, 'Karma is the byproduct of all energetic action; its psychic appearance is as moving sheen and shadow and its elemental disposition is centripetal.'"

"But what exactly does that mean?" asked Stellium.

"Kyron demonstrated that karmic energy has the impetus to transcend time and space. Frankly, this wasn't exactly news to me, but I was unaware of the full disposition of karma until her demonstration. Even as a neophyte, I was familiar with positive and negative karma because karmic emissions were apparent everywhere I looked. When I began jumping to the fourth dimension, the evidence was overwhelming and I knew our karma pollutes adjacent dimensions. For some reason—maybe because of a conditioned rut in my thinking—I still never considered that karma was capable of invading the past from the future. However, it now is clear to me that karma is not bound by time."

I tried to lead Élan along with, "And the demonstration was?"

He took a deep breath and sighed; "I'm sorry; I still don't remember that part."

Stellium sat up on one of his elbows. "You mean to tell us that karma can jump backward in time, just as a Shardasko Warrior can jump backward in time?"

"Jumping seems like the wrong word because the way I understood karma is—it has no self-motivation or independent spark. Rather I would say that karma once launched has the tendency to move with a centripetal force, which is unaware of time or space."

I tentatively suggested, "Well isn't that what the four visions from the eighth dimension just demonstrated to us?"

"Now I remember!" Élan exclaimed. "Kyron said that when the eighth dimensional vision unwound within me, it would demonstrate how karma from the future would come back to claim me." Now that Élan remembered, he was eager to get the rest out. "We had a conversation about missed opportunities and miscommunications in other lives, followed by offerings of forgiveness and new promises of love. We talked about the repercussions of Dulce being the first soul in our group to approach *latturtimelda* and the underlying causes for his setbacks in his life. Kyron explained that because she was the first soul within our group to reach this elevated state, we were inexperienced about how to use and properly direct Dulce. He chose a difficult mission, to incarnate into this time and attempt to break the tyranny of the Trinity and Hectarian orders. Dulce told us that despite his evolvement, his failure still haunted his soul and he felt responsible for impeding Kyron and me. That's why he offered to relive this life through this new reality and glean more insight for our soul group. Kyron told me that she had incarnated to help set the stage for this adjustment. She surrendered to the earliest or past impact waves of Dulce's negative karma in this dimension, which began with me."

Élan hesitated and the next time he spoke his voice was quiet and reverential. "During this time, my feelings for Kyron evolved into deeper feelings for his female face. We shared a compulsion to be together. The feeling was more than wanting to be together; we want to be part of each other." Élan's outpourings stopped abruptly and he seemed to disappear into reverie. For a few seconds he was again dancing with Kyron. "Perhaps it's more accurate to say that once Kyron and I were one and when I remembered that oneness, I was filled with a compulsion to achieve that state of oneness again."

"You were given a wonderful blessing," I assured him, but that foreboding suspicion lingered and I still was waiting for the other shoe to drop.

"There's one more bit that I recall and it's extremely important," said Élan. "At the end of our retreat, our *Holder* brought us special gifts. We created a sacred ceremony and near the end, our *Holder* asked me, 'Élan, do you understand what we want of you?' I told it, 'Yes, I understand.' It said, 'You have swallowed the karma of your present life and now your soul mates and I ask you to dance with time to the tune of *latturtimelda*. The past and future will become your Now and lies waiting for your freewill decision. What is your reply?' I told my *Holder* what I told the *manatee* and already promised my soul mates. 'I will face the free radical specter in Michael's stead. I will help the souls trapped inside to freedom and if I cannot do that, I will die for Michael, so he will not have to.'"

Utter silence followed. This was my foreboding; this is what I sensed from Élan's *Emayre* when we first met her in room 21 at the Star Inn; this was the unprecedented opportunity/responsibility; the greater risk indescribable in words; that portentous and engulfing something too enormous for one soul to sustain. I had fooled myself. I allowed myself to believe that Élan's escape from Sutcay Tay meant that he was at liberty to live his present life in peace. Instead, his proximity to his future selves, Mellé and Michael, still trapped him, and he faced a greater risk than losing his life.

In my repository of understanding, I know of no challenge more desperate for a soul than an encounter with a free-radical specter of rage. When a specter interfaces with a soul, the specter interfaces only with the soul's incompletion and the specter feeds off this incompletion to fuel its erratic behavior. Eventually, the soul's incompletion imprisons it in a dark viscous sheath of its own creation. Trapped within this customized prison, the soul lingers in lonely self-torture as the specter sucks the soul down into Chaos. No soul can escape Chaos through its own volition. A soul's *Emayre* must petition its soul group for an escort that will accompany the *Emayre* into Chaos to attempt a rescue. When and if a *Emayre* succeeds in penetrating this imprisoning sheath of incompletion, the damage to a soul can be horrific. Souls retrieved from Chaos sometimes need "to sleep" for eons to recover. In truth, many of the most heroic souls in Creation are now "sleeping" in an effort to recover from their one fall into Chaos.

Élan so shocked me with this declaration that I exploded with, "Are you out of your mind? A few days ago, you were afraid of a few free radicals in the fourth dimension without Viobella's protection. Now you believe you are capable of engaging an aggregate specter of rage."

"A few days ago I was blind and did not remember what I remember now," he assured me. Stellium said nothing, but he already was sitting on the edge of the bed with his back turned toward us.

"What if you die? Dulce again will be born without ever knowing his father. How is he to succeed without your nurturing presence? Élan, you're a *latturtimelda* neophyte. Allow the advanced consciousness involved in this adjustment to deal with this specter manifested by Bell and Bastion. You certainly do not need to commit to such a dangerous undertaking. Maybe Stellium's *Emayre* was right about you. Maybe you do need to be a hero."

"I am a Shardasko Warrior," Élan said. "I possess the creative weaponry Michael and Mellé never had, to deal with this monster. I can make it dance to my tune."

"My sweet love, a monster does not dance, a monster devours."

"This crisis began with me and that's why it must end with me. This is the critical time. You know it's true! If I'm wrong, why has everything come to a boil at this particular time? If we ignore this challenge, we will only end up back here is this same place, faced with the same challenge. Besides, what good does it do for me to sit back and wallow in the comfort of this one personal life, when all my future selves suffer for my selfishness and lack of love? Isn't that the real insight into karma? We are not one merely with souls alive now; we are energetically one throughout time with all souls. That's why karma has no bounds."

"Must I remind you that the supreme high priestess that spawned this cursed specter was killed by it? True, she was corrupt, but certainly, she was no amateur magician. I must tell you, Élan, this new mission goes way beyond what I bargained for in my pre-incarnate agreement with Kyron. In fact, I think this new proposition jeopardizes my mission."

"This new mission simply carries your original plan one-step further and secures the future for Dulce and Mellé."

I got out of bed. "You've finally done it, Élan. You've stumped me. I don't know how to help you accomplish such a huge undertaking. I have no experience dealing with free-radical specters of rage."

"Well maybe this is your opportunity to learn what you need to know about the dark side."

Stellium got out of bed too. He collected his clothing and his valise and silently crept off to the bathroom without uttering one word. When he returned, less than a minute later, he was dressed and slipping on his raincoat. "I'm going out," he announced and he almost ran for the door.

Élan leapt up to intercept the fleeing Stellium and tripped over the loose sheet hanging over the edge of the bed. He fell on his knees and, in my opinion, that's exactly where he should have stayed, but he got up and yanked at the twisted sheet that was thin with age. The sheet ripped as he tore it free and he whipped what was left around his waist, to cover his nudity. "Please, Stellium, don't shut down on me. I need your support more than ever."

Stellium froze with his hand poised on the door lever and then gently rapped his forehead against the door jam. His shoulders began trembling as if someone was shaking him and the thought *I nearly made it*, sailed through his mind.

"Please," Élan begged. "Come back to bed and I will hold you and no fear would dare come between us." Élan touched Stellium's shoulder and he twitched as if he received an electrical shock. Then he spun around and for about three seconds, his expression turned uncharacteristically detached. In a bizarre and nonchalant manner, he relaxed and sidestepped away from the door. Sweeping his hands around his body, he created a locked energy-grid with his body inside. He put so much emphasis into the gesture that I felt the shockwave of rejection across the room. Never had I seen a Shardasko Warrior use his training in such a way until now, but I certainly would see it in the future. Stellium would teach this move and other Shardasko gestures to his students. Eventually this branch of Shardasko training would be known as Shardasko Defense.

"Back off!" Stellium said. "If you try to influence me with your energy that way again, I swear I will kick you in the root of your precious manhood. That ought to cure your oversized heroics, at least in this lifetime."

Élan was shocked. "I can't believe—"

Stellium chopped him short with—"can't believe what?" Tears trickled down his cheeks. "In the short time we've been together, do you realize how many times you've abandoned me?"

Élan stood there holding the torn sheet with one hand, while his other hand still reached out toward Stellium. "Never because I wanted to." Élan moved half in front of the door in a desperate attempt to prevent Stellium from leaving. "Please, let's sit down and we'll talk about this rationally."

Stellium started crying harder. "Get out of my way. Can't you see this is humiliating for me? I refuse to stand here in a puddle of my own tears and pour out my love, so you can ignore me."

"Ignore you? I listen with rapt attention to everything you say."

"No you don't!"

"I tell you I do. How can you think otherwise? My heart and soul are open books to you."

"If that's true, then why do I feel bewildered—yes bewildered, about what is going on in your private mind. In your tryst with your soul mates, did you consider your life with sprite and me? Did you even remember we exist? Do you think we love you any less than your soul mates? Humans have an expression you may not be aware of, my Earthly expatriate; the expression goes, 'A bird in the hand is worth two in the bush.' It means, don't sacrifice a sure thing for a doubtful outcome. Right now, I feel like your prosaic little bird—tossed aside for something out there in the bushes. With my last breath of love for you, I ask—why are you willing to sacrifice your life with sprite and me for a shot at becoming the most evolved soul in your group? Never mind! Don't answer that. I don't want you to lie and mar your new unstained soul." Élan's mouth dropped open in amazement and Stellium rolled over Élan like a bulldozer. "I see the truth much too clearly now. I'm still falling into my old patterns of behavior."

"No, Stellium, you're not."

"Yes! I'm what Earth Humans call a 'sucker.' I'm your adoring shadow and your zeal to evolve is squeezing me out. Since we met, the theme has been you and Kyron, you and sprite, you and Dulce, and now you and your split soul in the future. Sorry, but right now I feel split too; in fact, I feel ripped right in two. Half of me is screaming, 'If Élan doesn't realize he is more precious to you than life itself, then he doesn't deserve your love. The other half is screaming, 'Don't let Élan die alone.' You see both parts of me love you unconditionally, I just don't know what to do about it."

Élan put his hand to his forehead and I asked, "Are you getting another headache?"

"No," he said and he went and sat on the edge of the bed by himself. He glanced toward me and confusion wrinkled his brow. At that moment, I didn't feel like helping him, and in truth, I was his next problem waiting to happen. Élan gazed down at the floor before telling Stellium, "You're right; my first commitment is to you and Follie and this life. I've made a horrible mistake in agreeing to face this specter without consulting you first. Never should I take your support for granted. Please, will you both forgive me?"

Stellium laughed in mock hilarity before going right back to deadpan sobriety and his hand again was on the door lever. "You are a real ball-buster, Journey Cœur. No wonder you sired the ultimate ball-buster, Dulcerary Cœur. Our commitment is a plaster icon without our love to give it meaning. I'm not angry because you forgot our commitment; I'm furious because you forgot my love. You're more an Earthling than you seem to realize; your English simply is not as good as mine. On Earth we say, 'fuck it and fuck you.' Do you know what fuck it and fuck you mean, my Shardasko brother? Fuck it means, 'I've used it and now I'm done with it;'

and fuck you means, 'I've used you and now I'm done with you.' Go ahead, Élan; say it like a real Earthling, because your meaning already is crystal clear to me."

Now Élan was raising his voice too. "I'm sorry, what more can I say? If you don't want me to get involved, then I promise, I will allow the future to find its own way. I will break my vow to my soul mates and *Holder* and I will postpone my involvement with *latturtimelda* because you and Follie are far more important to me than any *latturtimelda*."

"Gee! Thanks for putting the responsibility for your evolution in my hands," shouted Stellium. "Here's another Earth expression to cover our dilemma: You've put me between a rock and a hard place. I'm sure your English is good enough to figure that one out for yourself."

"Well you've put me between a rock and a hard place too," roared Élan. "I said I wouldn't do it. What else do you want me to say?"

Stellium opened the door. "You've said plenty and as usual, I've said too much. I'm going out for a walk before I turn into a sea of tears and drown myself," and he walked out the door.

*New Delphi is difficult,* said my *Emayre*.

I was up and collecting my wet clothing off the floor too. "I'm not deserting you," I explained to Élan, "but right now I need some space too." I pulled a few pieces of clothing from my valise and dressed.

"It's cold and raining outside," Élan said. "Please, wear my coat." I slipped on his raincoat and we hugged each other for a moment. "I love you completely," he promised. "Don't ever forget that."

"I love you completely too," I assured him. "That's why this is so difficult for me." Outside, I stood in the pouring rain. My feelings were as real to me as Élan's confusion and Stellium's anger were to them. Despite the intensity of my feelings, experience advised me that the sort of feelings I now believed were real, were momentary sensations that I should not act upon or project onto others. For that reason only, I walked away.

Taking a deep breath of fresh air, I started walking toward New Delphi Village. The gray sky, from earlier in the evening, had turned to mauve, while the particle steams had morphed into green flecks of light. The particles, spiraling upward from the center of the Crystal, hovered for a moment before heading for space. Were they blessing New Delphi before striking out to explore the universe they themselves were creating? Creation was fresh here on New Delphi, especially at night when it was raining. The direct symbiosis of creator/creation was so efficient that it highlighted my dysfunction. Where could I find peace if, even here, on the edge of cosmic re-creation, I felt such unremitting agitation?

I was tired. A wave lifted inside me and urged me to find a cozy fire and sit, to take all the time I wanted to figure out what to do next. No sooner did the first wave ebb, than a second wave demanded that I decide immediately about whether I was going to join Élan, in this new daunting task. This wave wanted emphatic and clear-cut goals. The waves were harbingers, informing me of my obvious incompletion. These waves would attract free radicals, just as ocean waves collect bits of shell and sand. Once my waves caught free radicals, they would seek expression through me, through Stellium, and even through Élan. We would hear, feel, and sense each other's incompletion and distortions as our own.

Was I having a breakdown? My *Emayre* said, the distress you are experiencing means this is an opportunity to learn something important that you need to know. This is the challenge of the enlightened witch. She does not panic under attack, but uses the attack to increase experiential knowledge.

Thanks to Stellium's involvement with Envy, truth was emerging from my dark confusion. I knew each free radical has a voice capable of hiding its true nature. Now I saw Doubt in greater light. Doubt was not an authentic free radical. Doubt only was a voice, or effect of reticence, just as anger was one voice of impatience. Viobella had reminded Élan that impatience/reticence was a continuum. If a free radical sucked a soul down into its continuum, the soul would vacillate between any two arbitrary points, and that meant impatience/reticence, fear/courage, or doubt/surety.

****

No casual tourists wander this far up into the New Delphi foothills, especially on dark, rainy nights. Tonight, the solitude hovered with an eerie presence that made me suspicious and tense. As I trudged along the slippery cobblestone path, confusion engulfed me in thought. I was on New Delphi Island in an agitated state, so why was I surprised that my old tormentor—whatever its name—was capable of sending out an envoy to intercept me?

A chill ran up my spine when a shadow fell in behind me and picked up its pace. After a moment, it reminded me of the daytime peddlers hawking their wares along Jade Boulevard. "Look! Have a look!" they'd call. "Would *jaine* (miss or young woman) be interested in some fresh-cut orchids for an offering at the Witches' Temple?" Along with the flowers, hawkers sold incense spiked with inferior *tartan ratu*, sequined llexal talismans, and bright-paper fecundity bulls for the children. They even sold bits of broken crystals to those who believed the New Delphi Crystal was made of glass. "Have a look at these sparkling crystals, *jaine*; guaranteed, directly from Source." At night, the Crystal's lights coaxed out the enslaved souls, those who hawked their intangible wares. Many were *tartan ratu* addicts, rejected *privileges* that lacked the price of a windship fare to go home, and those, like Élan, who refused to leave until they got an answer to why they were there in the first place. The shadows, not as bold as enslaved souls, plied their trade above the hubbub of the lights, where I now roamed. *What say you this rainy evening?* asked the envoy that shadowed my every move.

I picked up my pace again, but my *Emayre* said, *let's stop and see what this vender offers for sale.*

*Please, wait jaine, there is an authentic question within me that might interest you,* suggested my opportunistic hawker.

"My pockets already brim with questions," I replied. "I have no answers even for myself, let alone a marauding ghost."

A rustle, like tittering wind, tickled my face and the rain paused for a few seconds. The sky's dark shifting clouds parted, revealing a fragment of the moon Trophy. On a clear night, Trophy appears as a pale orange disk in the Delphi sky. Tonight the clouds draped the moon and, for an instant, I caught a glimpse of a silhouette behind the clouds. It was a puzzle piece, shaped like a bearded old man. He was holding forth a lantern that glowed with friendly light-beams. Then the clouds churned and squeezed shut over the meaning and, again, I was standing in the dark. I wanted to shout—wait! Don't turn your light away. Don't leave me alone with this envoy in the dark.

I walked even faster and the shadow behind responded. *Don't be so quick to pass up a bargain,* jaine. Now glancing at the amorphous form almost running alongside me, I could see that it was a mimic. It was dressed in a raincoat with a hood pulled up over its head, just like me. *Special price, only for you because you are my first customer this evening.*

*Let's stop,* my *Emayre* again said.

I slowed my pace and naturally, the shadow did too. "Let me see your face," I said.

The shadow pulled its hood to one side and showed me part of its face. I stopped dead in my tracks, for what I saw was not ugly. The half-face was of an adolescent Gathosian youth with large haunting eyes. *You are shocked by my mild appearance?* it asked.

To which I replied, "May I see the rest of your face?"

*If you cannot see that I possess an original face from this small peek, then you certainly are not prepared to see the complete me.*

Now at a loss for words, I foolishly said, "I see."

*Do you?* asked the half-hidden face behind the hood. *Can you truly see that if I uncovered my entire face, this dark night would seem as day? Can you see that I am no different from you and your soul group of radiant light? Why do you spurn me? It seems that for all your pomp and surety about serving the light, you do not serve the light as well as I. Never have I fooled myself, as you now do, with the presumption of private thoughts. My inexperienced creators were naïve and forgot to build that one-way protective mirror around me, which prevents me from seeing out. So I ask you, as I ask all who stop to examine my humble wares. Am I the mistake or are you the mistake? And whom do you really serve? Which of us serves the light? I know I serve light because I offer safe harbor to all the questions and unfulfilled shadows that make the journey, but cannot glimpse their omega face. I shelter more shadows and questions than even you can imagine, so do not feel sorry for yourself on this dark New Delphi evening. Feel pity for me. These shadows pull me to them and I have no choice but to respond, whether I can assist or not.*

"I need to know—"

*Yes?* it asked expectantly.

"What's the cost of all this?"

*I'm still having a difficult time in deciding, but I am ready to deal—how about you?* The envoy reached inside its raincoat and brought out a shiny black ball that just fit in the palm of its hand. *This is a shadow prism,* and the envoy took the ball and bounced it on the ground to show me the ball was resilient and possessed a bit of life.

"It looks like a child's toy."

*Its appearance allows it to seem less intimidating.*

"What would I do with such an object?"

*If you took this shadow prism from me, the unfulfilled shadows inside could resonate with the free radicals now interfacing with your incompletion.*

"You want me to harbor more questions and unfulfilled shadows than I already own?"

*Together, they might realize they were not alone.* Then the envoy used the sacred word "understanding." *I understand there is comfort in this realization.*

"Are you the free radical that has pursued me all these lifetimes?"

*I am not pursuing you. You call me to you when you want to discard something uncomfortable about your life. Don't you want to discard your present confusion as quickly as possible?*

"If I purchased this shadow prism, would you finally leave me alone?"

*I could only promise that we would be finished with each other unless you left your questions unanswered or if you answered too quickly before all unfulfilled shadows had their proper say. If you honor the rules of proper decision-making, no place would be left within you, for me to interface.* Another trickling stream of truth got through my obvious blocks and every part of my collective consciousness took a leap forward. This mysterious envoy was suggesting that despite my incompletion, I could be whole if I allowed each shadow inside me, complete access to a voice. Since my emergence into *latturtimelda,* my fondest hope always was that through my efforts and the efforts of others, the third dimension would be able to play as an equal partner with other dimensions. Now I realized this could not happen unless souls in this dimension took responsibility for the karma that we create in this dimension. Every *Emayre* went to great lengths to bring love and understanding to its life. However, it was an abuse of divine love to ask a *Emayre* to remove our free radicals when they highlighted our incompletion. I realized then that Élan and I were wrong to drag Stellium to the blue galaxy and tell him it was okay to ask for relief. This was using our powers inappropriately. Élan and I forced healing on Stellium without allowing him to openly interface with his Envy and understand why his incompletion attracted Envy in the first place. Perhaps that's why Stellium's insights seemed superficial when he returned, because he discarded the free radical before realizing what it truly meant. Stellium's *Emayre* was right when it questioned our intension. Élan and I did act at our own convenience.

*I hear other customers calling out to me*, warned the envoy. *I must go because I have not earned the price of satisfaction for my unfulfilled shadows.*

My *Emayre* was quiet and I knew it was up to me. "Don't rush me. It's a big decision. If I make a mistake, I take my soul mates down with me."

*This is true. One of the largest communities within me is the unfulfilled shadows whose souls could not decide this question.*

"I certainly would not want to add to your community."

*Then your answer must be yes.*

"How do you propose we complete this deal?"

*I will go within myself for a moment and call the shadows forth that might find resolution through you. I will reflect them into this small black prism and when you decide to face them, bounce the ball against any hard surface and each shadow will animate and speak. However, be forewarned. When shadows appear, they always brag or complain. That they do quite well. You will find, just as I have, that unfulfilled shadows enjoy telling and retelling their stories endlessly.*

The envoy disappeared for a moment and I took the opportunity to draw a girdle of light around my aura for protection. When the envoy reappeared, the black prism ball sat waiting in his palm. *What do I owe you?* the shadow asked.

Startled, I replied, "I thought I was doing the buying."

*On the contrary, I owe you*, and the envoy pressed two copper coins into my hand, along with the shiny black ball.

****

Unaware of how far I walked, I now realized that the Hermit Inn, one of Dulce's favorite hangouts, was a short distance down the path. Thrusting my hand inside my left coat pocket—the opposite pocket from where I stashed the black ball and coins—I pulled out a few crumpled Gathosian banknotes that Élan had stuffed in there, earlier that evening. I hoped I had enough money to buy a "short plate" of *grash* and a carafe of hot tea. I went inside and spied Stellium sitting at the bar with a bottle of beer and a clean beer glass in front of him. I went over and sat down beside him. "I wasn't consciously following you," I explained.

He spoke to me in English saying, "I'm broke; how about buying me another beer."

Taking the banknotes from my pocket, I laid the money between us. "I left rather abruptly, so this is all I have."

He picked up the wrinkled money, smoothed it flat, and counted it with an exact efficiency that was the antithesis of his usual self. "It's the change from our landing tax. I remember the expression on Élan's face when he put these banknotes in his pocket. He glanced out toward the Crystal, which he really could not see, and said, 'I'm getting a real killer headache. Let's get going before I drop.' He really did drop—didn't he? And he's about to take us with him."

"Will you order me a carafe of razzleroot tea when you order your next beer?" was my only reply.

"*Sirlegram* (server or waiter)?" Stellium called and I swung around and sat with my elbows on the bar so I could take in the subdued ambience of the Hermit Inn. The Inn is what Humans might call a pub—walls and floor were raw planks of hardwood, with an open-beamed ceiling draped with fishnet and a few crystal lures. Tables were small and well spaced, perfect for private conversations, with comfortable upholstered chairs. The place smelled of age; a patina built, layer by layer, upon the comings and goings of souls and their unfulfilled shadows. How many times had Dulce been in this place? Was the Hermit Inn still anticipating him or was he a memory that left his fingerprints behind for me to find?

Tonight, the Hermit Inn hosted only about a dozen subdued customers. The interior artistry of the place was a slowly developing process and these few wayfarers were adding their brushstrokes to the scene, one hair at a time. Patrons were New Delphi natives—inconspicuous stylites—Gathosian men and women who stared facedown into their warm beers and imagined the origins of the Delphi light. Two elderly men in a corner chatted intimately and toasted each other with thimbles of *lume* wine.

Stellium swung around too and in the process put his arm around me. His arm felt warm and I snuggled into the comforting nook of his embrace. "I'm sorry that Élan and I dragged you to the blue galaxy," I said. "It wasn't our place to force healing on you. I should have known better."

Stellium leaned even closer and kissed me delicately on the edge of my ear. "I love you," he assured me. "You and Élan gave me an opportunity and I took what I needed just like a good Shardasko Warrior." At the moment, Stellium needed to touch someone, so I allowed him to toy with the collar of Élan's coat, bushing his fingertips against each collar point, to make them lay flat. He closed his eyes and sighed, "I'd like to wallow in the illusion that everything is going to be okay, at least for one more beer." He gestured with a backward flick of his fingertips. "The Hermit Inn reminds me of the Sutcay Tay campus and maybe Shardasko training in general. Both are insular, understated, and even provincially innocent."

The atmosphere of the Hermit Inn was purposeful darkness, alleviated only by the light of the drippy, ochre-colored candles on the tables.

Windows were small and high up, with the kind of cut-glass panes that impedes the viewing in and viewing out. The bar, installed against the rear wall, was an exquisite altar, a creation of handcrafted art, dedicated to the god of intoxication. Its carved facings were made of ubertian cedar, exactly like the altars in the finest New Delphi temples, and the bar-top was one solid slab of green jade, running the full length. On a sidewall was the cozy fireplace I longed for a short time before. Sitting opposite was the pièce de résistance—maybe the real reason Dulce came here in the persistent stream—an actual baby grand piano.

Stellium exhaled with an ironic huff before telling me, "Several of my voices are advising me to run away and save my hard-earned dignity. I have memories of the persistent stream too. Élan and I were light-years apart in that reality. Now I'm sitting here in the Hermit Inn and asking myself—who were the demons of light that made us the same sex, different species, and separated us by worlds?"

"Whatever happens, our new reality has proven its strength. In spite of all our handicaps, Élan knows and loves us both."

"But we've made not one journey, but two to secure his love. Was it worth it, sprite? Was it truly worth it, when he can so easily forget we even exist?"

"Please don't give up, Stellium. I can't do this without you."

"I'm shaky, but I am still here," and he drained his bottle of beer. "Do you think he will forgive me for my cruel words?"

"He loves you enough to postpone his evolution, even enough to doom part of his next incarnation to death, so I don't think a few harsh words will matter."

"That's what I like about you," said Stellium. "You really know how to cut through all my bullshit."

He was about to say something else, but the server brought my carafe of tea and I asked her, "I noticed your piano. Do you have entertainment here?"

"Not until later in the evening," she said. "Do you play?"

"Yes, I do."

"Help yourself," she offered. "If you're good, I'm looking for a person to play on alternate evenings. If you're lousy, please keep it down because our usual crowd hates noise."

"You play the piano as well as the flute?" asked Stellium.

"Not only will The Divine Dulce be my son, but my uncle was the composer Racquin Lanai."

Stellium leaned closer and whispered in my ear. "Play something Dulce wrote. I definitely want to hear a song from the future, something to inspire my hope."

I rubbed my hands together because they still were cold. A couple of minutes later, when I sat down at the piano bench, I felt goosebumps sprinkle down my legs. It really was not a chill. The goosebumps were part of the realizations of time jumping that causes the shiver that accompanies déjà vu. My consciousness loomed and overshadowed my body, asking, *has my body sat here before or will I sit here in the future*? The answer always was the same for a time jumper; my body of this moment would sit in this moment forever. My consciousness left my body of the last moment and joined the continuing me that ran a few muted arpeggios up and down the piano keys. The piano possessed a wonderful delicate action for a percussion instrument and surprisingly, it was in tune. I tried out the first few bars of the allegro of Dulce's "Blue Crystal Sonata," but felt semi-detached from the movement right away. The piece was too lengthy, especially for a hideaway like the Hermit Inn. Anyway, my mood demanded the adagio, the rondo, and definitely, the coda that ended in that last faint note of hope that Stellium and I desperately needed. I abbreviated the allegro, then slowed it, and blended it into the adagio and felt more comfortable there. A part of me remained detached and asked, *who is really playing this piano*? Was it Dulce? Had his soul drawn near his embryonic body because my fingers were dancing where his fingers someday would be?

I had played the "Blue Crystal Sonata" many times before, always quietly inside my head. I was afraid to play it openly at the *Emayre* School—afraid someone would hear the mere hint of transcendent sound within it and question my authority. Now I was on New Delphi, so close to transcendent sound, one needed to hide in places like the Hermit Inn not to hear. The adagio of the "Blue Crystal Sonata" starts out deceptively simple. It is leisurely and innocent and flows like a waltz. Then broad triplets insert themselves, repeat, and yet there is no hint of glib expression about the repeats. Each repeat is more poignant unless—as Stellium suggested about Denny Pratt's art—the artist's technique gets in the way. Emotion poured forth—my emotion—my interface between transcendence and music and I heard shades of meaning in the adagio I never heard, when I played the 'Blue Crystal" inside my head. I moved right into the rondo. The rondo from this sonata was one of Dulce's greatest masterpieces, an impeccable and highly disciplined piece of musical composition. His sublime, "Panansha Symphony" overshadowed everything else he ever wrote and the rondo of the "Blue Crystal" never got its due; but to any serious musician, this particular rondo was special. It proved that it was possible to apply pure logic to the art of writing music and still produce a lyrical masterpiece. No one heard the logic behind the music. All any listener heard was the music's beauty and captivating ability to lift one into a transcendent state. Finishing the coda, there was absolute silence in the room. The two elderly men toasted me with their thimbles of *lume*. The one with the mustache asked, "Would you please play another piece?"

Deciding the patrons should hear something upbeat, I announced, "Here's a *radee* written by my mother. A *radee* is a nonsensical song, not intended to make sense, but rather a device to transcend reason and suggest truth is beyond the ability of language to explain. Any *radee* was a thousand times more puzzling than the "Blue Crystal Sonata," which implied reality had a logic that a composer might capture in a song. I played my mother's *radee* through and then sang the chorus for the small crowd.

"Again-and-again, we-dance-through-time-and-space. We-feign-true-knowing-but-our-shadows-know-the-score. Where-are-we-going-and-what-are-we-rushing-toward? Undeniably, we-are-one-endless-encore. Then the door of the Hermit Inn swung open and in walked Élan.

I thought, *he has more tenacity than anyone I've ever known.* Despite his exhaustion and impaired vision, he walked the dark and twisting path to the inn by himself. He glanced my way and waved. Now I realized his vision was improved and that meant he remembered even more. He spotted Stellium and a moment later was sitting down beside him. Stellium said something to Élan and Élan said something in return, probably that he did not consciously follow us. Just the same, we seemed to be hot on each other's trail. Then, they reached out toward each other. For a moment they held hands. There was no grasping, merely a hesitation before letting go. Then Élan was ordering a beer.

I finished off my mother's *radee* with an improvisational bridge and then repeated the chorus one last time. As financially poor as I was in this life, it gave me comfort when the server offered me a job playing the piano on alternate evenings. "Thank you," I told her, "but I'm traveling through."

I sat down next to Élan and he said, "You're full of surprises."

"No more than you," I assured him and I kissed him on the cheek.

Stellium acted too happy and it was an obvious ruse to hide his misery. "What else do you play—an ocarina?" he joked. "How about an accordion or zither?"

I reminded him as he once reminded me, "An artist uses the tools at hand. When I was a child, I used to play a comb."

"You missed the best part," he told Élan. "She played a composition written by Dulce. It was one of the most beautiful pieces of music I've ever heard."

I wiggled my fingers in front of my face. "I couldn't play all the notes. He wrote it for five-fingered hands."

Stellium said, "When I was near the Blue Galaxy, I heard music emanating from it similar to what you just played, so it was easy for me to hear the missing parts. Your music got inside me and unlocked my love." He shrugged and glanced sideways at Élan. "I hope you don't mind, but the sound of the music allowed me to forgive myself for acting like a total fool and getting angry with you."

Élan laid himself down like a bridge. "You have every right to be angry."

Stellium ran right over and into Élan's arms. "No, never do I have the right to be angry, especially with someone I love as much as I love you."

Only the crisis was over. We were wet, hungry, and exhausted, so we fell into the spirit of the Hermit Inn and pretended we were okay. Perhaps we needed to do this to reestablish our reciprocal calm. Élan remembered to bring money, so we got a table and ordered food.

The three of us were approaching a new journey into progressive darkness—deeper and deeper into the unknown depths of something so terrible, we needed to pretend for just one evening that the danger was not there. We walked back to our cottage arm in arm; and we were tight with camaraderie and clever clips of meaningless humor, to mask our deeper anxiety. Élan spared us any more revelations concerning his three-day retreat with his soul mates and I didn't mention that a shadowy envoy paid me two copper coins to take responsibility for a black ball filled with free radicals. Stellium acted as if he and Élan had restored complete amity between them. We avoided even the obvious irony of our new situation. What we regarded as a difficult challenge—Élan blindness—had vanished just like the superficial voice of a common free radical. What was crouching beneath the obvious was always the specter of rage. Some people pretend for an entire lifetime and hide in places like the Hermit Inn, while we continued pretending just long enough to get back to our cottage and into bed. But it was a fragile pretending, especially for three souls born from the womb of Mother Truth.

# TWENTY

The following morning I awoke early, but pretended to sleep for another hour to avoid what promised to be a difficult day. Somewhere beyond our cottage, I heard the elusive sound of a flute and the music was melancholy. Feeling the bed on either side of me, I realized Stellium and Élan already were up. I got up too and ambled over to the window to see how the Crystal colored the new day. The New Delphi sky was lemon yellow and the aurora lights a crimson red. I cranked open the window and took a deep breath of fresh air. I listened for the flute music, but it had stopped. *Perhaps it was the sound of the Crystal singing against the wind*, I thought.

Then I saw Élan walking toward our cottage with a bag swinging from his hand. He had gone out to buy us breakfast. As I watched him approach, my love for him produced a collage of fleeting images. From the first moment I saw him poised on that overstuffed chair at the school, I had loved him. I even loved him the first moment I saw him in the persistent reality. This morning, Élan saw me leaning out the window and called, "You're still the most beautiful woman I've ever seen," and I felt the shiver of déjà vu. In the persistent stream, his fabulous good looks and his Humanity, in general, startled me. I had dropped the parishfruit in my hands and asked, "Still?" Blushing over his own boldness, he apologized and said, "We've met before—haven't we?" Another man might have used those words as a pickup line and I would have walked away. But as I stood there, startled by his beautiful blue-green eyes, it was obvious that his sincerity ran all the way to his soul.

Élan walked into the cottage without making a sound and the only noise was the crinkle of the paper when he removed the warm, fragrant bread from its wrapper. The bright yellow sky and morning air had lifted his spirits. "I'm so thankful my vision has returned," he said softly. "It's a beautiful clear morning," he said a bit louder. "After breakfast, Stellium and I would like to hike up toward the Crystal and find a place to meditate—what do you think?"

"I'd like to do that," I agreed.

*Was it the elusive flute player I heard that morning that made me decide to take my flute along?* After breakfast, we walked into New Delphi Village and bought three bottles of water, sandwiches, and pears for lunch. We fell into a meditative silence as we hiked past the San Delphi Monastery with its series of portico-sheltered buildings. The yellow sky had bleached to a buttery-golden hue and the aurora lights had turned a radiant blue. By then, we were at a higher elevation and the wavering of the particle streams easily touched the ground. The air crackled with excitement and sang with a faint "yowee-yowee" hum. Beyond the San Delphi Monastery, the path narrowed with frequent switchbacks and Élan, who was leading, consistently took only the paths that led upward, toward the Crystal.

By late morning, we reached the fence where the particle streams vibrate with a gnashing ferocity against the metal wires. Hectarians built this fence as soon as they established control on New Delphi. It no longer was necessary for guards to patrol the area, because everyone believed the Hectarian falsehood that beyond the fence, the Crystal was lethal. The fence was an ugly chain-link construction with spirals of concertina wire running along the top. Élan broke our mutual silence by saying, "I want to get beyond this point; are you game?"

Stellium suggested, "Maybe we could crawl under the fence if we could find a small breach somewhere. After all, the damn thing is ancient. It's bound to be broken somewhere."

We began tracing the outside border and about fifteen minutes later, discovered a spot where a landslide occurred, revealing the green underbelly of tons of fallen jade and quartz. An enormous wedge-shaped boulder had pieced the fence as if it were made of mere foil. As soon as we climbed through the generous-sized opening, the gnashing noise ceased, and we heard nothing but the reverential "aahing" of arising creation. The cedars were sparser at this elevation and huge outcroppings of jade and gray-green moss blanketed the ground. We observed several golden beams whiz close over our heads. As always, these beams seemed to be serious sentients—or at least pre-programmed starlets, created by the element Fire. We playfully extended our hands in an attempt to touch their sparkling light, but the beams would whirl as they bypassed us. About halfway up the mountain, we discovered a level spot where three huge cedars formed a natural cathedral. "This looks ideal to me," said Stellium.

"Okay," agreed Élan, however I suspected that he wanted to go all the way to the top ridge. We spread our jackets on the ground and sat. As we ate lunch, Élan kept staring at me in a peculiar way and the light changed color around him until he was dressed in a pale green hue. I felt compelled to ask, "What is it? You seem to be hanging by a questioning thread."

He leaned over and kissed me and said, "Golden light has created a web across your face."

"Look at Stellium," I said. "He is a beautiful orange and mauve pink."

Stellium bit his bottom lip. "We can't hide our feelings or our turmoil."

"I'm sorry," Élan said softly. "When I was with my soul mates, I did not remember either of you existed. Now I'm here—fully here and I am committed to you both."

"I need to confess something too," I said, " but my thoughts are only partly formed and I don't want to be vague."

Stellium, the extrovert, suggested, "Say it, maybe we can help you put meaning around your partial thoughts."

"It's difficult to explain and I dislike being vague," I protested.

"Say it," urged Élan and he could not help balancing my reticence to speak with his own impatience.

"I'll try. The three of us are so close that in a blink of an eye a free radical could easily jump amongst us. That means one of us might be holding a free radical, yet the voice of that free radical could be speaking through someone else. I think several free radicals entered me last night because I was the first to react."

Élan tried to spare me complete responsibility for our obvious difficulties and said, "The free radicals might have entered me first. Last night I was impatient to remember the truth and even eager to face this specter."

Not to be outdone, Stellium said, "It could have been me too. When Élan began talking about the rendezvous with his soul mates, I had a premonition that something ominous was going to happen. After all, soul mates don't get together to talk about the weather. I barely heard what Élan had to say because I was telling myself—this is so unfair. His soul mates can't make anymore demands on his life."

Élan reached out and took my hands. "Kyron told me that I should listen to you. She said you came as a teacher to our soul group to help us deal with this free-radical specter."

"If I have, I can't remember what I am supposed to teach anymore," I said.

"Let's meditate for a while," said Stellium. "Maybe through meditation we will discover how to proceed."

We fell quiet and half-closed our eyes to the light. For over two hours, we sat until Stellium said, "I urgently need to speak," and he waited for us to open our eyes. During those two hours, the mauve pink light had grown in intensity around him and now the light formed a mushroom-shaped cloud over his head. He seemed to be peering out at us from a beautiful translucent tent. "I was in a great deal of pain when my *Emayre* took me up to the blue galaxy," said Stellium. "Envy refused to let go and the closer we got to the blue galaxy, the tighter Envy clung to my chest and leg. We were just coming around on this side of the blue galaxy and my *Holder* said, the next time we head toward the far side of the blue galaxy, look straight ahead instead of at the seventh or eighth dimension. Look beyond, and you will see your true self.' When the time came, I looked where I was directed and saw a form radiating golden light. It was my omega self. Overcome with incredible joy, I flung myself toward this magnificent light. For a moment, I was part of it and it was part of me and through that few seconds of joining, I really did see. Then, just as suddenly, I again was with my *Emayre*, but now envy was gone. I had nothing to envy; I had seen my omega self and I was beautiful. I came away knowing love's true purpose was not to alleviate my suffering, but to macerate me into accepting my own glory. My *Holder* said, 'I gave you this glimpse of home, of our grand unity, to remind you where you need to go. This journey around is not simply for you, but also for others. Remember, you possess everything you need for this journey. Now your purpose is to remind others that they also have everything they need to solve any puzzle that confronts them on their journey.'"

"I think I understand," said Élan. "Your *Holder* is suggesting that we already possess the tools we need to face this specter, we merely need to recognize our gifts and learn how to use them properly."

I finally verbalized the truth that we already knew. "We can postpone our confrontation with this free-radical specter to another time, but we cannot avoid it indefinitely." The three of us held hands for several minutes of reverential silence.

Élan reminded us, "We cannot meet this specter with any malevolence within our beings. We each will need to reach an unprecedented state of internal balance to face it, so it has no place to interface with us."

"How we going to do that?" asked Stellium.

"I haven't got a clue," admitted Élan.

****

Despite our admissions that we would need to face this free-radical specter, the three of us felt so much better, we called our new resolve, the first miracle that day. Our renewed unity gave us hope. Toward late afternoon, Élan said, "I'd like to hike a little closer to the Crystal before we start down the mountain."

I was tired, but Stellium said, "I'll go with you."

"We won't be long," Élan promised. "A half-hour at most."

They walked away and a moment later, I took my mother's flute out of my pocket. I did not start playing immediately, but waited for inspiration to come my way. When it did, the light seemed to enjoy the round, high-pitched tones of the flute and in no time, an audience of red-orange light surrounded me. The light pattered with a definite rhythm against my face and sounded like drumming in my ears. I felt happy that we were making music together and I did not equate the red-orange light with the eighth dimensional consciousness that imposed the vision in Élan's head. But, as everything is one, in this case, it was one without hesitation or even chance for question. Maybe three minutes passed, and I heard the hammering vibration of running footsteps on the ground. I stopped playing and glanced toward the approaching sound. Stellium was running toward me through the soft violet light. He was shirtless and appeared terrified. "Come!" he screamed. "Élan has fallen."

Stellium and I seemed to be flying over the rocks and through the cedar trees as my psychic vision ran meters ahead of my body. Stellium and Élan had not hiked far, less than fifty meters away. I found Élan on the ground with Stellium's shirt wrapped around his forehead and the shirt was soaked in blood. Élan's head was thrashing back and forth and his body was rigid, as if he were experiencing an epileptic seizure. An occasional "ah!" managed to escape from his throat.

"Hold him still," I said between clenched teeth. I located the sizeable gash, which was right above his right eyebrow, and pulled the wound closed with my fingertips and used Stellium's shirt as a compress. The moment I touched Élan, I realized what was happening. Something had keyed the memory of Michael facing the specter. Élan had wanted to get closer to the Crystal because he was looking for the exact geographical location where Michael died in the future of the persistent stream. "You're having a vision," I kept telling him. "You're here—safe with Stellium and me." Then his eyes rolled back in his head and he turned absolutely still. It seemed as if death had stolen his fabulous blue-green eyes and left us with only the bloody holes.

"We were walking, simply walking," sobbed Stellium. "Élan clutched his head and fell over as if someone sliced him in half. There's the rock," and he pointed at the guilty rock that struck our beloved Élan.

Death was so close, it was a toss-up what would kill Élan first, the gash on his forehead or the vision inside his head. Taking his blood-soaked head in my lap, I held him close to the growing embryo that would soon be our son. "I've got you and I'll never let you go." But so many times I had lost him; and now it felt that despite all my efforts, the persistent stream would still have its way. "Help me," I cried. "Someone, help me?" My moaning and pleas on that sacred mountaintop must have sounded like a soul from the depths of Chaos. Then one of the golden beams emanating from the Crystal zipped past us and made a sudden U-turn, right back to us. "Please don't let him die," I shouted at the thin golden thread. Without further ado, the light beam wove itself into a web that draped across Élan's face. Perhaps ten seconds passed. The beam retreated and then dashed off on its merry way, before I could even offer thanks. The only evidence the gash was real was the blood split from Élan's body and of course, the memory in his mind. When Élan was able to stand, the first thing he did was to kiss the ground where he fell. We called his healing, the second miracle that day and, the fact that we recognized it was a miracle, definitely, the third miracle."

Afterward, as we picked our way down the trail, the "aahing" hum of arising creation seemed suggestive of secrets too fearful to examine. Humility subdued us and I realized how little we still understood. Later when we climbed into bed, we pulled the covers up under our chins. We kicked our feet like children and sunk into conversation like teenagers. We clung to the physical, the familiar, to what we knew. Arms reached out to embrace and offered safe harbor in the gathering storm.

Élan sighed with that same "aahing" tone I heard above the fence and then he said, "Let me tell the rest. It won't take long." His whispering voice was hoarse and its rough edge felt like the sound of a rasp. "Your flute playing unleashed the final bit of the vision. Don't ask me how or why. All I know is the key that unlocked the final bit was the sound of your flute."

Stellium and I held Élan. He relaxed, but his words remained a hoarse whisper. "For many phases, that abominable supreme high priestess, we know only as Bell, and her murderous Hectarian mate, Bastion, summoned free radicals to torture Dulce, yet they failed to contain what he started. People were asking the divine to connect directly with their hearts for the first time. Dulce was old; he had suffered the torment of free radicals most of his life. On a good day, he was melancholy, and on his bad days, he was high on *tartan ratu* and trying to write music. Bastion and Bell put on their sincerity masks and courted Dulce with praise and donations to his favorite charities. Bastion even made sure the Delphi Glee Club performed Dulce's cantatas. They both knew that Dulce could interface with the New Delphi Crystal as well as any priestess and they wanted access to his knowledge. Dulce did join the reclusive San Delphi Mystics, but he never wrote another note of music, from that day forward. He told everyone that his talent had faded. In a reduced state, the general distortions promoted by the Hectarians further affected his mind and Dulce believed the Crystal was deadly beyond the fence. All those phases on New Delphi Island and he never tried to get beyond the wire fence. When Mellé arrived, Bell and Bastion knew she was coming. Dulce had been quiet for years and no longer posed any real threat, but teamed with his soul mate, Mellé, a chance existed that his brilliance could resurge. Bell began summoning free radicals that she directed toward Mellé and the scheme with the hair *keylic*, was the pinnacle of Bell's evil plot. Mellé did not go to New Delphi to rescue

Dulce, but to free herself from her commitment to him. When she saw him, she became further convinced that if they went directly to the Crystal, a direct confrontation would break their bond. On that fateful day, when Mellé, Dulce, and Michael went to the top rim of the New Delphi Crystal, Dulce took two objects, your flute and my knife. He took your flute because he hoped to play transcendent music for the Crystal. Dulce had lost his ability to create, but he still believed in music and its ability to soothe and transform. Then the specter emerged."

Élan took a deep breath and let it all out in one ragged sigh. "Lost souls stuck out all over the specter. It fought with thousands of arms while virulent curses raged from between its gnashing teeth. It pummeled Dulce, demanding the music, and he prepared to die. Then, the specter snatched Mellé and began squeezing the spirit from her body and Dulce took out your flute and began playing not any sacred music, but The Sacred Music. The specter could not hear transcendent harmonies over the screaming voices inside it. Up to that point, it had not touched Michael, but when he jumped to Mellé's defense, the specter instantly made the connection between Michael and the hair *keylic*."

Then finally and at last, Élan scraped the bottom of his vision. "There's something else, something we all know is true, but so far were afraid to admit openly. The specter did not simply kill me, it sucked me down into Chaos." He cleared his throat. "There! I've finally said it. I've been in Chaos." Stellium and I were crying and Élan suddenly turned so quiet, he seemed to disappear. Through my tears, I gazed at his glowing face and that glow told me the highest of the high blessed him, yet they allowed him to sink into Chaos. Why? Élan's head bobbed rhythmically as if he were involved in a struggle to free his memory of a place he could never forget. "Listen to me," he said and the new strength in his voice startled me. "We will have help in dealing with this specter—that's a given—but we need to do our part, especially me. The specter is keyed to me and it will continue to be keyed to me until I neutralize its power."

*What a dark and dreary universe this would be without your sweet light*, I thought.

Stellium took Élan's hands. "I never, ever, will let you fall into Chaos alone. If we fail, we will fall together. We will hold each other and remind each other of the real until help comes."

# TWENTY-ONE

**O**ut of surrender emerges a resolution to work within the confines of what we know is true. Together, we decided that Élan should never go into New Delphi Village. A chance existed that a Trinity priestess would catch a psychic flash of how important he was. No one bothered us—either supernatural or corporeal—and that was fine with us. We didn't know how long it would take to prepare to meet the specter, but we needed to do it before my quickening. Once Dulce's soul entered my womb, I would be vulnerable. That meant we enjoyed the leeway of two moons to prepare and do the deed.

The following morning, I showed them the black prism ball for the first time. Élan and Stellium accepted what I did so easily, I questioned whether we were getting too blasé about the supernatural. For the time being, I set the ball and copper coins on a small makeshift altar we had put together.

Over breakfast, we agreed that we were still tired, but as soon as we finished eating, we launched into the task of interviewing the free radicals trapped inside the black prism ball. We created a restrictive space by folding the bed blanket into the shape of a triangle and laying it flat on the floor. I placed the two copper coins on either side, at the triangle base. At the apex, we lit a candle and fortified its energy by placing Élan's white feather close by. We prayed aloud, calling on the highest authorities we knew, for this was sacred ritual, and we were declaring our intent. If language could explain anything, then no higher language authority existed for us than the combined power of Wisdom and Understanding. "Great Wisdom and Immaculate Understanding, please be with us and bless us with your insights," was our only plea.

The three of us stood ready and alert, each of us guarding a side of the triangle. I tossed the black ball into the middle of the blanket and it did not come to rest, as I intended, but ricocheted off the cloth, with a force far greater than my gentle toss. Élan instantly assumed Primal Stance and guarded the triangle apex. "Razor Shardasko!" he communicated to Stellium. They both pirouetted and became a thin, black line intersecting the light. This maneuver was a further precaution, their effort to block the fourth dimension, so whatever was in the process of appearing had no chance to escape. Unexplainably, when Stellium stopped turning, he was clutching the black ball between the palms of his hands. The expression on his face suggested someone had just shouted, "Here! Catch!" Meanwhile, a dark figure was materializing in the middle of the blanket as a half-form. When the figure was complete, it stood perfectly still. Stellium nodded toward us before saying to the half-form, "Please lower your hood."

From beneath the cloak, a bony hand emerged that walked up its own body like a lateral moving crab and jerked back its hood. We saw a weary face that had lost its polish and detail. Its pitted skin was stretched taunt over a rigid jaw and the lips were thin as blades. Its jerky movement suggested the energy stutter of the elemental universe, which was still struggling to manifest this incomplete form. It continued to undress, first removing its cloak, then several filmy sheaths, until all its garments lay scattered around its feet. When it finally stood naked, its body was as pitted as its face and reminded me of a marble statue the elements had eroded through time. It was feminine yet the breasts were lifeless and her chest flat. The pubic area was hairless and her sex managed to convey a sense of brittleness, like that of a dead, curled leaf. Despite her appearance, she greeted Stellium with enthusiasm and offered him a faint smile. She showed him her palms, but they were devoid of lifelines and instead, filled with craters. "Honesty," she promised and her voice was a tinny echo.

"Tell me your name," said Stellium.

"I'm an orphan without a name," she said. "Would you like to give me a name?"

Stellium glanced toward me for advice and I shook my head no. "What is your purpose?" he asked.

The figure astounded us by proclaiming, "My purpose is to create perfect balance through the power of All-There-Is," and the way she spoke the three words, all there is, made them sound as if they were one word. Stellium raised his eyebrows in surprise and fell into deliberate thought. Her tinny voice called out in fear that Stellium had deserted her. "Hello? Where have you gone, soul?" Did her empty eyeholes mean she was blind and could not see him standing so dangerously near? Her head jerked to one side as she leaned closer to the edge of the blanket and listened, while Élan raised his arms and again moved into Primal Stance.

"Who created you?" asked Stellium.

"I thought you ran away," she admitted and then she answered more confidently.

"All-There-Is created me."

"Is All-There-Is a what or a who?"

"All-There-Is is both a what and a who. All-There-Is is cause and its own effect, while I am one hesitation in the multitude of hesitations of All-There-Is. Many of my kind are much older than I am. I am a young orphan, born behind the green galaxy when it was forming." Again, we were in shock. Was it possible the lush perfection of Paradise was capable of producing a free radical as lifeless and cold as this one seemed? "If you step into this space, where you have confined me, and look into the windows of my eyes, you will see All-There-Is in its full glory. If you wish, we can become one and your name will become my own."

"For now, let's each hold our separate spaces," Stellium said. "Tell me about how you join with a soul."

"The fourth dimension is where I meet souls. There, great aggregates of my kind act as transporters and assist me in locating suitable hosts."

"Are there many great aggregates in the fourth dimension?"

"There must be multitudes, for I never have a problem finding one to give me transport."

Élan tried to insert his own question by asking, "What kind of souls attract you?" The free radical did not answer and it did not take us long to realize it heard only Stellium.

"What kind of souls attract you?" repeated Stellium.

"Various sorts," said the free radical. "I just came out of a Hectarian Mystic named Brother Remette. I can show you how he seemed to me."

Serious eye contact was going on among the three of us. "Go ahead, show me," said Stellium.

The figure began moving and again we were on the alert. She jerked her head and twisted her limbs, rearranging them like ghastly three-dimensional puzzle pieces. When she ceased moving, she stood deadly still. Her strange new silhouette reminded me of a tree clinging to the vertical side of a mountain. The free radical possessed the same features as Remette, yet she was an obvious impersonator. "Remette worked hard and used his power to become what he called, 'an expert on moral authority.' Every time I spoke, he tried to silence me. After many phases of ignoring me, I resolved to leave him; but naturally, I could not escape until he died. I began nudging him toward death, so I could escape sooner."

"Why do you believe Remette would not listen to you?" asked Stellium.

"He told me I impeded his perfection and sense of organization, which were important to his moral authority. He called me a liar and never believed I sought perfect balance and my way home to All-There-Is. When he died, his soul group called me forth and I told my story of living inside his life."

"Ask her how Remette died," I said.

Stellium repeated my question and the figure said, "Remette died in the recent meteor storm on the planet Sutcay Tay."

Stellium communicated, *do you want me to follow up on Remette*? I shook my head no. "Could you tell me more about your appearances before soul groups?" asked Stellium.

The free radical said, "All-There-Is expects me to make appearances, although I cannot say I'm always a welcome guest in your halls of light."

"Do soul groups blame you for a soul falling short?"

"I'm blamed only if I do not speak honestly. The soul takes most of the blame because it can interface with your universe more easily than I can. What never ceases to amaze me is many souls believe they can stand before their own soul group and lie. For instance, Remette hid behind his self-importance, portraying himself as all goodness and light, yet I was there to unmask his oppressiveness. I told his soul group the truth. 'This soul lived as a close-minded hypocrite.'"

"Shortly after Remette's death, I hailed an aggregate and told it to give me someone simple." The figure began twisting and this time, she turned into a man with a barrel chest and large bony head, but of course, the free radical still was itself shining through. "When I got into Scopas, I found him easy-going, agreeable, and even self-effacing. Then he started having health problems, which he chose to ignore. He avoided me by humming or whistling to drown out my voice. That's when I realized he was utterly simplistic and believed he could fix every problem with a dust mop and broom. He angered me and I aligned with his physical problems, so I could escape sooner. Between his health problems and me, we finished him off in a matter of a few moons."

"What did these two souls have in common?" asked Stellium.

"They both lacked common sense," said the free radical.

"Do you believe common sense is the path to your perfect balance?"

Her voice brightened considerably when she exclaimed, "You do understand. I'm attracted to those who listen and even more to those who understand. I think I would like to be inside you. Maybe together we could create perfect balance and through you, I could find my way home to All-There-Is."

"First, tell me more about your views on common sense."

As casual as can be, the free radical offered us this nugget: "Well, without common sense, there is no wisdom or understanding, which always form the two moving perimeters of each creation." To say the least, the three of us were astounded. It was as if this free radical told us, when building any new creation, the building code requires that the walls must be of the sturdy materials of wisdom and understanding. Was it an authentic glimpse behind The Creative Line?

Stellium asked, "Based on your travels, what do you believe the consequences are for a soul who ignores common sense?"

"I observe the same pattern in souls that host me. They ignore me in favor of their preoccupations and this brings them to failure."

"How do you react when they ignore you?"

"I become angry. In the end, they force me to beat myself against them to get free."

"So what would be the reward for listening to your advice?"

The free radical further amazed us by saying, "I have a vision of what the reward might be. I dream too. I dream of perfect balance and that I might leave a soul with strength, success, wealth, and finally victory; and of course then an aggregate would take me home to All-There-Is."

Stellium hesitated and the three of us stared at each other. We needed to talk in private. "Okay," said Stellium. "I might have more questions later. For now, I am going to toss the ball your way and you jump back inside and take a short rest." Stellium tossed the ball toward the stony figure and the power of the black prism ball sucked up the figure along with the clothing around its feet.

Stellium spoke for all of us when he said, "My previous understanding was that free radicals were somewhat stupid. This free radical was a quantum leap smarter than I imagined free radicals to be. In fact, it's smarter than some people I've met."

"And it seemed to have no amnesia between lives," I said. "Do you realize that if free radicals have an awareness of multiple lives, then they are knowingly dragging their karmic legacy into unaware souls and superimposing their disposition on those souls?"

Élan was pacing back and forth at the top point of the triangle. "Did you notice that it interpreted its motives as completely righteous? It suggested souls were seducing it, impeding its ability to return to All-There-Is. I sensed no love or loyalty for the soul that gives it host, only a sense of duty to report when the soul is off-balance." Élan let go a meaningful, "hum! I see a pattern here. Despite the lack of love and loyalty, a yearning exists within this free radical to go home." Élan thought for a moment and moved his empty hands in front of his face as if juggling some invisible objects. "See if this makes sense to you. The green galaxy produces an instinctive energy that fuels our physical senses and enhances our ability to create new forms. Frustration of that energy would make it difficult for our basic physical senses to interpret reality. What do you think the strongest force within that frustration might be?"

Without hesitation, Stellium said, "Rage! Sprite, do you recall the discussion we had about my mom and the Earth doctors when I was an infant? Stellium explained the details of the conversation to Élan and said, "Sprite broke each person's motivation down into fear, shame, and rage."

Élan listened carefully before concluding, "If fear, shame, and rage are the motivating forces influencing free radicals, then I bet the aggregate gave us three shadows and two more shadows are still inside that ball."

"So which emotion motivated the energy of that particular free radical?" I asked.

"Well if it truly was born behind the green galaxy then perhaps—rage?" guessed Élan.

Stellium started pacing too. "It seemed too innocuous to be rage."

"If pushed hard enough, aren't we all capable of rage?" asked Élan. "If a free radical can align itself with death and bring about the death of a soul, that free radical possesses a force as lethal as rage." At that moment, I noticed Stellium's pacing was rather jerky and uncharacteristic of a Shardasko Warrior. We needed to be careful because it appeared as if the free radical was able to affect us, even without direct contact.

"That free radical chose me," said Stellium. "It cast itself against me because I'm the one it was attracted to. It showed itself in the most favorable light to gain my acceptance. I believe we saw only its surface and not its true nature."

**\*\*\*\***

"Well, let's see if my rage, fear, and shame theory holds up," I said and I picked up the ball and again tossed it gently into the center of the blanket. This time, the ball rebounded to me and again, we saw a figure with a hood pulled up over its head. "Let me see your face," I said.

The hood came down and the filmy sheaths came off, just as before. This time a nude man stood before us. The round abundance of his fleshiness was in direct contrast to the first figure. Fat hung in folds over his belly and hips. His arms and legs seemed too short for his rotund torso; and his penis hung flaccid, while two acorn-sized testicles seemed lost inside his overstretched scrotum. His cheeks were cherubic and his pate bald and shiny. His appearance was silly, as silly as the first figure was horrific. Except for the empty eyeholes, he could have passed as a bedraggled festival clown. He showed me the chubby palms of his stubby-fingered hands and promised, "Honesty."

"Speak your honesty," I said.

Then he threw out the lure just as the first free radical did. "My honesty is better experienced close-up."

"First, tell me about the souls you've lived inside."

"Many souls have been similar to you."

I felt offended over his presumptions. Did he think I was transparent or simply easy prey? My gut response was to distance myself and depersonalize the connection between us. "How do you know they were similar to me?" I asked.

"The aggregate told me they were similar to you." He coughed and his coughing sounded of thick phlegm. Was he evoking an effect or was his cough an authentic clue to his nature? "They usually are old souls, blessed with many gifts. Their desire is to experience all life can offer. They've cleared many of the hurdles associated with controlling their primal senses and now they seek to experience the abundance, love, and happiness that life can offer. I work with them, and if they listen, I can be an adaptive advantage that helps them evolve."

"Do these souls appreciate your help?"

"In the beginning everyone appreciates my help. In the end, most souls are indolent, many depraved, and a few become involved in debauchery. In my opinion, they cannot handle abundance." He showed me exactly what he meant by masturbating his penis for a few seconds. His masturbating had no effect on his physical penis, but his masturbating left me with the impression that the action was relieving the phlegm in his throat. "When these souls return to their groups, they often feel shame because they have been blessed with much, yet have failed to bring their blessings to fruition."

I was getting telepathic messages from Stellium and Élan. *There it is!* they both thought. *This free radical has a link to shame.*

"I was in your son Dulce and he was a personal disappointment to me in many ways," said the free radical.

"Did you warn him about the dangers associated with his gifts?" I asked.

"Of course! I always advise perfect balance, but he would drown me out with another glass of champagne or another whiff of *tartan ratu*. He was quite a libertine when his energy was plentiful, but quite apologetic as an older man."

"What first motivates you to speak inside a soul?"

"I speak only when a soul begins to block their blessings. Then I must balance that block with an opposing energy to maintain the balance of All-There-Is." This free radical was telling us its function was critical to the stability of reality."

"How does a soul go about blocking their blessings?"

"Blessings still get through, but in the process, distortions occur. My job is to stand at the point of distortion and accurately report what I see to the soul."

"In your opinion, why would a soul choose to block such blessings?"

"Choice! Choice is freewill and as long as freewill exists, my kind will be here to help maintain the balance of All-There-Is."

"Does your kind have a common name?" We were about to find out a lot more for I finally posed the right question. The free radical said, "We are the children of the Prism of Dark."

Élan and Stellium were nodding in agreement so I asked, "Tell me more about the Prism of Dark."

"As a light prism refracts light, breaking it up into the primary colors of your spectrum, a dark prism refracts dark, breaking it up into the primary shades of the spectrum and creating me. Together, Prism of Light and Prism of Dark make up All-There-Is."

"Can you show me specific souls, besides Dulce, that once gave you host?"

"The first of my kind, which you previously interviewed, is different from me. She is younger, and chooses to mimic souls to show them where they are off balance. My design is subtler and I would prefer not to mock the many souls I've been inside. I will tell you this: I'm attracted to a soul that interprets its primal motivations in terms of a caretaker or enabler. Those that presume to be motivators, role models, paragons of virtue, the status seeker, the artist, the romantic, the dilettante, and even those that consider themselves tragic victims. You fall into several of these categories. All these paths have their pitfalls and I am forever available to these souls to point the way to All-There-Is."

"So where does your energy come from? What are your origins?"

"I am made manifest by the power of All-There-Is and I know my origins in a place before the creation of your universe."

We were flabbergasted. Was it a liar? Insane? Presumptuous? Whatever it was, it was a new perspective with a language that was different from our own. We were anxious to learn as much as we could. "Do you wish to go home to this place before the creation of this universe?"

"More than anything."

"How did you get from before the creation of my universe into what is going on now?"

"I came in a great aggregate, for it knew your creation would give birth to many children and we would be needed. Now, between my host souls, I do return to All-There-Is, but All-There-Is always sends me out again on the continuum that takes me toward the fourth dimension. In the fourth dimension, an aggregate will approach me and again introduce me to a soul that will inflame me with their mission."

"What is most important to you personally?"

"All-There-Is is the only important thing to me."

"Why are you able to focus on only one soul at a time in your efforts to return to All-There-Is?"

"Because, just like you, soul, I was created to work on a one-to-one basis."

"In your travels, can you say if All-There-Is is a place or a being?"

"My experience suggests that All-There-Is is a drifting energy that is capable of organizing and dissolving at will. All-There-Is acts as desire and is an accurate witness of the way things truly are."

"Do you think it would be possible for a large aggregate to come fully into the third dimension?"

The figure coughed and cleared its throat before dropping this bomb. "That should never happen, but if it did, it would tear the time threads between the third and fourth dimension and that would be difficult to heal."

"Do you think it would have the power to take souls back to All-There-Is?"

"The motivation of the children of the Prism of Dark, including aggregates, is to return to All-There-Is. Aggregates are evolved children who have volunteered to stay in this alien place and help less evolved beings, such as me, find our way home. Any aggregate that would mistake a soul for a dark child would be like one of your golden ones taking a dark child into the strongest light." I grew quiet and thought about Élan falling into Chaos. I thought about souls taken against their will into interminable darkness, where the reality was so alien they could only interpret their experience in negative terms. "Are you there?" called the free radical.

"Thank you," I said. "We are finished with each other," and I tossed the ball into the triangle. The shiny ball promptly sucked up the free radical inside, and the ball returned to me again. "It's obvious they have organization just as we have organization," I said.

"And great purpose," added Stellium.

"Wait a second," said Élan and he waved his arms around like a real Gathosian. "Now I see I have been looking at this whole problem through a too narrow scope. In persistent reality, the aggregate tore a hole between the third and fourth dimension; now, through this patch, we have a chance to mend this rent."

"Hold up!" said Stellium. "I suggest that you wake up from your heroic dream and sense the real danger here. This Thing, whatever its name, came into our third dimension and its purpose was very personal. It hunted you down and took you into Chaos. The only difference is This Thing is much bigger than we originally imagined. We still know nothing about it, Élan. Messing with it is like standing before Source and expecting to direct its energy."

"The next free radical is bound to be mine," said Élan. "Give me the ball, Follie. I have to know where I still fall short."

I hesitated and then gently handed Élan the ball. "Be careful," I said.

"I love you both, never forget that," he said and then he tossed the black prism ball into the center of the triangle. This time, when the hooded figure appeared, it held the ball in its own hands. The three of us exchanged expressive and questioning glances. We had lost control—that much we knew for sure. The figure lowered its own hood, but did not disrobe as the first two free radicals had done. The figure showed itself as a young man. His body looked well muscled under his cloak. His hair was short and dark that he wore slicked down. His complexion was ruddy with obvious good health. He appeared angry and defiant even without speaking and his expression suggested a street rowdy sporting for a fight. He turned toward Élan and taunted him with, "If you want my knowledge, then you must open your hands toward me."

Élan was completely compliant. He picked up his white feather and placed it in the palm of his hand before saying, "All my honesty, I swear upon my *Holder.*"

Then the figure promised, "And all my honesty in return, Brother Élan. However, do not presume to question me, for I am the child of the Dark Prism who has come to question you." Then the figure fired the ball toward Élan and he was forced to let go of the feather. It twirled around in the air, but did not fall to the floor as expected; instead, it lifted until it sat as a guardian above his head. "Nice catch!" mocked the figure. Then the free radical cast the lure, just as the first two had. "I hear you are a clever shadow dancer. Do you want to dance with me?"

"I don't dance with strangers," replied Élan.

"Give me the ball," demanded the free radical and he cupped his hands in front of him. Élan gently tossed the ball back to the figure. "I will grant you this. You are a refined soul. Your inner light peers out proudly from behind your eyes. What else could your soul group call you but enlightened? Even as we speak, they chatter congratulations amongst themselves. They call you the great and enlightened Élan Journey Cœur, while no one mentions my part in your life. Tell me, who am I?" and he fired the ball back toward Élan.

This time, Élan jumped backward to avoid getting hit in the solar plexus and the feather over his head quivered with anticipation. "I didn't realize you existed," said Élan. "Now that I know, I thank you for always questioning my intent, helping me to innovate, and find a better way. You have mocked me and played the part of my critic. You are my guardian that keeps my feet upon the path. You challenge, yet support my bravery in every aspect of my life. Still, I fear you, for some strange reason."

"What do you feel at this moment?"

Élan held the ball between his thumb and forefinger and peered at it. "I feel a little awed by your assured presence, as if you are stronger than me."

"Good!" cheered the free radical. "I've found an honest soul for a change." The figure extended its hands. "Give me the ball," it said.

Élan looked toward Stellium. *Be careful,* Stellium thought.

Élan glanced my way and the mere hint of a thought emerged from him, *I don't know how to stop this.* Then he gently tossed the ball back to the free radical.

"Did you know I gave Kyron your first conundrum?" asked the figure.

Élan winced. "'The brightest light hides the darkest shadows.'"

"And now you finally understand."

Élan nodded. "Together we are one. We are chaos and order, futility and hope, strife and harmony, sorrow and joy, rage and compassion, shame and honor, and fear and courage. We are All-there-is. Forgive my allegiance to my previous limited perspective, but it felt safer in the light."

"Where has your limited perspective taken you?"

"To the edge of a situation I am unprepared to face," admitted Élan.

"What do you want from me?"

"I want you to help me figure out how I may face a free-radical specter that broke through the timeline and how I may redirect it to where it needs to go."

"And what will you do for me in return?"

"I will be sure the aggregate takes you back to All-There-Is. You will be there and I will be here. Together we will be in perfect balance." With that, the free radical stepped outside the triangle. Élan went into Primal Stance. I presumed it was a protective gesture, but I was wrong. Élan was preparing to jump with the child of the Dark Prism to—we knew not where. The free radical fanned open its cloak and it made a snapping sound as it engulfed Élan and the feather. In an instant, the three had vanished.

****

Stellium and I were stunned. We stared at each other for several seconds, until Stellium screamed, "We have to follow."

A split second later, Élan reappeared in the middle of the blanket. He was changed and had hair on his face. "How long was I gone?" he asked.

"About fifteen seconds," said Stellium. Élan sank down in the middle of the blanket and held his head in his hands. "Are you okay?" asked Stellium.

"Okay?" asked Élan. "I can tell you this, real night lasts infinitely longer than any day."

"What happened to the free radical?" I asked.

"Nalé?"

Stellium sat down near Élan and became tender. "Darling, that's your name spelled backward."

"I know; it became a joke between us. Nalé is here too; he came back with me." Élan took the black ball out of his pocket and handed it to Stellium. "Here, be careful with that. It contains a few dozen free radicals, we picked up along the way."

I sat down next to them on the floor and asked, "Where did you go?"

"Nalé showed me that our Creation is a miniscule piece of what's going on. There's more darkness out there than our consciousness can imagine. A million to the power of a million are the cycles of darkness that support our puny little creation of light."

"How did you get back here?"

"Kyron helped me and so did Nalé. He took Kyron and me into All-There-Is, what we call Chaos. Once, Nalé and I were at war there, but this time it was different."

"What about the free-radical specter?" Stellium asked. "Do we still need to face it?"

"More than ever," said Élan. "Now I truly have the knowledge to do it right. Nalé is going to help." Élan stood up, went to our thermos, and made a cup of tea. As he steadied himself with sips of hot tea, he began unrolling his plan like a carpet. "Kyron will take us to the correct future time and show us which cottage Mellé and Michael rented. I will jump to that time, find the cottage, and replace my hair with Michael's hair. Then Nalé and I will have the power to redirect the aggregate toward All-There-Is."

# TWENTY-TWO

**T**he next morning, the weather on New Delphi was dreary. Rain clouds sat near the horizon and the rain would last all day. We ate breakfast in total silence. With nothing left to say, the everyday sounds of creaking chairs and the sound of footsteps landing against the floor seemed louder than usual. *What do you know* hung in the air, without anyone uttering the words? We could not pretend that we were inconsequential in what was about to happen. We knew within our *Emayres* that we never hid from a challenge and we worked long and hard to create balance in our lives. We participated in creating a reality where love and trust were elevated to divine status. Still the question lingered, *what do you know*? The question no longer excited us, but rather sat inside us as a confession that we still knew very little.

After we finished breakfast, Élan said, "Let's stash our belongings in one spot. As soon as we return, I want to leave New Delphi."

Stellium brightened with hope. "By tonight, we could be on our way to Earth." Élan still could not live up to his Shardasko moniker. He was heroic, serious, and introverted. He touched Stellium's cheek in a loving gesture, "I mean it," Stellium swore. By tonight, we will be on our way to Earth."

We stripped off all our clothing and packed it away in our luggage. Élan saved out only two items for our mission, his white feather of authority, and the black prism ball filled with free radicals.

"What are you going to do with your knife?" asked Stellium.

"All manly weaponry must remain here in the past," said Élan.

"I'm going to take the prayer beads," I told them.

They both nodded in agreement. "Okay, let's do it," Élan said, and we jumped to the fourth dimension. As soon as we cleared the breach, Élan placed the white feather in the palm of his hand and blew upon it. "Kyron,

353

take me forth," he commanded. The feather immediately morphed into an infallible white hawk and, again, a red rose appeared in its beak. The bird lifted, like hope, and took flight. The translucent whiteness and brilliance of its fluttering wings was an awe-inspiring sight. We followed and it flew to our left, heading into the future along the drifting threads of the timeline.

We cleared the breach a second time and landed outside our cottage, number 22, on Auric Lane. We were just a few meters away from where we jumped seconds before. The time of day was the same. It was mid-morning, but now the sky was clear and the color of dusky roses. We were thirty phases into the future yet the place looked older and shabbier. The whitewashed shutters on our cottage were gone and one of the windows cracked and mended with sticky tape. The huge old cedar that stood to the left of the cottage door was a dead stump. I barely noticed the old cedar in the past and now it was an important landmark because it was gone.

We hid in nearby bushes for our nudity would shock any passerby. Kyron the hawk was careening around the immediate area, waiting for new instructions. Élan whistled softly and the hawk came like an expectant lover, landing on his shoulder, and cuddling its white-feathered head against his neck. "Kyron, take us where we need to go," he whispered in its ear a second time. His obedient and loyal guide again took flight and we followed, skirting along behind the bushes. We did not have far to go. The hawk landed on the roof of a cottage six doors up the path from where we were staying. This time when the hawk returned to Élan, he blew gently into its ear and the hawk fell into that familiar white feather in his open palm.

We waited while the sky turned metallic gold and then faded to violet blue. While we waited, we strategized. "This first part is going to be tricky," explained Élan. "I need time to switch the hair *keylic*." Élan went behind the cottage and managed to pry open the window, so he had easy access when the proper time came. Stellium and I hid in two separate locations, near the front, with a good view of the path that came up from Jade Boulevard. Stellium and I planned to be lookouts and warn Élan when we saw Mellé and Michael on the trail. At the same time, we were alert for Beltania, who soon would come to steal the hair *keylic*.

Thirty minutes later, Stellium, who had a better view of the lower trail than I did, sent the critical message. *They're coming.* A moment later, I saw them too. Mellé and Michael might have been brother and sister or even twins. Even more startling was they both looked like Élan. I don't know why their stark resemblance shocked me, but it did. Finally seeing them in the flesh felt like hard evidence that Mellé and Michael were Élan's poor split soul in the future. All three were blonde with those wonderful Human blue-green eyes. Michael's skin was pale, even for a Human, and I knew it was because the Tyrowsian scientist Jana Revba had tinkered with Michael's

DNA. Any dark Gathosian would have said Michael looked ill, but to Tyrowsians, beautiful skin was porcelain white. Mellé and Michael were taking turns pushing a cart with their luggage along the stone walkway. Mellé stopped just a few meters from where I was hiding and complained, "This is quite a hike."

"It shouldn't be too much farther," said Michael. "Let me push the cart the rest of the distance." His love for her was obvious as he linked his arm to hers. They arrived at their cottage and went inside. Ten minutes later, they reemerged.

*They're leaving*, I immediately relayed to Élan.

They hesitated for only a moment outside the cottage door. Michael assured Mellé, "I know the way," and they walked up the trail toward the Crystal. We knew they were headed toward the San Delphi Monastery because they had a strong hunch that Dulce was there. A question drifted through my mind as I watched them walking arm in arm. *Who gave them that hunch?*

I had no time to ponder my question because, a few seconds later, the situation again turned busy. Stellium was communicating—*Beltania is coming*.

I knew Élan needed more time to switch the hair *keylic*, so I created a few seconds of illusion to stall Beltania. My illusion stopped her and asked, "Do you know the correct time, sister?"

Beltania was preoccupied with her daunting task of stealing the hair *keylic* and said, "Sorry, I'm not wearing a watch today," and she brushed right past my projection without a second thought. I chided myself. *Why didn't I ask for directions to the Witches' Temple, something that would have taken her more time to answer?*

*Get out*, Stellium and I were communicating to Élan. *Beltania is coming around to the rear of the cottage.*

Nothing. Dead space.

Three minutes later, Mellé was trudging back up the hill toward their cottage. I had no idea where Élan was hiding, but Stellium and I were doing our part and communicating with great urgency that, *Mellé is poised to open the front door of the cottage.* Holding my breath, I was certain Beltania, Mellé, and Élan were doomed to a face-to-face confrontation. Then Beltania dashed around the side of the cottage and disappeared down the trail toward Jade Boulevard. A few seconds later, Mellé reemerged and walked up the trail a second time. I had not moved from my crouched position for the last ten minutes, yet I was breathless. As soon as she was out of sight, Élan opened the front door and beckoned us.

Stellium and I made a mad dash for the front door and went inside. "I switched the hair *keylic*," said Élan. "Inside Mellé's suitcase, I found a hairbrush on top of the clothing. I had no time to escape so I hid inside the closet. From there, I was able to watch and it happened exactly as it did in the vision. Beltania came in through the window I left open, stole the hair *keylic*—only this time it was my hair—and Mellé walked in just as the hem of Beltania's green skirt disappeared out through the window. Mellé went to the window and closed it, exactly as she did the first time. It's obvious she thinks she saw something suspicious."

"Odd!" exclaimed Stellium. "Who left the window open in the persistent stream so Beltania could get in and out so quickly?" It was another unanswerable question.

The three of us rifled through the luggage and helped ourselves to clothing. We politely avoided underwear. Élan was delighted. He discovered a pair of Michael's shoes in one of the bags that fit his feet. "My *Holder* loves me," he said. "I have shoes." Meanwhile, Stellium and I found a couple pairs of socks so Stellium could wear Michael's slippers and I could wear Mellé's shoes.

"Bring their luggage," I decided. "With luck perhaps we'll be able to persuade them to board the mid-afternoon windship back to the mainland."

****

The San Delphi Monastery was two kilometers straight up toward the Crystal. On our evening hikes, we avoided the fork in the path that led to the monastery, but now we took it and walked straight up to the front gate. The monastery sits on a carved-out part of the mountain. The ascent is steep and twisting and the trail turns into stairs toward the end. A flimsy rope handrail provides the only barrier between the precipitous cliff edge and the rugged rocks below. "We can't be more than twenty minutes behind," said Stellium.

"Let's give them a few minutes alone with Dulce," decided Élan. We watched from a distance as Michael and Mellé got into a debate with the Hectarian guard outside the entrance; then he opened the gate and allowed them inside. "This is getting weirder," said Élan. "They did not know the moniker Dulce was using as a Hectarian. Telepathically, I just told Michael that Dulce calls himself Equipoise and I'm sure Michael heard me."

"It's going to get weirder until the two realities mesh," I warned him. We waited for a few more minutes because we didn't want to spoil their reunion with Dulce. Mellé and Dulce had not seen each other in over eighty years and Dulce had seen Michael only in dreams. Twenty minutes later, the three of us approached the Hectarian gatekeeper ourselves. Stellium told him, "We're here to visit Brother Equipoise."

"Is he having a party?" asked the Hectarian.

"Today is his birthday," said Stellium and the three of us smiled deferentially.

"Brother Equipoise is in building E, floor 3, cell 2. His name is on his door." The Hectarian laughed. "Tell him to save a sniff of *ratu* for me. I'll be off duty in about an hour."

****

Up on the third floor, we scanned the dark hall for cell 2. Near the opposite end was the door we sought. Élan knocked and we heard muffled conversation inside, but no one answered. Élan tried the lever and the door opened. The smell of rose-scented incense flooded my nostrils. The room was dark and the only light came from a burned-down candle sitting across the room. Dulce, Michael and Mellé were sitting on the floor and Dulce was crying uncontrollably. "Trust me," Michael was pleading. "Take a chance. You have nothing here except torment and memories. Come out of this place. I swear I can make you whole again."

"I want to believe in someone again," Dulce moaned.

"Start by believing in me," Michael urged.

"But where can we go?" asked Dulce. "The Trinity Witches know all. They will be after us."

We realized we were still a micron distance outside persistent reality and that's why they did not see us standing there in the dark. We made some noise and moved into the candlelight. Élan said in a clear and rather loud voice, "Excuse me, we've come to help and show you the way to safety and freedom."

The situation turned weirder still. Mellé did not know who we were, but Michael said, "You've come! I knew you would come."

Meanwhile an expression of terror gained strength on Dulce's face. "Mother?" he questioned. "You're alive?" Dulce grabbed Michael by the shoulders and shook him. "See! The Trinity Witches can steal a personal memory and create an illusion as real as this."

"They're not illusions," said Michael confidently. "At this moment, they might be more real than we are."

Élan crouched down on the floor and patted his future self on the shoulder. "Let me try," said Élan. "We're not illusions, Dulce." Élan put his hand on his son's cheek. Disguised as a simple touch, Élan gave Dulce a direct transmission. It might take Dulce days or even moons to figure out exactly what the transmission meant, but he would know Élan's point of view in a matter of seconds through that one simple touch to his cheek. "Do you feel my warmth, my love for you?" asked Élan.

"You're my father," said Dulce with sudden realization. He looked clever. "You might even be real. I have no memory of you, so the Trinity Witches could not recreate you from my memories."

"I am real. I am your flesh and blood father and this woman is your flesh and blood mother. We are here to help you change the future. Know this my three children, without our intervention, Michael will die in the next few hours."

357

"No!" moaned Mellé. "I can't lose Michael; he's the only good thing I ever made with my life." I leaned over Mellé and put my fingertips on her forehead. In an instant, I gave her the same transmission. "How did you do that?" she asked.

"I did not do it," I told her. "My *Emayre* leaned out through the window of my forehead and touched your forehead with its hand."

"Oh—" she said vaguely. She looked up at Stellium and said, "And your name is?"

"My name is Stellium. A Trinity Witch stole a hair *keylic* from your suitcase a short while ago and that witch is my soul mate."

"Yet you've joined ranks with Dulce's parents?" asked Mellé.

"Yes, and if you allow me to touch you, then you will know my point of view too."

Mellé lifted the short hair that covered her forehead and said, "Okay, put it right here, next to what Dulce's mother just gave me." Stellium did just that. Over the next few minutes, there was a great deal of touching among the six of us and with that touching more information was exchanged. Still, so much remained unsaid. It takes time to talk in depth, to express feelings and we did not have that time. Our focus was getting Mellé, Michael, and Dulce off New Delphi as quickly as possible. In the time we did have, Élan, Stellium, and I attempted to gather the complete flavor of their situation, from their point of view.

"One question still haunts me," said Michael.

"Only one?" asked Stellium.

"If I do not fall down into All-There-Is, will your new reality continue to support my existence? I'm worried I might die anyway, you know, simply disappear."

"You will live," I said. "After we deal with the errant aggregate that the Trinity Witches are now preparing to call forth, we will avoid the timespan that supports your future existence. This will protect you as well as Élan. I see no impediments and I believe Michael can live to a ripe old age, if you pay attention to what's important."

Dulce said he owned a few personal possessions he wanted to take with him and he went to a chest to collect the items. He had my mother's flute, the tarot cards I gave him on his tenth birthday, and his father's knife. He showed the knife to Élan. "This is all I ever knew of you," said Dulce. "You didn't tell me in your transmission why you ran away and left mother and I alone."

"I was afraid," Élan said simply. "I'm no longer afraid and I want to give you, Mellé, and Michael everything of myself in a great exchange. Listen for me in meditation and I will come and sit with you. I can do this and I will come—this I swear. We are one consciousness and no time—be it persistent or alternate reality—would dare block our communion of love."

I took the prayer beads from my pocket and gave them to Mellé. "Many souls have charged these beads with their energy, so guard them well. Use them in meditation and souls will come to you, advise you, and guide you to your own enlightenment."

It took a short time to get down to the place where the windships landed. As we hoped, they boarded the mid-afternoon windship back to Logan's Point. "Don't tell us where you're going," cautioned Élan. "I don't want that knowledge to be in my mind when I face the aggregate."

"You have done so much for us," said Mellé. "What can we do to help you?"

"Live and love each other," Élan said simply.

"I know something you could do for us," said Stellium. "You could give us a few banknotes for food."

Mellé tried to give Stellium a great deal of money, but he said, "Just enough money so we can buy some food and water. We can't take money through the fourth dimension and even if we could, we have a different kind of money in the future."

Élan embraced Dulce and called him, "My precious son. You have knowledge of Gathosian stealth. Use all your stealth in getting away from this place. Do your work and pray for us."

It felt so strange to me, to embrace my son and send him away on a windship while I was carrying his waiting fetus inside me, but that is exactly what I did. We watched as the windship disappeared in the afternoon glitter upon the Iris Sea. We looked around at the peddlers, pilgrims, and tourists and the atmosphere was perfectly calm. People brushed past us as if we were not there.

****

Again, we had time. We bought sandwiches, drinks, and a small roll of utility paper. We hiked up the trail past the cottages and New Delphi Village, the Hermit Inn, and the fork in the trail leading to San Delphi Monastery—all the way up to the fence. We traced the fence to the spot where we discovered the breach and the fence still was broken in this time. We climbed through and went past where we sat and meditated and finally past the place where Élan fell and almost died. This time we went to within a few meters of the rim. "This is far enough," said Élan. "This is the exact spot. Now we must wait until Bell and Bastion manifest the aggregate and it finds us."

Bell and Bastion were even now about their nasty business of manifesting the specter. Beltania was watching through the cleft in the rocks, and soon the blue and crimson curtain would catch fire. However long it would take the specter to find us, we were prepared to wait. Where had the aggregate gone when it fled Bell's temple? I had a vision, but did not know if it was real. I saw the aggregate cutting loose upon creation. In a maniacal joy ride, it was picking up bits and pieces of perverted consciousness wherever it went.

We ate our sandwiches and drank water. "There must be something special about this exact spot," I told Stellium and Élan. "The aggregate did not approach them in their cottage or along any footpath. The aggregate waited until they arrived here." The three of us knew the truth at exactly the same time. A breach existed here between the third and fourth dimensions."

"Let's move back a few meters," Élan abruptly suggested.

We picked up our food and drinks and that's when we became aware of the sound of the wind. It was making a shushing sound as if rushing through the cedar trees and telling them to be quiet. It was too late to retreat farther.

We heard its wailing moan in the distance and then spotted it as it cut right through the tops of the huge ubertian cedars. The aggregate was spherical in shape and dark, like the shiny, black-prism ball. This aggregate's mass was several thousand times larger. Its auric energy was pale yellow-green and out of its aura, extended arms of lightning. The mouth was huge, with several rows of teeth, which we were about to discover had the ability to speak. Staring at the aggregate in terror and awe, I knew I might never see anything as awesome as this again. It definitely was an angry god from another dimension and the only thing comparable, in this universe, would be an entire soul group, rolling itself into a ball of energy and descending into the third dimension. The aggregate's power was stupendous, but it was lost and confused and tragically, the souls inside were imprinting the specter with their rage, shame, and fear.

"You miserable bug!" the aggregate shrieked several times. Then one of the auric arms became a hand from which a finger emerged. A sapphire blue light poured forth from the finger and scorched the ground. "That's for my mother's mother that you screwed, impregnating her with your rotten seed," the aggregate howled. It was repeating what it heard from inside itself, from Duebel. "I will kill you this time—rip your limbs from your living body and consume them as you watch," it raved. The whole scene might have been ridiculous, if the energy was not primal rage. Then I realized something new. I knew rage was the final tearing in any continuum stream; and if rage succeeded in delivering its payload here on New Delphi, neither persistent reality nor alternate possibility could repair or reconciled the damage. The aggregate moved around the area in a trance, acting out something it imagined was real. "It's not that easy," it snarled. "No one will rob me of my pleasure. No one will deprive me of my revenge. You will obey me or pay the consequences. Remember the madness? Remember the terror, the pain, and the emptiness of a body without a soul? You remember it all—don't you Dulce?" The words were the echoes from the high priestess. It was obvious the specter had sucked up her soul along with countless others.

Élan waved his arms and shouted, "Are you looking for me?" The aggregate abruptly stopped moving and even seemed to listen. "I'm right here." We moved toward the aggregate and it focused upon us and began to move toward us.

Now something happened that none of us anticipated. The New Delphi Crystal sizzled with new energy and a howling roar. The Crystal unleashed a ferocious wind, as the elemental universe attempted to purge the alien energy from its system. "I think the elemental universe is getting pissed off," Stellium warned.

The three of us fell to the ground as cedar limbs began crashing down around us. Struggling against the wind, Élan took the shiny black ball from his jacket pocket and fired the ball, with all his might, toward the aggregate. The ball struck the ground just below the aggregate and out popped dozens of free radicals. Among them were the three that had appeared in our cottage the day before. The aggregate saw them and descended upon them like a hungry whirlwind. Only Nalé turned toward us and gave us a defiant smile and thumbs down before surrendering himself to the aggregate's hungry mouth.

Despite the strong wind, the aggregate abruptly turned quiet. Something was going on inside it. The aggregate then opened its mouth and expelled specks of colored light. We heard mumbling and bits of vision emerging from the lights, remnants of unfilled lives. Then the aggregate closed its mouth and began to spin. Faster and faster it turned, becoming darker and more concentrated as it rotated. Then it headed for the sky, disappearing from sight. It would take centuries to learn that the aggregate did not make a clean exit from the third dimension. Instead, it headed for a weak spot in our universe that later would become known as The Door to the fourth dimension. It would eat every star and planet in its path on its way to this weak spot. The closest planet to survive was Dellaremos. At the time, Scientists on Dellaremos would identify the phenomenon as a fast-moving rogue comet, probably an anomaly created when the Afen Comet came in conjunction with the star, Insanio.

****

On the planet Delphi, the approaching evening was instantly tranquil with its milky wash of pastel hues. "Let's go," said Stellium. "That's enough excitement for my entire lifetime."

Élan smiled in agreement and added, "I'll say—"

We hiked back down the mountain to Mellé and Michael's cottage, stripped off our clothing, and made the jump. Inside the fourth dimension, all seemed quiet. Élan took the white feather and animated it into his hawk. "Kyron, take us back to our natural time," he ordered. Clearing the breach a second time, we found ourselves standing a short distance from our cottage door, thirty phases into the past. We dressed in our own simple clothing and left the key to the cottage on the table.

Just as Stellium hoped, we left New Delphi that night on the last windship out. Three days later, we booked passage on a spaceship headed for Earth. Again, our cabin accommodations were wonderful. We retired to the regrav unit for a nice long sleep. Our third day out in space, I felt the quickening inside me and I awoke Élan and Stellium to tell them, "Dulce is here."

They took turns putting their ears to my belly and listening to the sound of growing life inside me. Élan was ecstatic with joy. "I told you we were going to get to the easy stuff soon. Now do you believe me?"

"Raising children is not easy," insisted Stellium.

"Do you think a child could shake our composure after what we just went through?" asked Élan.

"Stellium is right," I said. "After all, the finest consciousness of your soul group is going to manifest through Dulce and Kia and they might have a few new hoops through which we must jump."

"Kia?" asked Stellium.

"Dulce just told me that Kyron wants us to name her Kia when she incarnates." They both started laughing as if something was hilarious. "What's so funny?" I asked.

"Oh nothing!" said Stellium. "Absolutely nothing."

"Everything!" said Élan, who finally was growing into his name.

# EPILOGUE

My brother Dulcerary received my parent's journals as a gift when he was eighteen years old. Four years later, he gave the journals to me on my eighteenth birthday. While my father Stellium is a well-known and respected artist, my brother Dulce's music has made him into a phenomenon Humans call, "a legend in his own time." While Humans generally regard celebrity as favorable, my father and brother continue to struggle with the Shardasko principle that fame and public acclaim bring labels that attempts to define and limit their art. In addition, the media is so invasive with their speculations, of late our entire family has become more reclusive than we actually prefer. As Dulce often says, "Focus is askew when the messenger becomes more important than the message."

I want to state briefly that my family believes that only a few Gathosians and Humans now realize the dire ramifications involved in the destruction of the planet Pybatium six months ago. Tyrowsians are now migrating to Human and Gathosian worlds in large numbers and bringing another perspective upon reality into our conscious midst. Now, more than ever, Humans and Gathosians need clear focus and compassion concerning Tyrowsians.

With that in mind, later this year, my family will release the twenty-one volumes written by Kyron and the additional two volumes written by Viobella, my father Élan, and me. The title of the twenty-third volume will be *The Twenty-Third Key: The Nature of Free Radicals*. While it is true that soul groups did produce the archetypal free radicals, every soul continues to produce free radicals based on those archetypes. Every soul carries a speck of energy within it from The Source, which shelters its original face and acts through the power of creation. Any deviation away from the path of our original face produces some kind of free radical. This is neither good nor bad per se, but rather the way reality works. Perhaps if a twenty-fourth key emerges, it should focus on "why." Humans sometimes say, "Be careful what you ask for because you are liable to get it." I would carry that a step further and say, "Take conscious responsibility for what you think, feel, and, especially, do, for your freewill is creating a free radical discharge with its every move."

My mother and I are publishing edited portions of the journals she and my father Élan wrote as a prelude to understanding these twenty-three volumes. The work of translating these journals was quite a challenge for us both. English still lacks words to express some modes of Gathosian thinking and we sometimes needed to exercise English elaboration to explain one Mescale word. It's our hope that the release of this new information will curtail the growing rumors concerning my family and, especially, the messianic rumors surrounding Dulce. Our focus remains simple: we hope our efforts will support universal fraternity and allow both Humans and Tyrowsians a glimpse into how Gathosians think, feel, and live. We want to share what we know is true so all people everywhere can fulfill their original intent.

In conclusion, now that I am a woman with a family of my own, I have a bit of perspective about my life here on Earth. Dulce and I had a very different upbringing from what Humans consider normal. Our parents shielded us from public view and told us we were "lucky" to have two fathers instead of one. Education and love were the focus in our family. Like the vaspray of Gathosian worlds, we began jumping dimensions as soon as we could stand. We lived in a large house in central North Carolina on sixty acres of surrounding woodland. Cerebow, Taro, and their three offspring lived with us. They roamed the surrounding woods and wandered into our house whenever they were in the mood and Dulce and I learned to communicate with them at an early age. Our parents taught us that everything was conscious and our mother taught us how to understand the language of nature. It was a great shock to me when I learned that many Humans believed we were crazy. Many people, both Human and Gathosian, came through our doors and some stayed for months and even years. We enjoyed the camaraderie of a large extended family. The tiny Gathosian headwater planet of Sutcay Tay never recovered from the devastation of the Afen meteor storm and consequently, the Sutcay Tay School fell on difficult times. Master Dalini was the first Shardasko Warrior to leave Sutcay Tay and join my fathers and mother in helping them establish the first Shardasko facility here on Earth. I will never forget the day Master Dalini arrived because it was on my eighth birthday. He told my father, Élan, "I am here because I've never been able to forget your bright auric glow when you emerged from the fourth dimension." Brother Aytinous joined us three years later. I am very proud that my fathers made me the first female Shardasko master in June of this year.

Afen,
Master Kia Lanai Esay

# ABOUT THE AUTHOR

Martha Fawcett was born in Tiffin, Ohio. As a child, her dad stoked her imagination with talk of future inventions, space travel, and meeting alien species. In addition to writing science fiction, she now takes delight in the protocols and absurdity of politics, a June garden in the morning, highly polished gemstones, and the beautiful flow of life. She enjoys time with her husband Bill and their two children, Penelope and Adam.